Dest:

CW00539191

DESTROYER
OF
LIGHT

A NOVEL BY
RACHEL ALEXANDER

for Robert, my muse

PROLOGUE

"JUST A LITTLE FURTHER, MY LOVE… A LITTLE further." The rabbit pelts bundled around his feet had kept out the snow, but not the cold. The wet leather straps holding those flimsy wrappings around his ankles chafed and bit into his skin.

"Why…"

"There's food ahead in Eleusis," Dimitris said. "Everyone says so."

She stumbled, leaning on her husband to take one more step. "Everyone?"

"Yes, love," he said gently. "Everyone we've met and all we walk with. We're nearly home. And Eleusis is not far beyond. " More feet crashed through the snow onto their path, a caravan of the starving and sick, bound for the promise of food, praying to all the gods that they'd make it. Dimitris pointed at the shadowy outlines of those around them, some walking faster, driven by hunger or by grief for the dead they had left along their journey. Others trudged slowly across the frozen landscape: those with children, the elderly, and the ones refusing to abandon their dead. "Demeter is in Eleusis. There's food there. And so many people."

"You said that about Athens."

I

"This is different."

She coughed violently and he stopped again, the third time in the last hour. Dimitris stroked Melia's back and held a rag against her mouth to keep her from breathing in the chill air and the blinding flurries of snow. She leaned harder against him, her coughing subsiding. He pursed his lips when he brought the linen away. More bright flecks of blood had joined the ones that had already dried brown. She wheezed, and dropped to one knee. "Dimitris, please. Let's stop. Build a fire."

"We can't," he whispered. "There's no more kindling. And the branches are too green to burn, and frozen through."

"Oil, then," she rasped. "Burn the oil."

"It's the only thing that keeps you from coughing. We shouldn't—"

"There's nothing—" she coughed again. "There's nothing that can stop it. Please. I just want to feel warm. Just once... just once."

Dimitris looked around them for shelter or anything that could stoke a fire. Oil could set a branch or two aflame. They had nearly reached their small farm. Surely these reserves could be spared. He tilted her head up. "Melia, my heart. Look there. You see? You see the grove there?"

"Yes." She smiled for the first time in days. "We were married there."

"Yes, we were." He spoke low and stroked her back as she coughed again. "And I will wager that none of these people know that our grove has scattered kindling. Enough to make a fire. It can't be seen from the road. They would have missed it." He forced a smile.

"Go gather wood there."

"Alone? Melia, it's only half a mile—"

"I can't." She sat still closing her eyes. "I need to rest."

He nodded to her, somewhat relieved. By himself, it would take a third the time to collect wood. And with the sun setting, time was in short supply. He wrapped the extra blanket securely around her, and propped her against their meager provisions and belongings. Dimitris kissed her on the forehead. "Stay warm. I'll be right back."

Dimitris struck off from the road, trudging through the drifts and banks. His feet sank through new fallen snow and crunched against the packed ice, the cold biting at his shins. He grabbed the branches above for balance and kept himself from sinking into a fresh drift, then plowed into the center of the grove.

He shook his head. Melia had told him the morning after their wedding that Kore, Demeter's flower-bearing daughter, had been there to bless their union— that she'd felt the young goddess's presence at their ceremony. Dimitris had brushed off her fancies. Why would a goddess pay a visit to two lowly mortals on their wedding day? They weren't royalty, and neither of them had divine blood.

He chuckled. Dimitris had always thought Melia was a goddess among women. She always wore flowers in her hair. A daughter from the next farm over, he had known her since childhood, and they had secretly promised themselves to each other in youth. When she came of age, Dimitris had begged his father to speak with hers and make the arrangements, even though he was still too young to marry. The second happiest day of his life had been when Melia's father gave his approval.

It had been sunny the day of their wedding. He still remembered the taste of honey and barley cakes and her soft lips. The day after was eerily calm, and other farmers reported strange fallow spots in their fields. They'd thought nothing of it until the next day, when the sun had disappeared behind clouds, the wind howled, and all the wheat and flowers died.

"If you're there, Maiden, as she thought you were that day, then please…" Dimitris whispered in prayer. "Please…

please let us reach Eleusis. I'll sacrifice the rest of our stores. Anything. Please help us. Help her."

Dimitris reached the clearing. The trees above had shielded it from snowdrifts and passers by, but the ground was bare. Every piece of fallen wood had been gathered, the shrubs had been uprooted, and even the lower branches of each tree had been hacked away. His prayers were unanswered. The Maiden Kore couldn't hear him anyway. She was in the Land of the Dead. His shoulders dropped. He would return to Melia empty-handed.

There wasn't time to fell any trees. He had to get back to her. He'd carry her on his back if he had to. They only needed to get home. Eleusis could wait. He could tuck Melia into bed, safe from the wailing wind and burn everything they had in the hearth— chairs, tables, linens, and oil. She would be warm while he went to Eleusis to bring her food, and perhaps a healer. Surely there would be one among the throngs that had traveled here. He tripped and fell into a bank, the snow suffocating and wet on his face. He jumped back up and brushed his clothes off before it could melt and chill his bones.

Dimitris reached the road and quickened his pace. A man and his son trudged past him, bound for Eleusis, their bodies cloaked and faces bundled. Through the haze of drifting snow he made out the outline of Melia, her knees huddled against her chest under layers of shawls and blankets, leaning against their packs.

His strides became longer. He would pick her up and carry her. It wasn't far. If the grove was so close, then their home was just beyond the ridge. They needn't build a fire here. They could wait for home. Home…

"Melia!" He called out, waiting for her to turn. She didn't move. "My love, it isn't far. Let's get you up. It's time to go home. Melia?"

She lay still.

"Melia!"

4

1.

INDIGO WAS THE COLOR OF MOURNING, SHE THOUGHT. Mourning was the unwillingness to accept that the time spent above was a fleeting moment in the journey of the soul from mortal to shade and back again. Hecate pulled the darkly dyed himation tightly around her body. She longed for her familiar crimson, the color of the living, beating heart— and long ago the color of the Olympians' proud banner. She didn't begrudge the mortals their displays of sorrow. They knew no better. Mortals' numbers grew every century, and for many souls these days, this was only their first lifetime; and any that had returned from below remembered nothing that would help them understand the path their soul had walked.

But as for the Goddess who encouraged them to keep their sad vigil… she expected better from her onetime student. Here, indigo meant more than mourning— it represented unmitigated suffering. Desolation. Demeter had isolated herself here at Eleusis, her inconsolable grief threatened to destroy the world, and with it mortals and gods alike. Hecate held a long, four-headed torch in each hand to light her way. The flames guttered in the wind, clinging to the torches and turning ghostly blue every time she passed between buildings.

She hadn't set foot in Eleusis in aeons. She remembered it as a tiny village, all mud huts and warm fleece and scattered grains. The priestesses here once blessed the fields with the tribal lords, praying for the fertile harvest with the ritual rhythm of their bodies, giving of themselves to one another to ensure that their people would not go hungry. Now great houses with cold stone floors stood in place of the earthen homes, and women were shut away indoors to be sold by their menfolk into childbearing as if they were sheep on two legs. Though all the worlds were open to Hecate, it was little wonder that she preferred Chthonia above all others— even when the earth had been warm and green.

She squinted. Wind-borne ice stung her eyes. In the fertile countryside, vestiges of the old ways had remained mere months ago, but the famine and cold had killed off the country folk, the warmth of love matches, and the maidens who would choose their husbands. Desperate and starving, mortal men had scrounged and scraped for the last arable land, and divided the earth, their chattel, and their women among them.

Hecate waited, listening for the sound of the *koudounia*. The veiled girl standing at the door represented Demeter's lost daughter, her bells a promise to the worshippers that Kore would return. The Goddess of the Crossroads thinned her lips. The child was as frail as a baby bird. In six or seven years, as soon as she flowered, her father would sell her off to her new husband— a stranger over twice her age. She shook her head. A little bird girl standing in for the powerful, regal, fearsome Iron Queen of the Underworld. The only being the Keres would obey. Demeter wouldn't even recognize her own daughter were she to walk through the doors of the Telesterion this very moment.

The future, what little she could see of it these days, was awash in pandemonium and forked into infinite paths. Some of them wavered and changed, many more were too terrifying to follow, but Hecate knew one thing for certain— this day was the tipping point. If she failed to convince Demeter to relent...

She wouldn't consider that possibility. She *must* succeed. The Lady of the Harvest had once been her cherished student. Now she was the only Olympian receiving offerings— powerful beyond her wildest imaginings. Demeter herself might not even realize the extent of that new balance of power, thanks to her isolation. The Goddess of the Harvest would allow no guests from Olympus. Hecate watched initiates file out of the Telesterion, once the home of pastoral King Celeus. He was now her highest servant. Him, and the boy. Hecate looked for Triptolemus, wondering if Demeter's lover was among the crowds exiting the temple. But she only saw women. They were the sole keepers of the food in Eleusis, and in a world where gold could no longer buy grain, these women were the apportioners of all that mattered anymore. *A pity*, Hecate thought. *You are greater than you ever realized. You could have righted the course for untold generations to come.*

As the worshippers filed out one by one, each took a sip from the golden cup held by dark-robed Metaneira, the queen turned priestess, a woman ever grateful to Demeter for saving her sons. Hecate moved to walk past her.

"My child," the mourning woman said, stopping Hecate in her tracks. "I have not seen you before. Are you just arrived today?"

Hecate turned to her. Child. If she were indeed mortal as her appearance suggested, she likely would have a couple small children in tow. In three days, it would be the full moon. Though she was aeons older than even this woman's mistress, today Hecate looked as though she were only twenty. "Yes, my lady. My path has wound through here... many times. But I cannot linger long."

"Please stay. You have come to the right place. All are welcome in the sight of the Queen of the Earth."

"Queen of the Earth." Hecate smirked at the title. "I would see your queen."

"The evening's bread is already broken. The other children of the earth will gladly share theirs with you. You can come back tomorrow for our morning devotional," she said, starting to close the great oak door.

"I do not require bread, priestess. Only a word with your mistress."

Metaneira wrinkled her brow. "That is rather presumptuous of you, girl. To think that the Lady of the Harvest would speak to—"

Hecate let her torches flare hot. For the briefest moment, Metaneira saw in triple: two other faint forms of the one before her held the torches on either side of the woman and faced away— one very young, the other very old. The hood of Hecate's indigo cloak fell back, revealing her otherworldly countenance. Long waves of red hair interwoven with selenite beads gleamed in the torchlight, and a silver moon sat on her forehead. Her expression was calm, but resolute. Hecate watched the mortal woman blink incredulously, thinking that her mind was playing tricks on her. Hecate smiled reassuringly. "Peace, Metaneira, daughter of Polymnia, your eyes do not deceive you," she said in three voices, that of the Maiden, the Woman and the Crone. "I would have you either stand aside, or show me to your queen."

Metaneira swallowed and bowed her head to the unknown goddess. "O-others have come f-from Olympus and our lady has turned them away..."

"I am not from Zeus's court," Hecate said with a single voice, and walked past the frightened mortal. She stopped in the center of the room. The braziers warmed her skin, and she looked around. A great oak throne taller than Thanatos was raised up on a stepped dais at the back of the hall, sheaves of barley and wheat lay all around it. Empty. She waited.

Her awareness spread further than the stone walls of the Telesterion's great hall, and Hecate could sense Demeter. Her former student was happily mating with Triptolemus this very minute. She could sense it just as intuitively as when Aidoneus was with Demeter's daughter. These days, that passing understanding was as common a sensation as breathing. She smiled. They had found joy in each other.

Hecate was also glad that Demeter had found happiness. She sighed, knowing innately that their current activities, though not intentionally, were being practiced in the old way— the goddess and her consort ensuring the fertility of the earth. It was natural for Demeter. Perhaps her newfound love would make this easier. She could only hope that it would soften Demeter's heart enough to hear her words. So few elements were on her side in this…

Finally, a door creaked open behind the throne and out walked the Lady of the Harvest, her face flushed with health and youth. Demeter tucked a stray lock of hair behind her ear. She hid a serene smile and picked up her long indigo skirts, walking toward the center of the room. Suddenly, her face fell and she stood stock still, her eyes wide. She could barely draw in a breath.

"Too many seasons have passed, acolyte."

Demeter clenched her teeth together and rasped. "Get out."

"I think I will remain."

"Of all the beings in this cosmos," Demeter said, her voice shaking as she advanced on Hecate, "there is only *one* I wish to see less than you!"

"Indeed? Enlighten me."

"You…" she shook her head. "Do you think me an idiot? You are in league with him! Get out, Hecate. Do not think to show your face here again!"

"Walk with me," she said, holding a torch out for Demeter.

"Are you hard of hearing? I just told you—"

"You certainly did," she said, looking at the vast room and the indigo cloth draped from the rafters. "You've dyed your crimson darkly, I see. No. Abandoned it, I should say."

"*You* abandoned *me!* You told me to make *my* choice and—"

"And I ask that of you again. To make a choice."

"To acquiesce," she spat out. "To acquiesce to my daughter's rape!"

Hecate shook her head patiently. "She is Kore no more, but Persephone would not color it thus, nor do I."

"Get out!"

Hecate ignored Demeter and slowly strolled around the room, pausing at the tapestries of the House of Celeus, as though she were admiring their handiwork. "Your roots have taken a firm hold here. The Queen of the Earth, they call you. It would be a shame, Demeter Anesidora," Hecate said, raising her voice almost imperceptibly, "if you were to find the pathway to the rest of the earth choked with thorny brambles. How sad and limited is the existence of the local, rustic god. How long, do you think, before the Eleusinians realize that?"

"You wouldn't dare..."

Hecate stood still, staring placidly at Demeter. Both knew that it could be done. The white witch held dominion over the ether, and could bar Demeter from traveling that path if she willed it. She smiled at her former student and offered the torch again. "Walk with me."

It was more command than request. Demeter roughly grabbed the torch from Hecate's hand. The goddesses made their way to the back of the palace and stepped through the doorway onto the portico. The small garden below was alive, the last place outdoors that grew any food, mercifully shielded from the wind by the amphitheatre of the hills above and shielded from Demeter's wrath by her protection of this village. But the fertile rows of wheat, barley and millet were not Hecate's destination.

"Do you feel it? The cold?"

Demeter didn't answer.

"I thought not. Propitiations come to you now like ants to spilled honey. I would be surprised if any sensation could touch you."

"Why have you come here, Hecate? Why pull me out into the snow?"

"To show you your daughter."

"Kore…" She stiffened. "Did you bring—"

Hecate's silent glare stopped her. She motioned for Demeter to follow her. The hillside was steep, the northern wind growing stronger the higher they climbed. The torches smoldered orange, the barest blue flame flickering at Hecate's bidding.

Demeter recalled the last time Hecate had led her uphill by the light of a long torch, both of them stumbling up a rocky path at twilight to the heights of Olympus. She remembered the low fire Hestia had created with pine, cypress, and oak, shielding any light that might alert their enemies on Mount Othrys of their presence. Hera had nervously looked about and braided a peacock feather into her rich brown tresses. Poseidon had argued tactics with Zeus by the fire. Aidoneus had sat apart from the rest, looking out over Thessaly, blood dried onto the sword he always wore strapped to his back. Some of the rebelling Titans came as well— Tethys, with the split nautilus she would always wear around her neck, and Metis, who had dutifully recorded all with her stylus on the clay tablet that never left her arms. The clever trickster Prometheus and his hot-tempered brother Epimetheus were there that night.

The night she conceived Kore.

Demeter followed Hecate up the hill, the waxing moon lighting the wide bay and mountains. She heard a groan coming from the south, and for the first time saw blocks of ice scattered across the water, cracking and grinding against each other, the sea rolling beneath them. She pursed her lips. It served Poseidon right for how cruelly he'd mocked her.

"What do you see?"

"Eleusis and the sea," Demeter said, frustrated, the wind biting through her clothes.

"Look again. Northward."

"Hills. You said you would show me my daughter! Where is she?"

"You glance with you eyes. Look. As I taught you how to look."

Demeter scowled, then acceded, closing her eyes and facing north, the wind whipping the veil back from her diadem. North, across the hills and beyond. And further still, until the north abruptly stopped, replaced by a great blanket of ice, fathoms higher than mountaintops, crushing all in its path.

"Now do you see? How it crawls closer? The wall of ice descends from Hyperborea. It's not far; it has advanced even further from its icy den than when your father wore his crown."

"What has this to do with me?"

"Everything."

"None of this is my—"

"Everything," Hecate repeated. "The world dies beneath the ice, and the mortals will die before then, and the gods themselves *end* if you don't stop this, Demeter. The frozen maw that swallows mountains will not spare your worshippers. More ice rises from below the Heliades, a southern beast no less ravenous. And when they meet, it will end us all. But we will not see that day, for before it dawns, the chains of the new order that bind the Titans to Tartarus will be broken, and all we have made will be undone. *Worse* than undone. Every tree we grew from a seed will be uprooted,

12

shattered, burned, the ashes scattered and the ground salted. What they will do to your daughter, the Queen—"

"This is Hades's fault!" she snapped. "If he hadn't stolen Kore—"

"You swore on the Styx, Demeter. Long ago. There was no theft, no violation, and they are husband and wife now. Children separate from their mothers. They find their mates. It is the way it has always been done. So will it always be."

"Oh yes, Hecate, her *mate*, surely," Demeter scoffed. "Which is why he had to burst out of the earth and drag her screaming into the depths. I spoke to Helios! He saw it happen."

Hecate's serene, placid gaze jarred for a moment, her lips set firmly. "You know better than I what inspired that haste. You know what bitter fruits his complacency would have borne."

Demeter paled, preparing to deny it, then realized it would be futile. "I… I could have never gone through with it. I would have found something temporary. Something—" Her eyes stung.

"Something that would *still* allow you to break the sacred oath you swore on the Mother River?"

She turned away from her former priestess, tears blurring her vision, freezing on her cheek in the wind. "It was different, then. I made that oath when I thought my daughter would grow up to at least be the queen of the earth or the seas, if not Queen of Heaven. I didn't make it to condemn her to the grave!"

"That was never for you to decide; the Fates wove that pattern. And now your whim is to heave us into peril once again."

"You told me to make a choice, and I made it."

"Careless planting delivers a poor harvest."

"What do you mean? We won the war. I did my duty. *You* didn't approve of my choices and *you* abandoned me to utter powerlessness and ruin after that night."

13

"We took the field that day. But we lost the war. Our king who now sits Olympus follows his father's crooked road more closely than most would admit, and he allows those same scales that tipped during the rule of the Tyrant to lean further askew. You remember my lessons: its imbalance will one day finish us all. Now little more than an aeon remains."

"The future is not fixed. You, Gaia, Nyx... none of you know that for certain."

"Look around you, Goddess of the *Fruitful* Earth. Look and *see*. Many more women than men make their new homes on Other Side. Though wars end many young men, more and yet more women die at their husband's hands, and are met by infant girls left to the elements, while those still alive are kept in ignorance and slavery. Worse awaits those who choose otherwise. Half a century ago, an Athenian woman practiced my ways, as mortals may: she midwifed and used herbs. First came the ugly rumors, then they called her a witch, and then they stoned her. Then they stoned her friends, and they stoned her young sister. Then the mob turned on her sickly mother, and drove her into the wilderness."

"So what if a few of your worshippers died? You're not alone in this. All mortals die."

"Is it to be that every woman who refuses to marry, or who wishes to learn, who has the sight, who has a free spirit and a free heart should be put to death? That is where our guiding star leads. The *hieros gamos* that night on Olympus was bound to the decision of the Fates. Your tyrant father threw the cosmos into peril, and you were one of the instruments by which the balance could be restored. You knew your duties and knew how the Fates had called upon you."

"I chose the man I loved! The *right* man to rule the gods."

"Bad planting, bad fruits. I say now as then, you chose poorly. Ruled only by passion. And see where you lie now. Hmm? Is he yours still?"

"So you disowned me, abandoned me, because I chose differently? I did everything you asked of me! Your words to me that night were to 'listen to my heart and let it make my choice for me.'"

"Would that I could have spoken more carefully."

"You once called me *daughter* and yet you left me alone in this world— wholly reliant on Zeus while I grew with child. You would not speak with me, Gaia would not help me, what would you have had me do?!"

"If you had made the choice I laid out for you…"

Demeter looked away in disgust.

"…You would be Queen of Heaven even now. And he, according to his birthright—"

"I could just as soon have fallen in love with a stone!" Demeter yelled over the wind. It howled past them, the sea shimmering with new ice.

"Love was not my request. I offered you a way to sway the will of the Fates, asked you to do that for all of us. Love would have come in time."

"Why him? Why has he been your *obsession* all these aeons?" Tears clouded her eyes and for a moment she was back on Olympus the morning after the *hieros gamos*. Hecate's voice filled Demeter with guilt; the new and pleasant ache between her legs turning painful, shameful at her words. "What is your sick fascination with him, Hecate? Aidon was always, *always* your favorite! I sacrificed everything to be your acolyte and you *still* loved him more! I wonder sometimes, *priestess*, why you never broke your vows of chastity to have him for yourself!"

"Because he is my son." Hecate glared at her, her voice trembling. "We share no blood, certainly, but our spirits are true kin."

Demeter rolled her eyes. "Why did you even take a vow of chastity to begin with? You have tried in vain your whole life to create your own twisted version of a real family. To mother children you can't possibly have…"

She ignored the slight. It was a different time at the beginning of Kronos's reign: take the vow or be forced into a marriage— or worse— to one of the Titans. "Though you see Aidoneus as a crude and ugly statue, your daughter has found warmth behind his stony visage." Demeter looked up at this, her eyes wide. Hecate smiled knowingly. "Is it impossible for you to believe that she has fallen in love with him?"

"You lie," Demeter said quietly. "I know my own daughter. In all the cosmos there is no one more opposite her than Hades."

"Perhaps that is their greatest strength." Hecate smiled for a moment. "I told you I would show her to you, did I not?"

Demeter clenched her jaw shut. "Where is she?"

Hecate pulled a single bead of selenite from her hair and held it up. It shone in the light of the waxing moon, taking on a glow of its own as Hecate took her hand away. The bead sat suspended in mid air, then flattened and expanded. A perfect reflection of the two goddesses appeared on either side of it before their visages faded in ripples of silver and crimson. A window through the ether was created in their wake. A scrying mirror.

"Ask of it," Hecate said. "In the way I taught you. Tell it what you desire to see, so you may have no doubt of what it has to show you. So you know this is not one of my witch's tricks."

Demeter closed her eyes and thought about her lost daughter. When she opened them, she saw her Kore's face up close, a large male hand covering her eyes. Kore's lips were parted. She hadn't seen her daughter in almost two months. Demeter sputtered a short cry, her eyes burning. She wished she could reach through the mirror and pull her girl back into the land of the living, or let her know that it was all right, that she was doing all she could to rescue her from the grave, even if it took letting Zeus's worshippers die of starvation until the King of the Gods acted.

16

Hades's fingers wrapped around Kore's eyes, blinding her, pinioning her back against him. Demeter took a sharp breath as she saw the Dark Lord's lips whispering close to her daughter's ear, words she couldn't distinguish, the mirror silent. Hesitantly, she willed the scene to pull back so she could see more. Black marble and malachite. Though she'd never visited, she guessed that they were in his dreary palace. Kore was clothed in a long white peplos, its borders burgundy. Heavy jewels adorned her neck and the fibulae that held up her dress.

His other hand gripped her arm, leading her forward, blind. What was he doing with her? She felt angry bile well up in her throat as two of his fingers unwound from Persephone's arm and deliberately brushed against the side of her breast. They walked forward together. Her daughter said something that looked like 'where are we?', but the image wavered, and Demeter couldn't be sure. Hades's mouth twisted upward unnaturally and he lifted his hands, taking a step back. Kore blinked a few times before her eyes grew wide and she drew in a sharp breath, startling Demeter.

She watched her daughter run from his side and bound up the stairs of a dais. Hades stood back and admired her, watching her reaction. Was he smiling? Her daughter ran her hands along the arm of a wrought iron throne, airy filigree in the shape of hundreds of hateful asphodel, equal in height and stature to the austere ebony throne beside it. She sat down and looked back at Hades, kicking her feet underneath her like a child on a swing. Persephone stood up and ran back toward him, then jumped from the second step, throwing her arms and legs around Aidoneus and nearly knocking him off his feet. His face was almost as shocked as Demeter's, but while she fumed, Aidon's mouth turned up into a surprised smile and his hands came up to hold her.

She watched her daughter kiss him, and saw his eyes close as he brought her deeper into their kiss. He pulled back and wrapped his arms around her shoulders, twirling her around, her legs flying out away from where he spun her. Was he laughing? Aidon was laughing. *Kore* was laughing with him. Hades carried her back up the steps; her limbs still awkwardly wrapped around him, and plunked her down on her throne. He took his seat beside her, and they both leaned over to kiss once more. Persephone whispered something in his ear that made his eyes widen before he turned toward her with a surprised, then lascivious grin. He slowly rose, and she rose with him. He pulled her into his embrace, both standing on the wide dais holding each other, their mouths heatedly locked together, his hands everywhere on her, her hands trailing down his chest and stomach, reaching for...

"Enough!" Demeter cried. The scrying mirror broke into thousands of pieces, showering down between her and Hecate, the glittering fragments lost in the snow.

"Your own eyes tell you—"

"Lies!" Demeter shouted. "That was no Aidoneus I have *ever* seen!"

"No, indeed," Hecate said with a smile. "A rather good thing, wouldn't you agree?"

"You *conjured* that vision. I knew him better than any of the other Olympians. That was *not him!*"

"I no more conjured it than you conjured the walls of ice. You know this."

"If the sorcery isn't yours, then it's his! He has trapped her down there so long that the smallest kindness, the *tiniest* grain of affection would draw her into his arms. He abducted and *raped* her; he convinced her that she is bound to him as wife and that he loves her. Once she finally gave in and accepted his prison fantasy, even the tiniest grain of tenderness he could muster would convince her to do anything he wanted!"

Hecate stood silently and listened. *Please let this be the end of your grief*, she prayed. *Please, kindly Fates, great Chaos, lead her into acceptance. Please...*

18

"And maybe, just maybe, the pure goodness that radiates from Kore was enough to soften him ever so slightly. But if you expect me to believe that he has become smiling and gentle after such a short time, you must think me the greatest of fools. We're the deathless ones. We're aeons old, teacher, and we don't change for *anything*. I know Aidoneus. I know him *far* better than you do— than you *ever* will. You forget, *priestess*, that I was imprisoned with him inside Kronos for aeons, and Aidon is, through and through, his father's son!"

"He loves her and she loves him. Please see what is so plainly in front of your eyes, Demeter."

"Hades isn't capable of love; he never has been, he never will be. He only knows violence and death! He's a blood-soaked murderer who *reveled* in exacting his vengeance on anyone in the way of his sword. Don't you remember? He came back *every night* covered in gore, invigorated by the kill-ing. Zeus and Poseidon didn't!"

"He bloodied his sword so that we might survive. He did it for all of us. And for you in particular."

"No. He *enjoyed* it. During the war, Hestia and I were cornered by a demon of Echidna, and Hades came to our aid. He appeared out of the ether before us and skewered its head on his blade, killing it instantly. But oh no, that wasn't enough for him. He hacked away at it even after it was dead, yelling as he did, stroke after stroke, spattering us with fetid blood, with this *look* in his eyes. And when the Keres came and wrested the demon's spirit away to Tartarus, Aidoneus smiled. It was the one time I ever saw him do so. And thanks to you, Hecate, he has... has corrupted... and destroyed my daughter," she said, shaking. Demeter turned away, her last words sputtered through tears.

She wouldn't let Hecate see them. But the Goddess of the Crossroads felt them. Anyone could. She let Demeter cry, then took a step forward and placed a hand on her back. "Child..."

Demeter turned to her, tears wet on her reddened cheeks.

"Daughter…" Hecate stroked her arm. "You can make this right. But you must let go. This is not a war; there is no defeat, no cause for shame. She will still see you, and you her. They asked me to be their voice, and in return I will also speak for you. Ask it of me and I will entreat Persephone to walk the world above with you. As often as you wish it. You would be welcome in her realm— to see her, and to know the truth of her marriage."

"I don't believe you," she said, wiping away her tears with a sleeve. "How can I? You come here to shame me for what I've been *forced* to do to have even a chance at getting Kore back, to mock my grief as foolishness, then try to soften my heart, as if I should just forget all the aeons you forsook me."

"How should I apologize first, Demeter? For leaving you to Zeus, after you chose him? If that will right this, I will fall to my knees this instant and ask your forgiveness."

"As patronizing as you always were, Hecate…"

"It was never my intention."

"What of the Eleusinians? They *need* her now, and nothing short of her return will suffice." She thought about Metaneira and Celeus, Demophon and Triptolemus. The deaths of her lover's sisters would be in vain. Demeter imagined Triptolemus accusing her of betrayal, spitting on her and cursing her name. She would be cast out from her own temple. The worshippers she had garnered throughout the winter would despise her, burn everything down, smash her altars. The rest of the Olympians would shun her and never come to her aid again if she relented now. Not after this. She would be an outcast among men and gods.

It was too late. Demeter looked at the groaning floes of ice that covered the sea. Poseidon might be angered enough that he would make good on his abominable suggestion and force himself upon her in the vilest way imaginable. And after all she'd done to weaken the rest of Olympus, the others would only be too glad to stand by and watch.

"Let us protect you," Hecate said, reading her thoughts. "If it is the vengeful storm of sky and sea that you fear, then ally yourself with us; with your daughter who loves you. You are the goddess of all that grows upon the earth, and those who dwell beneath it would welcome you with open arms."

"I will *not* accept exile! To become yours and Nyx's docile pet as my influence dwindles to that of a nymph? The Eleusinians—"

"Your mind buzzes about this village like an insistent fly! Your *accomplished* lover and his family are here, but what of the rest of humanity who you starve and freeze?"

Demeter's breath halted at the word *lover*. Then she bit at the side of her cheek. Of course Hecate would know that. Hecate knew everything, she thought angrily. "I leave Zeus's followers to Zeus. Whoever wishes to come to me is welcome. I welcome all at Eleusis, slave and freeborn."

Hecate slitted her eyes. "So your precious Kore is not at the heart of this. This is about your power. Your pride…"

"This is *entirely* about Kore. She was taken unwillingly. Stolen from me. And you dare speak of power? Hypocrisy! A trade was done between kings— between two of the three who divided creation itself— with no regard for her or for me. Do you think when I made that oath at the Styx I would have been *allowed* to say no? To the likes of Zeus and Aidoneus? My daughter was bartered like chattel before she even came into the world and sold off to a man twice her age! I thought you were against that on principle!"

Hecate sighed and bit at her own cheek. Demeter was right, in that at least. "What is time like that to beings like us? What was done is done. Would you have me remake her maidenhead? Uproot her blossoming love for Aidoneus? Slip her a dram of the Lethe and make her forget she is a venerated and powerful Queen? These are things that will not happen." Hecate paused, taking a slow, even breath. "But I am endowed by Persephone, Queen of the Underworld, and Aidoneus, her divine Consort, with the ability to grant your desire. Name what you will, Demeter, and I will do my utmost to make it so."

For the briefest moment, she considered it. Then she weighed it against the scar in the field of Nysa where Hades had violently ripped her daughter from the world above. She thought about Kore's stolen innocence, and her unfeeling, blood-soaked adversary in his dead kingdom. She thought about the borrowed helm and the bargain she was forced into once her plan to win back her love went awry. She thought about the Eleusinians. Celeus. Triptolemus. Metaneira. All she had done, all the death and destruction, in vain. Demeter stiffened and stood tall. "Annul the marriage. Bring her back to me. I will accept nothing less."

"Demeter—"

"*Nothing less!*"

Hecate stared at Demeter for a long moment. She finally stepped back and shook her head. "I tried, Nyx."

She vanished and Demeter was alone again. Hecate's torches lay in the snow, crossed over one another, their lit ends burning out. As wisps of smoke rose from the extinguished pitch, Demeter heard her former teacher's voice on the wind.

I tried.

2.

"CAREFUL!"

Persephone smiled. "Pay him no mind."

Merope dipped the comb in olive oil again, cautiously pulling it through Aidon's hair. "Beg pardon milord, but if your purpose in judging kings is to meet them as a king yourself and dispel whatever hubris they still have, it might serve to look as they look. All the Peloponnesian kings wear their hair pulled back this way. If they haven't cropped it at the neck, that is."

Aidon pursed his lips.

"Would you rather I cut it all off?" Merope asked.

He tightened his jaw and turned sharply, giving her a withering glance.

Persephone laughed, and Merope suppressed a smile. The nymph shrugged innocently. She yanked the comb through another unruly curl, and he growled. "They know who I am. I don't see why this is needed."

"Then why I am I wearing *these*?" Persephone said. Merope had woven rubies into her hair amidst the asphodel, and the weight of the jewels and her pinned-up hair strained her neck. Merope paused, unsure whether she should continue.

Aidoneus relaxed his shoulders and motioned for her to resume. "Forgive my obstinacy, Merope. We've never had a servant before."

The nymph tied back his hair with a gold band and braided his hair. "You needn't apologize. You've dressed for judgement many times since I've been your wife's maidservant without my assistance. What's the occasion? Are you seeing someone important today? A demigod, perhaps?"

Hades and Persephone glanced at one another, unsure how to answer. Neither wanted Merope to know who would be coming before them today. Her nightmares had subsided, and she could sleep through the night without Hypnos's poppies, but even so, she'd awoken half the palace earlier that week with a scream.

Aidon refused to cause her further pain. He forced a smile. "It is my queen's first time sitting the throne with me for judgement."

"A special occasion, indeed," Merope said, looping sinew and gold thread tightly around his last few braids.

"And as such," Aidon said, standing up from the chair, "one must look the part." He fastened a gold torc around his neck. His normally gray himation was deep black and bordered in a thick meandros of gold. The same pattern was etched into the wide golden bands that he wrapped around his biceps. Merope helped fasten smaller versions of those bands onto the arms of his wife.

"I hope you'll tell me how it went."

Aidon's eyes met Persephone's again, his expression set tightly. She tilted her head at him and he softened, nodding his approval.

"I will, Merope," she said. They would have to tell her at some time. And it would be easier when Sisyphus was in Tartarus— once justice had been done.

Persephone stood in front of the mirror, hair glimmering with jewels, a noble compliment to her dark-haired husband. She looked every bit the wife of Hades Plouton, the Rich

24

One Beneath the Earth. Merope picked up a heavy apron of gold, fire opal, garnets, and rubies, and fastened it over Persephone's black dress. She clipped it together at Persephone's neck, and then fastened it at her waist. Jewels cascaded from collarbone to ankles. The girl that was Kore chafed under their weight. Kore no more. She shared a bed with the Receiver of Many. She had walked the Fields of Asphodel and weathered Tartarus itself. She was Persephone, Queen of the Underworld.

✻   ✻   ✻

Hades and Persephone Chthonios sat in their thrones, receiving the dead one by one. Rhadamanthys stood at the door, allowing kings, archons, and magistrates to enter, one at a time. Minos sat below the dais on their right side at an ebony table, a scroll laid out before him, carefully recording all he heard and saw onto the parchment. The judges had never seen so many in one sitting, and all were anxious to receive their final 'guest', the king of Ephyra. Aidoneus held his raven-crested staff in his right hand.

Two departed leaders, an archon and a magistrate of Athens, had stood before them earlier in the day. Both were well educated and spoke to Hades and Persephone in their own tongue— the divine language of the Theoi. Early in his career, the archon had accepted a substantial bribe; the magistrate had fathered a child out of wedlock and had hid the girl from his wife, but had provided for her and the mother until his death. For their sins, both were terrified of being condemned to Tartarus. But they had otherwise lived good lives, for the most part.

The archon had fallen to his knees, begging for mercy until Aidoneus shook his head and bid him stand and not fear him. Persephone noticed that her husband's judgement was almost conversational, asking after the men's families and relaying to them the details of their own lives, and how their livings acts had influenced his judgement. Each guest was thrown off guard, expecting a catalog of sins to be read aloud and thus condemn them. At the end of each judgement, Aidoneus pronounced that the archon and the magistrate were free to drink the waters of the Lethe and join the souls in Asphodel, giving them the chance to return to the world of the living once they were ready.

"How do you know?" she had asked under her breath as the magistrate departed.

"They are part of this realm from the moment they arrive. I can see into their hearts," he replied, grasping her hand. The rings of the Key of Hades glinted off his fingers in the muted light of the throne room. "I see in each of them *what* was done, but I speak with them to know *how* it was done. A king is just a man, and kings go to war. They kill and decide to kill others. If a man has ended someone's life, even if he is using another's sword, I want to know why."

"What happens to most?"

"Asphodel. Once they drink from the Lethe, they are no longer kings and queens. They are just shades in my kingdom. Most are brought before me knowing exactly what they did. Their perceived sins make a prison for them in life and they come here terrified that I will send them to Tartarus. But all men err, some more than others. Our responsibility," he said, gripping her hand and turning to face her again, "is to determine whether or not they have learned from those mistakes within their lifetime."

She smiled at him. He returned it, then turned solemn once more and stared forward.

"I don't care what power or wealth they had in life. They can't take it with them, though many think they can. They think it will sway me, somehow. Mortals and immortals alike say many things about me in the world above. But my reputation for being inexorable is well earned."

Persephone smiled wryly. Draped down the front of her clothes were more jewels than the oldest, richest dynasty could hope to acquire in all its generations, much less a single mortal in a short lifetime. Any one of the rubies in her hair could ransom a princess.

Minos stood up and nodded in a cursory bow to the royal couple. "Your Excellencies, there is one more to be judged before we bring in the Ephyrean," he said. Minos refused to even breathe Sisyphus's name. His shame at his mistake with Merope was too great. Aidoneus had made the same error and had quickly forgiven Minos and Rhadamanthys, but the Mycenaean brothers still held onto their guilt at recommending an innocent soul for Tartarus.

"Who is it?"

"King Hebros of Thrace."

Aidoneus sat back on his throne. Hebros, son of Heamus, whose parents were turned into two Dacian mountain ranges after daring to compare themselves to Zeus and Hera. He sighed. "Send him in."

Rhadamanthys opened the door and a man entered, his himation plain and black like all the others. But Hebros's arms were covered in the ink markings of his people— a dark pattern of horses and sunbursts. His hair was a mass of auburn curls with streaks of gray at his temples.

"*Hebros. Zin na Heamus i Rhodope od dieza na Thrakos. Nositel na alopekis na mezenai zibythides,*" Aidoneus said, continuing in Thracian, "*You died three days ago when you rode your horse across a frozen lake. The ice broke underneath you, no?*"

Persephone listened to him speak in perfect Thracian. The language, hard on her ears, rolled smoothly off his tongue, as if he spoke this way every day. Her heart beat a little faster, listening to the calm baritone of his voice. The words were unknown to her, and the only clues she had as to what he was saying were the reactions of the Thracian king.

"*Hades i Despoina, zibythides,*" he said, falling onto his knees, his forehead touching the cold stone floor. Despoina. That was the name the fisher folk on the outskirts of Hellas had called her when she was Kore. Her husband's head shook and he raised his hand to stop him.

27

"Ne, ne. Tya ne e Despoina. Tya e Persephone," Aidoneus corrected him, *"My beloved wife and your queen now that you are here as our guest."*

"Forgive me, my lord," he replied in Thracian, cowering before the dais.

"Think nothing of it. Stand," he said, waiting for the Thracian king to rise. *"How is your queen, Hebros?"*

"Pardon me, my lord?"

"Your queen. The Dacian woman. What is her name? Nevena?"

"Yes."

Aidoneus leaned back on his throne. *"You took her from her father's family... unwillingly?"*

"Nevena was promised at birth to me by her father's father. Therefore she was mine."

"How did she come to your marriage bed? Did she desire to do so?"

"Does it matter? She was my woman! They should come to the marriage bed whether they are willing or not. The gods decree—"

"I am the only god you need answer to anymore," he interrupted darkly.

Persephone watched the Thracian's face go pale, his feet shifting under him. She stared straight forward, a flutter forming in her stomach, feeling the respect and power her husband commanded here. She wanted to look at him— to look at the face that she loved so well— but remained poised, eyes fixed forward, remembering that her presence here meant they were speaking and passing judgement as one. She felt Aidon's hand cover hers as he ran a finger over her upturned wrist. His touch sent a shiver up her spine and reminded her of the vision from Tartarus— the two deities enthroned, and life swelling within her. She tamped the thought down. Hecate would return soon. She would speak to her about that then.

"Yes, forgive me," he said, bowing once more, *"Our people made our due sacrifices to you, Lord Hades."*

"And if you had made more or made fewer it still would not sway me. Perhaps you didn't understand my question. Did you, Hebros, rape your wife and then make war on the Dacians, her people?"

Hebros stood shocked, his mouth open, a nervous smile curling his lip. *"My lord, surely you must know... the Dacians... they're barbarian sheep fuckers that worship wolves. They raided our lands from the mountains and... and..."*

"Go on..."

"I... I did it to stop the raids."

"Did you, now... Couldn't you could have sent just a few of your forces to patrol the borders instead of sending your armies to pillage the city of Arcideua and burn it to the ground?"

Hebros was stunned, his mouth hanging open as he took a step back and looked at Minos, his eyes cast down to the scroll, transcribing Hades's words. He darted a glance at Persephone, her face cold and serene as the Lord of Souls languidly stroked her wrist. They were implacable. King Hebros fell to his knees and wept, extending his clasped hands in the air toward them. *"Please, please, your Excellencies, do not send me to Tartarus! Yes; I took my wife against her will, and I shouldn't have, I knew I shouldn't have the moment I looked down at her face. She was crying for me to stop. It was three years after our wedding night before she would even speak to me!"*

Hades raise his eyebrows at that and shifted in his seat. *"What changed?"*

"Our son— Ardeskos. We both loved our son. I apologized to her for his sake so we could be a family. I was faithful to Nevena. I grew to love her. And in time, she forgave me and loved me as well. I would do anything for her, and turned my armies around after Arcideua to come home by her request, with no further burning or rapine, not even on the way back. But I'd beaten the war drum too loudly before we left. I couldn't tell my men that turning back was my wife's decision! They would think I was weak and soft. Any of my rivals would have murdered me, then Nevena, then our son! I'm begging you—"

"Save your pleas. I'm not sending you to Tartarus. You did what you thought was right. What your father taught you, and his father before him.

But Arcideua did not deserve your wrath, no matter how much your wife's father insulted you or raided your lands."

"Am I to go to... Asphodel?"

"No."

"B-but..."

Since she could not understand his words, Aidoneus tapped her on the hand, signaling that it was time for them to stand in judgement. They rose in unison before he spoke again. "Hebros, son of Heamus and Rhodope, you will not be given the water of the Lethe. Instead, you will stare into the Cocytus until you understand the pain you caused others in your mortal life. We will see you again in one century to determine if you have learned enough to peacefully join the other souls in Asphodel."

The Thracian looked up at Aidoneus, tears staining his face. "I will have another chance?"

"Yes. Now go. Aeacus will show you the way," Hades said. Rhadamanthys opened the door once more.

"Thank you, my lord! You are merciful and just."

Persephone waited until the Thracian king was led away. She watched him pull his black himation over his head, using it as a cloak before the door shut behind him. Minos wound black ribbon around King Hebros's scroll and secured it with a gold clasp. The three-headed image of Cerberus sealed its contents, to be opened again when the Thracian returned to this room in one hundred years. He set the parchment aside with the others.

Her husband sat beside her and took a deep breath. She laced her fingers within his. "You spoke in his own language."

"It only seems fair..."

"Oh, I agree," she said. "But... you can speak Thracian as well as the king of Thrace. How many languages do you speak?"

"All of them," Aidon replied, turning to her.

She drew her hand away and looked at him in surprise.

"I've had an eternity to study, and learned the languages of the mortals from the shades themselves. It's fascinating— they keep changing as the centuries go by. You too will learn them all, one day."

"But I can't hear the dead once they've drunk the waters of the Lethe. Only you can."

He contemplated that for a moment. Aidoneus had possessed the Key for almost as long as mortals had been coming to and from the Underworld, and couldn't imagine what overwhelming silence Asphodel must be for her. "Perhaps you'll let me teach you myself, then."

"You would have to, if you want me to sit at judgement with you."

"Yes, I suppose. Sadly, I cannot read or write as many languages as I speak," he said, his admission surprising her again. "The writing of Hellas is all I've been able to learn."

Persephone smiled at him. "I can only read a few words, mostly what mortals write on the sides of temples. Which reminds me— what are those strange symbols written on the floor in our antechamber?"

"Minoan," he said. "The words themselves are just labels on the map. Few in the world above can write in that ancient tongue anymore. Minoan is also the language the Keres use to call you their Queen." Persephone recalled a painting she'd seen in Knossos, the ruined capital of the old empire on Crete, when her mother had fled with her from Attica's bitter war. She had seen those symbols there, but had thought they were only crudely scrawled pictures of animals and tridents, flowers and birds. She remembered her mother pulling her away from statues of proud and tall bare-breasted goddesses and queens; her favorite had gray-blue eyes and long skirts, and held snakes aloft in each hand. She remembered paintings of men with linen wraps around their waists, trimmed beards on their chins and long dark hair pulled back from their faces.

"Perhaps you can teach me to read it one day?"

"I'd be delighted. And maybe we can learn more together. There are people outside of Hellas who have written down all sorts of things I want to read." Aidoneus felt a corner of his mouth twist into a smile. "I'm glad you want to learn."

"Well, I liked listening to you speak in Thracian."

He looked straight forward, speaking under his breath to Persephone. "I thought you didn't understand Thracian."

"It was the sound of you speaking; the way it made me feel."

"And how is that?"

"Aroused," she said with a serene face, and glanced down to see his knuckles turn white on the arms of his throne. He bowed his back ever so slightly and drew in a long breath.

"When I speak in a foreign tongue?"

"Yes," she said with a hint of a smile.

"Well then, my queen… it seems there are all sorts of things I can do with my tongue that please you," he crooned, glancing out of the corner of his eye and smiling while she tried in vain to sit still, her thighs squirming together. He laced his fingers with hers and stroked her palm with his thumb. Aidon turned and studied her. "Do you know any languages besides our own? Any place we can start?"

"I speak the language of Attica, but not perfectly," she said, turning her head only slightly so she could see his eyes. "You'll have to go very slowly with me." She watched him bite down hard on the corner of his mouth and shift in his seat when he caught her double meaning.

"Gladly," he said, leaning toward her. "And what would you like me to say?"

"You could… tell me what you're thinking about right now," she said. Her stomach fluttered at just how dangerous that request was, so soon after teasing him. Aidoneus leaned over and cupped his hand to her ear. His breath tickled her neck.

"Se skeftomai sinehia. Se thelo, glykia mou... agapimeni mou... gynaika mou," he whispered in her ear, *"Meta to souroupo, otan kanoume erota... otan eimai mesa sou,* maybe then, I can tell you... in detail... what I'm thinking about right now. All though I'm sure my actions will make it evident..."

Fire bloomed within her and she gripped his hand tighter, hoping that Minos didn't hear her shortened breath. She looked straight ahead trying to maintain her composure, then shivered as he inhaled sharply next to her ear.

He caught the scent of roses on her skin and smiled before sitting back on his throne and speaking low once more. "Trust me, my love. Right now, my thoughts are not appropriate for mixed company."

Persephone thought about what she was going to do to him tonight for teasing her like this at her first judgement hearing, and knew that he was likely thinking the same. Their passions calmed, and they resumed the appearance of a king steadfastly holding his queen's hand while the room was at recess before their final hearing.

Rhadamanthys cleared his throat, drawing the attention of Hades and Persephone back to the door. "Your Excellencies, do you wish for Hypnos and Thanatos to bring forth the Ephyrean?"

Aidoneus turned to his wife. "I will help you, but he is all yours."

"Are you sure?"

"You questioned Merope; not I. You sent Thanatos and Hypnos after Sisyphus. Her testimony is instrumental in the judgement we will pass on him today. You *must* take the lead."

"But I can't hear his thoughts," she said.

"Leave that to me, my love. I am right here with you," he said, squeezing her hand.

Persephone faced the door. "Rhadamanthys, please send him in."

"Yes, my queen."

The door opened loudly, the ebony frame swinging wide. Rhadamanthys pushed open the second door, allowing Thanatos and Hypnos to escort the accused king into the throne room. After roughly releasing his arms, Death and Sleep stood on either side of Sisyphus. His hands were bound in front of him with iron manacles. A length of heavy chain, crafted to hold back the Titans, hung from his wrists. It scraped loudly across the floor.

Persephone narrowed her eyes at Sisyphus. His features were noble, like all the members of the House of Aeolus, with piercing blue eyes and gold-flecked dark hair. His shoulders were broad, but his legs were slightly short for his frame, as if he were somehow meant to be taller. Though he had seen at least forty-five years, his features were unnaturally youthful and magnetic— a convenient side effect of his sorcery. Only the darkened circles under his eyes disrupted the glamour of youth about him.

"Sisyphus," Persephone began. "Born Aeolides, son of Aeolus and Enarete, Prince of Thessaly and King of Eph—"

Her words were interrupted by low laughter from Sisyphus and she pursed her lips together, struggling to not react or be intimidated by this creature. She could feel rage and fire emanate from Aidoneus, but intuitively knew that his face was unchanged. She did her best to copy her husband, listening to the iron Chains of Tartarus rattle as the mortal king brought both bound hands up and pointedly wiped a tear from his eye.

"Hades, honestly," he guffawed, "is this your way of putting me in my place? To have your sweet little arm decoration punish me instead of dealing with me yourself? Or are you hiding behind her because the father and king of the new gods stands before you?"

Aidoneus felt a smile tease the corner of his mouth as he shifted on his throne and sighed. Neutrality aside, he would enjoy seeing Sisyphus punished. Without turning, he spoke to Persephone. "This one before us is a mortal man of Thessaly; a charlatan. A master of sleight of hand who calls himself a sorcerer—"

"Actually, I like to think of myself as a philosopher king," Sisyphus interrupted. "Not unlike yourself, Hades. In truth, I'm glad Thanatos found me. I've never spoken with you before. I know the other immortals quite well; I even took a nymph as my consort as Poseidon did. But I've only ever heard you spoken of in hateful, hushed tones. Even the gods are loathe to speak your name above ground. Which makes me curious. Why have you never risen against the tyranny of Zeus and claimed your birthright as the King of the Gods?"

"Forgive me, my lord," Thanatos said, pushing at Sisyphus's shoulder. "I forgot to mention that this one does not shut up. Ever."

Sisyphus glared back at Thanatos and gave him a wolfish smirk before facing the thrones again. "Also, Hades— by your own laws, Thanatos had no right to take me. All of you know that I was not properly buried by my family, nor did I pay Charon for passage across the Styx."

The Lord of Souls reached into the folds of his himation and flicked an obol with his thumb, the small coin rolling to a stop at the feet of Sisyphus. "There is your fee. We'll see that it reaches the Boatman."

Sisyphus swallowed, then composed himself quickly. "You are a fair god, Hades, and are as all-seeing with the souls of the dead as Zeus claims to be all-seeing with the living. Surely you know that I was wrongfully persecuted by him?"

Aidoneus remained silent.

"I was certain that there would be justice in *this* court for a man who saved the daughter of one god from being ravished at the hands of another," he said. Sisyphus looked pointedly at Persephone. "But clearly, that is not to be. Gentle Queen, do you know why I was originally condemned to Tartarus? What set me on my course? I helped poor Asopus find his precious, missing daughter. When he found her underneath the King of the Gods, crying for help, the lowly river god reacted as any decent father would, and I was blamed. This was when I was young, before I learned the ways of the world— before I learned that there is no justice. Only obeisance and tyranny. If the roles were reversed, if I had helped Zeus save one of *his* daughters from ravishment, I would be lauded as a hero and songs would be sung about me. Instead, I was condemned to the Pit— forced to take my fate into my own hands, which led to some... unfortunate circumstances. It would have been a different world, a better world, Aidoneus, had you drawn the right lot. But I couldn't imagine a realm such as this in worthier hands. If you are wise enough to decide in my favor, then I'll let you keep the Underworld when I overthrow Zeus."

Hades cleared his throat and turned to speak to Persephone. "You remember, my lady, on our journey to Tartarus when I showed you the fate of Salmoneus?"

She stared forward, a smirk threatening the corner of her mouth when she saw Sisyphus flinch. "I remember, my lord. The clatter he made in life, pretending to be my father, throwing thunderbolts and terrorizing his people, now echoes in his head unceasingly as he wanders the Fields of Punishment. He screams almost as loud as Ixion." She slowly turned to meet Aidoneus's gaze. "Dear husband, this cannot possibly be his brother, could it?"

The sorcerer king swallowed.

"One and the same, dear wife." They both turned back to face Sisyphus, their expressions unmoving and pitiless. "His father, a kinslayer, is in Tartarus for throwing his incest-born infant grandson to dogs, and then entreating his daughter, poor Canace, to kill herself. Another brother, Athamas, was driven to madness. His niece, Tyro— the rape of whom is one of the charges levied against this one— made the decision to kill her children before she took her own life. I am tempted to think that their entire bloodline runs with poison, and I will receive their children and children's children as guests of Tartarus as well. Now, this charlatan stands before us, declaring himself a god. Should we take pity on his madness, my queen, as we shall surely do when we finally receive Athamas? Or should we reunite this one with Salmoneus?"

"Salmoneus was a fool. I claimed his throne for a reason," Sisyphus said. "I care not that he suffers in Tartarus. It serves him right for trying to imitate Zeus so crudely. Not to mention his many slights against me."

Persephone thought about how Aidoneus had judged the Athenian magistrates. "How is Glaucus?"

"What?"

"How does Glaucus fare without his mother? He's just recently a man of fifteen, is he not? Surely he misses his mother, Merope— the wife you murdered to declare yourself an immortal before Ephyra?"

"She sacrificed *herself* to our new order; to me. Willingly."

Aidoneus turned to his wife. "I am amused that this one thinks he can lie to us in our own realm. A place where every thought in his head could be on full display for all assembled if I chose to lay it bare."

"Ephyra was a pile of pig shit before I built that great city!" Sisyphus yelled, his eyes flashing deep blue. "Now our walls are impenetrable; our treasuries overflow with gold! Before the sea became thick with ice, our ships sailed to every port of the Mesogeios delivering the grain your mother still withholds, Kore!"

Persephone flinched and squeezed her husband's hand.

"Oh yes, little Queen, I know *exactly* who you are. Kore. The lost daughter; the captive concubine, raped by the Unseen One day and night. That's what they say in Eleusis, at least— that you were ruined and soiled by Hades. Your mother now sits there as the self-appointed Queen of the Earth, giving their land grain as she decimates the rest of the earth. My people need me now more than ever! Is it fair to them for me, a savior and a living god of the Ephyreans, to die from something as trifling as an infection from a tooth-ache?"

Persephone willed her face to stillness, but his words bit hard. She sloughed off the baser insults, but felt her stomach twist knowing that her mother was starving the earth. What insults and wailing from the condemned must her husband have had to endure all this time? She turned to Aidoneus. "This one thinks he can sway us with pity and pride. That his shallow accomplishments mean anything after death; that his station is of any consequence. This one believes that his bones should not be returned to the earth from whence they were formed. To answer your question, my husband: no. I do not think we should take pity on him."

Her calm in the face of the condemned king's insults didn't go unnoticed. Aidoneus squeezed her hand until she looked into his cold eyes. They warmed only for her, for just a moment. Their first meeting in the dream came back to him— her voice and her words when she had challenged him. He knew now as he knew then that she was born for this. "Perhaps it is you who should deliver our judgement, my queen."

She turned her gaze to Sisyphus. "You stand before my husband Hades Isodetes, the great Leveler. Your wealth was vast, but your acts were vile. In utter futility, you tried to cheat my husband of your soul. From the moment you were born until the moment you died, Sisyphus, it belonged to him. And now you are here at last to return it. Salmoneus may have displeased the King of the Gods to earn his pun-ishment. But anyone who cheats the Lord of Souls of his due should expect his fortunes to be grave."

A smile twisted Sisyphus's mouth as he stared at her, unmoved and silent. Persephone stood, and Aidoneus rose tall beside her.

"Abandon all hope Sisyphus, son of Aeolus and Enarete. For the murder of your wife, the violation of your niece, for offenses against my father, and offenses against my husband and myself, you will not be given the waters of the Lethe. In the sight of my husband Hades Aidoneus Chthonios, firstborn son of Kronos, I, Persephone Praxidike Chthonios sentence you to burn in Tartarus for all eternity as you burned Merope on the pyre. Thanatos and Hypnos, Minos and Rhadamanthys, will escort you to the Phlegethon. The Erinyes will cast you into the Pit where the Hundred Handed Ones will exact your punishment."

She spoke as his queen. Aidoneus felt warmth course through him at the sound of her voice. Thanatos and Hypnos grabbed Sisyphus roughly by each arm and left the room, followed by the Mycenaean judges. The same smirk still decorated Sisyphus's face. Rhadamanthys shut the heavy ebony doors behind them with a slight bow, a broad smile for his queen's first hearing hidden by his gray beard and lowered head.

When she heard the echo of the heavy door slam shut, Persephone sighed, relaxing her shoulders. She gazed up at Aidoneus, handsome with his crown of golden poplar, regal with his raven crested staff held in his right hand. A smile slowly spread over his face.

"That went well, didn't it?" she asked quietly.

He chortled and shook his head. "You were incredible; majestic. I couldn't have done better."

"Aidon, that's... high praise," she said, dropping her gaze. "This was still my first trial. Surely there's much I can improve on for next time."

In a rare sight for anyone but her, his smile widened, his teeth visible. "I was being serious." *You were truly born for this, my queen,* he added to himself.

"So am I," she said earnestly, looking up at him.

He looked away and bit at his lip, playing over each detail of the judgement of Sisyphus, before turning his gaze back to her. Persephone shuddered as his pupils dilated and darkened.

"Well, after we've given our judgement to the condemned, it's customary to send only two escorts with them instead of four…"

"Oh," she said, her cheeks reddening. "Well… is it terrible of me that I was purposefully trying to clear out the throne room?"

Aidon drew closer to her. "And why would you want to do that, wife?"

Persephone couldn't hide her smile any more. Her husband closed in on her; the coy expression on her face was the only answer he needed. Aidoneus tilted her chin up with his left hand and bent forward to kiss her. She crushed her lips against his and jumped when she heard the staff clang against the dais after he dropped it to wrap his arms around her. She ran her hands up his bare arms, feeling his muscles cord under the gold bands. Persephone raised herself on tiptoe to lean closer to him. She canted her head and tasted him.

Aidon gripped her waist to press her closer, then grunted in discomfort when the heavy apron she wore slammed against him. He broke away from her for a moment, cursing. "Damn these ceremonial clothes!"

She grinned and unlatched the gold clasps at her shoulders and waist. The entire piece slumped loudly to the floor, a haphazard pile of red jewels and delicate gold chains strewn at their feet. He smiled and drew her in again, holding her against his body, feeling the heat growing between them.

"I'm glad I sent them all away," she whispered against his neck. She kissed him at the pulse point above his collarbone and felt him push aside the mantle she wore. He reached over the edge of her chiton to cup her breast, and then pulled the nipple over the edge, licking his lips and dipping his head to taste her. She gently pried his hands off her. "Aidon, this is the throne room! What if someone walks in on us again?"

"Sweet one, Hermes… *unwisely* disturbed us… but he's not part of our realm. I assure you, no one we rule over would be foolish enough to burst into any room where I am alone with you."

He looked down at her with an expression that someone unfamiliar with him would have mistaken for annoyance or frustration. And it was frustration, in part. He wanted her. He wanted every barrier standing between him and his entry into her body removed in that instant. He'd said as much amidst the heated words that had rolled off his tongue when he'd spoken to her in the language of those who worshipped her in Eleusis. Persephone teased him— dangerously stoking the raging fire. She moved her leg between his thighs and grazed past him again, listening as he hissed sharply at the contact. Persephone nipped at his jaw line, moving her hand down his stomach to splay her palm against his arousal.

Aidoneus exhaled sharply and spun her around, holding her from behind as he sat them down on his throne. He thrust his groin against her. Pinning her limbs to her sides with one arm wrapped around her waist, he firmly held her by the hips with the other.

"Are you regretting giving me a separate throne, my lord?"

He kissed her beneath her ear, her pulse fluttering under his lips. She squirmed on his lap when he lightly pulled at her earlobe with his teeth. "Now that you mention it…" He barely held back a laugh. "Can you imagine the look on my judges faces if we held court like *this*?"

"Aidon!" She giggled, half-heartedly slapping at his hands as he groped her breasts from behind and pulled her back against him. She felt him squeeze upward again, and their mirth faded back into desire. His arousal dug insistently into her rear as he nibbled at her earlobe and ran his thumbs over the hardened nipples ghosting through the front of her chiton. Persephone gyrated against him until she felt him nestled between her cheeks through their clothing.

He pulled back and whispered softly in her ear, his voice vulnerable. "Would you consider letting me take you this way?"

He pushed up again to drive home the implication. She blushed and looked around. "Right now?"

"No, no no…" he soothed and lightly kissed her neck with a smile. "In our own bed, of course, with… careful preparation. Someday, when we're both thoroughly relaxed and able to go slowly."

Persephone's breath caught at his suggestion. His fingertips danced across the underside of one arm, causing her whole body to shiver and grind seductively against his once again. "I didn't know that interested you, husband…"

"Knowing you in every way possible is what interests me, wife." He lightly grazed her arm with his fingernails, until he found where she had jumped before. When he reached it, he was rewarded with another wiggle of her bottom against his groin. Heat pooled low in her belly, matching his heat below her.

Her legs shook and she turned to kiss him. He wrapped an arm around Persephone to support her, turning her further still until she pulled her feet up onto the hard ebony arm of his throne and sat sideways in his lap, mating her tongue with his. She broke away and leaned her forehead against his. "Yes."

"Yes?"

"I want to know you in every way possible as well," she whispered. He heatedly locked his lips against hers again. Persephone delighted in his taste until he broke off, breathing heavily. Hades grabbed one of her slender ankles before moving his hand up her leg, drawing a slow path inward. "Perhaps very soon we can—"

A bang on the door thundered through the quiet throne room. Both sides burst open with enough force to gutter the torches.

"My queen! Lord Hades!" Hypnos flew in, his silver wings beating furiously as he cleared the doorway and alighted in the center of the room, out of breath.

His eyes flared in anger as Persephone scrambled to get out of his lap. She stood awkwardly next to the throne, righting her clothes.

Hypnos brought his hands up as if to shield himself from Aidon's rage. "Aidoneus, please. I wouldn't have dared to *knock* on the door, much less come in, if it wasn't deadly serious!" Hypnos nodded to Persephone. "Forgive me, my queen. A thousand apol—"

"Say your piece and *get out*, Hypnos!" he bellowed, his previously aroused mood stoking his anger. Aidoneus watched his friend cower and his wife jump at his voice and forced himself to calm down. "You can apologize for this incident later."

Hypnos took a deep breath. "He's gone."

"*What?*"

"Sisyphus escaped."

"That's not possible!"

"It gets worse. Aidon, my brother…" The silver haired god's lip quivered. "Minos and Rhadamanthys are with him, but…"

"Where are they?"

"The shores of the Cocytus. Aidon, we need you there. You'll want to bring the staff."

Aidoneus paled and stood up. He looked back to her contritely. "Persephone…"

"I'm coming with you," she replied. There would be time for apologies later.

3.

WHILE HYPNOS WENT TO fiND NYX, AIDONEUS and Persephone hurried down the staircases to the entrance of the palace. Without saying a word, he pulled her close against him and enveloped them both in dark smoke. They emerged from the ether at the farthest ends of the Fields of Asphodel, the darkness dissipating around them. Aidon grasped her hand and walked quickly toward the River of Lamentation, his long strides forcing her to walk briskly. The gray earth and flowering stalks became scattered and shorter as they went, then disappeared entirely, replaced by jagged rock.

Along the silent River Cocytus, black hooded shades stared into the waters, weeping despondently. The stench of the water made bile churn in Persephone's throat, bringing her back to a day long ago, when Attica had gone to war and the fields of wheat were razed. Demeter had shielded her from the sight of crows picking apart the remains of horses and hoplite soldiers. But her mother couldn't conceal the acrid smell of blood and decay. It was as if the Cocytus had washed through those fields, and preserved all the foulness within its stagnant depths.

Wailing and cursing interrupted her morbid reverie. Just ahead, Thanatos writhed in pain, his wings beating incessantly against the ground like an injured bird.

Persephone picked up her skirts and quickened her pace, feeling sharp rocks abrade her ankles. She winced at the first scrape, then set her jaw against the pain. Aidoneus jogged next to her in long, heavy strides, his staff level at his side like a spear. She cried out in the direction of the judges. "Minos! What happened?"

The judge joined her, following as she ran to where the Minister of Death lay. "My queen," he said, out of breath, "we don't know!"

"What's wrong with Thanatos?"

"The Ephyrean was here one moment," Minos shuddered, "then the next, the chains…"

Persephone blanched as Thanatos turned toward her. *A master of sleight of hand…*

The manacles that once held Sisyphus's wrists were now on Thanatos's arms. The links of iron chain laced through flesh and bone, grotesquely exiting his skin on the other side. There was no blood, no other sign of injury; he was a god. But, there was pain. Against all instinct, she forced herself not to be sick. The bile welling in her throat since she reached the shores of the Cocytus abated, replaced with empathy. The sight of her husband's friend, her friend, in such agony superseded the ghastly sight of the chains impaling his arms. "Thanatos! Stay still."

"My queen, you do *not* need to see this!" he yelled out, turning away from her.

Aidoneus walked to him, his heavy staff thumping on the ground with each step. Persephone ran over to Thanatos and knelt down to cradle his head, narrowly avoiding a thrashing wing.

"Please," he said through gritted teeth, "Don't… This was my fault—"

45

"No. This wasn't," she said, wiping beads of sweat off his forehead with the cloth of her mantle.

"Sisyphus planned it all along," Hades snarled, speaking to Thanatos. "He spent the entire judgement distracting us. Throwing us off guard. I should have read his thoughts... I should have been reading them the whole time. I let this happen." He knelt next to Thanatos and placed a hand on his shoulder. "I'm so sorry, my friend. This is going to hurt more than you can imagine."

"It already fucking hurts!" he screamed.

"What are you going to do?" Persephone said, looking up at her husband.

"Break the chains, pull them out," Aidon said quietly. He inspected the chains. "Most of them are missing..."

"Just do it already!" Thanatos gritted his teeth.

"You may want to look away—"

"No," Persephone said. She remembered from her youth when one of the Naiads had tended to another, removing a forgotten fishhook stuck deep in her heel. Persephone took the edge of her chiton and tore a strip of it away, wadding it up in her fist.

"What are you doing?" Thanatos said dizzily, the pain making him nauseous.

"Making sure you don't crack your teeth," she muttered, twisting it into a bit.

Aidoneus kept his voice calm and motions steady. "You will heal. But the pain—"

"Of course I'll heal! I'm a fucking *god*, aren't I?!" He forced a smile around the pain.

Persephone twisted the wool again and put it between Thanatos's teeth. He looked up into her eyes. The mask of anger, his feigned mastery of the pain, melted into fear. His eyes widened in panic, a vulnerability he only allowed her to see for a moment. She stroked his forehead. "Just be still, Thanatos."

She held him and watched as Aidoneus rolled a small boulder over to where he lay.

"I thought nothing could break the Chains of Tartarus."

"Everything has a weakness," her husband said quietly, raising the raven standard. "Hold him steady!" he called out to Minos and Rhadamanthys.

Aidoneus draped the center of the chain over the boulder, stretching out Thanatos's arms. The judges gripped him at the elbows and held his wings while Persephone leaned his head in her lap. "It will be all right," she whispered to him.

"On three," Aidoneus said. Thanatos started breathing hard around the twisted wool, bracing himself. Persephone nodded. "One, two…"

The staff landed with a resounding crack, and Persephone flinched away from the noise, feeling the ground lurch and shake. Death bit down hard and screamed through his clenched jaw, his arms flailing, flinging Minos to the earth while Rhadamanthys desperately maintained his grip. The boulder beneath the chains was broken into rubble. She tried to calm Thanatos, and saw Minos grasp his free arm to still him. The chain lacing through his wrists burned red hot from where it had been struck. Persephone smelled seared flesh and tried to push it from her mind so she wouldn't retch. She focused on Thanatos's face again, wiping away a tear that trailed down from his right eye. "Thanatos. Please! Be still… I'm sorry. I'm so sorry…"

A female hand appeared from behind her and rested on Thanatos's forehead. Persephone saw a beautiful, pale face framed in weightless black hair come into view beside her. The woman whispered to Thanatos. "Shhh…"

His head slumped to the side and his eyes shut. Thanatos stopped moving his wings and lay still, his breathing light. The strange goddess gently pulled the twisted wool from between his teeth. She hovered above Persephone, then moved as though she were swimming through the air to face the young goddess.

"You did nothing for which you should ever apologize, Aristi Chthonia," she said softly. "No matter what anyone tells you."

Aristi Chthonia. The name the House of Nyx and the Hundred Handed Ones called her. There was only one being this could be. Persephone kept Thanatos's head in her lap and bowed her head to the last of the Protogenoi. "Lady Nyx."

The elder goddess smiled and lightly lifted Persephone's chin until the Queen's blue gray eyes met her silver rimmed ones. "You never need bow before me, Queen of the Underworld," she said, smiling. Her face grew solemn again as she stroked Thanatos's unconscious forehead. "Especially not after showing such kindness to my son."

Hypnos alighted on the ground behind them. "Mother—"

"He'll be fine," she said, and caressed Thanatos's sleeping forehead again. "My poor, sweet boy..."

The Goddess of Night grasped Death's right arm in one hand before closing her eyes. The alabaster flesh on it disappeared for a moment and released a chain, the links falling neatly between the bones and onto the rocks below. She opened her eyes and his arm was made whole but for deep pits on his skin, the edges darkened where the broken chains had burned him.

"Hades..."

The bone of his left arm was squeezed within a link of chain. Aidoneus knelt down and stared at Persephone, his jaw set tight. *Just this once, my love, look away...* his eyes seemed to say to her. She kept her gaze trained on his face as he focused again on his task. Hades yanked the link out, snapping the bone in two as he did so. The sound made her stomach turn. Her husband winced as he pulled the metal away. Though he was unconscious, Thanatos jerked to the side, then stilled, his head held steady in Persephone's lap. Nyx patiently waited until the bone healed, knitting itself back together, before she released his arm. His scarred flesh appeared over it once more.

"We are all healing more slowly these days," she said, then looked to Hades. "Where is the rest of the chain?"

He sighed, frustrated. "Sisyphus stole it. I almost wonder now, Lady Nyx, if he allowed himself to be captured. The things he said at trial... If I had read him, none of this would have—"

"This is not your fault, Liberator," Nyx said, placing a hand on his shoulder. "Nor yours, Persephone."

She gathered Thanatos's limp form in her arms, the fringes of the darkness that surrounded her rushing in around him. They gingerly touched Thanatos, the wavering tendrils drifting softly over his limbs as if to comfort him.

"You'll know what to do," she said to Aidon, pointedly.

"What do you mean?"

"That you'll know what to do," she repeated. Nyx looked back to Persephone. "The tidings Hecate brought to me were ill, indeed. We must hold strong together, now more than ever. They will look to you, Aristi Chthonia, for guidance." Nyx rose upward toward Erebus, carrying her son, until she disappeared into the mists that hung above the riverlands and the darkness beyond. Hypnos nodded quietly to Hades and Persephone, worry etched across his face, then followed his mother and brother into the fog.

Persephone turned to the others, her heart sinking under the weight of Nyx's words, and saw her husband staring at the ground, his brow furrowed, his mouth set in a thin line. She walked over to him and laid her head against his chest. He brought an arm around her shoulders.

She looked up at him. "Has this—"

"No; never before."

"How did this happen?"

"I don't know," he said under his breath, looking out across the Cocytus and the shades weeping at its shores.

Persephone leaned into him. The pathways leading toward the palace from the marshlands of Acheron teemed with shades waiting to be judged. The emaciated, spectral forms desperately tore the asphodel roots from the gray earth and bit into them, heedless of the fact that whatever hunger they still felt was an illusion— a shadow of the manner in which they died. Their bellies were distended by starvation. Another boatload disembarked with Charon's guidance and walked solemnly toward the Trivium. She remembered what Kronos told her in the Pit and shuddered. Again, his terrible prophecy played out in her mind in all its vivid detail. Destruction, violation, rape, the end of all things...

Rules that bound the cosmos were bending, twisting, and disintegrating. The world above was breaking apart— and with it, she realized as ice poured down her back, the world below.

✿   ✿   ✿

"Merope."

The nymph startled awake. She sat up in bed, looking around her small room for the voice. Her eyes adjusted to the darkness and shadows cast by the single oil lamp burning low beside her bed. Ever since Queen Persephone had given her this room she'd kept it lit to hold back the encompassing dark. Merope looked to the door, then the plainly decorated walls, and lastly to the small ochre vases arranged on a table opposite the bed. The chair in the corner was empty but for a soft fleece thrown over its surface. She turned and glanced at the dark curtains draped across the window. A flash of light caught her eye.

The oil lamp's flame glinted again before she saw the shape of a man crouched on the window ledge, a face staring out from under a black hood. Her heart leapt into her throat, choking back her ability to scream. Merope backed up on her bed in fear, pulling the sheets up to her neck.

"It never ceases to amaze me," the shadow said, hopping down from her window and examining the flashing sickle that terrified her, "how this instills fear even in those already dead. Perhaps because it's the last thing they see before coming here."

"Th-Thanatos?" she said, trying to calm her racing heart. "Gods above, you scared me!"

"Seeing as how the gods above despise me, it's best not to swear to them in my presence. I am, after all, the antithesis of every prayer ever offered up to them," Death said, pulling back the hood of the himation with which he'd cloaked himself for the journey to the world above. Thanatos gave Merope a familiar and comforting smirk.

"Apologies, milord, but what are you doing here? And why do you have… *that*?"

Thanatos sat back in the corner chair and spun the sickle's handle in his fingers. "Well, this was given to me at the end of the war. It was the only thing I asked for, much to their surprise… no realm or palace of my own, no special honors… especially given the despicable thing I did to help win the Olympians' cause— something no one else seemed willing to do."

Merope shuddered, knowing full well what Thanatos meant. In the early days of the war against the Titans, the entire race of the Golden Men had been wiped off the face of the earth in the course of an afternoon by Death himself. Many of those who benefitted the most from what he did still hated him for having done it.

"Justice exacted on the ones who nearly destroyed my family was enough reward for me. To this day, they're baffled as to why I only asked for Kronos's sickle. I think it unnerved them, but in the end they thought it was appropriate for who I am. For what I do. The way I figure, the weapon that the Tyrant used to castrate my uncle, to maim my elder brothers when he came to power, was a fitting reward. And if such a weapon can injure gods and kill lesser immortals," Thanatos said, looking at her pointedly, "then surely it can handle a fucking abomination like your husband."

"But— he's— if you and Hypnos are back, that means he's—"

"Did you not hear? Sisyphus escaped," Thanatos said, setting the sickle against the wall. Merope paled in fear, panic seeping into her at the thought of her tormenter loose in the Underworld. He sauntered over to her, wings outstretched, his upturned arms presented to her. "But he was kind enough to gift me with these before he left."

Merope gasped, and cupped her hand over her mouth as she stared at the deeply pitted scars decorating his arms. "Are you alright?"

"Mostly. Where it counts, at least," he said with half a smile and his lower lip caught between his teeth. "Don't worry about me, my lady. I'm a god; it won't take long for the scars to disappear. By morning, I doubt you'll even see them."

Merope was too distraught to catch his insinuation. "How did he escape?"

"I was hoping you could tell me that." Thanatos narrowed his eyes at her. " When did Sisyphus learn how to bridge the divide between our world and the world of the living? What *didn't* you tell us?"

"I... I don't know how he—," she trailed off in fear. Nightmares of Sisyphus, Tartarus, the Keres, burning, screaming, choking... "Please, you must believe me! For the last eight years he hid everything he did from me! Don't send me back to the Pit, I beg of you! I swear to you, I h-had... n-no idea he could-d..." Her words were lost. She broke down crying, tears obscuring Thanatos's softening expression. "I..."

"Shh..." Thanatos ran his hand along her cheek, cupping her face, trying to soothe her. She sobbed and shook and he felt her tears trickle over the back of his hand. He shook his head. This was not going the way he'd wanted, and he weighed whether or not he should even be here. Thanatos had spent the last month hunting down the sorcerer king, thoughts of Merope haunting his every step. He wasn't used to waiting for women. For Thanatos, the time between desiring a willing woman and having them on their back was never greater than the span of an hour.

Once he had returned to Chthonia, he'd waited three agonizing days at his king's bidding before coming here. Aidoneus had told him to wait until Sisyphus was in Tartarus. And so he waited. Against every instinct he'd ever had, he waited, until she became a torment in his mind. Sisyphus was gone, and he wasn't about to wait *another* month. Merope was killing him just as surely as he, Death, was the end of all things. He'd read all the signals she'd given him since the moment they met, her eyes examining him just as carefully as he had looked at her. But now, when he was so very close, she was hysterical and feared him utterly. *What in Tartarus did that bastard do to you, Merope?*

"Merope, it's alright. Look at me," he said, waiting until her eyes met his. Maybe she was too damaged for what he really wanted. Or, he thought, maybe this was the perfect means by which they could both have some brief peace together and forget about the cruelties of the world above. Her deep hazel irises swirled in fear, then swam in relief when he studied her calmly. Another tear fell, caught between his fingers. He brought it to his lips and darted his tongue out to drink its saltiness, hoping that wasn't the last taste of her he'd have this evening. "Merope, I'm not him. You have nothing to fear from me— ever. Even if you *weren't* under the protection of the Queen." He leaned forward and kissed her on the forehead. "I just came here to make sure I had everything I needed before I left."

"E-everything?" she said, confused by the grin on his face.

He looked down and laughed quietly to himself.

"What's so amusing?"

"Nothing. You're an innocent, in every *true* sense of that word, Merope. It's an uncommon quality in a nymph, especially one who lived as long as you did." Thanatos smiled at her, reassuring the woman that he wasn't patronizing her. "I like it, truthfully. And since my attempts at subtlety obviously don't work on you, I think I'll have to be a bit more explicit," he said.

He leaned in and brushed his lips past hers until he felt her sigh in acceptance. When Merope opened to him, he pressed them to hers, their unexpected warmth searing through her. She hadn't thought the kiss of Death would hold any warmth at all, that he would feel cold. Thanatos started with her bottom lip, lightly nipping at its soft fullness. His tongue flicked against her teeth, tasting honeyed date wine, deep and sweet and fermented, before her mouth let him in. Her lips slanted against his and her hand came up to rest on his shoulder. Merope tried to gain some sense of balance against the relentless vertigo of his tongue stroking and battling against hers, filling her mouth with the heady, peppery first press of olives. She deepened their kiss and tasted him in turn, her head tilting back to allow him greater access. Merope broke away eventually, lightheaded, her head buzzing, her lips tingling, and for the first time since the pyre, her heart beating. An ache, a flood of liquid heat, dead and absent to her far longer than her fiery sacrifice in the *agora*, overtook her with a fierceness that made her gasp.

"Thanatos... I..."

"I'm leaving at dawn to kill your husband, Merope." He took her head in his hands on either side of her temples and pressed his forehead to hers. He spoke low, almost breathless. "But before I go, I'm spending the night in your bed."

"Why now?" The hand holding the sheet to her breasts clutched harder at his suggestion, as though she were afraid she would drop it right then, or that he would take it from her— rend it in his hands. Her breath hitched, realizing she

54

didn't mind either possibility. He drew away from her. When Merope shuddered, searching out his lips again, he knew that he had her, and would deny him nothing. Still…

"Because when I reap him, I'd like to do it for you. If I do it for the sake of my own vengeance, it will cloud my judgment. And I think spending tonight together will give both of us a chance to… lick our wounds. I've seen you," he said shrugging off the weight of his cloak and letting it fall to the floor. "I know you," He listened to Merope's breathing waver in anxious delight. Thanatos lounged across the foot of her bed and continued. "I know you desire me as much as I *clearly* desire you, but I will warn you now— Do not expect me to return to your bed after tonight. When I take someone, I only take them once. Now… knowing that, if this is what you want, I'll stay. If not…"

She glanced down the length of his body as he reclined unashamedly naked, unmistakably aroused, at the foot of her bed. Thanatos let her examine him, giving her complete awareness of her choice.

"Yes or no," he whispered.

Merope looked him in the eye. "Did you come here, come to me, to take revenge on him?"

Thanatos drew back for a moment, contemplating his answer. Truth, raw truth, had always been his ally. And if she didn't like his truth, then he would cordially leave now and find another to slake his unrequited lust. Tasting Merope's full lips, feeling her respond to him, had been satisfaction enough. He cocked his head to the side. "Maybe."

She nodded and saw his sinews tense, preparing to leave at her refusal. "You gave me your terms, Thanatos, now I'll give you mine."

"Go on…" he smiled. He relaxed his shoulders.

"I suffered Sisyphus in my bed and in my soul for seventeen years. And I won't do it ever again. So if you've come to me, thinking about my husband when you should be thinking about me, then I'll ask you to leave right now. But if you can put our scars aside," she said, leaning back and letting the sheet fall to her waist, "and allow us to enjoy each other for one night— then yes; you may stay."

"I'm certain I can agree to that, my lady." He smiled at her and slowly pulled back the rest of the sheet, hand over hand, until she was fully exposed to him.

He took in all the things about her that had haunted his imagination for a month. She sat up to meet him as Thanatos crept forward. His knee parted her legs and his arms held him aloft on either side of her. He brushed back the tight ringlets of her hair, tucking them next to her ear.

"Every night, my brothers have quelled your nightmares and healed you while you slept…"

Thanatos kissed across her cheek, and lightly stroked his fingers down her neck and collarbone, caressing the outside curve of her breast, a dark berry nipple beading against the gentle pressure of one digit.

"Now that your eyes are open, it's my turn."

His next kiss lowered her to the bed. Their limbs feverishly tangled together several times before dawn, alabaster hands on olive skin, male and female, awake and alive, both marveling at the contrast. She needed this, and though his ethos didn't always permit him to give women what they wanted, he always managed to give them what they needed when he had them. He wasn't upset at himself for bending his rules with her; it was all within the course of one night, and he wouldn't return to her. He knew in the back of his mind that even if he did want to see her again, it would be impossible. Their last coupling was leisurely and sublime, and as he rocked gently within her, Merope finally let go— ready— at peace. When light started filtering through her window, Death quietly draped himself in the black cloak that lay pooled at the edge of the bed. He planted a kiss on the nymph's sleeping forehead and walked to the window, sickle in hand.

"Goodbye, Merope," he whispered.

4.

"SHE WENT TO AEACUS TODAY TO DRINK THE waters of the Lethe."

"Who?" Persephone asked. "Merope?" Aidoneus nodded. She sighed and sat on the divan.

He walked behind her, brushing a hand down her back. "Does that upset you?"

"Only a little, and mostly for selfish reasons," she admitted. "I enjoyed having someone from my... previous life... that I could talk to, but every conversation would drift back to all the pain she endured. I don't understand why she insisted on clinging to those memories day after day."

"Many do," he said. "Sometimes, it seems those who've suffered the most are the least willing to let go. Merope is not the first such soul I've encountered; and I assure you, she will not be the last."

"Truly? I'm happy she finally decided to find peace in Asphodel." She stilled his hand on her shoulder and laced her fingers within his, looking up at him. "Any idea what convinced her?"

"I have my suspicions," Aidoneus said darkly. "Aeacus said that she was smiling, and calmer than he'd ever seen her. Merope told him she was ready and it was long overdue. She wanted to say goodbye to us, but told Aeacus it would only make it harder."

"I just wish there were something more that we could have done for her."

"What more? Merope is at peace now."

She slid over so he could sit next to her and gazed out over the Styx beyond the terrace. Persephone shook her head. "I'm not sure. It is true; Merope will be at peace in Asphodel..."

"But..."

"...She will be reborn one day. And while the living world is a place of joy and sunlight..." she paused when she saw Aidon cast his eyes downward. He looked exhausted. She stroked his cheek and reassuringly looked him in the eye once more. "There is still so much suffering. Needless, endless suffering. And it's so strange to think that she will come back as a mortal with no recollection of the aeons she was alive."

"Not for a while, rest assured. Her circumstance is... unique, but we are the caretakers of the souls. We can't make special exceptions in a cycle as old as mortality itself. But if we could, what would we do differently? What would you want?"

She smiled and dropped her gaze, tears in the corners of her eyes. No matter how vehemently the House of Nyx and the Hundred Handed Ones had insisted that this realm belonged to her, she was still amazed that Aidoneus sought to include her as his equal. "I'd let the better souls rest."

He raised his eyebrows at her. "The better ones?"

"Merope, for instance. Surely she has done enough good and suffered enough ill?"

"Who else?"

She thought for a minute. "Tartarus is there for those who spend their lives destroying the lives of others, is it not? But what about their opposites? What about those who made the lives of those around them better? What about

58

those who sacrificed themselves for others, those who were especially brave or kind…"

"And sacrifice their usefulness to the world above? Won't the living world only deteriorate if we cloister them here?"

"If they decided to leave, they would have that right. And new souls are made here every day. They can take the place of those who wish to stay. People can change."

He frowned. "You have more faith in them than I do, I'm afraid."

"They can. After all, *we've* changed, and it certainly took less than a human lifetime. I would be unrecognizable to someone who knew me only before I met you. And you've changed as well."

"Oh?" he said with a smile.

"Well of course you have," she said, brushing the lines near his mouth and eyes. "This, for instance. You were so very grim and serious when I first arrived."

"I was afraid."

"You? Of me?" she said with a teasing smirk. He nodded. "The warrior who fought Titans?"

He lowered his head, the half smile still on his face. "Doesn't compare to the terror of starting my married life with you, sweet one." He chuckled when her nose scrunched up. "I don't mean that to offend. Remember, it took me all the time from when you reached majority until two months ago to muster the courage to ask for you. And nothing in my life frightened me more than the possibility that I'd lost you forever, thanks to the manner in which I brought you here."

"But nothing frightens you now?"

He looked away, exhaustion evident on his face once more. He'd barely slept the night before. She'd drifted out of sleep a few times over the course of the night, just as worried as he was, and each time she'd seen Aidoneus staring at the ceiling, willing himself to rest. She held his hand. "Sisyphus."

"It's more than just him. So many things have transpired that are *not* supposed to happen. And after what we were told— what we saw in Tartarus..."

"Husband, none of that was true."

"There were grains of truth. And now..." he shook his head and paled with anxiety. "A mortal... a *living mortal* has stepped through barriers that *gods* cannot cross, and he could have done so at any time. But he chose that *last* moment, on the final leg to the Phlegethon. He only stayed as long as he did to observe our strengths and weaknesses. And I don't know what he learned or what he'll do with that knowledge, much less with the Chains he stole."

"How can he possibly have done that?"

Aidon said nothing.

"The Titans are infinitely more powerful than he is, so if Sisyphus was able to escape, why haven't *they*?"

He remained silent. All he could see was the last vision of Kronos.

"And why didn't Hecate—"

"Because she was busy trying to reason with your mother!" he snapped. He looked at Persephone, her shoulders tensed, her face drawn. "Wife, I'm sorry. Forgive me."

He dropped his forehead into his hand and shut his eyes. Persephone leaned against him. "It's all right. I shouldn't expect you to have all the answers."

"I don't think anyone has the answers right now. Too many impossible things have happened since..." he silenced himself, knowing where this led.

"Since you brought me here," she said, and watched him scowl. "Not all of them are bad things, Aidon. The grove, for instance."

"Well, our grove— and everything we know— will either end in flames or vanish into nothingness if she—" he bit his cheek and took a deep breath. "If this continues much longer."

"Do you think to somehow protect me from what my mother is doing?"

"No."

"Then why are you holding your tongue?"

"Because you asked me to. It was the first thing you ever asked of me."

"I recant. Speak your mind." The gravity of the situation demanded honesty, but Persephone was quietly pleased that her husband had been so loyal to his promise.

Aidoneus opened his eyes as wide as the floodgates she had just parted. "There's so much I've held—" he swallowed. Where would he begin? "When I took you from the fields it was because Demeter was willing to sacrifice all, including you, to keep you from me. And even now, her stubbornness is destroying everything from the heavens to the depths of the Pit. I don't understand why I became the target of her wrath when it was your father who mistreated her in the first place! He deceived and abandoned her, left her heavy with child, he killed her lover—"

Persephone's mouth went agape. "Her… My mother's what?!"

Demeter's policy of keeping Persephone ignorant had stopped surprising Aidoneus a while ago, but this instance didn't stop him from shaking his head at the injustice done to his wife. "Some years after you were born, a mortal farmer came across the shores of the Styx with stories about Demeter, and an infant goddess named Kore. His name was Iasion— a very skilled farmer, in truth. The greatest mankind had produced in those early days. Zeus had caught them… coupling… and struck Iasion down as he lay beside your mother. He died instantly— he didn't even know what happened."

"Why would Zeus do such a thing?" she said, horrified. "He'd already abandoned my mother! Why couldn't he just leave us alone and let her be happy?"

Aidon pursed his lips. "Because he still loved her, in his own selfish, foolish way. He sought an alliance with Hera because she was a better match. And that was the most frustrating thing for me. I always knew that Hera was a better choice for him, but what could I have told your mother? Hera was craftier, more influential— clever in all the ways Zeus wasn't, and they complemented each other perfectly. But that didn't mean he loved Demeter any less."

Persephone scowled, angry, wishing she could have known at least something about Iasion, this singular man who had never caused her mother any grief. She also puzzled at why her mother hadn't made her lover immortal— especially when he had given her so much joy.

"After I learned what I could from Iasion," Aidon continued, "his shade drank from the Lethe and was at peace in Asphodel, his name forgotten. But I could see what manner of man he was. He was too valuable to the world above to languish below, and when the time was right, after mankind regained Prometheus's fire, I returned him to the mortal world. Before he left, I did something I had never done before, and had his shade drink from the Mnemosyne before departing."

Persephone shivered, remembering the flood of memories when she'd sipped a few drops of the Mnemosyne. "What happens to shades when they drink from it?"

"The Pool of Memories gives them a chance to recall fragments of their previous life when they return. It would be a dangerous thing to give mortals *all* their memories back; they would go mad. I've only allowed rare souls the privilege. Iasion had more to do, more to teach to his kind… but another part of me…"

She held his hand, tracing the lines on his palm.

"…I had hoped that when his soul returned it would find Demeter, somehow. Give her some happiness, be it as a friend or lover."

"Aidon, why didn't you ever tell my mother this?"

He clenched his teeth together. "Hermes was not yet born. Without the Messenger of the Gods, I had no way to tell her, short of rising out of the earth myself, which our pact forbade me to do. I later learned my efforts were for naught. Demeter had long since made her home in Nysa, where mortals cannot go. The shade returned across the Styx after a full life. She had been a mother of six, a grandmother of twenty. She milled wheat, baked bread with her husband, and bartered it at market. Her whole village mourned her death and buried simple, tender gifts for her to carry here with her. I was glad for it, but didn't interfere with Iasion's soul again."

Persephone shifted and sat across from him, holding his hands. "This is why I wish there was something we could do for souls such as Iasion's. A way for them to keep their memories, to rest, to be rewarded for a life well lived."

"Sweet one, I only have what I was given when I came here, and this order existed well before you and I, before the current race of mortals even came into being. There is Asphodel, and there is Tartarus. It would be a torment for shades to walk the Fields with memories of their lives— imagine when they meet those they knew and loved, stripped of everything that made them alive. That fate serves as a temporary punishment for the shades that stand at the Cocytus, and eternal agony for those in Tartarus."

Persephone bit the inside of her lip while she digested his rebuttal, helplessly sympathizing with those noble souls trapped by aeons of tradition. She lifted her feet onto the divan. "Will Thanatos be all right?"

"He already left to hunt down Sisyphus."

"But he was seriously injured! Why did you send him?"

"I didn't," Aidon said, pulling away. "Hypnos told me this morning that his brother left in the middle of the night."

"I didn't mean to sound accusatory, Aidon," she said. "How did they capture Sisyphus in the first place?"

"He was in Chios, and they snared him in the Chains while he was—" Hades stopped cold and stood up, his mind turning. He paced across the floor of their antechamber. "Gods..."

"Aidon?"

"That... *gios enos kakodaimonos suagroi...*" he snarled, cursing in the common tongue.

"Aidon!" she said incredulously, scrunching her nose in surprise at his profanity.

"I don't know how I didn't see it before!" He turned to her, eyes alight with new understanding. "Everything happening in the world above... it largely rests at your mother's feet, but he's been exploiting and *worsening* it! That's why he was going from city to city, priestess to priestess... I *knew* this couldn't be all Demeter's doing..."

"What do you mean?"

"The earth has ways of restoring itself, with or without Demeter. She is *not* the only one watching over the earth. There's Gaia, Rhea... It could not have become this bad unless there was something else at work. And the *something else* is Sisyphus! He's been using the wise women who've been trying to restore the earth to sap its vitality even faster."

"How?"

"The *hieros gamos*," he said, sitting down again. "The mortals' version of it, at least. What Hecate and others have taught the nymphs and mortals is that they are surrendering themselves to creation, distilling the primordial energy of the earth and returning it to their fields and villages. Sisyphus was using them to steal that for himself! With all he'd amassed before coming here, he was able to escape. And since the Olympians barely keep to the old ways, he's been able to do this right under their noses!"

"But why would he purposefully get caught, come down here and steal the Chains?"

"It was all in what he said...all I dismissed as delusion. He means to overthrow Olympus. He had the last Book of

Tantalus, for Fates' sake… Seeking immortality, seeking the means to bind the gods themselves…" he brushed his hand back through his hair and began pacing again. "He sees himself as a damned hero…"

"But he wouldn't have been able to do any of this if my mother weren't…"

Aidon thinned his lips and looked down.

"Aidoneus, we have to do something. You and I—"

"How? We have no say over the world above. Zeus will speak to Dem—"

"My father isn't going to convince her of anything!" she said, wrinkling her brow.

"You didn't know them *together* as I knew them. She will listen to him."

"She will not! You don't know them *now*, Aidon. Zeus was the one who consented to give me to you in marriage. If she was going to bend to his will, she already *would* have. Do you *honestly* think Zeus has the power to convince her to do anything?"

He put his head in his hands, his fingers pulling back through his hair. Aidoneus shook his head. "Then what should I do?"

They will look to you, Aristi Chthonia, for guidance…

"Are you looking for advice?" she said cautiously. "Or are you just curious about my opinion, as you were with the fate of mortals who had led good lives?"

"No, Persephone. I am legitimately seeking your counsel. I'm lost," he said. Lines appeared on his forehead, and he met her eyes again, his expression filled with pain and uncertainty. She knew he would never allow anyone else to see him like this. Persephone wanted to wrap her arms around him, but she fought to stay where she was and listen without distraction. His voice wavered. "What Demeter wants is untenable. This world needs you too much. *I* need you. I cannot give her what she desires. I'm lost. I didn't ask for the weight of this to fall on us."

65

Persephone nodded. "I must go, Aidon."

He looked up and felt his heart nearly stop. He had always sworn to himself that he would let Persephone go if she asked it of him. And now the fate of the world hung over their heads. It was the rational thing to do; a decision Aidoneus would have made himself— before she had awakened everything within him. He tried to speak around the lump in his throat, to calm himself. Showing his distress would only make it harder for her. "Back to Demeter..."

Persephone watched him heroically try to mask his panic, but she could sense what he feared— that she was about to leave him forever for the sake of the mortals. "Not *back* to her, Aidoneus. I need to tell her that I've made my choice. That it's mine to make," she said, and saw faint hope flicker in his eyes.

"If you do this, it cannot seem as though I'm exerting any influence over you."

"Then I need to go to her alone." *Tell him.*

"What will you say?"

"I will tell her that this has gone too far, that too many have suffered. I'll say that she can come visit us whenever she chooses, and I can see her when it doesn't interfere with my duties as Queen." *It's time*, Persephone thought. "I'll say that I need her acceptance. I am married. I am Queen of the Underworld. She needs to understand that you are my husband." *Tell him.* "That it's not just duty that keeps me, but that I choose to stay with *you*."

He stared at her as she took a deep breath, her heart beating out of her chest.

"And I choose to stay with you because... I love you."

"You—"

"I love you, Aidoneus."

Aidon expected to feel a change once he finally heard her say it. Perhaps he did— a sensation of everything clicking into place, a sweeping sense of rightness and peace pervading his being. He'd given her time to think it over and consider its meaning.

"My love?" she said, tentatively breaking the lingering silence. Her voice came out meek and small. "Are you alright?"

He smiled softly at her. "More than you know. Because now I can finally speak the words I've been longing to say since the moment I met you."

"What would those be?" she whispered.

"I love you, too."

She felt her cheeks and eyes burning hot. It wasn't until her vision wavered and she felt teardrops fall onto her peplos that she realized she was crying.

"Why are you weeping, sweet one?"

"I don't know," she smiled, brushing a hand across her cheek. It was futile. The levee had burst and everything she'd held back for days streamed down her face in a torrent. "I don't know why I am when what I feel is... relief. I can't explain it. I haven't felt this since I— not ever! Not even when I lived in the world above. I've never felt so..."

He reached to her and brushed away another tear.

"...So free," she said and reached up to hold his hand. "I love you. I waited to say it, and I'm glad I had time to think on it, but... Aidon..."

Persephone said nothing more. His lips were already on hers, slowly savoring her. Aidon kissed the corner of her mouth, where one of her tears had trailed, and brushed his lips across hers to peck at the other corner. He drew back and looked at her, his eyes warm, rare flecks of gold appearing in his dark brown irises.

He looked away from her and smiled broadly. She placed her hands on his chest and he looked back at her, both their eyes swimming. Aidon grasped her at the back of the neck and pulled her lips against his, sampling them before canting his head and feeling her open to him. She tasted like sunlight.

Persephone hummed softly and Aidon brought her closer, wrapping his arms around her and feeling the room itself tilt, losing himself in her. He wavered between staying here to enjoy this moment or carrying her to their bedroom to celebrate this revelation more fully.

She decided for them. Persephone grasped at his robes and stood, bringing him with her, then pulled at his himation until it dropped around his feet.

"What would you have of me, my love?" he whispered against her lips.

Persephone stopped and flushed pink. "I... want to hold you."

"To hold me?" The corner of his mouth twisted up.

"It's... such an uncomfortable angle here on the divan. I thought we would... be more comfortable, that is, if—"

He chortled at her stumbling words. "Are you sure that's all?"

"I— Yes," she said, not meeting his gaze.

"Why so shy? We've lain in that bed many times over."

"It's just very... everything feels *heightened* right now." How could she put it into words? When they were, as Aidon had phrased it several days ago, merely friends and lovers, she had no hesitation at all. Half their encounters she had initiated herself, much to their mutual delight. Her chest felt heavy and her throat closed again, tears forming before she could speak. "I don't know. I feel... exposed."

Aidoneus nodded and held her closer. "I understand."

"You do?"

His mouth remained set, but his eyes smiled. She gathered at once that this was how he had felt after his declaration burst out of him the day she arrived. That such a time spanned between their confessions made her heart ache.

"My sweet Aidoneus, I'm sorry."

"Don't apologize—"

"I was scared. I thought if you knew you'd won me that you would lose interest and abandon me, the way Zeus did

68

to my mother," she said warily, and saw an incredulous half smile quirking the corner of his mouth.

"Can the sun find its match in anything but the moon? Can the heavens lose interest in the earth?" Hades pulled away from her and stroked her cheek. "Can death exist without life?"

She looked away from him. "But, I waited so long…"

"No you didn't," he said. "And I was willing to wait far longer."

She stared up at him, her eyelids growing heavy, her body urging itself closer to his. "I think… we'd be more comfortable elsewhere, my lord."

"After you, my queen," he gestured toward the bedroom. "We…"

"Not unless we both desire it. And right now I need the same thing as you."

Persephone relaxed her shoulders and led the way, almost regretting her shyness. Her heart was beating faster than it ever had around him, and she sat at the edge of the bed before hitching up the skirt of her peplos to scoot back on the sheets. Aidon clenched his jaw, studying her bare legs before joining her. She lay on her side and he nestled in behind her, his hand stroking her arm. For a moment she was reminded of their first meeting in Eleusis, and her thighs closed together around a familiar empty ache. She waited for it to pass. When she relaxed again and fit her body to his, she felt him pressed against her rear.

"Ignore it," he muttered through his teeth.

She rolled over to face him with a smile. "Hard to ignore."

"As are you," he said. He wound his fingers into the hair at the nape of her neck and pulled her close, kissing her forehead. He whispered her name against her skin.

"Aidoneus…" she answered. "I love you."

He spread his hand across her back and pressed her closer still. "And I love you. It pleases me to hear you say it aloud."

"But not for the first time."

"That day at the Lethe," he said under his breath.

"That's not what I speak of. I said it a few days ago, once I knew you were asleep," she shyly admitted, "and every night since."

"I wish I had heard. I wish I'd been willing to hear you say it."

"But you were right. We weren't ready."

"What changed?"

"Everything. I couldn't go any longer without telling you. Not with what I have to do. It was time."

"Time." He laughed dryly. "To think— I've only had the pleasure of hearing that, of feeling that, for such a short time. *Minutes*, for Fate's sake, and now you have to leave me."

"I should go first thing tomorrow."

"So soon?"

"I won't be long. And it must be done, my love. Every day we delay, more die."

"Their journey here is inevitable. They're mortal."

"I know. But to come here all at once is neither fair nor just," she said. "The balance of everything—"

"Please stay with me a few more days. It will make little difference in the end."

"Husband, this— I don't understand. You've always looked beyond yourself to the greater good."

"You think too highly of me, wife. Please, please permit me a shred of selfishness," he said, kissing her. "Stay. Just a day or two longer."

She sighed softly. Maybe she should stay and enjoy this. All of her time here had been spent trying to find where they stood in each other's lives, and now she would leave just as soon as they had found it… "I'll think about it, Aidon. But we know I must go eventually."

He nodded and brushed stray hairs from her forehead.

"How will I get there?"

"There are many ways. The long roads are by way of the passages through which the souls descend to the Styx. They wend through the caves and chasms in the world above, and on foot the journey can take days. The short road, through the ether… to traverse those same boundaries requires the Key."

"Which means you'd have to go with me."

"Which we cannot do, or Demeter will not listen. And I don't like the idea of stranding you in the world above, sweet one."

"Neither do I," she said. The sleeve of her peplos slipped down on her shoulder and she saw Aidon's eyes follow it. "What if they don't let me come back?"

"There's no 'let' for one such as you," he said, and nudged the edge further down her arm, exposing more of her collarbone. She leaned into the brush of his fingers.

"There is if I am unable to return here. And we both know that Olympus doesn't hold me in quite the esteem that this world does." She shifted closer to Aidon and he pulled the fibula away from her shoulder, setting it aside. "Is there any way to borrow the Key?"

"No way which I am aware of," he said reaching for the pin holding up the fabric of her other shoulder, the motions familiar, then remembered her desire to just *hold* each other. He looked at her and spoke low. "Is this alright?"

She nodded.

"Are you sure?"

"Yes," Persephone looked into his eyes. "I need to touch you."

"Is that all?"

"For now I just— I want your skin on my skin."

This felt like the first time he'd lain with her, when they cautiously joined together in her bed at the other end of the palace, the oil lamps' low lights barely flickering across their

71

skin, hidden from one another. This time, they were well versed with each other. Just the same, Aidon moved slowly. He unhooked the other shoulder of her peplos, carefully untied her girdle, and brushed the fabric off her shoulders and waist until she was bared to him. Her hands moved down to his waist, unfastening his belt. He pulled out a fibula at one shoulder, shrugged off the other side of his tunic, then his loincloth, before gathering up her clothing with his and casually tossing it to the floor.

Aidoneus gathered the sheet around them and held her close. The feel of her naked skin was torment enough without the sight of her soft curves flush against the angles of his body. He lay on his side and pulled her against him, stifling a groan when her stomach pressed his arousal between them, the tip seeping with want. The scent of roses and lilies and all things uniquely Persephone filled his senses. It would take very little effort on his part to pull her leg over his hips and slowly sink into her welcoming heat, and he imagined she would offer him no resistance. Instead, he bent forward and kissed her, then pulled her toward him, achingly slow, until they were face to face. She ran her left hand along his arm and up to his shoulder, her body wrapped and enfolded within his. Her right hand rested over his heart, feeling his pulse quicken the longer her lips stayed locked to his. He held her fingers beneath his free hand and pulled away to look at her.

"Is this what you meant by holding each other?"

"Yes," she said against his neck. The feel of him against her soothed and inflamed all at once, and she felt the low throb between her legs start to ache, begging her to claim the hardness nestled against her thigh. But right now, she wanted only this feeling of security and sureness, new yet familiar. Persephone glanced at his hand over hers, over his heart, the rings glinting dark and sanguine in the hearth light. "How were you given the Key?"

He inhaled and tensed. "Nyx… burned it into me, so to speak. It originally belonged to her and Erebus."

"Did it hurt?"

"Unbelievably so. It knocked me senseless, and I stayed unconscious for a long time after. But the Key is a part of me. These," he said, holding up the rings, "are symbols. When I take them off, the Key remains within me, but its power becomes more distant. So merely pulling the rings off my fingers and placing them on yours would do nothing."

She sighed and looked down. "How will I go, then? How will I come back?"

Hades pursed his lips. There must be a way to do this. He recalled the day on Aitne at the end of the war, when he was so certain he would draw the lot for rulership over all. The Key had fueled his hubris. Now it was the very last thing he had that she didn't. Everything else he'd given her— or had taken from him. This was the last piece— his ability to move freely from one realm to the next— and the prideful, fearful part of him clung to that desperately. Once Aidoneus realized that, he knew what must be done, but didn't know how to go about it. "I need to give you the Key."

"How?"

"I don't know," he said, perplexed. Aidon held Persephone closer, trying to think his way through their dilemma. Her skin moulded against his, perfectly fitting them together. *Almost perfectly*, he thought ruefully. He could feel and hear her heart beating against him, her chest rising and falling in time with his. If Nyx was willing to give him the Key, it meant that the Queen of the Underworld was to one day have it. "She never told me—"

You'll know what to do.

What do you mean?

That you'll know what to do.

She felt his whole body tense when he stopped mid-sentence. "Aidon?"

He looked into her eyes, feeling as if a fog had been lifted. Aidoneus wasn't supposed to *give* Persephone the Key...

Why not just be King and Queen to each other, Aidoneus, and to Tartarus with what anyone else says?

...he was supposed to *share* it with her.

"Persephone," he said, weaving his fingers into her hair. He stared into her eyes. "I need you to trust me..."

He'd said the same to her on their descent to the Underworld, when he'd revealed himself to her. *Trust*, she thought. *Give yourself over at last.* "Yes," she said, nodding her head, ready, prepared.

"Just let go," he said, closing his eyes. The words were meant for him as much as for her. He grasped her left hand within his and leaned his forehead to hers, much like when he had eased the torment she'd suffered in the Pit. She felt him reach carefully into her consciousness, trying to pour himself into her. He opened his eyes, hers following his lead and staring up at him.

Persephone drew in each breath in time with his, conscious of each inhale and exhale only when his eyes locked to hers. Aidoneus rolled her onto her back and followed over her, clasping her hand tightly within his, resting his body-weight on his right elbow. She moved with him out of instinct, as though this were a dance, the edges of their consciousness blurring. As he lay astride her, cradled by her, he stared into her. Through her. He lowered himself, their hands linked between them, each against the other's heart.

Warmth pervaded her and she felt a strain between them, as though they were at the edge, about to push through, so close, so close... She looked up at him and felt the rise and fall of his chest with hers, felt her heartbeat increase its tempo, catching up to his. Her eyes met his and she quaked. His presence in her mind was palpable. She met him equally— thought for thought, soul and soul intertwining. He blinked as though something had dawned on him, and she understood, the same realization sweeping through her. *This isn't about sharing the Key*, she thought. *It is already shared. He and I are one.* Almost. She nodded at him and urged his hips forward with her free hand.

His flesh joined hers, and they were drawn inward, together into one space, one moment— oneness. She felt the glorious stretch to accept him and gasped once he finally sheathed himself within her. Her voice sang out and his teeth gritted, each momentarily overwhelmed by the intensity, and then concentrated again. Sensations, thoughts and will coalesced, wrapped around each other, winding, melting. They gazed directly into each other, through each other, unflinching. Their breathing slowed together and she felt his heart beating against the back of her hand, and hers against his, falling in time with his.

Blinding fire seared between them at every point they were joined, cycling through and around them in bursts of heat and trails of light at the edges of their vision. Persephone felt her left hand burning as though it had been thrust into coals. She winced, but held steady, enduring it.

From a distance, she heard whispers. *Theos... Pater... Sotir... Anax...*

"Aidon?" she broke her gaze and looked down at her hand clasped within his. Red stones burned on his fingers.

And upon hers.

Thea! Sti Thea!... She's here!... Annessa! Annessa kai Anax!... Pater kai Metra, hear me... Theo kai Thea...

The shades in Asphodel. She gasped in shock. They were speaking to her. Goddess. Queen. Savior. Mother.

"Oh gods," she said, "I can hear—"

It's alright, my love, my sweet wife... I'm here; I've got you.

She startled and looked up at him with a sharp inhale. "Your voice!"

He shuddered. A deep part of him knew, but it shook him nonetheless. "You're able to hear..."

Your thoughts, she finished as he held his breath.

75

He could hear her as well. Persephone saw his mouth part in awe. She spoke within his mind as he had within hers. Then his eyes closed in pleasure, realizing where he still was. She moaned when he surged forward.

Then hear this, my Persephone, he said, focused and intent. *I am yours. I am yours alone and I love you. Don't ever doubt that. Not ever. I was as dead as this kingdom before you came to me. I am alive with you.* He withdrew and sank into her again. *Within you.*

She brought her hands around him and clawed at his back. *Aidon... You showed me everything... I had nothing, I was nothing, I was a scared little girl...*

To me, you were always a woman, Persephone. My queen. Always. He cupped her face with one hand and kissed her. *I only showed you what was yours. What has always been yours.*

They stilled, clinging to each other, feeling their love-making within and through each other, the sensations and movements too much. She sensed each thing he shared with her. Persephone listened. His breath was ragged against her left ear and she could feel his body straining between the instinct to move within her and the enveloping bliss that gripped him when he did so. She could feel those sensations warring within him, she realized. Her hands moved soothingly over his back and she squeezed around him. He groaned, his fingers clenching her skin.

She listened, letting her perception broaden. *Theos... Annessa... Anax... Pater... Sotir... Metra...*

The voices of Asphodel. And deeper than that, welling up in fear and anger, the voices of Tartarus.

Annessa, you freed that nymph bitch! Free me! I do not deserve to be here... The chains are weakening... Anax, she deserved it!... They have upset the balance further... The end nears for them and we will be free... Briareos can do nothing...

Persephone felt Hades's jaw clenching, knowing that he heard them too. The damned. The Titans. She'd had enough of their presence in her thoughts, in their moment together, and cast them away like darkness running from torchlight.

Be silent. Now! You will intrude on us no more...

Their voices stopped.

Aidoneus looked at her with wide eyes. "What did you do?"

"I..." she licked her dry lips. "I told them to be silent."

"I know you did, but..." he said, confusion melting into admiration. "Persephone, this is the first time they've ever truly been quiet."

Her breath came out unevenly around her words. "It's... it's still for you now? *That* is what you were hearing day and night for aeons?"

"Yes. But you..." He gathered her up in his arms, sitting back and raising her with him, her body sinking down upon his. *My love, you don't understand... I could quell them before, but now...*

"Aidon, we—ah!" She clung to his shoulders as he pushed deep into her.

For the first time, for the first time since I arrived, they are quieted. More importantly, Persephone, he *is silent. Completely.*

You cannot hear Kronos's voice?

No, sweet one, you freed me... My love, my light, my sweet wife... my queen...

She gripped his back, her fingers tracing the long scar, and held onto him as he drove into her, joining with her again and again. On the edges of perception, they heard the voices of Asphodel.

Sto Theo, sti Thea! Aristi, Aristi! Chthonios kai Chthonia...

They were calling out to them. Chanting. Celebrating. They knew she could hear them— that the Queen could hear her subjects at last. Ululated trills arose from the voices; the celebratory cries of women, echoing through all of Asphodel, millions of voices in a rising tide.

Aidoneus glanced to the open door, out to the balcony. He heard them too, and turned to his wife, spurred on by the joyful noises outside. Persephone didn't spare him her voice either, each plunge eliciting a sweet cry from deep in her throat.

Do you hear them? He kissed her roughly. *It's the old way… the ancient way,* he said. *When they wanted the priestesses' mating to bless the fields. Their collective ancestral memories… This is for us. For this…* he said, clasping her left hand.

The thought drove her wild, a primal heat gripping her as he rose within her, pushing, thrusting, her legs winding around his back. She leaned away, watching sweat bead on his skin. She needed him to touch her. Unprompted, Aidon traced the sheen between her breasts, down her stomach and over her navel, ending in the thatch of hair that hid the center of her desire. She rode him, the voices pushing her on. She was immersed in the sensations of fingers and lips, tongue and phallus, working together on her and within her.

His hands… *oh Gods, his hands…* moving all over her in concert with hers on him, sliding over slick skin, holding each other, their movements echoed, reverberating. Every part of her that she wanted him to touch, he touched. It was as though he could sense her every desire— *no, he could,* she realized, *completely.* He gripped her waist tighter, knowing what she needed, and pushed her against him. Her head was thrown back, and she grew lightheaded from the pressure of him against that spot deep within. She shook. The fingers of his other hand circled, strumming at her front in perfectly balanced gentleness and roughness, manipulating, teasing and caressing just as her own hands would move and respond. Her sensations were his. His were hers.

She felt something building within him, powerfully singular, focused and strong. *His peak is approaching,* she thought briefly. *Oh gods, I can feel it…* She could feel her own climax growing closer. His was so similar to hers but lacked the anticipatory strain, the contracting waves she felt rolling inside. Persephone knew from his untempered voice that Aidon could feel her spasms starting in earnest. She felt her pleasure sharpen powerfully, tinged for the first time by his approach, burning white hot. Fire rose from their joined cores, through their hearts, their throats, their minds overtaken by the sensation building higher and higher. She wondered, they wondered together, if this was what it always felt like for their mate.

And then everything shattered— gone in a radiant burst as brilliant as the birth of the cosmos. Mingled with the rapturous song torn in unison from their throats, they could hear the women's voices ululating as though it were a wedding, a death, a rebirth, an anointing—

The coronation of a Queen.

Persephone collapsed against his shoulder, almost sliding off of him against frictionless perspiration, his skin burning, his muscles taut and holding her to him. Aidon's fingertips had left a radial of quickly fading bruises on her hips. His arms came up and glided over her back to support her. They heard the joyful noises of their kingdom die down and fade back into whispers.

Thea… Metra… Pater… Anax… Annessa… Theos…

She wondered if he had heard that strange celebratory cry every time he was with her. If, in their occasional haste, when he hadn't time to remove his rings…

"No," Aidoneus finally breathed, hoarsely answering her very thoughts. "That's never happened before. Just the usual whispers, if that. At least, I'm almost certain. I'm usually… distracted," he chortled.

"The rite you and Hecate speak of…" she struggled to speak, still overwhelmed, her tongue thick in her mouth. "Was that it?"

"I don't think so," he said between labored breaths. Aidon allowed the maelstrom of his thoughts to collect again. "No, it wasn't. The *hieros gamos* is performed deliberately, steeped in ceremony. There was none such tonight."

She carefully lifted herself from him, and they each felt a momentary pang of longing as he slipped from her. They both needed to breathe, needed to collapse beside one another.

We're gods. We need no ceremony. To whom would we swear ourselves?

Persephone remembered him saying those words a month ago. "Ceremony..."

"I want that for us," he whispered. "I want to wed you in the sight of all."

"Gods have none to swear by..."

"I don't care. We'll swear by the Fates. We'll swear by the cosmos itself. And I want more than that— so much more..." He swept her hair away from her face. "I want to perform the Rite with you, Persephone. I want to bind us as one..."

"On the full moon?" She said, gleaning from his thoughts what little he knew of it. "That's nearly here. Tomorrow. We'll never learn it in time. And I still must go..."

"Not tomorrow. The very next one we're together..."

"I am no one's acolyte, and never was. I know nothing. To fulfill my role—" She reached for him in the dark, the fire playing against his skin.

"I will guide you. As your consort, I will learn... and I will guide you. It is one of the last things Hecate has left to teach me. I will go to her while you are in the world above. I want to seal myself to you."

Persephone ran a hand over his forehead, playing with one of his wayward curls, feeling affection and a hint of impatience course through him. She didn't need to hear him ask, and she gave no answer. Persephone reached for Aidoneus as he moved over her, then within her. She wanted the same thing he sought— to spend the rest of the night exploring this new connection, this newfound pleasure, for as long as their intertwining bodies would allow.

5.

T HE DAY BEFORE THE FULL MOON, THE TELESTERION opened its doors to all the people of Eleusis. Those who had patiently waited for their womenfolk to bring back food each day could now bask in the warmth and sustenance provided by the Corn Mother.

The gardens outside yielded enough, but the steady flow of new arrivals had not wavered, and the stores were wearing thin. Demeter contemplated the idea of extending fertility to Athens' fields, enough to feed the people traveling in on the sea road. She clenched her jaw. The patroness of that city had betrayed her: Athena had all but handed Kore over to the Lord of the Dead to curry favor with her father. It would do the supposed Goddess of Wisdom no good. Demeter knew from bitter experience that Zeus cared nothing for his offspring. Athens would go hungry. Its temples would stand empty. Let its people come to her instead.

Eumolpus and Diocles stood below on the first step of the dais, one holding a bundle of wheat, the other a sickle. They watched over the men, women and children filing silently forward, each placing a sheaf of millet or barley on the steps, muttering their blessings with eyes averted. Cups of *kykeon* were passed to the congregants as they took their seats.

Triptolemus stepped forward from his place next to the Queen of the Earth, glancing back at veiled Demeter, who smiled at him from beneath the linen. The hall was silent as he picked up a single sheaf of wheat and raised a short iron knife. He split a single grain from the end and held it up.

"A single corn, reaped in silence, for the Maiden's return from the halls of the Unseen One."

The room stayed silent, watching. He placed the grain into a kylix of olive oil. Taking a red-hot coal with iron tongs from a brazier, he set it aflame, holding the offering above his head.

"For the Maiden's return!" he said louder as it blazed brightly and produced a plume of dark smoke.

"For the Maiden's return," the room echoed as one, raising their cups.

"To the end of winter!" he said as the flames calmed.

"To the end of winter," they repeated and drank the barley mead.

On their last word, Demeter sat up straight. A distant rumble rolled across the hills outside and echoed through the temple. No one else had heard it through the din.

Once the offering dwindled into a thin wisp of dark smoke, Triptolemus handed the empty kylix to Diocles and spoke to the assembly. "Our holy Mother revealed to me that I am to teach her Mysteries and wisdom to the world, to spread her worship and knowledge far and wide once her daughter is safely returned so that no man—" Thunder rolled again, stronger this time. He paused, feeling the Telesterion vibrate. "...So that no man or woman, slave or freeborn, will ever go hungry again."

Demeter's breath quickened. *He wouldn't come here... He wouldn't dare...*

A bolt struck the frozen oak tree outside, splitting the solid wood with a deafening crack. The congregants startled, their cries and shrieks multiplying when they heard the groan and crash of an ancient branch falling to the ground. Another blinding flash of light framed the doors at the back of the hall. The hanging censers shook and rattled on their chains. Demophon started to cry. Metaneira gathered him in her arms and took him from the room with Celeus close behind her, their shoes clacking against the stone floor.

A nervous murmur spread through the chamber. In the second row, a rust-haired boy pressed his hands over his ears. A gaunt woman huddled closer to her husband. Demeter watched the Eleusinians shift about, turning and whispering to each other. Everyone could feel the electric prickle in the air, arcing across wool and skin and separating hair.

Triptolemus swallowed and started again, trying to stand as tall as he could to reassure and quiet them. "Sh-she has given to me her char—"

The doors flew open, each side slamming against the wall. The little veiled girl with the *koudounia* ran behind a column and dropped her copper bells. Wind whistled through the rafters, sending a drift of snow into the hall. The fires in the braziers stuttered and nearly extinguished. The posted guards ran inside, taking refuge from the sudden storm. At the back, several congregants strained to push the doors shut, leaning hard against the great entry to close it, then hoisted a heavy wood beam to bar it against the gale. No one paid any attention to the figure that had strolled in amidst the cacophony.

No one but Demeter.

The wind outside ceased and the room fell utterly silent. She stood and pulled her veil back from her face. Those in the audience averted their eyes from the face of the Mother and instead turned their cloaked heads to follow her gaze. A broad shouldered man stood in front of the sealed doors dressed in the same indigo as Demeter's other petitioners. But his feet were sandaled, in stark contrast with everyone else, who wore leather wrapped in linen and wool up to their knees to keep their toes from falling off in the snow. His face was stern, and all in the Telesterion stared at him in curious wonder.

"I come to speak with your Queen of the Earth."

He brushed the hood from his head and took a step forward. The man produced a bundle of wheat in one hand and a bundle of barley in the other. Offerings. He slowly dropped to one knee and knelt with arms extended, as her petitioners often did.

Demeter slitted her eyes and tilted her chin up before she spoke. "You are not welcome here, Loud-Thunderer."

Gasps went up in the crowd. A single name was on every tongue. Zeus.

He arose and took another step forward. The crowd flinched back as a single mass, eyes darting from the Sky Father to the Earth Mother, unsure what to do. No one was foolish enough to place themselves in the middle of a confrontation between the two immortals. A few began to slowly move toward the exits, and then others followed carefully, all the while murmuring to one another. Then they hurried their steps, quietly opening the heavy doors and filing out into the cold, giving the King of the Gods a wide berth.

Zeus turned to watch them go, pausing on the rounded flare of a brunette maiden's hips and imagining all the things he could do to her once this winter was over and she got a little more meat on her bones. His fingers itched, clutching at the bundles of grain. The two priests were the last to go, their himations drawn over their heads. Zeus casually watched them leave, then willed the doors to slam shut behind them.

"Come to chastise me? Plead with me as your wife's handmaiden Iris did?"

"Neither, my lady."

Demeter stood cold as stone, except for a finger brushing against Triptolemus's hand.

That single touch made Zeus boil on the inside. He could hear the boy's heart thundering in his chest the closer he got to the dais. With a slow cast of each hand, he spread the offerings of grain at Demeter's feet, as though he were a mortal supplicant. Zeus spoke low. "Your pet may go."

Triptolemus puffed his chest up, then reflected on who stood before them, swallowed, and dipped his head. "Your grace, I am here *only* by my lady's leave."

He smirked at this young hero's bravery, then looked him up and down. "I can see that you are *deathless* now."

Triptolemus nodded.

"Congratulations to you, boy!" he said loudly, smiling with white teeth, his eyes speaking a different story. Triptolemus imagined this was how a wolf must look at a cornered hind before it lunged. "It's been a little while since we elevated one of your kind to our ranks. I believe the last one was my cupbearer… about five hundred years ago, or so. I brought him to Olympus, even. Deme, what was his name, again?"

"Ganymede," she said through clenched teeth.

"Nice boy, Ganymede… served me well. Isn't that right, Deme? Still does, sometimes. Much like how your *catamite* serves you."

Triptolemus clenched his fists and ground his teeth at the insult. His fingertips danced along the hilt of the knife he'd used to cut into the blade of wheat. If this were any man other than the King of the Gods, he would have used its point to open his throat.

"Typhoeus was deathless too, and about the size of a mountain. They sing songs about what I did to him." He watched Triptolemus— how he hated the very *sound* of that name— take a step up the dais, retreating toward his mistress. Zeus tried to banish the creeping images of him putting his filthy, calloused, mortal-born hands on Demeter— *his* Demeter. He quelled them, at least enough to resist the temptation to strike down her young lover where he stood. That wouldn't help his cause at all. "Ask your lady what happened to the last deathless one that defied me. Or perhaps I can show you myself. Prometheus has been lonely too long— has only an eagle tearing at his liver each day for companionship. He may need some company…"

The Eleusinian prince shuddered and looked to Demeter. She nodded to him and squeezed his hand. "I'll be alright," she whispered, then leaned up to kiss him. "Go."

Triptolemus cautiously crept down the dais. Zeus could still hear his heart drumming in his chest; see the cold sweat beaded on his brow. He feigned a lunge toward the youth, eyes wide and intense. Triptolemus flinched back, then quickened his retreat. The King of the Gods chuckled after the greenhouse door slammed shut.

Demeter sat back down on her throne. "How dare you threaten him?"

He shook his head and guffawed. "I suppose we all need our amusements. Don't we, my heart?"

Her nostrils flared and she stared at him, shocked. "How— You have no right *whatsoever* to call me that!"

"And why not, Deme? I remember when you loved that name."

"That was aeons ago. You lost that right," she said, stiffening. "You will address me formally, or not at all!"

"As you wish. Demeter Anesidora, the Bringer of Many Gifts, the Cerulean Queen, Holy Daughter of Great Mother Rhea and Goddess of the Harvest, then?" he said, sky blue eyes sparkling. Zeus drew in a long breath. "Will that suffice?"

"The Eleusinians call me Queen of the Earth," she said, quietly.

"The Moirai might have something to say about that… but if you insist."

"When have you *ever* cared for what they say?"

"Oh, I care a great deal. If not for the Fates, I wouldn't have claimed Olympus."

If not for my choosing you, she thought. "What did you come here to say, Zeus?"

"What would you have me say?" he crooned.

She flushed. "Stop that."

"What?" he said softly.

"Stop it! Just stop it!" she said slamming a fist on the arm of her throne. "I'm not the blushing, naïve girl you knew me to be! And I refuse to get drawn into this… this *nonsense* with you! Say what you came here to say, then leave the way you came."

He smiled at her and seated himself in the first row, leaning forward and resting his elbows on his widely parted knees. "Do you know why I fell in love with you, Demeter?"

"The same reason you've *fallen in love* with every other woman. For the heat between her thighs."

"Hardly," he said folding his hands. He smiled lightly and she swallowed, remembering that look. "It was your passionate stubbornness that won me over. You were a fighter. You refused to give in to anything. Most of all me."

She snorted and rolled her eyes.

"Scoff at me all you want, Deme. I had eyes for no other in the early days. You know that."

"You've had eyes for everyone else since… and you were chasing Metis almost as soon as you rose from my bed."

His smile disappeared. "But I *loved* you. You know I did, my heart."

"I said don't call me—"

"If you had shown *half* the resolve during the war as you have over this," he interrupted, looking around, "I would call you that still."

Her face fell.

"It's hurting my neck looking up at you, Deme." He ran his hand through the hair at the base of his skull for effect. "Fates, woman, your throne is set high! Why don't you come down here so I can speak with you?"

Demeter drew back and gripped the armrests.

"I'm not going to try anything with you," he said with a reverent smile. "I respect you too much for that."

Respect? Her daughter was passed off to the God of the Dead like chattel and he dared talk about respect? She roiled with anger and looked away so he couldn't see it. "You must be joking."

"I only wish to talk with you... see if we can come to some sort of accord."

"You mean you want *me* to give in and submit to—"

"I never said that, Deme. I want us to *discuss*— to come to an agreement that leaves all of us satisfied," he said. Zeus reached across the aisle and patted the seat across from him. "Come speak with me, my lady."

Demeter didn't move, her mouth a line, looking down at him. His playful eyes belied his serious intent, his relaxed demeanor that of a prowling lion. His essence was wrapped in the same contradictions that had left her guessing in the early days when he had loved her— ones that made him so delectably unpredictable and made her feel alive. Looking up at her now, his expression was set with the loving reverence that had captured her heart the moment she first blinked in the sunlight and saw Zeus as he gently carried her away from Othrys.

He was dangerous, she remembered. How many had he seduced, ravaged, buggered, and raped with those crystal blue eyes and handsome smile? His mouth twisted up, then his face fell, his expression pleading with her. It was a ploy, she knew, but he was still her only chance at getting her Kore back. Only Zeus could sway unbending Aidoneus. She stood and stepped toward him, her veil catching on the arm of the throne and falling away from her head. She glanced back at it.

"Leave it," he whispered, his voice rasping as he said it.

Demeter shivered at his tone and descended the steps of the dais at a careful, measured pace, as though she were ready to bolt from the room at the first move he made. She knew that if his intentions toward her were in any way sinister she wouldn't have time to run, but couldn't help approaching him with trepidation. Demeter examined him carefully as she drew closer. More lines than usual traversed his cheeks and forehead, and his normally blond hair was streaked with brittle strands of white and gray.

The corner of her mouth ticked up. This is why he wasn't coming to her with threats or edicts. This is why she wasn't chained in the sky or cast into the Pit for ruining the earth and bringing the mortals to the brink of annihilation. Zeus couldn't do anything to her. He hadn't come here to talk; he'd come to *beg*. He was weakened.

And she was strong.

Demeter gracefully sat down across the aisle from him, folding her robes behind her and plaiting her hands in her lap. "Well?"

"I want to apologize first," he said quietly, not taking his eyes off her.

"Ha!" She sneered at him. "For what, Zeus? Where would you even start? When you started dallying with Metis? When you sold our unborn daughter to Hades? When you broke your promises to me? Left me helpless and pregnant? When you took Hera as your bride the very day I was screaming with labor pains to deliver your child?!"

His brow furrowed, not from age or diminishment, but from what looked like genuine regret. She knew better. Zeus didn't have a remorseful bone in his body. He cast his gaze to the ground. "That and more, Deme."

"More?"

"Yes," he bit his cheek and looked up at her. "I should have taken better care of you, Demeter. And when you fell into the arms of that... mortal..."

"Iasion," she whispered.

"When you turned to Iasion for comfort, I should have let you be happy with him until he passed or you tired of him. I should have insisted that you stay at Olympus with the rest of us, to Tartarus with whatever Hera said. I should have seen through her. I should have seen through her when she brought that... crippled *thing*, Hephaestus... into being without me. I should have banished her *permanently* and taken you back when she tried to usurp my power. And you stayed loyal despite everything. Fates; I shouldn't have left you in the *first place,* or doubted you. I should have made you my queen like I promised. I was an idiot."

"You *are* an idiot, Zeus." Her eyes stung. "There's no past tense about that."

He clenched his jaw. "When it comes to matters of the heart, yes. I am. I'll admit that. I've come to you with no pride, Demeter."

"Words," she whispered. "I think I've heard enough of your meaningless words to last me a thousand lifetimes." Tears filled Demeter's eye and she turned her face from Zeus. How long had she wanted to hear him say all these things? To show a hint of remorse for all the aeons she'd spent alone and abandoned? She seethed. He'd waited until he wanted something.

"Deme..." he said brushing a hand down her back.

She spun around. "Don't you touch me," she spat out. "You think I will just relent because you came and... *apologized* for aeons and aeons of ill treatment that I'll be appeased?"

"No, I didn't—"

"Next thing you'll be expecting me to spread my legs for you as a thank you for *lowering yourself* enough to—"

"I'm not worthy of you, Demeter," he said, jaw clenched.

She straightened in surprise and wiped her eyes with the sleeve of her mantle. "I'll have you know, *my lord,* that true apologies come with reparations."

"They do," he said. "And I'm prepared to give you those reparations in full."

Demeter held her breath.

"Except for one condition."

She scowled at him. "Then it's not a true apology at all if it's conditional. Unless you are willing to make amends for everything, you will get nothing from me."

"Damn it, woman! Will you just—" He drew in a breath and swallowed his frustration. "Please let me speak, Demeter. If, by the end of what I have to say, you *still* won't accept my sincere apology and recompense for all the ills you've suffered at my hands, then I promise I will do everything I can, *within reason.*"

"That comes with an oath, Zeus, or you can leave. If you mean what you say, you'll *swear it,*" she said, narrowing her eyes.

He pursed his lips. "So be it. I, Zeus Aegiduchos Cronides Olympios, solemnly swear on the great River Styx that if what I have to say— to *offer* to you— does not meet with your approval, that I will do *everything in my power* to bring Persephone—"

"Kore."

Zeus had to bite his cheek. This denial was laughable. The whole cosmos knew that Hades had divested Kore of anything that would still make her... a *kore.* He'd even heard a rumor that the Lord of the Underworld hadn't waited to consummate their union until he got to his palace— that he'd had her on the way there. When Zeus had first heard that bit of gossip he'd stared at Hermes in open-mouthed disbelief then laughed long and loud, smacking his thigh so hard that the sound of thunder rolled through the valleys of Thessaly. To think that cold, taciturn, law-abiding Aidoneus had done something rash and passionate for once in his long life! When Hermes had returned earlier this very week, his face pale and wincing, Apollo had grilled him until he gave up the news that he'd barged in on Hades and Persephone enthusiastically twisted into a position that only lovers who had happily known each other fully and many times over would have attempted. Kore she most certainly was not. He wouldn't allow Demeter to labor under that delusion, no matter how much he needed to tread lightly with her. "I will do everything in my power to bring *Persephone* back to you."

She sat still, her heart racing. It was done. He'd sworn. She'd done the impossible and made the King bend. Her daughter would be freed. She would see her again, and deliver her out of the hands of her cruel abductor. Demeter was no fool. She knew that Aidoneus had deflowered and defiled Kore. Her daughter had been raped; she was Persephone now, no longer a maiden. But Demeter had succeeded. All the suffering, all the sadness and waste and ruin had meaning. Her daughter was coming back from the Land of the Dead.

"But…" he said, swallowing. "No matter how you decide, you will let go of your terrible wrath against the mortals! And against the gods who rely upon them. Are we agreed?"

Her breath caught in her throat, disbelieving that she had just heard such joyous news. "We are agreed."

He opened his mouth to continue, and Demeter interrupted him.

"*But…*" she said, trying to keep a gleeful smile from twisting her features, "my end will only be upheld once you fulfill your promises, Zeus. Not a moment sooner. Am I understood?"

"Yes, my lady."

"Then I will listen."

"Demeter…" he started quietly. "Do you want to retain your title as Queen of the Earth?"

"If you mean to take it away from me—"

"I do," he said. "In a manner of speaking…"

"What manner would that be?" she rasped.

"By giving you one greater."

Demeter felt ice pour down her spine. "You surely don't mean…"

"You are the earth, Demeter, and I am the sky. When and where I am the sky, then and there you are the e—"

92

"Do not repeat those vows to me! You used them to lie to me and seduce me, and you fouled those words just weeks after we said them! Those words were meant to be sacred—to bind us to each other forever as male and female, but—"

"What if they still do?"

"You actions alone prove—"

"Demeter, hear me. You said you would," he rumbled, raising his voice ever so slightly. When she stilled, he continued. "What if those words still hold true? What if I *made* them hold true?"

"And by doing so you would undo everything between then and now? Divorce your wife? Have her children declared bastards as my child was deemed a bastard by her?" Her lip curled up. "I have a feeling the Goddess of Marriage might take grave offense at this."

"I will deal with Hera myself. She is the goddess of *nothing* without me."

Demeter widened her eyes and turned away from him.

"But you," he murmured, his voice warm and soothing. Zeus carefully moved next to her on the bench. "You are so very much a goddess in your own right."

She flinched and stiffened at his closeness but didn't back away or face him just yet. He caressed one of the tresses falling from her diadem and brought it up to his nose, inhaling. She could feel his thigh pressing against the outside of hers and her heart tapped a rapid staccato.

"You are the bringer of life. You've shown me how much power that holds. How much power *you* hold…"

"That you would then take from me?" she said, her voice far smaller than she'd hoped it would be.

"No. That is power that I would exalt and venerate and glorify. You and I were meant to be, Demeter. Like Gaia and Ouranos before us."

"On Olympus…" she breathed.

"Yes. In the palace they built to bridge the heavens and the earth. Fitting for us, isn't it, my heart?" He whispered next to her ear. "My wife?"

"Yes," she whispered. Her pulse drummed so fast it made her lightheaded.

"Our daughter," he said with the lightest of kisses on her shoulder, "will be my acknowledged firstborn. She will be made legitimate…"

Demeter closed her eyes as his lips touched her skin and shivered. How many aeons had she waited for this? His touch was electric, his scent like approaching rain. How easily he seduced…

…How likely he was to do it again. She thought about Triptolemus, his pure love for her, his devotion, his soul bound to hers since he met her aeons ago as Iasion. Zeus had killed Iasion.

Her anger boiled under her skin, undetected by Zeus. She thought about stone-faced Hera, witness to thousands of indiscretions and bastard children. The shame and the embarrassment of knowing that three of those same children, conceived in other women's beds, and that crude seductress from the East who claimed she was descended from Ouranos, had been elevated to sit side-by-side with the Children of Kronos. She remembered Aidoneus warning her about Zeus, long ago. Demeter had felt like a fool when he'd been proven right. Never again.

She clenched her jaw and coiled, ready to strike. "What if Hera objects or rebels?"

"Metis met an… unfortunate end. Hera would be wise to avoid that fate."

Zeus stroked her arm and her stomach turned, remembering the nebbish gray-eyed Titaness. She felt sick. To whom else would he make this promise in the endless years to come? If he were willing to go to such lengths with Hera, would she too meet the same fate when Zeus needed to bargain with another goddess?

"What say you, my heart?"

"You would have me trade places with Hera?" Her voice was low and sultry like warm, dark earth.

"Yes."

"I would be your queen."

"You would, my heart."

"My throne would sit with yours on Olympus…"

"Yes, Deme."

"…from where I can watch you fornicate with every goddess, nymph and mortal from here until aeon's end?"

His eyes grew steely and he backed away from her. His jaw set tight when he saw her turn toward him and lift her chin triumphantly. He grimaced. "If this is a bid to keep that— your *lover*, I'll let you. Though you have no idea how much I compromise to do so… But fair is fair. Poseidon has his own *arrangement* with Amphitrite, after all."

"It has nothing to do with Triptolemus."

He ground his teeth impatiently. "Then *what*?"

"Not long ago, you said to me that I wouldn't want you for a husband as you are now."

"Deme, my heart, I can amend my—"

"Don't insult me! You might be able to crawl back to the bed of that *cow* over and over with your empty capitulations, but don't think *for a moment* they would work on me!"

"You know what I am, Demeter! I am offering you everything. You would be Queen of Heaven for Fate's sake! You would have my protection, my fealty, my willingness to put you *above* all others, you would have my love…"

"You don't have the capacity to love," she spat out.

"And you know that's a lie! We loved each other once."

Demeter stilled for a moment, her eyes shining like cool jade. She nodded. "We did. You're right, Zeus. There is one thing, however, that would make it impossible for me to accept your offer…"

"What is that?"

"I love my daughter more than I ever loved you."

Zeus felt everything sink. She was going to say no before he even started speaking. He'd walked into her trap and made an oath. *The* oath.

"Annul the marriage."

"Demeter—"

"You swore."

He was caught between one Stygian oath and another. The end of all things sat in one hand, the breaking of the oldest sacred agreement among the gods in the other. And worse— if Aidoneus had grown as attached to his bride as everyone said he had become, if he would do anything to keep her, it could mean the end of all things by ways he dared not consider. If Demeter had withdrawn all fertility from the earth and killed scores of thousands to reclaim Persephone, what unspeakable things could the Lord of the Dead do to humanity?

The winds outside rattled the Telesterion, an icy draft permeating the room and wrapping itself around the back of his ankles. Zeus cast his eyes down and slumped his shoulders in utter defeat. "I'll send Hermes."

*　　*　　*

Aidoneus curled against her, his breathing steady against her neck. Persephone had never felt him sleep so heavily— as though he'd never slept before. She wondered if he truly had. Though the noises from Tartarus had faded into the background of his perception over time, they must have always been there, bleeding through the edges of his consciousness. And before that, the war. And before that, Kronos. His arm was heavy, cast over her in the same place it had fallen after the last of several couplings, his hand splayed against her stomach. She smiled. Her hip was still tender. Aidon had taken her in the same position they lay in now, hoisting her knee with his forearm, his hands free to roam across the front of her.

96

Most of her was tender, truthfully. That wasn't the only way they'd had each other. Each position they'd settled themselves into was familiar yet completely new, changed forever by their heightened connection, their bodies and spirits bound together. The rings sat heavy on her hand, the same sigil of responsibility her husband had borne all the aeons of his rule. She drew her palm down her abdomen until it settled over his hand, and listened to the voices of Asphodel.

Metra... Soteira... Annessa...

Her titles. Could they tell that she was awake and he was not? The words were infrequent, and if she just listened to the syllables, they almost sounded like crickets chirping at night. They relaxed her in an odd way, and she started to pick out a few individual sentences within the din.

Thea, we're so happy you're here, so glad you hear us now...

Annessa, I'm ready to drink from the Lethe. I'm prepared to return...

Metra, please. Please watch over my husband, Ioannis...

She held her breath at the last one. That voice came from the Trivium— a shade who had not yet been judged... who hadn't drank from the Lethe. Once it knew its voice had been heard it started again in earnest.

Metra! Metra, please! Our infant was too young for me to leave! Ioannis cannot feed him! Send me back, I beg of you...

It grew panicked and then other voices joined it.

Annessa, my children. I'm already gone but spare my children. Please!...

Soteira, my brothers— they starve; they have the fever. End their suffering as you ended mine...

Persephone felt her throat close and gasped for air. The voices grew frantic when they discovered she could hear them.

Save me! Save me, Soteira! I don't want to be dead! I was to be married next month!...

Thea, I loved them truly, but they were all that was left to eat. They were already dead, I swear! Do not send me to Tartarus! Please...

Annessa, why? Why? Why am I gone while my neighbor who stole my pigs was spared?! Punish him! Punish him!

She choked, her breathing rapid without really drawing in any air, her body cold and shaking. A hand gripped hers firmly and she yelped in surprise before realizing it was Aidoneus, awake and angered.

Silence! His voice resounded above the fray. They did as he bid and stilled. Hades spoke to the newly arrived shades calmly, countless millennia of experience lending weight to his words. *Peace— all of you. Let go of the lives you led. They are ended. You will drink from the Lethe and be freed of your burdens soon enough. Until then, have respect for your queen and be silent!*

She trembled and he wrapped an arm around her. A few voices started again— the peaceful crickets of Asphodel.

Thea. . . Annessa. . . Soteira. . .

"Persephone." His strong arm rolled her over to face him, his face etched with worry. "My love, are you alright?"

Air finally entered her lungs again, and exited as a cracked sob. She looked away from him, not wanting to show weakness. He'd heard these voices for so very long, and she'd folded after mere moments. "There were so many…"

"Sweet one, I'm so sorry." He drew her close, holding her, and tucked the blankets tightly around them to secure and comfort her, letting their warmth surround each other, until her tears stopped and her breathing returned to normal.

"I don't know how you do it, Aidoneus," she said quietly.

"Because I must. They're the responsibility the Fates gave me."

"Our responsibility."

He stroked her hair. "I shouldn't have burdened you with this…"

"It's not a matter of burdening me. These are *our* subjects."

"We've never received so many guests at once. It was too much—"

"This is why I must go tomorrow." She felt him wilt, their debate settled, knowing once and for all that she was right. "Aidon—"

"I know." He held her tighter. "I know."

"I'll be back as soon as I can. It could only be a matter of hours—"

"Or days," he muttered.

"I don't know that. I can't tell you for certain."

"I know, sweet one," he said, and cradled her until she was resting her head against his arm. "Let's not keep you up, then. You have a long journey tomorrow."

"I'll be back before you know it, Aidoneus." She nestled into him and sighed. "I love you."

"And I you. Just rest, my love. I'm right here. I'll always be here."

He rubbed her back with his free hand until he heard her breathing lightly, steadily, then closed his eyes and joined her in sleep and dreams.

The fruit hung heavy on the branches, the seeds now grown. Ripe. The offspring of the ones that had taken root in gray earth and grown life in the land of the dead. They sat poised, crammed together, ready to fulfill whatever destiny the Fates decreed. The arils pointed every which way, row upon row, each path different, each outcome the same. Why they were there, they knew not; they needed to know. Eagerly and desperately, they called out, saying: 'Come to us! Come and see what you brought forth. Come and see. . .

. . . before it is too late.'

6.

WE FORGOT TO SHUT THE DOOR LAST NIGHT. IT WAS THE first thought to enter Persephone's mind when she awoke. She could see the wan light of the Styx from behind her closed eyelids. The gentle and distant rush of the falls, mingling with the steady breathing of her husband, almost lulled her back to sleep.

The bed felt so much harder this morning. Her body was stiff, the sheets damp and cool beneath her, and her head was pillowed against his arm. She sighed, savoring the pleasantly aching after effects and still-vivid memories of the sensual delights they'd shared the night before. The bedclothes tickled her skin as she leaned into her beloved's side, luxuriating in the warmth of his body and his earthy scent.

Cool air nipped at her, causing gooseflesh to rise from her ankles to her neck. Strange. *We must have kicked the covers off, too,* she realized. The fire usually made up for that, but it was easily remedied. Her hand reached for the sheets...

...and closed around a clump of grass. Persephone's eyes popped open and she jerked upright. Aidoneus let out an annoyed groan and yanked her down, pulling her back against his chest. "Too early..."

Persephone began to push herself up again and he muttered what might have been a 'no'. Aidon enclosed her within his arms, this time nestling behind her. She cleared her throat nervously. "But, my love…"

"Mmm…" He sighed and gave her a slight nudge against her bottom. At least *one* part of him was awake.

"Ah, Aidon? We—"

"Wife, it's early. Just stay in bed with me until I can wake you up properly," he mumbled and heatedly pressed against her once more.

"That's what I'm trying to tell you; we're not *in* bed!"

Aidoneus cracked his eyes open. Gently releasing her, he sat up and looked around. The surrounding trees came into focus, their drooping boughs dangling overhead and heavy with ripe pomegranates. "Persephone… Did you…"

"…bring us here?" She hugged her knees to her chest to cover herself. "No, I-I don't think so. We did dream about them again."

"I know," he answered, "but that's… never taken us here before."

"Maybe last night was special," she said with a shy smile. He returned it and ran his thumb under her chin.

"Very," Aidon said brushing his lips against hers. He nipped at her lower lip to coax them open, then darted his tongue across her teeth. His hand wrapped around her ankles to unbend her legs, trying to get her to lie back down beside him.

"We're in the garden, my love," she warned, whispering against his lips.

"Indeed." He pulled away. "And?"

The corners of Persephone's mouth ticked up despite her concern about their exposed situation. She turned a charming red, almost matching the fruits above them. Aidon pounced and caught her at her waist. He drew her down next to him so quickly that it left her breathless, then planted his hand in the grass beside her shoulder before looming over her.

It's plain on your face but I'll ask anyway, he said to her with a thought, a fire deep in his eyes. *Are you thinking what I think you're thinking?* He kissed her slowly on the lips. *Do you desire what I also desire?*

Aidoneus, she began, tracing a single fingernail down his chest, *are you trying to make this my idea instead of yours? Answer that for me, husband*, she teased.

He drew in a breath and covered her body with his, pressing her into the earth. She realized belatedly that he meant to show her, not tell her.

"Wait!" she said out loud. "Aidon, we can't—"

"Before you protest, let's consider this," he said quickly and held up his thumb. "First, this is *our* garden. Second, I am almost certain Askalaphos already saw us sleeping here, and likely took off in the opposite direction as fast as his fat little legs could carry him!"

She giggled.

"Third," he continued, holding up another finger, "Hermes was just here and has no reason to come again, and probably thinks I'll throw him head first into the Cocytus the next time he walks in on us."

Her giggle turned into a full-throated laugh, and Aidon couldn't help but kiss her cheeks and tuck a lock of hair behind her ear.

And lastly, he said, winding a trail with his upheld fingers down the valley between her breasts, meandering across her stomach, then gently caressing her sex. *I want to give you a reason to return to me as soon as possible.*

She arched and answered him with a kiss. *As though you haven't given me reasons enough already?*

Play along with me, wife. He smiled against her lips. *Let me give you a proper send off.*

"Proper?" She laughed shakily when he kissed the pulse point just under her jaw line, then closed her eyes in pleasure

102

as his fingers dipped into her heat ever so slightly. A sharp, aching need thrummed through her in their wake. "Aidon, we're outdoors... in a grove! A-about to—"

Our grove. More than anywhere else in existence, this place is most thoroughly yours and mine. A light pluck at the peak of her breast made her gasp and she looked down to see him rolling the puckered flesh between his fingers again. *And don't tell me you haven't thought about this... or something like it.*

She sighed. "Yes..."

When the world above is healed, I want to make love to you in the cypress grove. In Nysa. In the sunlight. He perused her thoughts as he mentioned it, and found a peculiar, enticing vision. The two of them weren't in the grove at Nysa, but surrounded by poppies and grass in a wide-open field, his body driving hers into the earth, flowers bursting from the fertile soil all around their wanton joining. His mouth replaced his fingers, which in turn made their way back to her core. *Oh, so you have been thinking about it, then? Where is this grassy field, wife?*

"Eleusis..." she answered breathlessly. "Near the oak glade where I saw that wedding. The day you were at Olympus."

Outside Eleusis... That is where your fantasy lies? Aidoneus said through thought, his mouth otherwise occupied. He delved deeper, surprised by his findings. *And me carrying you off over my shoulder, like some conquering king taking away my spoils...*

"Yes!" She grew hot. "Gods, yes. If the arrow had struck true..."

Not the beginning I would have wanted for us. And the beginning we did have—

He paused, looking into her eyes while she explored his thoughts. Scalding recollections flooded through her— feelings, sensations. She felt with his lips the unforgettable first kiss they shared in the darkness of Erebus. And felt her own warm weight in his arms when he knelt to wrap her sleeping body securely in his cloak and carry her home once the chariot had stopped in the stable yard. Every moment in between, every detail of her abduction from the world above was seared indelibly into his mind. Both were awash in desire when the memories flooded through them. And then, beyond the desire, a palpable twinge of regret.

Persephone shook her head. "No, my husband, my love. It was not what either of us had envisioned for our first time, but… it was as the Fates intended. We're here now because of it. And you love the memory of it," she said, looking into his eyes, "and so do I. So why are you upset?"

Fates, Persephone… He settled over her and closed his eyes remorsefully. *I had planned everything so carefully…*

"The Fates seldom listen to our plans, my beloved," she said, brushing her hand over his forehead and tangling her fingers in his hair.

He looked away from her and smiled, his mind decided and clear. "I'm fine with that," he said aloud, positioning himself at her gate.

"You *ah…*" Persephone felt a growing fullness as he joined himself to her in the most elemental of ways, the earth under her tilting back and vanishing. "You are?" she gasped between heavy breaths.

"Oh yes," he answered, his voice roughened by the tides of her slippery heat. "If they deny me for the rest of my existence, I can still live happily. As long as they decreed that you should be mine."

She smiled up at him. "I love you, Aidoneus."

"And I you," he whispered into her ear with the first surge of his hips. "My Persephone…"

She clung to him, feeling his pulse reverberating within her. The ground was unyielding against her back, and she winced. Their bed always cushioned his thrusts, but the hard ground of the grove made his entry into her difficult. When he sensed it, he stopped and withdrew part way, lifting his body from hers. She reached to grasp him at the root, trying to return him to her fully.

I want you, Aidon. I don't care about the pain, she said, the corded muscles on his neck prominent as he restrained himself.

But I do. He gently moved her hand away and pushed in shallowly, the flared tip raking repeatedly over her most sensitive spot until she was lightheaded. He settled his fingers on her pulsing bud and drew circles around it. Aidoneus closed his eyes, focusing intently on the rise and fall in her sensations. When he could feel her pleasure starting to throb, he drew his hand back, teasing her inner thighs with feather light touches until her hips lifted from the earth and inched along his length to reclaim him. He strained as her body tried to swallow him and his thumb returned to brush and press against her bud in earnest until Persephone lay gasping underneath him.

He felt her grow hotter, clasp harder around him, grasping desperately at him, and saw the tips of her breasts pucker deliciously. His thumb left her folds to gild her aureole with her essence. She mewled and squirmed, and he rewarded her with a deeper plunge before pulling back to taste and suckle at her breasts, her sweetness caught on the pink flesh. Persephone moaned and threaded her fingers through his hair, impatient and wanting.

Her reservations about making love in the grove were forgotten. There was only him, only his flesh surrounded by hers, his hands, and his tongue, all working in concert. She felt her body screaming for him, begging for him under this delicious torture. She wanted him— she *needed* him, not just to bring her to her fast approaching peak, but to push deep within, to the place only he could reach. To wildly give himself over to her with abandon— mercilessly and without his ever-present control.

Aidon felt her tighten around him in urgent pulses, knowing she was close. He returned his digits to her center, strumming until her channel pulsed around him.

Aidoneus... My love, please... please...

I'm right here. . .
I need all of you. . .
Sweet one, you will. . .
Now!
Come for me. . .

Pleasure broke over her like a storm and she arched her back, her mouth open and crying without a sound. With a single motion, he gathered her up in his arms, holding her at the curve of her back. He sat on his knees with her, pulling her down and sheathing himself to the hilt. Her silent cry broke into a full-throated scream when he filled her, her eyes squeezed shut and her fingers grasped at his back. Skin slid slick against hot skin, and he tilted his head back, reeling in the exquisite delight of her climaxing around him, her pleasure his as he throbbed within her tightening channel. When she came back to him, he stood, still intimately joined with her legs wrapped around him.

"I need you, Persephone," he slurred huskily against her neck. "Before you go... in the way I first took you." She nodded, dazed, and he pushed up hard inside her, bending to brace himself and spreading her thighs further apart. He plunged into her in long strokes while slowly walking forward until her back was against a sinewy pomegranate tree.

He needed more. Aidon cushioned her shoulder blades with his forearm, the bark scraping against his skin and sparing her naked back. He filled her once more, leaning into her tentatively at first until he was sure of their balance, then thrusting wildly, lost in sensation. Through fluttering eyelids she saw his brow furrowed, his jaw clenched. Persephone braced herself, holding a low branch at her side and the trunk behind her, offering him greater resistance, pushing back with her hips. A low growl rumbled in his throat, a feral harmony to accompany the primal rhythm of flesh against flesh.

She moaned in awe at his raw passion, aftershocks of her peak having left her wordless. Her world was compressed, consisting only of the branches gripped in her hands, his arm supporting her back, her body moving at the insistence of his. She felt his need in full while he took his pleasure on her, every thread of control unwound, moving ever faster. His voice broke and sang with hers in sighs and curses. His skin grew flushed and his muscles tensed. When he drew close, Persephone let go of the branches, needing to feel his skin pressing against her. His body was on fire. She clung to his shoulder with one hand and grabbed the flank of his rear with the other, feeling each quick flex as Aidon's uncontrolled lust burned into her.

His eyes rolled back, and tension fled from his face and body in one glorious moment, then violently returned as he bucked into her, bowing his back as though every bit of heat he could offer was pouring into her. It seared through her in rapid pulses, fast and potent, and she heard him call out her name and his love for her to the branches twined about and above them. They stilled and fell against each other. She carefully brought one leg down, then the other, reluctantly uncoupling from him. Aidon's knees shook. He held her close and breathed harshly, his softening organ pressed against her stomach and slick with their shared essence.

"I love you too," she whispered in answer against the center of his chest. "I love you, Aidoneus, and I'll be back before you even know I'm gone."

He chuckled at this and kissed the top of her head, inhaling her scent before he spoke at last. "My love, there will not be a moment you're gone that I won't experience deeply. Painfully. I assure you."

"Only a day…"

"Misery."

She smacked playfully at his arm. "Oh, don't be so dramatic, Aidon! What if it takes two days?"

"Agony," he smiled, and kissed her forehead.

She laughed. "And three days?"

"Unbearable," he sighed against her cheek. "Any longer than that, and I'll split the earth and claim you again."

His tone was playful, but she sensed the promise behind those words, especially when he tilted his head and claimed her mouth in a passionate coda to their lovemaking. When he separated from her, Persephone rested her hand against Aidon's cheek. "It won't take long. After I speak to my mother, she will return everything to—"

"Let us not," he stroked her hair, "let us not speak about Demeter right now. Let me just enjoy this time with you. Only you."

They inched to the ground and rested in the grove, sated and blissful. Aidon leaned his back against the tree and Persephone against him, his hand resting lightly against her abdomen. She felt the rise and fall of his chest behind her head. She smiled at the thought of them reclining here as though they did this every day, uncaring that they were as naked as the day they were born. This moment felt inno-cent— as though they were the only two beings in existence and all of it was new and theirs.

"That's interesting..." Aidon said, motioning to the cen-ter of the grove. In the place where they had awoken, a perfect, six-pointed narcissus had sprouted, its saffron-colored trumpet reaching upward.

She gaped at it. "I-interesting?"

"Yes," he said, twining a lock of her hair around a finger, and quaking in silent laughter. "After all the little miracles you've brought down here, *this* is the one that leaves you dumbstruck?"

"But... I thought I wasn't able to..." Was that single augural flower, the same she'd plucked in Nysa, the first thing she'd grown here outside of a dream?

"I think we should come out here more often and see what else we can grow," he said, nuzzling her neck. Perse-phone jumped when Aidoneus broke her reverie, and he chuckled against the shell of her ear at her reaction.

"Aidon, Do you think this place *itself* brought us here last night?"

"More likely than not. It's what I'd like to believe, at least." He stared up at the pomegranates. Reaching for the lowest branch, he pulled at one of the fruits until the bough bent, then released the ripe globe into his hand and rebounded, shaking above them. "Until they started growing here, I'd never actually seen a pomegranate."

"Really?" She turned around to sit cross-legged in front of him. He followed her lead and played with the rough-skinned fruit, tossing it back and forth.

"I had no opportunity— too busy fighting in ash and fire. The mortals don't hold feasts to honor us, and these aren't given as libations to the world below or buried with the dead, so there's no way they would have come before me." He examined the perfect, six-pointed star at the bottom and the stem at the top, turning it over curiously. Aidoneus lifted the pomegranate and smelled it, then opened his mouth to take a bite.

"What are you doing?" She blurted out. He halted, mouth wide open.

"Eating it," he replied matter-of-factly.

Persephone laughed until she almost fell backward, drawing a quizzical look from her husband.

"This amuses you?"

"Aidon, it will taste horrid!"

"Then why would anyone eat these? I thought pomegranates were sweet."

"The *arils* are sweet, but the flesh is bitter," she said, taking it from his hand. "Here…"

Digging her thumbnail sharply into the pomegranate, she scored the hard skin and pulled it back carefully. Dark red spray from a pierced aril cascaded across her neck and collarbone like a smattering of garnets. Aidoneus leaned forward and swept his tongue across the trail, eliciting a surprised squeak from his wife.

"Mmm. It *is* sweet," he remarked. "Of course, that could be due to how it was served…"

Persephone bit her lower lip and smiled at him before she broke off a section of the scored rind. "I've had so very few of these, I forgot how difficult they are to open without a knife."

"Why? Are they rare?"

"Not at all. I just wasn't… allowed to eat them."

Concern overtook his features. "Are these fruits poisonous?"

"…No."

"What was it then that forbid you to eat them?"

"People say they have potent properties. Something about stopping seeds from taking hold in the womb—" She doubted it would affect her. Women had been eating pomegranates and having babies for as long as they had been harvested. But when she saw his jaw set tight at her words, she banished that line of thought from her mind. For now. She still needed to speak with Hecate. "The main reason Mother didn't allow me to eat them was because pomegranates are… amatory."

He raised his eyebrows and looked at her blankly.

"It's a food meant to arouse passion," she offered.

"What a cold sounding word for it," he mused, and then pulled at one of the arils. It burst on his fingertips and he licked up the juices before digging out the two next to it. He tossed both into his mouth and crushed them, smiling at the burst of juice and the crunch of the seeds between his teeth. The next one he delicately rolled along the roof of his mouth, feeling the shape and texture of it. He closed his eyes and rapidly flicked the tip of his tongue over it, thinking about how very much the little aril felt like a favorite part of his wife's body. When it gave up its essence, he sipped and savored it— dark and sweet, tart and heady— the taste and recollection sending a fresh jolt of desire through him.

"I take it you like it?" she said, reading his expressions.

"Very much so. I could eat these with you all day long. I think I can see why they claim this arouses, though I'm certain sure my present company helps."

Persephone grinned widely at him and pulled a ripe aril from the exposed rind. She lifted her fingers toward her mouth, only to have Hades wrap his hand around her wrist.

"Don't."

I am already bound here, Aidoneus. She looked into his eyes; his jaw was set seriously. Persephone held up her left hand, her fingers adorned with the Key. *Is this not telling enough, my love?*

"That is by choice," he answered aloud and loosened his grip on her. "But this grew in the Underworld. And if it is anything like the asphodel roots that feed the shades, the *fruit* that bound *me* to Chthonia, then it's… final. Those are rules governed by the very order of the cosmos itself, ones that supersede the will of all others— the Gods, the Fates…"

I choose to stay with you, she said. *To love you. To be your queen.*

"And because that is true, I don't want Demeter thinking that I drove you to eat the fruits of the Underworld— that I trapped you here, unawares. It would undermine every word that came out of your mouth. If you taste even one of those seeds, you might as well stay." She paused, considering the choice, then nodded in agreement. He lifted her hand to his lips and sucked the aril from her fingertips, leaving a soft kiss in its place. "Just… wait. At least until you speak with her— convince her to relent."

"When I get back, then?"

"When you return, I'll feed you those seeds myself, if you wish it. But with everything hanging so precariously in the balance, let's not alter the order of things any more than we already have."

"Alright," she said, kissing him, his lips made sweet by the pomegranate. "We can wait."

7.

H E SHIVERED AND CURSED. DESPITE THE HEARTH fire, the cold air bit at his skin as he hurriedly put on his tunic. Hermes's feet danced on the freezing floor for a moment before settling, thankfully, on a thick fleece rug. The nymph lying huddled under a pile of furs atop her bed giggled. She'd whimpered for him not to get out of bed, that it was freezing, it was the middle of the night, and now he could almost hear her biting back an 'I told you so.'

Daeira. An Oceanid, he remembered, who'd come to shelter in Eleusis. She'd been pleasant company this afternoon. More even than the heat within her, Hermes appreciated the warmth of just lying beside her. He usually didn't sleep next to women after he coupled with them, and certainly not all day. But between the bitter cold, his eventual destination, and what he'd been tasked with, it was a welcome comfort. Long dark hair fell and pooled on the indigo himation she'd rolled up as a pillow, and she stared at him quietly with turquoise eyes. Their color reminded him of a pond he'd played in as a boy near Kyllene. He vaguely remembered saying that to her before he untied her seashell girdle.

Hermes adjusted his belt and tunic and wrapped his chlamys over his left shoulder. It was too spare a garment for a night as cold as this, but he would only be outside for a few moments. Then he would fly through the endless caves and passages that twisted every which way through the depths of the earth. Those long roads would be warmer. The irony of that! He usually hated the descent because of how much colder it was in the Underworld. But there hadn't been any warmth in the living world for weeks, and it was as dark as Erebus outside, storm clouds obscuring the moon and stars. He planned to arrive when there was daylight on the Other Side, dim as it was.

His goal was to enter the Underworld when Hades was likely occupied, and Demeter's daughter hopefully alone. Hermes lifted the heavy wool high on his right shoulder and held it fast with a finely crafted gold fibula in the shape of a caduceus. It had been a gift to him from his father, made by the Blacksmith.

"I'm between the tides." He jumped at the voice and spun around. Daeira lay resting her head on one arm.

"Oh?" Hermes answered. "I thought the ice froze the tides. That's why you left the sea."

She tittered. "No, milord. I mean that I am fertile. You probably gave me a child this evening."

"That would be nice, sweetling," he smiled, and studied her face. Hermes cleared his throat, then went back to lacing up his sandals. "But there's nothing being born right now. No one is having children."

"Except for here, you mean."

He turned to her. "Hmm?"

"The Great Lady Demeter restored fertility to Eleusis, silly! A tabby cat in the basileus's stables just birthed four kittens last night."

"Well, is a child what you want from me?" He cringed hoping she wouldn't shove him out into the snow with what he said next. "I... ahhh, I don't want to give you the impression that I don't *like* the idea of making a child with you, it's just…"

Daeira sat up and clasped her hands in her lap, bundling the fur around her shoulders. They were silent for a moment, and then she started laughing. "Look at you! You turned as pale as the Lord of the Dead! I'm not looking for you to *raise* it with me, so stop worrying your pretty head. I'm just curious how a babe by the famed Argus Killer would look."

Hermes shuddered at Hades's mention, relaxing only slightly when the nymph brought up the hundred-eyed giant he'd lulled to sleep and bludgeoned aeons ago. At least Daeira wouldn't give him any grief in the coming years. *Do I even have such a thing as 'coming years'? Or is this all going to end in fire?*

"Your woman doesn't mind, does she?"

"What?" He slung his satchel over his shoulder and patted it to make sure its terrible cargo was still within. "No. She—" *She's used to it*, he thought. "Penelopeia doesn't mind. Just don't… If we did conceive, be mindful of her feelings, would you?"

"Of course I will." She purposefully let her cleavage poke out from the fur. Hermes grinned as she spoke again. "And if nothing took hold the first time, milord, you can always come back to my bed tomorrow."

If I'm not thrown into Tartarus for this, he worried. "I wouldn't mind that at all, sweetling."

"Hermes?"

"Yes?" He pulled his petasos onto his head.

"When you come back," Daeira crooned seductively, laying back and lengthening her body in an inviting arch, "can you… you know… do that little thing with your tongue again?"

"What little thing?" Hermes gave her an impish smile as he opened the door. She blushed. He wasn't going to press it. It might be fun to rediscover what she meant without the encumbrance of words. "I think that can be arranged."

114

When it closed behind him, he went pale again. *If Hades doesn't cut my tongue out first.*

✳   ✳   ✳

"Is it lopsided?"

Aidon leaned around her, studying her reflection in the polished hematite. "No."

"Are you sure?"

He straightened his crown of golden poplar leaves and cocked a half smile at Persephone. "I don't know why you're fussing over your appearance so much."

"I'm nervous," she said, rearranging an asphodel flower for the fifth time.

"Why? It's only your mother." He considered the implications of that statement, and his smile faded.

"I haven't been above for two months, and when I *do* see her again, I want her to see me as Queen. Not as Kore."

"You'll always be Kore to her."

"Yes, but I need to look like a queen," she said, pulling at the edges of her mantle. The fine linen draped over her shoulders, held in place by ruby clasps. She wore the necklace he'd left on a table for her when she'd first awaked in the Underworld, garnets and fire opals cascading from her neck to her collarbone. Aidoneus was formally dressed, ready to see to the numerous shades waiting to be judged. He stood behind Persephone and met her eyes in the mirror.

"You look like a queen even if you didn't have a single flower, a single jewel, or a stitch of clothing on you. It's who you are, and they can never take that away from you." He planted a kiss on her cheek then looked at her askance. "Even if your hair *is* lopsided."

"Wait! You told me it—" she stopped when she saw him biting back a smile. She scrunched up her nose at him, then playfully smacked his chest.

"You look beautiful," he said, smoothing his hands down her shoulders. He remembered that Merope was no

115

longer there to attend to his wife and good-naturedly tease him. Having a servant had been strange for him. The Olympians had plenty, but he'd seen no need for them in his kingdom, more so because Olympian gods were known for having their nymph attendants see to other wants, a service he'd had no need of. Aidon watched her push a stray lock behind her ear. His face fell. "As beautiful as the moment I first saw you in the moonlight…"

She turned around and gazed up at him. "Aidoneus…"

"I know it will be only be a few days at most."

"I'll miss you, too. And I'll be back as soon as I can."

"At least there's work to keep me busy while you're away. I have to oversee eight judgements today. And nine tomorrow. The bloodiest wars don't yield this many rulers. I haven't had such numbers come before me since recruiting the three judges."

"You'd think that after this, you might want to just let them judge the rich and powerful in the same manner as everyone else, hmm? Aren't all equal in death?"

"And risk impartiality?"

"Are your judges trustworthy or not?"

"They are, but…"

"Aidon, how long have Minos and Rhadamanthys been here?"

"Fifteen centuries."

"And Aeacus?"

"Thirteen."

"And they were kings of men?"

He grunted in acknowledgement.

"Aidon, they've all been dead for well over a millennium. Their bones, their *empires* crumbled long ago. The Minoans, Mycenae… they're all gone. There are only the scattered cities in Hellas and Ilion now."

"Maybe you're right. I'll consider it." He kissed her forehead. "Unless, of course, I am receiving a direct order from my Queen."

"Oh, Aidoneus, honestly!" She smiled, shaking her head. Persephone rose up on tiptoe to peck him on the cheek, only to have him lean into it and steal the kiss from her. "Will you walk me at least as far as the Styx?"

"I'd go further if I could."

"I should go alone— and leave from the opposite side of the river. This is my first time crossing between worlds on my own. But I would love to have you with me for the first leg of my journey."

"Charon will be glad to take you to the far shore. He's been pestering me to see you again."

"And why *ever* haven't we paid a visit to dear Charon?" she asked, coyly.

"Well, we've been... otherwise occupied. I'm sure he understands. We're newlyweds, after all..."

She bit her lip and smiled.

"And though we don't make an exhibition of it—"

"We didn't make an exhibition of it until this morning, you mean," she teased.

Aidoneus pointedly cleared his throat and continued. "Even though we don't, what I feel for you is no secret here."

Secrets. Persephone licked her lips and debated whether this was a good time to tell him about her suspicion— that they may both be harboring a greater secret yet. "Aidon, there's something I—"

A loud knock at the door to their antechamber interrupted her, and she halted her words.

"Your majesties?" a muffled female voice said.

Hecate, Aidon said with a silent thought. He walked hand in hand with Persephone from their bedroom to the antechamber, where they sat next to each other on one of the divans. *It wouldn't surprise me if she already knows that you're going to see your mother.*

Nor I, she answered, then called out through the door. "Enter, please."

117

The Goddess of the Crossroads, dressed in a crimson peplos, pushed open one side of the antechamber doors. Her eyes were red, the lids swollen from lack of sleep, and she looked pale and gaunt. Worry lines creased her forehead, foreshadowing by a week the transition into her aspect of the Crone. "Good full moon to you, Queen Persephone, Lord Hades."

"And you, as well," Aidon replied.

"Is something troubling you, Hecate?"

"Only a single fork in a solitary path, my queen. One of many. And there is another matter," she said, giving Persephone a knowing look. "I should speak with you about it *later*. Tomorrow, perhaps?"

Persephone swallowed. The Goddess of the Crossroads already knew. And if she intended to speak with her about it tomorrow, then Hecate already knew Demeter would relent after only a day. This heartened her. "Thank you, Hecate."

Aidon quirked an eyebrow at the exchange, then moved on. "Since you're here, I assume you're aware that my wife intends to journey to the world above and put some sense into Demeter?"

"Yes," she said distantly. "Yes, I suspected she would. Especially after the torrent of voices in Asphodel last night when you two shared the Key…"

Persephone turned pink and felt sheepish embarrassment wash over her husband. "Is there anything else?"

"Unfortunately, yes." Hecate pulled a pomegranate— *their pomegranate*— from her sleeve. "It seems that someone has salted the sacred soil of you grove."

The pink that colored each of their cheeks turned a brilliant shade of red. The King and Queen exchanged a furtive glance and squeezed their hands together.

Hecate cleared her throat. "I see. I suppose I'll offer an apology to Askalaphos."

"You didn't go too hard on him, I hope?" Aidon chortled.

"Other circumstances may have colored my… accusations," she said. Hecate held up the fruit, its torn skin plainly visible to both of them. "Six seeds are missing. My queen, please answer with crystalline clarity: did you eat *even a single seed* from this fruit?"

"Don't worry, Hecate," Aidon answered for her. "I picked the fruit. Those seeds are missing because of *my own* curiosity. I'd never eaten a pomegranate before."

"I was going to," Persephone added, "but we decided it would be best to wait until after I return from Eleusis."

Hecate paused a moment, her face falling further. Her voice wavered. "I see."

"It would be foolish to bind myself here prematurely. I need to speak to my mother first, and she would blame Aidon if I ate anything in the Underworld."

The Goddess of the Crossroads blinked back tears. "Yes. Yes, I suppose she would." She forced a smile. "I shouldn't linger and keep you from your goodbyes."

"Are you sure there is nothing else?" Aidon asked, perplexed by her reaction to so simple a thing.

"No, my lord," she said solemnly. "A twist of fate, so to speak. All will follow the will of the Fates. I must go." She walked to the door and dipped her head before she departed. "Farewell, my queen."

* * *

"I love you," he said quietly, for what must have been the ninth time since they closed the palace gate behind them. They stood at the Styx, his voice the only sound disturbing the peaceful lapping of water against the gravel shoreline.

"I love you too," she replied. The golden poplar tree hung overhead as Aidoneus and Persephone gazed across to the other side. It was taking Charon longer than usual to reach them. Of course, given the number of souls departing his boat on the road to the Trivium, that was to be expected.

Aidoneus didn't mind the delay. It gave him a few extra moments with his wife. The shades waiting for his judgement— the high priest of Delphi, three kings and two magistrates from Hellas, a prince from Ilion, and an Amazonian tribal queen— could wait just a little while longer. They had eternity to do so. "Promise me, no matter what they might say to you…"

She let herself melt into him as his arms closed around her. "I know who I am, husband. They can't take that away from me."

"I only say it because you are entering a different world. They will only respect my protection of you up there— not who you really are. If you need to use that to your advantage, do so."

Persephone turned to face him, his hands now resting at her mid back. "It's only my mother that I'm speaking to, Aidon. What worries you?"

His stomach did another turn as he thought about Hecate's strange reaction to the pomegranate and the look on her face when she learned that Persephone hadn't consumed any seeds. "Nothing."

Her mouth twisted into a half smile. "We know that isn't true."

"I'm *worrying* over nothing, more accurately. Demeter cannot do anything to you. Even by the laws of the world above, you outrank her now. Only one among the immortals could stop you from returning here, and he swore an oath that your place was with me— gave you to me, by his understanding."

"So did my mother."

"This is different."

"Tell that to her."

"I thought that's what *you* were planning to do," he said with a rueful smile.

Persephone leaned into him again. "I'm going to miss you, Aidon. I'm going to miss *this*. Even though I've only been here for two months, it seems like a lifetime has transpired."

"Oh?" he said in confusion.

"Not in a bad way," she giggled. "So much has happened in so little time. It's like my time as Kore in the world above was a dream I awoke from."

Aidoneus was about to respond when he heard the swish of an oar through water. Both looked up to see hooded Charon rowing across the Styx at an even pace, until the prow of his boat raked against the rocky shore.

"Can your majesties forgive my tardiness? The boat was full."

"Full?" Aidoneus said, his voice betraying his surprise.

"Yes, full. Even for a craft such as this and beings as insubstantial as they. But to look at the far bank, does it surprise you?"

"Concerns me, is all." He straightened and lifted his chin. "Charon, can you permit us a moment?"

"Of course, my lord."

Hades turned to Persephone and cupped her face, staring down at her. *I will be here waiting for you.*

No, she answered. *More important matters await you. As they await me. Give me a few days, Aidon. I can reason with her, I can say goodbye, and I can arrange to see her again.*

He knitted his brow.

Briefly, she said with a smile. *But I must concede some things. I think visiting her from time to time is fair.*

He grimaced and gave her a heavy sigh, grinding his teeth together. *I suppose.*

Aidon, only to visit. This is my home. You *are my home.*

Persephone tilted her head up to look into his eyes, then closed them as his lips descended to hers. She held his shoulder blades, the sinews of his back cording under layers of cloth when he drew her closer. Aidon pulled away slowly and brushed a thumb over her cheekbone. "I will miss you, my queen."

"And I you, my lord. Take good care of our realm while I'm away."

"I always have," he said, giving her a warm smile. "And I always will."

Aidoneus suddenly bent down and swung Persephone off her feet and into his arms, to her delighted surprise. He walked to the edge of Charon's boat, the Styx drenching his himation up to the knee, and carefully sat her on one of the bracings. The Boatman cocked an amused half smile and said nothing.

Aidoneus held Persephone's hand for a long moment before placing a light kiss on her upturned wrist. "Farewell."

"And you."

He walked to the prow and leaned into it with one shoulder, giving the boat a mighty push. It rocked and settled into the water, gently swaying to and fro before the Boatman steadied and guided it the rest of the way with his oar. Persephone watched Aidon walk backward until he was standing once more on the shore. A quick brush of his hand instantly rid his clothes and sandals of the cold water clinging to them. He grew smaller in her sight as Charon rowed them away into the slow current.

Persephone locked eyes with him one last time before Aidoneus opened the gate behind him and walked inside. She raised her hand in a farewell as the door closed, then repositioned herself on the bracing opposite Charon, quickly losing herself in thought.

"My lady has a smile on her face, though she departs her realm?"

Persephone glanced up at him. "What? No, not because I am leaving. That's not why."

"Does it have anything to do with the celebration last night?" he asked with a slight smirk that reminded her for a moment of his younger brothers.

"In a way." She bit her lip. "Yes, in fact. Absolutely and completely." Persephone smiled and leaned back with a sigh.

"I'm in love, Charon." She stopped, tears welling in her eyes. "I'm sorry. I shouldn't be making a scene."

"And why ever not? Should our Lady not make it known that she loves our Lord?"

"I know. I only—" she sighed. "I love him so much. I can't explain it without feeling ridiculous or wanting to burst apart at the seams. Do I sound foolish to you?"

"Of course not." Charon smiled. "To hear you express your joy and know that is it returned… what could make my heart happier, my queen?"

As they retraced the path she had first taken across the Styx over a month ago, she saw the multitudes at the far shore. The asphodel that had once grown there were long gone, dug up by hungry shades who couldn't yet fathom they were dead. They had no way to know consuming the asphodel roots made no difference now. Persephone shook her head. "So much suffering. So much needless suffering…"

"Suffering is the mortal condition, dear lady," Charon said as his oar lapped gentle waves against the boat, "and all reach this shore, inevitably. It's been this way for aeons— ever since mortals came to be. They come, they go, and I bring them home so they can be reborn again."

"The shades *are* at peace once they are a part of our realm." *Our realm.* The last time she sat in Charon's boat she'd scarcely imagined ever referring to the Underworld as her home, much less taking responsibility for it. "But it's not *their* suffering I speak of. It's the ones you never get to see, Charon— the loved ones they must leave behind. Mothers. Children. Friends."

Charon merely nodded. Persephone could see the contemplation on his face and knew that he didn't truly understand what she meant. He might have heard the same words from a shade— from countless shades— explaining what it meant to leave those they loved behind, but the

123

mourning of living mortals lay beyond his understanding. "And you mean to set all of this right?"

"I must," she replied. "I know that because of everything that's happened, your family doesn't look on Demeter too kindly."

"Humph," he grunted, darkly.

"I know her, though; she's my mother. She's grieving. She grieved for Eleusis after they burned down her temple a century ago, and the fields throughout Attica didn't grow anything for nearly a month."

Charon thinned his lips. "I remember that famine. Not so harsh as this; none have ever been so harsh as this. But we had more souls waiting for passage than I would have liked. Thin. All so thin, just like these. And so soon after Ares's petty squabble with Athena made such a mess of things..."

"My mother would only do this if she thought I were in danger, or if she thought I was here against my will. I must tell her that she needs to stop this at once, that I am here of my own free will as Queen, and that I truly love Aidoneus."

Charon gave her a dry smile, then faced away from her, looking into the mists of the river.

"Charon?"

"Yes, my lady?"

"Have you ever been in love?" She realized at once that it might have been rude to ask such a thing of the Boatman.

He read the expression on her face and smiled. "Why fear asking me something like that? In truth, yes— I was once in love."

"What was she like?"

Charon sighed. *How many hundreds of aeons has it been?* he thought. "This was well before your husband was born. Before Hecate, before Hypnos and Thanatos, even. Back then, the only sons Nyx and Erebus had were Morpheus and me. There were so very few deathless ones then. Consciousness itself, the very idea of existing and being alive— much less gods or nymphs or spirits or whatever we were going to call ourselves— was still new. The woman I loved was older than me." He chuckled as Persephone's eyes grew wider. "Hard to imagine, indeed! But she was, just the same. Immortal, like you and I. Of course, nothing mortal existed back then. It was a concept beyond our grasp."

Persephone settled onto the bracing and brought her knees to her chest as she listened.

"Her eyes... the deepest blue you've ever seen. Like the bottom of a lake. I could see myself in them. Her hair was black as a raven's wing, soft, and she dressed in white— always in white... as I once did. Such pure brilliant white that floated about her, as if she were in the water. As though she *were* the water." He snorted and a smile curved his lips. "She was skinny, too. A bit too frail to be considered a true beauty, but I quite liked it."

"What happened to her?" She asked quietly.

His smile turned wistful as he looked back at her. "She was only slightly younger than my parents— one of the first born of the Protogenoi, when we were still piecing together how to make more of ourselves... and whether or not we should. Funny enough, she was also one of the first to become one with her divine domain— as my father eventually did."

"Were you happy with her?"

"No," he said, surprising her. "At least not as much as I had hoped to be."

Charon sat down across from Persephone as the boat caught a slow drifting current. He laid his oar across his knees.

"She loved another. Saw me as a trusted friend and nothing more. Sadly for her, she and her love could never be together." He looked out at the rocky slopes leading to the mouth of Tartarus and the glow of the Phlegethon. "I believe that was why Styx decided to become one with the river she watched over. Of course, I begged her not to. But after Ouranos claimed power over all of us and created the

125

Golden Men, she saw little reason to cling to a changing world."

Persephone sat quietly as Charon leaned over the edge and dipped his hand in the water, small wakes forming behind his skinny fingers. Charon's eyes met hers.

"I'll tell you a secret, Aristi Chthonia, *the* secret down here, if you asked your husband."

She raised an eyebrow and grinned. "It wouldn't have anything to do with the coins, would it?"

Charon chuckled. "Aidoneus always wonders what I do with them once I collect them from the shades. Oh, but don't tell him! It's one of the last things I still have on your husband. Where do those coins go, hmm? I can't fly up to the world above and spend them on riotous living. Although I could fly, once…" he drifted off, his eyes dulling for a moment before his wandering mind returned. "Look at me now! I wrap myself in a dusty cloak with no adornment, and my oar is my most treasured possession. I don't even wear shoes on my feet. I'm a rather boney creature, my queen, and I suppose I'd look rather frightful walking through some sunny *agora*." He laughed again, more freely this time.

She was unsure whether or not to laugh with him.

"I made a promise, long ago. I told Styx that I would give her everything I had, if only I could have her at my side for all eternity. It was the last time I saw her before she made the river's course her own. So to this day, every coin I receive, I give to her. Neither she nor I knew that the Fates would place me here and give me charge over the river lands of Acheron. But I got what I always yearned for in the end, I suppose."

She knitted her brow, her eyes cast down.

"How many others in this cruel cosmos can say they have lived countless aeons never having been parted from their beloved?" he said smiling. Charon leaned over the edge again and stroked the back of his fingers through the water, caressing it, whispering to the surface. "That is one thing I can say. Can't I, my dear?"

When his eyes drifted up to meet Persephone's gaze once more, a tear had rolled down one of her cheeks.

"Do not be sad for me, my queen. With any luck and by the will of the Fates, you will be with your beloved for just as long."

The lapping of the water grew louder against the craft, and the boat scraped against the shoreline before lurching to a halt. Persephone stood up carefully, regaining her balance before taking Charon's proffered hand.

"Are you sure you'll be alright, my queen? The stories I've heard from the shades…"

"It's not going to be the world I left, I know. But trust me, Charon; I'll be fine."

"Trusting you is not my worry. What of those petty gods above?"

"I am Hades's Queen," she said, hopping from the prow to the shore. "That alone should be enough to keep me safe."

His jaw set in a grim line for a moment, then he bowed farewell to her. "I'll be eagerly awaiting your return." Persephone smiled shyly, and Charon continued. "I shudder to think what a foul mood Aidon will be in while you're away," he said, smirking, and she laughed.

Persephone scanned the shore, seeing the tops of hundreds of heads bowed toward her. The recently arrived shades stood, walking once again toward Charon's boat.

"One obol… one obol… one at a time… one obol… a drachma! What did they imagine *that* would buy you here?…Yes, yes, I'll take it… one obol…" she heard as he allowed each of them aboard. Persephone walked on, watching shades respectfully lower their heads at her approach. She listened to them whisper amongst themselves. They created a wide berth for her, parting as she walked further up the shore away from the throngs so she could concentrate.

The dark passageways leading back to the world above stood in front of her. Spirits wandered in, looking around in awe and terror as they took their first steps into the Underworld. A few had coins in their hands, some in their mouths, others removed obols from their eyes to behold the vastness of Chthonia. She felt a cold brush of air on her left and looked to see a soul wandering back toward the passageways. It had become as faint as pale smoke, wandering away as a ghost bound for the world above.

There was nothing she could do for these newly dead, nor for the lost souls. They were part of Chthonia and would find their way back, or Hermes would return them eventually. She had to concentrate on those she *could* save in the mortal world and let her husband look after these. Persephone stretched her left hand in front of her and shut her eyes.

Eleusis—

"Kore!"

Persephone's eyes snapped open. She swore she recognized that voice.

"My Lady Kore!"

She glanced to her right and saw a shade running toward her. Persephone held her breath and took a hesitant step back. Did this soul want something from her, like the voices from the Trivium had late last night? She looked side to side, worried she was about to be surrounded by pleading spirits. The female shade stopped several steps away and prostrated herself. Persephone hesitantly reached out and touched her on the shoulder. "How do you know me by that name?"

The woman raised her head. Their eyes met and Persephone stumbled back.

"No…"

"My lady, we worshipped you in Eleusis. I would know the image of our lost Kore anywhere."

No, no, gods please no! She cupped her hands to her mouth and her vision blurred behind tears.

"My lady?"

Her throat was dry and her heart was beating out of her chest. "You… please, it cannot be you. You couldn't have died… Please…"

"I do not mean to trouble you so, my lady… Forgive me, I'll go."

"No; wait!" Persephone cried out. Her chest felt heavy. "I know you."

The woman turned to face her, then pushed a lock of black hair from her face. "How could you know someone as humble as me, my lady?"

"Two months ago. On the day of the full moon… do you remember?"

"That was…" The shade's lip trembled and she looked away. "That was my wedding day."

8.

Y OU KNOW AS WELL AS I DO THAT ELEUSIS CALLS ME TO *bear witness to their marriages*, Demeter had told Kore. *I can foresee their fates and cannot stop her from passing to the Other Side...*

It was the bride from Eleusis— the one whose marriage she had seen consummated in the wedding tent. Her mother had prophesied her death, but Demeter had thought it would be from bearing children. Little did she know, little did any of them know that it would be because Kore, Persephone, was in Hades. She tried in vain to hold back a sob, her breath shallow and tears running down her face. "I was there."

The woman's eyes widened. "You," she stammered in shock. The slightest smile lit her face. "I knew it! I told Dimitris the next day that I felt your presence there."

"Dimitris?"

"He's my husband. He—" she stopped, choking on her words. "He *was* my husband."

Persephone wiped her tears away with the edge of her peplos. "Where is he now?"

"At home. He— Dimitris had to bury me two days ago. He couldn't stop crying."

"What is *your* name?"

"I was called Melia, milady."

"How did you know I was there at your wedding?" Persephone choked out.

"I *felt* you there. Watching over us. I felt it with every heartbeat. Dimitris didn't believe me. Especially in the coming week when it grew so cold…"

"What happened?"

"The crops outside Eleusis withered overnight. And it was nearly harvest time. Dimitris and I took all we had and journeyed east. Surely Athens would have food, we thought. But it started snowing when we were on the road, slowing us down, and by the time we got there their grain stores were empty.

"We heard from other travelers that the Lady of the Harvest had returned to Eleusis. We started back almost as soon as we got there, and took the road by the sea. On the way there, we could at least fish. But the trees were frozen too solid to build a fire. Even the withered grasses had been pulled up for fires. Nothing remained. The sea froze over—"

"It… it what?!" Persephone gaped, horrified.

The shade looked perplexed by Persephone's ignorance. "Everything is frozen, my lady. The sea, the ground, the air is cold as ice. They can barely dig deep enough to bury the dead. You see all those there?" she said pointing to a group of shades huddled together away from the river. "They don't even have coins. No one was left in their village to bury them. And they built pyres out of abandoned homes in Athens because their dead were too numerous."

Persephone looked away from her. It was so much worse than she had even guessed. She'd expected the land to be brown, stripped of fertility, as it had been when her mother's temple had burnt down a century ago, but not this. Not a frigid blanket of death covering the earth, with nowhere for the forgotten souls to go once they reached the Styx.

"Everything above is gray. Nothing but a gray waste. And the ice covers everything else. People fleeing from the north told of great crushing walls of it overtaking mountains…"

Persephone's legs wobbled and she stared aghast at the Eleusinian bride. That was why the shades were eating the asphodel. They couldn't help themselves. More food grew in the world below than in the world above. The Fields must have looked like a *paradise* compared to the ruined earth. "Please. Tell me more. What happened to you and your husband?"

"Dimitris… he… I miss him so much," she said, shaking and wringing her hands. "He's all alone now. And he tried so hard… so hard to take care of me when I got sick… but it was too late by the time we got back. He refused to send my body with the carts headed for the sea." She looked away, her throat closed. Persephone's eyes stung with tears as the Eleusinian bride continued. "He chopped down his family's old fig tree. Then Dimitris burned it so he could soften the ground enough to bury me properly."

Persephone heard other shades wail mournfully as they passed by her, their voices a chorus of sobbing and confusion. Women, men, and children milled about, lost. The shore was empty. Charon's boat had already departed, laden with souls to ferry to the other side She sputtered another cry and took the Eleusinian woman's hands. "I'm sorry. I'm so sorry!"

"No, my lady, this isn't your fault."

"I—"

"You were stolen. Ravished."

Persephone looked up at her in shocked silence.

"Weren't you? You wouldn't have abandoned us, would you?"

She stayed silent. "I—"

"But you are going back?"

"Yes."

"You are escaping, then!" Her hand tightened around Persephone's. "Quick! Let me help you! That is why you are on this side of the River, isn't it? I can show you the path back to Eleusis!"

"No, I didn't escape. This is my home now, and I—" the shade wrenched her hands away from Persephone's and took a step back, her eyes growing wide. Persephone felt her mouth go dry as fear washed over the woman's face. Her voice rose, pleading. "You don't understand. I'm going back to see my mother. But I *will* return here after I do."

"Then you— you did abandon us..."

"Hades is my husband. I am his queen."

"But everything is *dying* without you!"

Persephone swallowed. "I know. But I will set it right again—"

"Destroyer," the woman whispered, shaking her head and backing away. "*Destroyer!*"

"No, please..." Persephone whispered.

"Destroyer!" another shade wailed as it wandered past. "Destroyer!" "*Katastrofeas!*" she heard in the common tongue. The voices blended together in Theoi, Attic, Thracian, and other languages. "*Despoina, torelle mezenai!*" "Persephone!" "*Ekeini pou katastrefei to fos!*" "Destroyer of Light!" "*Perephatta!*" "She who destroys the light!"

They weren't speaking to her, but around her. It was as though her conversation with the Eleusinian woman had rippled outward, affecting the shades. The shoreline became a shrill chorus accented by wailing and sobbing. Destroyer of light. Ice poured down her spine and Persephone doubled over as though the wind were knocked out of her.

A balance has existed here for all the years you've been alive, Praxidike, Kottos had said. *You are the one who transcends and connects the worlds. You are the embodiment of balance...*

She was caught between her mother and her husband, and the fate of the world was bound up with her, just as the Hundred Handed Ones said it was. *No, please Fates, no...*

133

"Please, I didn't mean to—"

"My Dimitris was right," the shade hissed. "You weren't there to bless us. You did nothing but curse us!"

Carrier of curses...

"I didn't... this wasn't... Please, you *must* believe me," she cried, nearly hysterical. "I had no idea that it had become so terrible! It's why I'm going back. I— Please, tell me what I can do to help you; to take away your pain. Please!"

"Take me with you."

Persephone blanched. "I am sorry, I cannot."

"I must see Dimitris. He *needs* me!"

"You *cannot* ask that of me. You know there's no going back to the world of the living."

"Please, Soteira, take me back!" she cried frantically.

"Do not ask this, please..." Other souls began to take notice.

The shades around them began to cry out to her, their voices a cacophony. *"Aristi, my children!" "Metra, please, spare me..." "Just once more, Thea, let me see her once more..." "Soteira, voithiste me! Voithiste me!"* someone cried out in the common tongue.

The shades circled her, begging her to spare them. The Eleusinian woman backed away from her, fading to translucence. "My lady, I will not go. I'm not ready. I must see Dimitr—"

And with that she was disappeared— a soundless ghost bound for the world above.

Persephone crouched and shut her eyes. She clapped her hands over her ears to block the wandering shades out, crying loudly to drown their voices. They stopped their petitions and started weeping as she was. They milled about, wailing and moaning, their cries incessant as she huddled close to the ground, too distraught to rise.

My mother isn't strong enough to undo this on her own, she realized. The weight of it sat on her shoulders like the punishment that had been doled out to Atlas. *She needs me.*

It wasn't as simple as talking to Demeter. It was easy enough to blame her mother, stay implacable and do nothing. She needed to restore balance. Persephone was a goddess of the earth, like her mother, her grandmother, a lineage stretching all the way back to Gaia herself. Even if she was Queen below, the earth was still her domain. A reality, cold as the world above, struck her.

Caught between her love for her husband and her mother's love for her, she'd forgotten why she existed in the first place— for them. The mortals. To look after their eternal souls, not just when they were here, but during their brief time in the sunlit world. To feed them. To protect them.

If Demeter would not take responsibility for what had been done and, she thought woefully, if Hades could not, then the obligation fell to her. She would need to stay above far longer than a few days— *months*, even— to truly right all that had gone wrong. She would have to break her promise to Aidoneus. Persephone slowly stood and stretched forth her hand, ready to create a path back to Eleusis.

"Kore? Persephone?"

It was a high tenor voice, almost lost to her amidst the weeping shades. It sounded so clear and distinct that she thought that it was an illusion.

"Lady Persephone!"

She looked up through her tears to see a young man wrapped in a chlamys, his face hidden by a golden petasos. He descended from above and landed next to her.

"Wh-who…" She knew who he was. Hermes. Persephone blushed hotly, thinking about the last time he had caught a glimpse of her. "Why are you here?"

He lightly took her hand, barely touching her fingers. "You're free."

"What?"

"Persephone, I was sent here by our father to bring you back to your mother, Demeter."

"We never asked for you to— what..." she drew in a breath as he grasped at her wrist. She wrenched it away from him. "Let go of me! What are you doing?!"

"You've been freed from Hades's captivity. I'm here to bring you back to your home in the living world."

"Freed from— Hermes, I don't know what you've heard, but—"

"There isn't much time. Please! Zeus insisted I take you back at once."

"No!" She stepped away from him and backed toward the Styx.

He looked at her, bewildered. "What do you mean?"

"Who gave you the right to haul me away from here? From my realm?"

"Your—" he looked at her dumbfounded. "The King of the Gods! Are you going to obey him or not?"

"But... Zeus said..." she stilled, her blood freezing. If her father, the one who had permitted her union with Aidoneus, had told Hermes to take her from here then that meant... "Hermes, you need to talk to my husband right now and get this straightened out."

"I'd rather not," he snorted, then smiled to cajole her. "Look; it will be easy. I'll fly us back, quicker than you can fathom. You'll be gone from here before he even knows you went missing."

"No!" she cried out. This isn't happening! She felt her limbs go slack, felt helpless and crushed. "You need to tell him—"

"Please, Lady Persephone," he pleaded, "If we do that, it will only complicate matters."

He grabbed her wrist again and closed his fingers tightly. She struggled against his grip. "Let me go!"

"Persephone, you're already on this side of the river—"

"Let go of me now!" she cried out, finally wrenching away.

"You and I can avoid all that and—"

"While you are here, God of Thieves," a gravelly voice said behind them, "I suggest you follow the rules set out at the division of the cosmos."

Persephone stifled a cry of relief when she saw Charon, whose long oar stood beside him. His jaw was set grimly, his eyes steely, his skin frighteningly pale underneath his hood. Though thin of frame, he towered over them both from his place atop the stern bracing. She relaxed her shoulders as Hermes took a step back.

The Messenger swallowed. "I-I have my orders, Charon. You cannot stand in my wa—"

"The realms were divided equally, *Thief*, and this domain does not belong to your king. You know that, I know that." His voice sank into a low growl. "And if you touch our queen again, boy…"

"You'll what?" Hermes said, narrowing his eyes as Charon tightened his hand around his oar. Hermes rose an inch from the ground.

"Enough!" Persephone said. "Both of you!"

The Boatman inclined his head to her. "Say the word, my lady and—"

"Charon, thank you." She gave him a relieved smile and turned to Hermes, her eyes narrowed. "Hermes Psychopompos, you have no right to take me from here unwillingly. If you have orders from Zeus, you are to bring them before my husband!"

Hermes set his lips in a line, his worst fears realized. "Give me a moment then. I'll fly to—"

"No, you will not," she said with a scowl. His eyes widened.

"But—"

"From now on, if you come here on official business, you will enter our realm as all do."

A smirk curled the Boatman's lips as Hermes stared at her in disbelief. "You cannot be serious…"

"I suggest that you make your peace with the fact that your only path across the river is through Charon. And since I am empowered by my husband to speak on his behalf, I suggest you not disobey me," Persephone said, raising her voice.

Hermes stared at her blankly, trying to form words, then jumped back in fright when a blazing ring of fire appeared in front of the little flower goddess, pointing her way through the ether.

"We will see you in the throne room once you arrive." With that, she stepped through and waited until the gateway closed. When it shut, she curled into a ball and cried until she screamed. They were going to take her away. Forcibly.

Captivity... Obey...

She grew nauseous. Persephone wouldn't get the chance to speak with her mother or fix anything. They were dissolving her marriage. She felt as though the very walls around her were collapsing and disappearing, and realized that she wasn't in the throne room or the palace, or the Underworld itself, even. She was still in the crimson and silver twisting vertigo of the ether.

What if she just stayed here forever? Hermes didn't come here. Hecate would surely welcome her, and no one couldn't pull her from here. She held a Key that gave her access to every corner of every realm.

She chided herself. *Hiding like a little girl, are we? Aren't they trying to take me away from because they still believe me to be little innocent, ignorant Kore?*

Persephone wiped her tears away and focused. She had to speak to Aidoneus. Quickly. She willed herself to open a pathway to the palace, and stepped through. Persephone stood in the pomegranate grove.

Fates! Why have I been carried here again? She picked up her skirts. Her sandals crunched across the gravel as she ran past a confused Askalaphos, her shoulders knocking against the carefully manicured asphodel, racing for the portico and the palace beyond. She had to find her husband. She had to get there before the Messenger.

✻   ✻   ✻

"Delaying this isn't going to make me disappear, Boatman," Hermes said, shifting from one foot to the other on the center bracing.

"Would that it would."

"Excuse me?"

Charon had remained silent, pushing slowly off the banks of the Styx and winding his way through the shallows into the river. "Is there a problem?"

"It's not me you have to worry about, Charon."

"How fortunate are you that it was I who discovered you, and not Hades? What could you have said just then, with your hand around his wife's wrist, to keep him from tearing you limb from limb? I wonder..."

Hermes mouth went dry. "Wh-when Zeus—"

"And who am I to argue with the currents of the river?" he said slowly, deliberately aggravating the Messenger. "Or argue with the Queen?"

"Kor— Persephone is Hades's consort. His— his duly acquired bedmate, for Fate's sake. Not a Queen. Not in any real sense— she has no power. And I don't care what your mother says."

Charon lifted his oar out of the water and let the boat drift to stillness. The bow turned in an eddy and the Boatman turned with it to look back at Hermes. "Really, then? In your heart of hearts, I wonder... which one of our sovereigns would you rather deal with, coward?"

Hermes opened his mouth to speak, but couldn't get a word out before Charon continued.

"Answer her name, and you're a fool. Answer his, and you're a liar. You came here thinking to take her right out from under her honored husband's nose and thought none of us would mind?"

139

"This goes beyond what any of you should be concerned with."

"Perhaps I am wrong about you, Hermes. Perhaps instead, you are very brave if you think you can lay your hands on the Iron Queen without consequence?"

Hermes stayed silent. Charon plunged his oar back into the water, pushing the boat forward, a tiny wake the only disturbance on the crystal clear surface.

"Or perhaps, you are exceptionally stupid?" Charon added with a grin.

Hermes face grew red. "I only wanted to... speak with her. This is extremely urgent."

"Urgent?" He slowly sunk the oar into the water again, the opposite shore growing minutely closer.

"Yes, urgent! Do you think this is amusing?" Hermes said, gesturing back at the rows of shades awaiting passage to the Other Side.

"I am the one who must deal with the shades you petty Olympians send down here every day," Charon spat back at him. "Why would I find any of this amusing?"

"*Your* people call me Psychopompos! I am the one who has to find lost souls and bring them back here. Don't act like you're the only one who has to deal with this, Charon!"

"Then you should keep to your business and let us to ours. Why waste our time and intrude on us? Why try to spirit away our queen, God of Thieves?" Charon asked as he rowed the boat through the currentless marshes.

Hermes impatiently looked at the emaciated souls waiting at the river's edge. "I wasn't trying to spirit her—"

"You're a poor liar for a thief."

He snorted and rolled his eyes. "I don't know why I'm even answering your questions, Boatman. I outrank you."

"Did you come here as Zeus's errand boy or as a cut purse to steal our beloved queen, you half-hardened prick of an immortal?"

Hermes bit the sides of his cheek.

"One or the other."

"I have no time for this, Charon. And I know you can get us there faster than *this*!" he said, shifting again from one foot to the other. Charon looked behind him with wide eyes and a threatening grin and removed his oar from the water once more. The boat drifted slower, at the mercy of the current. "I come as the voice of the King of Gods."

"And which king of the gods would that be?" Charon said with a smirk. "I only recognize the one."

Charon rowed forward, silently delighting in the Messenger's shocked expression. Hermes bristled. "That's... heresy! When my father—"

"I do not see him here. Do you? Or are you merely seeing his handiwork," Charon rasped, pointing a thin finger at the droves of souls standing on the banks of the river, "and calling *that* power?"

Hermes faltered, swallowing, and looked around him, "I—"

"This is Chthonia, boy. The eternal realm. You are an interloper from the corporeal world. And if you doubt my prior question, then remember that we didn't come begging you for the flow of shades to stop. If Hades were to consign you to the Pit, there wouldn't be a thing your lofty king could do to stop it. If our queen decided to have you flayed and scourged by the Erinyes for daring to touch her..." he said as the prow raked the shore and lurched underneath them. "...I would only be too glad to watch."

Hermes paled and stared up at the black marble monolith of the palace, the towering gates, and golden poplar looming above them. The Messenger swallowed.

"Best remember those things, Psychopompos, when you stand before him who rules over the souls of all mortals, living and dead."

9.

"WHO'S NEXT?"
"The last one today. Inachus of Argos."

"Your scrolls are out of order, Minos," Aidoneus said with a measure of annoyance. "We received him a week ago."

"Yes, my lord, we did," the judge said, not looking up. "This is his son."

Hades sighed and leaned back in his throne, recalling the judgement of Inachus the Elder, third in his line: sent to Asphodel. And his wife, Chryseis: Asphodel. Their son had been five years old, and with no suitable living regent, the prince was crowned king. Now he was dead as well, and his bloodline with him. It had been ages since a small boy had come to this room of judgement— ages since Aidoneus had even been in the presence of a child who wasn't already a resident of Asphodel. A trial felt unnecessary, as there was nothing one so young could have done to warrant it.

Perhaps his wife was right. When the glut of newly deceased had been dealt with, perhaps he would turn over all hearings to his judges and only have a hand in the most disputed decisions. But right now, the child was his responsibility. "Get me the waters of the Lethe."

"Doesn't Aeacus usually—"

"Just do it!" he growled. "*Scores* of thousands of common folk wait on the Plains of Judgement, and the four of us sit here *coddling* the few souls of the rich and powerful! Take Aeacus and your brother. I'll handle this myself."

"Should I summon Inachus, then, my lord?"

"Yes."

Minos left one of the ebony doors wide, and stepped outside to murmur some words to Aeacus. He returned with an earthen bowl, handed it to Aidoneus, then quickly retreated from the room. Hades held the red clay kylix and stared into the clear, dark water from the River Lethe. Nothing. The water itself couldn't even remember a reflection.

Hades saw a pair of brown eyes and a small hand poke out from around the door, then a thin boy with dark curling hair slowly walked into the room, terrified. A tiny indigo chlamys clung to his shoulder, pinned over a child's black chiton— the garments he'd been buried in.

The child crept into the room, his eyes cast down. He was too fearful to look upon Hades, the dark god his family had told him scary stories about whenever he fussed or talked back to his wet nurse. The boy's face crinkled up as though he were about to cry.

"I'm sorry you had so short a time," Hades muttered.

The little shade didn't make a sound, trying to be brave, trying to hold back his tears and be a man like his departed father told him to be. Aidoneus stood, and the little boy gulped and took a step back.

"Don't be frightened," the dread King of the Dead said gently. The child's lip trembled, and Aidon realized that Inachus didn't understand. He awkwardly started again. "*Mi me fovasai.*"

The boy looked up in silent recognition. The Lord of Souls walked slowly, descending the dais with the kylix in his hand, his robes trailing behind him on the steps.

"*Ksereis poios eimai?*" he asked in the common tongue.

143

The little boy nodded. *"You're. . . you're the Invisible One, m-my lord."*

Aidoneus knelt down, his gaze level with the child's wide, fearful eyes. *"But you can see me now, no?"*

Little Inachus nodded again and brushed a knuckle past one of his eyes before looking up.

"Ela," Aidon said, motioning him forward. The boy remained rooted where he stood. *"It's alright. I'm not as scary as you'd think."*

The shade took one cautious step, and then another. *"But you're scary sometimes?"*

"Only when I have to be," Aidon said, the hint of a smile tugging at the corners of his eyes. He held up the bowl. *"You know what this is?"*

"They told me it makes you forget. And stop being sad."

"Yes. They were right."

"But I don't want to forget Mana!"

"Was Mana your nurse?" The boy nodded. *"You loved her very much, then."* Another small nod. *"Well. . ."*

Persephone walked toward the entrance of the room of judgement, her steps uneven. Drawing nearer, she heard the welcome sound of her husband's voice— and that of a small child, faint and trembling. She stopped just beyond the doorway, out of sight. The boy was already scared enough. He didn't need to see the Iron Queen in this state, with tears streaming down her ruddy, panicked face.

"You'll see her someday," Aidoneus continued. *"But I will not lie to you. You won't remember her as you do now. But the love you have for her here,"* he said tapping two fingers where little Inachus's heart would have been, *"that you will always keep."*

She stayed out of view, and fresh tears filled her eyes. If she weren't already in love with Aidoneus, this moment would have made her his. Persephone wanted to rush to his side and kiss him. She wanted to tell him what she suspected, that she might be carrying their child, that they soon might have a little boy like this. She bit down on her lip and

144

cupped her hand to her mouth, then squeezed her eyes shut and crumpled against the wall. Persephone cursed herself: she had waited too long for the right moment, waited to speak with someone else first, and now it was too late. Their world was coming down around them. She folded her knees to her chest, so the layers of her peplos would muffle her sobs.

Aidon's insides twisted with sudden agonizing grief. He quickly schooled his expression, hiding his alarm so it wouldn't frighten the boy. *"How did it happen?"*

"I was so hungry. Mama and Papa. . . they went to sleep, Mana said, and then she said she had no food left."

He tried to listen, tried to stave off the dark emotions flooding into him from... Persephone. He was certain that something had gone terribly wrong He had to find her. Aidon pushed down his rising panic as best he could and shut his eyes, drawing a deep breath before opening them again and focusing on the little king. He placed a hand on Inachus's tiny shoulder, hoping that it would comfort the shade, and took it as a good sign when the child didn't recoil. *"Then what?"*

"I was cold, it was hard to breathe, then I was burning up. I couldn't move and I heard Mana crying," he said. *"I can still hear her crying."*

Hades saw the boy dip his head to hide his face so the Lord of the Underworld couldn't see it contort into silent weeping. He crouched lower. *"It's all right; it's over. All the pain is over. You're here now as my guest."* He gently tilted the little shade's chin up until their eyes met again. *"You're home, Inachus."*

"Home?"

"Yes." Aidon forced a thin smile. *"Everyone is waiting for you."*

"Mama and Papa are here?"

"They are. But you must do something for me."

Inachus swallowed.

"You must let go."

145

"Of what?"

Aidoneus smiled sadly. *"Of… the things you knew. Of the hunger and hurt and sadness."*

The young boy thought for a moment, eyeing the kylix nervously. *"Mana too?"*

"You won't forget her love, Inachus. Only her tears." Aidon offered the vessel to him. *"Be brave, little one, and drink the waters of the Lethe."*

Persephone shook, weeping quietly, the effort starting to hurt her throat and chest. Any doubts she'd had about whether they could be parents were erased. She listened to Aidon, and rested her hand on her womb. If she was pregnant, if that was why her moon blood had stopped, then she would bring his child into this world joyfully and without hesitation. She wanted to give Aidoneus piles of children— to fill the palace with as many of their offspring as she could. The thought filled her with happiness, even as it overwhelmed her with sadness. She may not have the chance. Persephone might be taken away from him forever. *Captivity.* Hermes had said her *captivity* was over. Did Zeus call it that now, to make her union with Hades easier to dissolve?

Too late, too late, she thought, angry at herself. *You should have told him you loved him! You should have shouted it from the porticos and passageways of the palace that you loved him! You should have told him a month ago that he had your heart… that you are his and he is yours. But you were a coward. A scared little Kore…* She wanted to scream at the injustice of it, but choked back her voice. It was too late. If she told Aidoneus what she believed she was carrying and they tried to take her away, he would tear apart the cosmos to keep her here. And then Kronos's dread visions would truly come to pass. She needed to be strong. She needed to lock this knowledge away, find a way to set all of this right, or it would be the ruin— the death— of them all.

"Are you ready?"

"Are there others here to play with?"

"There are quite a few, recently arrived," he sighed. *"You'll find many friends. And one day, when you're ready, you will go back to the world above."*

Inachus looked up at him with his dark eyes. *"You promise?"*

"I have no reason to lie to you."

The shade turned his head to the side and considered him, unsatisfied.

Hades relented. *"I promise. As a king to a king."*

"Will it hurt?"

"Just the opposite. You'll be free of all pain, all sadness."

Inachus nodded and reached for the kylix. As he lifted the heavy clay cup to his lips, Hades held it steady for him.

"Slowly now," he said while Inachus sipped the water.

The boy finished his draught and smiled. *"The water is warm,"* he whispered.

Inachus watched his hand become translucent and tittered, experimentally wiggling his fingers. He reached for the cup again and gulped down more of the Lethe, then laughed, his form shifting about, visible one moment, then a clear blur the next. He took a few steps, looking at his feet, then darting his eyes around the throne room.

The shade turned toward the door, voices calling him to come play in the Fields, and then broke into a short run. He spun on his heels before he faded from sight and whispered. *"Efcharisties, Theos…"*

Then, he was gone.

Aidoneus nodded, then went to the balcony and set the kylix on the ledge, peering at the banks of the river, looking along the shoreline for his wife. He heard the heavy door of the chamber slam shut, then muffled sobbing behind him. "Persephone?"

Her face was hidden in the palms of her hands and she leaned against the door, crying.

"Persephone!" He ran to her and pulled her hands away, looking down at her tear-stained face. "What happened?"

"He... They're going to t-take me— The woman from Eleusis— th-the one I told you about... I s-saw her and..." She could barely speak. Aidon wrapped his arms around her and held her.

"My love, calm down," he said stroking her back. "Be calm. It cannot be as bad as all that."

"Aidon... it's worse— *so much worse* than w-we thought," she sobbed.

"What do you mean?"

"All ice, everywhere... leveling the world. It's dying, Aidon! The earth is... dying. Everything I ever knew is gone! It's just flat and gray and ice and cold and there's no food for any of them, and even Eleusis will run out— And they... the gods above..."

"That's why you were going to Demeter, sweet one. To help stop this. What happened on the way?"

"Hermes."

He darkened and looked her in the eye. "What about him?"

"He tried to take me from here. He said that m-my captivity— *captivity*, Aidon! That was what he said— he said that it's ended and— and that he was o-ordered to take me *h-home*."

Aidoneus seethed, grinding his teeth together. This had gone too far. "Demeter cannot—"

"She didn't tell Hermes to come here!" Persephone cried. Aidoneus froze, the leaden feeling returning to the pit of his stomach. She wiped her nose and continued. "Zeus ordered him to take me away!"

He blanched. There must be some mistake. "Sweet one."

She looked up at him, her eyes swollen and red.

"Sweet one," he repeated, smiling reassuringly and slowly shaking his head. "They wouldn't *do that*. No one can; not even Zeus. They swore an unbreakable oath. The balance of power was built around *our betrothal*, Persephone. None of the

148

gods above would dare go against that." He raised an eyebrow and looked around. "Why isn't Hermes here now?"

"I told him to cross with Charon. To meet us here in the throne room. If he's not here yet then Charon must have delayed him long enough for me to tell you first."

"Wife, why didn't you call for me? I would have set this—"

There was a loud knock at the door.

She looked back at him and brushed away the last of her tears. Persephone shut her eyes and breathed deeply, trying to appear calm. *It's him, Aidon. We need to take our places. On our thrones.*

Persephone broke away from him and strode toward the dais. Aidoneus followed her. Perplexed, he sat down at her side. *Why bother to give Hermes a formal audience?* Aidoneus looked over at her. *I'd just as well have met him on the far side of the Styx to sort out this nonsense.*

No, she said. *I want the Messenger to come to us. If he has something to say, he'll say it here where it means something. I will not tolerate the notion that I can be spirited off like a little girl.*

You needn't worry, my love. He won't take you anywhere. By Zeus's very oath, he cannot do so. He squeezed her hand reassuringly and faced forward again, his features becoming grim and dispassionate. *And we won't allow it.*

The door groaned open and Hermes walked cautiously into the great hall. He dropped to one knee before he dared to look up at them. How much had Persephone told Hades about their encounter at the river?

"Rise," Aidoneus rumbled.

Hades and Persephone Chthonios, rulers of the Underworld, sat beside each other on their thrones. His was a solid mass of ebony, worn and polished by the aeons. Hers was of equal height to his, wrought from bright iron into a delicate pattern of twisting asphodel. There was no space between the thrones. Their fingers were intertwined and Hermes watched as Hades's thumb slowly brushed over his wife's. A silent wave of momentary distress crossed her face before she resumed a regal emotionless cold, echoing that of her dread husband.

A chill made its way up Hermes's spine. His position before the rulers of the Underworld and what he had been commanded to do came into sharp relief. Even Zeus kept Hera's throne on a lower dais than his own, and would never take an audience holding his wife's hand. He was well aware that they had consummated their union; that much had been etched in his mind forever, to their collective and eternal chagrin. But Demeter was wrong; they were all wrong. Persephone truly loved him; Aidoneus loved her. And Hermes's assignment was to part them forever.

Trying not to think about how these words might be his last before Hades threw him into Tartarus, he opened his satchel. The golden vellum scroll shook in his hands as he unrolled it. His mouth was bone dry. *Like Tantalus*, he thought darkly, cursing his own imagination.

What Aidoneus will do pales in comparison to what Zeus will do to you if you don't deliver this. He shivered again. *Probably send me to Tartarus.* His mind was made up. If he was to be damned either way, then so be it. Hermes stood tall once more. He was the Messenger; the voice of his father, the King of the Gods. Or so he kept trying to convince himself.

He took a deep breath as he unfurled the scroll. "B-by the holy order of Zeus Pater Aegiduchos Cronides, King of Olympus and of the Gods," he swallowed hard, "the marriage of Hades Aidoneus Chthonios, firstborn son of Kronos, Lord of the Underworld, and Persephone, daughter of Demeter, Maid— Lady of the Flowers is hereby annulled. The histories shall hereafter state that Persephone tempted the Lord of the Underworld by picking a flower sacred to his realm in order to draw him up from the depths. Hades then abducted Persephone from her garden in Nysa by force, committing rapine against her, and dragged her unwillingly to the Underworld to force her into unlawful marriage. Any

titles bestowed upon Persephone by Hades are hereby re-
scinded and any issue from their union will be
considered—"

The parchment burst into flames, swirling embers turning to ash between Hermes's singed hands and vanishing
before Hades's outstretched curling fist. The Messenger
gasped and stumbled backwards as the Lord of the Underworld closed on him. Hermes didn't see Hades's hands wrap
around his throat; he only felt his voice, his breath, cutting
off. The dark god stared down at him, gritting his teeth, his
eyes lit with fires of murderous rage as his fingers tightened
around the young god's neck. Hermes tugged and clawed
fruitlessly at Hades's grip, his gold petasos clattering to the
ground. His knees buckled underneath him, and his senses
began to fail him. As if from a great distance, he heard Hades's wife call out.

"*Aidon, stop!*"

Hades released Hermes and watched the Messenger
crumple onto the marble floor at his feet. As Hermes
coughed and sucked in rasping breaths, Aidoneus bellowed
at him. "You dare to abduct my queen from the shores of
Styx, you insult us both, and then you announce that the
oldest oath your king ever made is now broken?!" Hades
kicked the crumpled god's petasos clear onto the terrace outside. "That he plans to end my marriage and *steal my wife*?!"

Hermes held up his hand, trying to shield himself from
Hades's wrath, his breathing still labored. "I'm only the
Messenger…"

"You are a coward hiding behind Zeus's skirts!" He
picked Hermes up by the front of his tunic, shaking his limp
form. "Answer for what you have said to me in my own
halls!"

"Please, Aidon…" Persephone said quietly, taking a step
toward him. Hades looked over his shoulder at her and
paused, collecting himself, then dropped Hermes and retreated a step back.

"You are no longer welcome here, Hermes Psychopompos," Aidoneus said with a growl as he turned back toward the dais. "Do not ever come to the shores of the Styx again."

"You need me now more than ever," he said as he coughed, slowly getting to his knees. "The dead are too numerous for Charon's boat. The unquiet souls will wander back into the world of the living and sap what's left of its vitality even faster. They *must* be returned here, and who else will do it but me?"

"That is not my concern," he said quietly.

"The borders between the realms are collapsing! If you do nothing, every man, woman and child will die, Hades!"

"I said that's not my concern!" Aidoneus shouted. He sat back down on his throne, motioning for his wife to sit with him. He narrowed his eyes at the boyish god before him. "Strange that the rest of the immortals care so much for them now, when century after century it fell to *me* to clean up the messes you made with your petty wars, your pestilence, your famine and floods! Need I remind you how aeons ago *your king* left only *two mortals* alive when he flooded all of Hellas?"

"This is diff—"

"How?" He slammed his fist on the arm of his throne. "How is this different?!"

"Because this isn't Attica or Crete or even just Hellas. Humans are dying *everywhere.*"

"Mortals begin their slow march to my realm from the minute they draw their first breath! Some arrive faster than others."

"Please, Hades… You must return Persephone to Demeter—"

"I *must* do nothing!"

"Hades, I'm begging you. Our worlds are intertwined. Have you not noticed that souls are no longer drinking from the Lethe and leaving your realm to be reborn? That mortals are openly crossing back and forth as if no border existed? Don't think we haven't noticed that Sisyphus of Ephyra—"

"Sisyphus is *mine* to deal with, and I assure you my justice will be hard and swift," he growled.

"You'll never get the chance to exact it, Aidoneus!" Hermes said. "The world is ending. Because you *insist* on keeping *her* the world is ending!"

"Hasn't your *king* taken enough from me already?" He leaned forward and gripped the arms of his throne, his knuckles turning white. "That scroll you delivered was a *declaration of war!*"

"Aidon, my beloved, no—" Persephone said, her voice low. She placed a hand on his. He turned to her and caught it in his grasp.

"What choice are they giving me?" he pleaded, wide eyed. "What choice do I have? You heard what he said!"

"Reason with your husband, madam. The world cannot survive—"

"You will be silent, Hermes!" she said, her voice ringing through the hall. She turned back to Aidon and stroked his cheek. "My love, think about what you're saying."

"I have, sweet one," he rumbled. "I've thought about this from the moment Charon ferried me across the river all those thousands of years ago." He turned to address Hermes. "If it were not for me, if it were not for every *moment* I spent planning, fighting, *killing* in the Titanomachy, they would all be in Tartarus right now! I *won that war* for them and this is the thanks I get?! Is it not enough that I was forced to be the warden of Tartarus, night and day, for all eternity?"

"But, Aidon—"

"If it were not for my own accursed suggestion to divide the lots, I would be sitting Olympus right now, ruling over all by birthright, instead of being *discarded* down here! I should have trusted my instincts and *never* left the rulership of the cosmos to that bloviating, philandering fool!"

153

She turned to him, shocked. "Aidon, what are you saying?"

"That I should have done this aeons ago, and now is the time to correct my mistake! They are weak. Look at them cower before us even now," Hades said, pointing dismissively at Hermes. "Every moment that Demeter starves the earth only enriches our kingdom and weakens theirs."

Persephone watched the rims of his irises begin to glow with the fires of the Phlegethon. She shook her head gently, considering her next words carefully, and spoke to him where Hermes could not hear them. *I cannot support you in this. Aidoneus, please. Tartarus is reaching through you. Kronos—*

This has nothing to do with my father! He turned away from her frightened gaze. *He has no power over me.*

But these are not your words, she said. *They sound like his!*

Can't you see what is happening? His eyes returned to dark brown and grew wide, his panic palpable. *They are separating us forever! Their oaths, their laws, now mean nothing and they are making you and I and every mortal on earth victims of their capriciousness! They care nothing for us, and nothing for them!* He gripped her hand in his. "Allow me to end their foolishness," he said aloud.

"These are not your words," she repeated.

"I am the eldest of my generation and you of yours. You and I are the rulers of the cosmos by *birthright*! It is time for us to embrace our fate, my love. Please, I need you." He knelt forward from his chair, and fell to his knees in front of her throne. Aidoneus took her hands in his.

She looked down at him, mapping the fear and desperation on his face, her heart beating out of her chest. Persephone considered acquiescing— considered telling him to unleash the Erinyes, the Keres, the Tribe of the Oneiroi, the Hundred Handed Ones, all their innumerable allies and go to war. Then she remembered what she had seen in Tartarus. The throne. The fall. The rising embers. Destruction. Rape. Death.

Aidoneus squeezed her hands, drawing her attention back from those frightful visions. "The Olympians have never taken responsibility the way that you and I would— look how they wantonly destroy the very threads of existence itself! You *know* in your heart that we can rule more justly than they ever did. Say the word, Persephone, and we will cast down these oath breakers. I will exalt you as the queen of heaven, the earth and the seas, of everything above and below. You and I will reign over the cosmos and restore order and honor and justice."

Persephone shook her head in horror. "Absolute power drove your father to madness, Aidoneus. Just as it did to your grandfather. It will do the same to you— and to me. And to any immortal. We are the rulers beneath the earth, and only there. And the earth above is *dying!* Chthonia's borders are weakened, and we must tend to our own realm."

"They're not as weak as you think," he muttered, out of earshot of Hermes. "And neither are we."

"You saw what happened when they tried to take Sisyphus to the Pit. Nothing is safe anymore, my love. You know what *he* showed us! Kronos and the rest of the Titans will break free if this disaster continues. They will kill *everything*. Destroy *everything*; destroy us! He is influencing you even now—"

"Please, Persephone," he supplicated. "My wife, my queen, I am *begging* you to join me! They'll take you away from me forever if you don't!"

He was right. She would never see him again. He would never hold her, they would never wake up in the grove as they had this morning, he would never be able to whisper to her again that he loved her. But if she supported him, they would witness the end of all things. The unthinkable would happen. They, the deathless ones, would die.

"Aidon," she said, and squeezed his hand. "Husband. You once told me that you've loved me forever; that you would love me until the stars were shaken out of the sky."

He squeezed his eyes shut to keep the welling tears from streaming down his face. Persephone brushed her hand along his cheek, and he shivered. "Persephone… *please*," he whispered.

"Are you ready for that? Do you really want that so soon?"

"No!" He looked up at her again. "No, sweet one, we have time. We can cast them down; you and I can save this world together—" he said, his eyes watering as his voice choked.

"Everything will end, my beloved. The heavens, the earth, you and I, everything," she said, watching Aidoneus's shoulders slump involuntarily, knowing in his heart that she was right. She ran her hand along his face, tracing his cheek as she spoke, her palm now wet with his tears. "But before it does, if you do this, Tartarus will be unleashed—"

"No…"

"—and every threat Kronos made against you and me will come to pass—"

"Persephone, don't!" His voice cracked over a whisper. "Please don't…"

"No, my lord husband. You asked for my counsel. But before you ask me again to join you in declaring war on Olympus, hear this," she shuddered, then composed herself. "You and I already know the outcome. We were there; we saw it. The last thing you will see before the end of all things, the very last time we will look into each other's eyes, will be as Kronos devours my violated body."

He stared up at her. Aidoneus was motionless, his eyes staring through her, fixed and dark and distant.

"Is that what you want?"

Silence filled the room. Then Hades Aidoneus Chthonios, Lord of the Underworld, crumpled forward, his forehead falling into his wife's lap. His entire body wrenched and shook, and he wrapped his arms around the small of her back. A long, tortured wail echoed through the hall, a sound she'd never heard before from him. Persephone ran her hands through his hair and huddled over him, shaking, tears pouring down. Aidoneus gasped in air around each sob. Hermes held his breath and took several steps back, the scene before him terrifying and unsettling. Hades shuddered quietly, going silent.

"I was finally happy," he whispered, his words muffled as his hands balled into fists in the skirts of her peplos. She sucked in deep breaths, trying to steady her voice and calm her heartbeat. She needed to be strong for him. Tears spilled out anyway. Persephone stroked her husband's back and hunched forward to kiss him on the back of his head. He whispered it again. "I was finally happy. Fates, for the first time in my life…"

"I will come back to you. I *will* find a way back to you; I promise…" she whispered against his neck. "They cannot keep us apart. I'll find a way… I love you, Aidoneus! I'll find a way, I love you… I love you…"

Hermes turned away as bile crawled up his throat, sickened at himself and his orders. He'd listened to Apollo singing about love, he'd used the word enough times to lay with nymphs and mortal women, and had even bedded the goddess of love herself. This was different.

Aidoneus wasn't his king, but he'd always deeply respected him. Having seen all that the gods did to mankind and to each other, even what he *himself* had done, he doubted he could say the same for many of the other immortals. Even his own father. Hermes walked out to the terrace and bent down to retrieve his hat. Hades was willing to tear down Olympus and end the world to keep her. Could he have ever said that of a woman, except when he was in the middle of seducing one? Who among the others loved their mate enough to not only stay true to them, but to wager their immortality to stay with them? Hermes looked out at the swarms of souls crowding the far shore of the Styx. *He could*

157

do it, the Messenger thought with a shiver. *Not easily, but he has no idea how weak we truly are right now. . .*

He toyed in his mind with the idea of 'we' a bit longer than he should have. Hermes knew his history. Prometheus and Epimetheus, the Titan sons of Iapetos, along with Helios and Selene, Hyperion's twins, had sided with the Children of Kronos during the Titanomachy. Turning against his kin and king wasn't outside the realm of possibility. He paused, grinding his teeth, trying to picture a cosmos ruled by the austere masters of this realm. *It doesn't matter,* he thought. *If it came to war, there would be nothing left to rule over.*

"Messenger," a low voice rasped from inside the throne room, breaking him out of his grim musings. Hermes felt every hair stand on end as he turned to walk back inside. Had she relented? Had they changed their minds?

His stomach dropped, wondering what was about to be asked of him. . . or done to him. Charon's veiled threats on the River Styx were still fresh in Hermes's mind. He nauseously recalled his encounter with beautiful and terrifying Tisiphone, when she had wielded her scorpion-tipped scourge against a man who'd viciously murdered his own mother. He tried in vain to drown the memory of the condemned mortal's screams, and the sounds of ripping flesh that accompanied them. He had ducked quietly behind a tree to empty the contents of his stomach, the buzzing in his ears not enough to drown out Tisiphone's sultry laughter. Words like *flay* and *burn* and *geld* played on the edges of his mind no matter how he tried to will them away. Somehow, his knees still worked enough to take him back inside the great chamber.

Hades and Persephone Chthonios, rulers of the Underworld, sat on their thrones, their hands clasped tightly between them. They were as somber as they had been before Hermes delivered his message, except for the redness swelling around their eyes.

"Y-yes, Lord Hades?"

"My wife and I have made our decision," Hades said, his voice grinding hard against the lump in his throat. "Persephone is to be escorted by both you and Hecate through the passageways of the Underworld until you find your way to Eleusis. There, she will be returned to Demeter."

Hermes sighed, his shoulders dropping in relief.

Persephone looked to Aidoneus and caught his gaze, tilting her head toward him with a pregnant pause. Hermes fidgeted, wondering what her eyes were telling her husband. The Lord of the Underworld pursed his lips and turned back to him. "I also want to express my regrets for how I reacted. You are only Zeus's messenger, Hermes Psychopompos. I take back what I said earlier. You are still welcome here, and you are right— you are needed now more than ever to escort lost souls back to the Styx."

He bowed low to the ground. "I thank you for your wisdom, Good Counsellor. You are a just king."

"How long?" Persephone choked out, fighting back a sob as Hermes stood up. "How long do we have?"

Hermes pinched his fingers around the bridge of his nose to rub his eyes and looked down. "Demeter demanded your immediate return. But Zeus in his enduring wisdom, thought it might… take time to persuade your husband, if I didn't find you alone— if I had to go before both of you."

Persephone looked back to her husband in distress.

"Your Excellencies," Hermes said, addressing them both, "the world will not end tonight. I must take Persephone back before first light on the Styx— sunset in the world above. That is the time all-seeing Zeus gave me to retrieve her."

"Thank you, Hermes," Aidon said quietly. "Now if you don't mind, I wish to conclude this audience so I can say goodbye to my wife in private."

"Of course, my lord. All I ask is a place to rest."

"You are welcome here as our guest. Hecate will arrive shortly. She will show you to your quarters for the evening."

Aidon was guessing at that. The departure of Persephone toward the world above would not go unnoticed by the Goddess of the Crossroads. In hindsight, her crushed demeanor this morning likely meant that she knew this would happen. Aidon didn't begrudge her silence. It would have changed nothing, and revealing her foresight would have likely made everything worse.

Aidoneus and Persephone rose. They nodded to the Messenger, who bowed low before them as they left the throne room.

10.

AS SOON AS THE DOOR TO THEIR ANTECHAMBER closed, he was upon her, kissing Persephone roughly, then breaking away from her lips and inhaling the scent of her hair. Aidon shuddered, and she realized that he was trying to hold back tears again, his breathing labored. He slid down until he was on his knees in front of her, holding her around the waist, his cheek pressed against her abdomen. His hands gripped her peplos, then untied her girdle and dropped it to the floor so his cheek was pressed against the soft cloth, not cold stones set in bronze.

Persephone cried, quietly at first, then with her whole body, shaking, unable to hold it back. "Aidon…" She could hardly breathe and slurred his name through her tears. "Aidon…"

"It's all right, sweet one. I've got you," he managed, haltingly. She realized that if he was calming her, it took his mind off the pain of losing her. Still, his grip on her waist tightened, and he buried his face in the folds of her peplos gathered above her womb.

Her womb. She felt him exhale into the fabric, the cloth warming as he tried to take a full breath and calm himself. If only he knew how close he was, or might be. Persephone needed to bury those thoughts as deep as she could. If Aidon suspected that she was carrying his child, he would reverse everything to which he'd agreed, regardless of consequence. The world would be undone and she doubted he would give her a say in it this time. He would be too consumed with defending the life they may have created together.

There had been no other signs that she was pregnant, but a measure of hope held strong within her. If she was separated from him forever, she would have that part of him to hold onto and remember him by. She thought about her mother and Zeus. She remembered Demeter constantly sheltering her, calling her back from danger, cosseting and protecting her from the cruelties of the world. Persephone was torn between potent anger and understanding, frustrated by the unfairness of it all.

In this moment, about to be separated from her love, Persephone finally understood. She knew why Demeter had felt compelled to guard her all her life. She understood why she would destroy everything living to get her daughter back. Persephone realized that she would do no less to protect any child she had by Aidoneus.

His hands found their way through the open splits along the sides of her peplos and touched her warm bare back before following the shape of her hips and pressing his fingers into her rear, made cold from sitting on her throne. Aidoneus tilted his head and looked up, gazing at her for a long moment. His forehead was creased with lines and his reddened eyes pleaded.

Stay.

I cannot.

"Please stay," he whispered hoarsely.

"We cannot go back on our word."

"What can they possibly do to us here?"

It's not about what they can do to us if I stay, she answered. *It's about what they won't do, and all who will suffer and die because of us.*

162

His grip tensed and he leaned his forehead against her. Persephone watched his shoulders shake, and heard him draw in a ragged breath.

He kissed her belly through her clothes, and kissed her again lower, feeling the heat of her through the layers and against his lips. He inhaled her scent and kept kissing her through the dampening fabric until it clung to her skin, his hands massaging her thighs, parting them with his fingertips.

A tear rolled down Persephone's cheek as she unfastened one fibula. Her peplos opened across the front and hung from her shoulder before she pushed the fabric to the floor. Aidon moulded his cheek against bare skin, first planting a kiss on one side of her triangle of curls, then the other. His lips trailed against her thighs until he came to her center. He buried his nose in the dark brown curls, and rasped his tongue against her.

Persephone doubled over, steadying herself on his shoulders. A last tear fell onto his head, and she shut her eyes, feeling him and only him, blotting out the sadness and loss with the heat of his mouth and the roll of his tongue against her folds.

She pushed his himation off his shoulder and lifted his crown from his head, casting the wreath of golden poplar leaves to the side. Persephone pulled out the pins holding up his tunic and it too fell into the heap of clothes pooled around them.

Aidoneus could lose himself here, surrounded by her taste, her heat, her scent. His mind could focus on this alone, let go, forget. But as soon as he consciously thought about it, the pain of losing her returned. He dove back in with redoubled fervor, like a starving man.

It became impossible for Persephone to hold back her sighs of pleasure, even though feeling bliss right now seemed strange, almost wrong. But there would be plenty of time— eternity perhaps— to dwell on loss. She put it out of her mind. Right now, Aidon was here, his fingers digging im-

163

pressions into her hips as he held her steady, his tongue setting her on fire.

She reached the precipice, felt her legs shake, and knew that he could sense it washing over her. He wanted to feel her peak from within her. Aidoneus gripped her thighs and wrested them apart, her knees bending, drawing her downward. Placing his broad hand in the small of Persephone's back, he eased her to the floor, sprawled and arched over his discarded cloak and her dress. Aidon rose over her and in an instant was inside her, hard and needy.

The weight and width of him pulsing within her launched her over the edge and she bowed her back, the tips of her fingers digging into his skin. He leaned against her, held himself deep within her warmth, and felt her tighten and convulse around him. She cried out and dragged her nails across his flanks, moving below him while he remained still and savored her every gyration.

Persephone's breathing slowed from its frenetic, gasping pace as she came down from her peak and felt him ready and waiting. She pulled at his hips, urging him forward.

"No," he growled into her ear. "I'll be damned if I have you here instead of in our bed. I'm not going to spend our... last time together embracing you on the cold floor."

"Husband, we have the entire night. There's time for that too," she whimpered, trying to form words. "But please, Aidon. Stay... stay... Just take me now!"

He gritted his teeth and pushed forward, grasping her at the base of her spine, holding her up. His other hand removed a few pins holding her hair in place and pulled the asphodel out of her hair. He buried his face in her locks, giving a punctuated groan as he withdrew, then drove into her warmth again.

She anchored herself to him as he moved faster. Aidon wanted to feel her completely, to savor every slow movement, prolong this moment, stop time entirely. But he couldn't concentrate. The only thing that drowned out the knowledge that he would lose her before dawn was raw intensity. He went faster. Harder. He gripped at her skin as though she would be ripped away from him at any moment. Persephone gasped and clung to him as he rose to a fever pitch, losing himself in her.

Soon— too soon, since he wanted this to last forever— he felt everything shatter. Fire raced up his spine and arched his back as he emptied himself into her. He gasped and shook, then buried his face in her neck, thrusting forward several more times as deeply as he could before he finally grew still. Aidon rolled onto his back, taking her with him.

He was desperate to stay within her, and kept pushing back until her body finally expelled him. Persephone felt sore and winced when she finally moved. It was a welcome ache, an aftereffect of how intensely he'd taken her.

He knew it, too. "I'm sorry."

"Don't. It's what we needed."

"Fates, when I first took you here I brought you nothing but pain. And now when you're about to leave forever, I..." He couldn't finish.

"My sweet Aidoneus, all will be right. I'll find a way to return. I'm wearing an immediate way back to you on my left hand, remember?"

"And then what? Your mother plunges the world into famine and ruin again?"

"There has to be a way."

"Not with the Key. The moment you use it they will know. And you must *never* let on that you have it. I don't want to think about what the Olympians would do to you if they wished to possess it."

Persephone saw visions of Prometheus bound to rocks, Hera chained in the heavens, Hephaestus's lame leg coursing through her husband's thoughts. "They won't ever know. It will only look like a few trinkets I decided to keep. To... to remember you by."

He held her as she started shaking, her fingers tightening on his shoulders. "There's a way to spare you this, wife."

She held her breath and looked up at him. "The Lethe?"

Aidon nodded.

"How can you even suggest that?" she whispered, shaking her head.

He couldn't bring himself to say anymore about it out loud. *It would be easier on you, Persephone. You could just… believe whatever they told you about me,* he said, shutting his eyes. *Whatever they need to say to justify this— that the Lord of the Dead took you from Nysa and ravished you. That he kept you prisoner in the Underworld, then stole your memories away. It will be easier. Your life can go back to how it was before, or as close to it as possible. You won't be forced to endure centuries of—*

I don't want my life to be as it was. I don't want to forget you, Aidoneus. No matter how painful losing you will be. She sat up part way. "Were you planning on doing this to yourself after I left so you could forget about me?"

"No, not ever," he answered aloud. "I don't want to think about you in pain. Especially since I cannot be there to comfort you."

"I won't do it."

He sat up and she rose to her knees, then stood with him. He wrapped his arms around her, his forehead leaned onto the crown of her head. She pulled loose an asphodel that had fallen into the waves of her hair and twisted it in her hand. The light started to change outside, the Styx transforming the mist into a wash of pinks and reds as light faded from Chthonia and dawned in the world above. They had only hours left.

Aidon… She looked into his eyes. They burned with a potent mix of determination, frustration and loss. Without another word, he picked her up and strode across their antechamber. Hades kicked open the door, then deposited her on their bed.

166

Laying beside her, he held her close, just as he had last night after she told him she loved him. Aidoneus clenched his jaw. Everything within him screamed to pin her to their bed and keep her here with him. He would create powerful wards against the Olympians, fortify the Underworld, make it impossible for anything to come in or go out. He would defy Zeus— whatever the consequences. His thoughts explored every possible path he could take, but they always found their way to the same place— scorched earth, ruination, the end of all things etched in fire and ice. What Persephone had described in the throne room was inevitable. He pulled her against him and silenced her approaching sobs and his dark thoughts with another kiss. And another; and another.

Before long, he was ready again and lifted her thigh to his waist, effortlessly sinking into her as they lay on their sides. She trembled with pleasure and sucked gently on his tongue, their voices muffled by their lips.

At least I can be as close to you as possible tonight, he said, not moving just yet. *At least I can have this before—*

Aidon. . . She clung to his back and pulled away from him, then returned, drawing him out and pushing him in again. *I'll come back to you; I will. My mother cannot watch me all the time.*

He looked her in the eye and frowned. "And act as if we're having some sort of tryst? Is that what you want?"

"There's nothing else can we do!"

"You are my wife. Not my mistress. I don't want to make our marriage into some sort of shameful secret. It would only be a matter of time before they caught us, anyway. Then what?"

"I don't know," she whimpered.

"Sweet one… we are bound by laws. I won't sneak around with you like the Olympians do with their whores. It's beneath your dignity. And mine."

"But at least I could see you!"

167

"Persephone, there's only one way around this, and that is to overthrow the order of things. And we cannot."

"Then what should I do?"

"Just be with me now," he whispered in her ear. She nodded and felt him move within her, then sighed and clung to him, wanting to wash away everything that was happening outside this room. Persephone wrapped her leg around his waist and dug her fingers into his shoulders as he took her in long strokes, leaving her breathless. Every part of her started to wind and tighten, then it burst apart, shaking her to her very core, and him inside it. Aidon groaned against her forehead, his entire body seizing. He tilted his head back and came apart, slackening his grip before he held her tightly again.

And then it was over. He pushed in again and again, as far as he could, until the intensity of the sensation bordered on pain and he could bear no more, and collapsed against her. He diminished and slipped from her, then lay on his back with her drawn into the crook of his arm.

It was easier this time for Persephone to hold back her tears and quiet her sadness-strangled voice. She simply had no more energy to cry; she just stared at her husband's profile. Aidon's eyes were shut and his breathing steady, but a teardrop caught by the light of the fire meandered from the corner of his eye, then lost itself in the hair at his temple.

"I cannot grow anything," he finally said. "But I promise I'll take care of our pomegranate grove. I won't let it fall into disarray."

"I know."

"That at least will give me something to remember you by…" Aidoneus trailed off, the path of the tear refreshed by another. His throat pinched shut. "I tried to be a good husband to you."

"I couldn't ask for anything better than what you did. This isn't your fault, my love."

"It is, though. I should have spoken to Demeter directly instead of involving Zeus. I shouldn't have been so stubbornly devoted to the *proper* way of doing things. I should have consummated our marriage right there in Nysa instead of taking you below, then made an arrangement of some sort with her— I just wasn't thinking clearly. Maybe I could have traveled back and forth between worlds for a year to make it easier on her— and you— to somehow prove that I'm not an unfitting husband before taking you here. The Underworld wouldn't have fallen apart in my absence."

"What about now? Come above and stay with me."

Gods, how he wanted to live under a blue sky with her. Aidon would gladly trade the palace for a humble mud and straw house on Sikelia, or further west, shaded from the sun by willows and sheltered from the wind by rows of cypress. She would tend a garden, he could herd sheep and gather wood. They'd have nights together by the fire, and live the passing centuries apart from gods and mortals, their lives quiet and free of the weight of the cosmos.

He realized that he was sharing his vision when he heard her weep again. Aidoneus shut those thoughts away and tightened his arms around her. He needed to be strong for her tonight, as she had been strong for him this afternoon.

"I can't, my love," he said. "There's too much to mend here. Our world has been weakened, as you said, though not as catastrophically as the world above. The Olympians cannot comprehend the extent of the damage, much less fix it, so the responsibility falls to us. I will set everything right below, and you above."

"But our marriage will be over! And by going back, I will have tacitly agreed to the *lies* they will say about you, and what we are to each other."

Aidon opened his eyes and managed a smile for her. "Sweet one, I have spent most of my existence ignoring what they say about me up there. I'll manage."

When will I see you? she asked. *Please…*

169

"I don't know," he said, trying to muster strength from within his grief. He couldn't say the undeniable truth out loud without breaking down again. *We need to resign ourselves to the idea that we might never see each other again.*

"I'll find a way…" she said under her breath, her limbs and eyelids heavy.

"Perhaps," he whispered and kissed her forehead. "But for now, rest. Sleep. You have little time to do so, and tomorrow will be… exhausting."

"I don't want to waste time sleeping. How can I?"

"With how far you must go and how much you'll have to endure tomorrow, what sort of husband would I be if I didn't insist that you did?" He grinned at her.

She shook again, and he kissed her face.

"Don't cry, my love," he said, settling behind her and wrapping his arms around her. Her heart drawn and her body exhausted, she started to drift off. *I'm right here. I'll always be here, and I'll always love you.*

✳   ✳   ✳

"My dreams," they whispered together, standing in the grove just after their return from Nysa.

"You've seen these too," she said.

"I hardly sleep as it is, and I see them every time I shut my eyes," he said. "They started when I brought you here."

"Last night, when I woke up and you held me," she whispered, "I saw these trees; then fire."

Praxidike…

Dark flames from the Pit twisted in the center of the grove, then filled with brilliant sparks, transforming them into blinding light. She saw the lifetime of the trees unfold before her. They grew from seeds that had lain dormant since the cosmos was created. Branches split away from sapling trunks which grew to twice the height of her husband, then filled out with broad leaves and blossomed in bursts of red. The petals fell to the ground and fruits crowded each other, weighing down the boughs, seeds darkening and ripening within.

"Don't."

"I am already bound here, Aidoneus."

Persephone and Hades were in the grove, where they had awoken this morning. She couldn't see him clearly, though— only his pale hand holding her wrist.

"That is by choice. But this grew in the Underworld." The recollection wavered, the seed held in her fingertips and the glint of the Key on their hands the only things clearly visible. "Those are rules governed by the very order of the cosmos itself," his voice echoed. "Ones that supersede the will of all others— the Gods, the Fates. . ."

She saw the fruits open themselves above them, seeds bursting and dripping blood red juice. It rained down upon them and stained their skin.

"I choose to stay with you," she said as crimson overwhelmed and washed away the vision. "To love you. To be your queen."

"I won't let it fall into disarray. . ."

The trees withered. Their trunks became hollow gray shards sticking out of the sterile ground. This was the Underworld, and her husband wasn't able to keep them alive on his own, no matter how desperate his desire to do so. The grove only thrived in their shared dreams, and had waited dormant for aeons for her to arrive and for them to join together. Without both of them ruling over the Underworld, it would cease to exist. She saw Hades sitting in the middle of what remained, stock still, his expression as lifeless as the six dead pomegranate trees.

"Aidon!"

She tried to reach out to him, call to him, but he couldn't see or hear her. He blinked, his only movement, then stared up at the shroud of mist above and further still into the darkness of Erebus. He lowered his head, studying the soil dispassionately, then sunk his arm into the gray ground.

"Husband, don't. . . Don't!"

She watched Aidon roll forward, color seeping out of his skin. A splash of dark smoke engulfed him, then dissipated. He was gone— as much a part of Hades as Erebus was part of the darkness that encompassed it.

"No! Aidon, no! Please!" She cried out fruitlessly as the vision faded to white.

"Six seeds are missing." Hecate spoke, but the voice was none of her three familiar aspects. It was a dark fourth: a blend of the brittle last words

171

of a dying old woman and a girl child so young her syllables were still unintelligible.

Then the clear, airy voice of Nyx. "They will look to you, Aristi Chthonia..."

The grove was alive again, consumed by fires that didn't burn the trees or ground, and Aidoneus stood in the center, his arms wrapped around her.

"I choose to stay with you..." Persephone's words reverberated.

Her vision filled with asphodel amidst the fire, the crown she had worn as she descended through the earth, made queen that day with the loss of her maidenhead. They were in the chariot. Persephone clung to Aidoneus and he whispered into her ear. "If you taste even one of those seeds, you might as well stay."

"To love you..." Kore was in the world above, lilacs strewn through her hair. She was lying with him in her shrine under the oak tree, the silvery light of the full moon shining on her skin.

Aidon was gently, carefully caressing her. They were seeing each other for the first time. "With everything so precariously hanging in the balance, let's not alter the order of things any more than we already have."

The scene changed again. They were lying in the pomegranate grove, entangled in each other's arms, markings gouged into the ground around them. Saffron robes lay cast to the side. Their heads were crowned with laurel and asphodel, narcissus and pomegranate. Their skin was anointed with sacred oil.

Six seeds.

"...To be your queen."

All went dark.

"I choose to stay..."

Persephone awoke suddenly and opened her eyes, then took a deep breath. She turned when she heard a halted groan. Aidoneus was sleeping, but not peacefully. His breathing was unsteady and his limbs jerked. He settled and rolled away from her before falling into a motionless stupor.

She climbed out of their bed and closed the curtain. She was terrified of what could happen if she failed— and moreso if she succeeded. The door to their bedroom was still open, and she saw silvery moonlight flooding in from the

172

Styx. She'd almost forgotten: Hecate had wished them a good full moon this morning. The last time the moon had shone through the river she had coaxed her husband's seed from him on the terrace next to the waterfall, the roar of the water drowning out his half-hearted protests, then his jubilation as she loved him with her lips.

Persephone's arms were cold and gooseflesh prickled her skin and hardened the tips of her breasts. She picked up her dress and held it for a moment before dropping it to the floor again, deciding to wrap herself in Hades's heavy wool himation instead. Persephone walked out to the terrace, the edges of the long cloak dragging on the ground.

She listened to the rush of the falls to calm and steady herself, resolved about what she must do. Persephone contemplated waking Aidoneus to tell him of her plans, that he should join her and witness this. She knew him too well, though. His rigid sense of duty and honor would compel him to stop her. He would remind her that they had already decided and agreed, for the sake of the cosmos, to obey Zeus and Demeter's decrees.

There's only one way around this, and that is to overthrow the order of things.

She couldn't tell him. Not even after the fact. If he knew that she'd done it surreptitiously, he might try to keep her here. And if Zeus and Demeter thought that she had eaten the seeds with his knowledge, they would accuse Hades of having forced Persephone to do so. It would, as he said, undermine everything. No, she needed to do this alone.

Walking back from the terrace, she very carefully shut the door of the antechamber behind her, tracing the outline of the poplar tree with her finger before making her way down the steps to the throne room. She heard a mournful howl in the distance, then a second and a third. Cerberus. He must know what was happening. It was little wonder, since this realm was its masters' through and through. What she and Aidon knew, it knew. What they felt, it felt. Stopping before their adjacent thrones, she concentrated, listening for the voices of Asphodel.

They were crying.

No, no... Metra, please don't leave us... You only just arrived, Annessa... Soteira, please, we waited so long.

Her throne would stand cold forever if she failed to do this. This wasn't just a matter of returning to her mother and never seeing Aidon again. It was the injustice of denying the Underworld one of its rightful rulers for all eternity. This place would stay as incomplete as it had been for aeons. And like their realm, Persephone and Hades would each be incomplete without the other. They'd already spent so many millennia apart.

Her walk took her to the great hall and past the tapestries of the Titanomachy, her parents, her husband. She ran her fingers over the white and gray threads of Demeter's chiton, and the bulge that represented herself, unborn. When she reached the door to the portico and garden beyond, she stopped, almost light-headed with the gravity of what she must do, and wrapped her fingers around the heavy bronze handle. There was no turning back once it was done. But if she faltered, she would never see Aidon, her realm, this very door in the palace, the Fields, the Rivers, ever again.

Persephone cracked the door open and peeked through, making sure that neither Menoetes nor Askalaphos, nor any of Nyx's sons, nor any of Hecate's Lampades was about. They mustn't know either. Not yet, at least, otherwise they would go running to Hades and tell him too soon. She realized she'd forgotten her sandals when her feet touched the rough gravel. Light reflected off the clouds and bathed the asphodel in silver. Poplars and myrtles stood silent, shadows dancing in the flicker of garden torches.

The twitching flames shed a warm light on the palace walls and garden gate. Persephone extended her hand and slowly, finger by finger, closed it into a fist. The light followed suit, dimming around her until the flames barely smoldered. No one should see her.

She winced as a sharp piece of gravel embedded itself in her foot, but kept walking. The path felt like it stretched on forever in the dark and she feared that at any moment Aidon would appear before her to stop her. She passed under the low branches of a pomegranate tree and stood in the center of the grove, exhaling in relief when her toes sunk into the soft blanket of grasses and moss. The narcissus that had poked its way through the soil this morning was still there. She considered plucking it so she would always have this immortal flower to remember her husband by if her plan failed, but stopped. She must have faith that this would work.

A sacrifice was required for both the land of the living and the land of the dead. With all the world above had suffered and all the world below had endured, there was nothing else to be done. If she dwelled here forever, Demeter would neglect the earth, destroying it. If she were only above for the portion of each year it took to make the plants flower, not grow, there would be too much damage to undo each time. There had to be a balance, as Kottos had said.

Six seeds.

Would they even accept this? Not just Zeus and Demeter, but her husband? There were too many questions in her mind, but the dream had been clear. She let the himation fall to her feet. The cold air hit her immediately, tightening every inch of her skin. She stood up on the balls of her feet and gripped a fruit, pulling it down until the stem snapped and the branch rebounded. The others jostled, pomegranates bouncing in the moonlight, and the leaves shook loudly against each other. She looked around to make certain she was still alone.

Persephone rolled the ripe fruit in her hand, trying to find a weak spot on the rough rind. She scratched her thumbnail along a fissure until it gave way. Her heart beat

175

faster. The skin tore back unevenly as she cut an edge through it, then dug her fingers in, splitting it open. She struggled, feeling a few arils break against her fingernails, drenching her cuticles and staining them deep red. The juices dripped down her hands. With a last wrench the whole fruit gave way, spilling seeds around her, a few broken ones bouncing against her thighs.

It had been so much easier to open the damned thing this morning when she could clearly see it and wasn't exhausted by grief. Her shaky desperation had turned this into a mess. Persephone brushed as much of the evidence off her skin as she could, then sat and wrapped Aidon's cloak around her, careful not to stain it with pulp. His scent of warm earth and cypress enveloped her.

Peeling back the bitter flesh, her fingers feathered over the dark seeds, each one flush against the other, crammed together, ready to burst. Her heart hammered in her chest.

There's only one way around this, and that is to overthrow the order of things.

She picked one seed from the pomegranate and held it up in the moonlight. The barest hint of red shone through it. Persephone lowered it to her lips and shut her eyes.

The skin cracked, a small burst of tartness on her tongue followed by sweet pulp. She rolled it along the roof of her mouth, and swallowed.

She opened her eyes and looked around her, then shifted her weight from one hip to the other. Persephone had forever bound herself to the Land of the Dead. Even if they took away her marriage, her name would forever be *Chthonios* because of that single seed. She expected some sort of change to overcome her, something physical that would signify the importance of what she'd done.

Nothing.

How long could she stay in the world above now that she was truly a creature of the Underworld? What *would* happen, she wondered, if they tried to keep her from coming back? Would she fall through the earth, the realm of the dead drawing her down like iron shards to a lodestone? Would it feel like dying?

She knew she would not be barred from the world above. Aidoneus had eaten asphodel roots and he was free to come and go at will. But she was a goddess of the earth. Just as it was an adamantine rule of nature that whoever ate the fruits of the Underworld was bound to it forever, there were similar truths for the world above. The time that passed from tilling and planting to the harvest of every grain, leaf and fruit was a changeless constant. To maintain the balance, she would have to stay for the duration of the season and protect the mortals' food from seed to reaping. Half the year.

Six seeds.

Persephone dug out a row of five more arils and held them in the palm of her hand like little polished garnets. She picked them up, one by one, sucking on each and breaking it with tongue and teeth. She savored the tartness and sweetness of the arils and the dry scratch of the seeds, then swallowed the pulpy mass whole.

She was tempted to eat more, to find every seed that spilled and eat the whole fruit— to consume every last fruit in the orchard if that was what staying with Aidoneus required. She restrained herself.

Her husband would hate her plan, but the just and reasoning part of him would understand. Her mother would feel betrayed. Persephone herself hadn't wanted to make her marriage into a half life when she declared her love to Hades, and her heart rebelled against her own scheme.

The Fates seldom listen to our plans.

A dark possibility settled over her thoughts. If nothing could stop her from returning to Chthonia now that she'd eaten the fruit, they might retaliate against her husband. If they thought Aidoneus was responsible for this, it could mean war between the realms. Despite Persephone's impulse to rush back to their room and rejoice with him that she'd found a means by which to keep him, even if only part of the time, she could say nothing. Reveal nothing. Persephone rose to her feet and pointedly set the opened pomegranate down next to the blooming narcissus, the missing seeds upturned and visible to anyone who ventured into the grove.

She knew her husband. He would come here soon after she'd left and he would find it: clear, undeniable proof of what she had done. Not now, but soon— hopefully after she had spoken with her mother. Her husband's shock would be her proof to Demeter and Zeus that she'd done this of her own free will. It would absolve Aidon of guilt, and save him from being punished.

It wasn't enough to have him discover it with surprise. Persephone herself would have to tell all what she had done, and she would need Aidoneus there if she was to prove his innocence in this. He would have to follow her above and face Demeter and Zeus *with* her. But how could she get him to follow without telling him what she had done?

Persephone turned back toward the palace and opened a path through the ether. Bright fire circled in front of her until she could clearly see the golden tree etched onto the door outside their chambers.

She didn't see the stout gardener peering at her wide-eyed from behind a white poplar tree in the garden. Persephone stepped through the gateway, letting it close behind her and returning the hallway to moonlit darkness. The door creaked open and she walked across the antechamber, casting off her husband's himation along the way as she crept back into their bedroom.

Careful not to disturb him, she shut the curtain and padded across the bed, the mattress sinking under her weight. Persephone nestled against his chest, rising and falling, deep in sleep.

"I love you, Aidoneus," she whispered. Her eyes drooped shut. "Forgive me."

11.

"**F**ATES..."

Askalaphos took a cautious step forward, his sandal padding softly into the grass. Cerberus howled in the distance, the unsettling harmony causing the gardener to jerk to a stop. He reconsidered his advance; Hecate had told him not to come here, that it was sacred ground and not meant for his care. The grasses and moss under his feet had grown in uncharacteristically wildly, stopping at the outermost roots of the intertwined trees. They were an untamed island in the sea of perfect asphodel and poplars that he'd spent millennia cultivating.

He heard a twig snap and held his breath, then realized that it had cracked under his own foot. The garden was still pitch black. Askalaphos had been finishing a final perusal of the grounds to make sure that Menoetes's ever growing flock of black sheep hadn't wandered in again, leaving their droppings, munching on asphodel flowers, becoming a toy or a meal— or both— for Cerberus. He was tired of cleaning up after them.

Just as he was about to retire to his bed, Askalaphos had seen all the lights in the garden dim. Then *she* had walked out, clad only in Lord Hades's cloak. He'd hid, not sure of what to do. She had dropped the himation at her feet and he had stumbled away and huddled behind a poplar tree, praying she hadn't seen him. He didn't dare imagine what the Queen— or, gods help him, *the King*— might do to him with the knowledge that he'd glimpsed her naked in the moonlight. Askalaphos had guessed that it was a ritual of some sort. He had never involved himself with any of the esoteric goings-on in Chthonia, and never questioned them. He'd heard rustling from Persephone's direction, then silence. It wasn't until Askalaphos saw the walls of the garden glow with the light of *her* fire, so very much like the Phlegethon itself, that he dared to turn around and slink from his hiding place.

He'd barely stepped into the grove when he saw it: a pomegranate, open, missing seeds, right where she had been standing.

"No, no, no…" Askalaphos wrung his hands and tried in vain to draw in a full breath.

Why did *he* always have to stumble into these messes? No one could find out about this… not Menoetes, not Hecate or Nyx… no one. Especially not Lord Hades! Askalaphos knew— *everyone* knew— about the rage that had beset Aidoneus in the throne room that day. Word traveled fast in the Underworld. Hermes was here. The Olympians had recalled Persephone to the world above, somehow, and she was to leave before dawn. If anyone knew that Persephone was now bound here forever, that she *must* return to Chthonia, and that Askalaphos had been present and could have stopped her in time, but didn't… *He* would be blamed for pushing the entire cosmos to war.

The pomegranate had been wrenched apart— a twisted, irreparable mess. He had to hide it.

Askalaphos took off his chlamys and shivered. Cerberus bayed and wailed in the distance, and his skin prickled again. He bundled up the fruit and as many fallen seeds as he could find, and pinned it closed. He darted his eyes around, praying that no one had seen him.

He took a few steps, careful not to leave any tracks behind him, and wiped his feet in the grass. Askalaphos ducked under a branch, then broke into a full run. A frightened bleat was all he heard before he tripped and sprawled in the dirt. A black lamb shook itself off and bounded away into the asphodel. His parcel rolled away from him, coming to rest against a rough ebony staff. The gardener paled and looked up at the crooked knees of the bondsman.

"Askalaphos?" Menoetes said, holding up an oil lamp. The light was blinding, and he couldn't see the man's expression beneath his hood, only the flickering flame.

"I… I…" he said, scrambling to rise and dust himself off. Menoetes leaned forward and grasped the gardener's hand. He still favored his right leg, injured a few months ago, but hoisted the portly man easily to his feet.

"Easy there, friend. What are you doing out so early?"

"I-I could ask you the same."

"One of the littler ones squeezed under the gate," he said, motioning vaguely into the distance where the lamb had zigzagged through the garden and away from Askalaphos's clumsy feet. "I almost had her when you came charging out of nowhere. What's your hurry anyway?"

"Nothing. N-nothing important, Menoetes," the gardener stammered. "I'll-ll just be on… my…"

Askalaphos trailed off, dropping his gaze to the bundle that now had Menoetes's rapt attention. A few seeds had spilled out, shining bright red in the flickering light of the bondsman's lamp. Cold raced down his spine when Menoetes poked at the bundle with his staff.

"What have we here?"

☼   ☼   ☼

"Sweet one…"
He didn't want to do this.

181

"My love…"

Let her sleep, his heart screamed at him. Let her rest, and let her stay here forever right beside him. But he had to awaken her. They were waiting.

"Persephone," Aidoneus whispered close to her ear.

"Hmm?"

"It's… time to wake up, my love. You have a long journey ahead of you."

Persephone felt his hand petting her shoulder, and drowsily opened her eyes. The crackling hearth fire lit her husband's careworn face. She blinked, wakefulness arriving along with recollection of everything that had transpired over the last day and night. She sat up and wrapped her arms around Aidoneus. He held her close, breathing against her neck.

She tangled her hands in his hair, and noticed a faint red glow. Her breath caught in her throat— it was coming from the rings on her hand, the Key. She breathed out slowly, hoping that Aidon wouldn't make the connection yet. Persephone pulled away from him and clasped his left hand, his three rings smoldering the same as hers. She opened her mouth in bewilderment.

Six seeds.

"I saw them too. Before I woke you," he said quietly. "I'm going to take it… as a good omen— that you and I will be together again, someday."

"Yes." Persephone nodded, then swallowed. "Aidon, when *did* you wake up?"

"An hour ago. I couldn't sleep."

She frowned. "You need rest. Today will be no easier for you."

"I'm not the one who has to face the Olympians."

Perfect timing, she thought to herself. "What if I asked you to?"

He grimaced. "Persephone, we discussed this last night—"

"This is different," she interrupted. "I want to speak to them and convince Zeus—"

Aidon snorted derisively and shook his head.

She continued. "I need to tell them that I *must* come back. That the Underworld *needs* me. And I need you there to support me, Aidoneus."

"Persephone…"

"The truth is as true today as it was yesterday, and as it will always be."

"Should we just forget everything that's happened and wallow in denial? Please, my love, don't make this harder on yourself. There are only two paths diverging from this moment, and one leads to the end of the world."

"Please be there with me."

He furrowed his brow. "You overestimate me, sweet one. Do you think it will be easy for me to face those who are separating us? To just leave you there and come back without you?"

"Please trust me."

"This has nothing to do with my trust in *you*, my love. I don't have that kind of faith in myself."

"But I do, Aidon," she said, stroking his cheek. "You asked me to trust you before. Many times. Please…"

He lowered his head. What would stop him from tearing Zeus and Demeter to pieces when he saw them? For betraying him and ripping away the one thing he'd ever wanted or asked for or cared for?

"Please," she repeated. "This might be the last thing I ever ask of you."

A knock at the bedroom door interrupted his answer.

"Your majesties?" came a muffled voice. Hecate had come to escort her and Hermes to the world above, Persephone knew. What she didn't know was how the three of them would travel. Would they all journey through the ether together? *About the other matter,* the white witch had said yesterday morning. *I can and should speak with you about it later. Tomorrow, perhaps?*

At least she would have an answer about *that*. Hecate must have known all that would transpire and had wisely said nothing. Persephone wrapped a bed sheet around herself and cracked open the door. "Hecate."

The kindly Goddess of the Crossroads stood on the other side, her hair wound up with strands of selenite, an oil lamp in her hand. "All the world above waits, Queen Persephone. You and I can speak candidly on the way there."

She nodded. "If you could wait outside and give us a moment to prepare ourselves?"

"Certainly," Hecate said, and nodded her head before leaving the antechamber through the double doors.

Persephone lit the torches on the wall with a wave of her hand.

"You can do that almost effortlessly," Aidoneus mused.

"Thanks to you." She was about to ask him again, and worried her lip with her teeth.

"I'll think on it," he answered, reading Persephone.

She gave him a pained smile. "We should get dressed."

The routine, mundane preparations for the journey ahead helped keep her heart from bursting out of her chest. It took all of Persephone's will to suppress and conceal every thought about what she was to do today, and what it would mean for her, her husband, her mother, the mortals— all the cosmos, in truth. She stretched out the two pieces of fine wool that made up her black peplos, looking for any signs of their lovemaking. Satisfied that they were spotless, she folded the garment perfectly so it revealed only her ankles and pinned up one shoulder. Persephone felt Aidon take the other side from her, fibula already in hand.

He slid the pin in place and picked up her jeweled girdle. "She's not going to like seeing you in this."

"Unfortunate for her," she muttered. "I'm not returning to my mother as Kore."

184

He let out a long sigh. "That much is certain, according to the scroll Hermes read yesterday."

"I mean I'm not going to my mother as a powerless, ravished victim, Aidoneus," she said firmly. "I will appear before her and Zeus as Queen of the Underworld. And as you said before Sisyphus's trial, one must look the part."

He nodded silently, fastening the catches of her girdle. Persephone wound her tresses up with a ribbon and started arranging the asphodel flowers that had spilled from her hair yesterday into a crown. Not one of them was creased or wilted. Immortal flowers did not decay. Persephone bade him sit in the chair in front of the hematite mirror. She ran a comb through his curls and pulled his long hair back with a gold clasp. His face was set in stone as he looked at her in the reflection. Persephone refrained from coaxing him to speak his mind as she normally would. There was a time and place for everything.

She set his poplar crown on his head and felt him bristle. He knew that she wanted him to present himself as the Lord of the Underworld when she confronted Zeus. The sinews of his neck tensed, and she stroked a hand down his back. "You said you'd think on it."

Aidoneus settled back in the chair and met her eyes in the reflection again. "I did. I still am."

"Please, husband. Follow me, but don't tell them that you will."

"I can't simply leave you there once—"

"Aidon," she said resolutely. "I trust you. No matter what. I'll…" her voice wavered, and she swallowed hard. She could still taste pomegranate seeds in the back of her throat. "I'm going to trust that you're coming. I won't even look back when we're on our way to the surface. I'll just trust that you're there behind me."

Her words pushed him ever closer to doing as she wished. As she had said, he might not ever get another chance to do so. They were separating him from his wife forever.

He immediately cast the thought from his mind. The more he dwelt on it, the harder it would be for him to let her go. He stood up in front of her, catching the scent of lilies and larkspur and a hint of pomegranate as she moved. Aidon felt her body heat against him as she arranged his himation to drape over his left shoulder, heard her steady breathing by his ear.

The sweet scent of pomegranate hung persistently in the air. He hoped it would last; when he shut his eyes, he could imagine that she was still there with her warmth and light. He pictured her lying against his chest yesterday morning, sated, blissful, the grass below and heavy fruits above, before everything fell apart. The trees in the grove were all that would remain of Persephone, the only trace that she had even been here at all. He violently banished that thought and focused on her.

Persephone was unnervingly calm, a serenity likely fortified by her desperately maintained notion that she could sway the King of the Gods to let her return. He cringed. He wouldn't be there when she was told with absolute and crushing finality that there was no going back. But Hades knew his wife well. She would almost certainly defy them. *Please, Sparing Ones, don't let Persephone be punished on my account*, he offered up in silent prayer to the Fates. *She'll insist, she'll petition, she'll attempt to come back. Please Fates, don't let her destroy herself because of me.*

"Aidon," she said softly, motioning him toward the antechamber door. He'd been lost in thought. Persephone was standing at the door, ready to open it. He watched her gaze across the room one last time, memorizing every detail. The antechamber and the bedroom were the first rooms he'd built— carved out of the cave he'd drunkenly retreated into after arriving in the Underworld. The rest of the palace was almost an afterthought. This was his sanctuary— a place for him to rest and meditate, to retreat. But it had only felt like home once he'd opened the door and let Persephone in.

He took a final look at the room, and then shut the door behind them with a hollow thud.

✻   ✻   ✻

Hermes stood still, listening. He was restless, wanted desperately to go somewhere, anywhere, but any step he took with his winged shoes would echo far too loudly in Hades's throne room. The room was pitch black but for the silver light filtering in from the terrace, the heavy silence broken only by an occasional howl in the distance. Cerberus. Hermes's wandering mind alighted on the very real possibility that Hades would change his decision, lock him up in Tartarus, and declare war on the Olympians for breaking a Stygian oath.

Hades has every right to go to war, Hermes thought, then urged his thoughts onward to less terrifying locales. He tried to discern which of Cerberus's heads were baying when the beast howled. He couldn't tell them apart.

"A wonder you slept at all, Psychopompos."

He startled so violently that his petasos almost fell off his head. Turning, he saw a woman in crimson robes with a half moon held by intricately wound selenite beads on the center of her forehead. "I wa-wasn't expecting you, Hecate," he managed once his heart slowed.

"Few do," she smiled. "A grim task you've been given, no? To sever a man from his lawful, beloved wife?"

Hermes pursed his lips before he spoke. "I have no choice. You know who my father is."

"In that, yes. But what of the horses whose reigns you *do* hold?"

Hermes blinked and shook his head rapidly. "What do you mean?"

"Selene proved herself a masterful storyteller— she spun such *intimate* details into her tale about your visit with Hades

187

and Persephone in the palace grotto last week. But I know *she* has seen no such things…"

"I…" Hermes fidgeted as Hecate narrowed her eyes at him. "You see," he tittered nervously, "er, that is, you can't imagine how persuasive my brother Apollo is. He insisted—"

"Your tongue is too easily loosened, Hermes." She walked to the brazier and with a flick of her wrist, brandished an unlit torch. Hecate thrust it into the coals. "And loose enough to risk war between the realms."

He took a quick step back when the torch flared white hot in her hand, illuminating the room as she approached him. Hermes swallowed. He'd heard whispered stories about what she'd done to her enemies during the war. "H-Hecate, I'm not stupid."

"Aren't you, now…"

"I'll not repeat a word of what happened yesterday!"

"Few of the futures I see are certain, Psychopompos. But this is one of them," she said, advancing calmly.

"Please; I promise!"

"Pretty words. I need strong words. Perhaps I should be more direct, and burn out your wagging tongue…"

"I'll swear!"

Hecate stopped her advance. The torch hissed menacingly between them.

He drew in a full breath. "I, Hermes Argophantes, swear on the Styx that I will not reveal a single word spoken by Hades in the throne room yesterday. Not one! To anyone."

"Hard to believe," Hecate intoned and lowered her torch. "You are known to do the bidding of *oath breakers*, Hermes."

"But I am not one myself," the God of Thieves said quietly. "Whatever else I may be, I take *that* seriously." Hecate's torch flamed out and disappeared from her hand. The lingering darkness left him almost blind. He waited for his vision to adjust and saw her calmly standing exactly as she was. "And despite what all of you think, I respect Ai-doneus."

"Respect." She raised her eyebrows.

"The very least," Hermes said through gritted teeth, "I'm afraid of him. Of... both him *and* her."

"As well you should be."

She glanced in the direction of the tapestry-shrouded staircase, the sound of sandaled feet descending from the chamber above. Hermes swallowed. A slender hand moved the cloth aside and Persephone peeked out, dressed in the same manner as yesterday, when Hermes had tried to spirit her back to the world above. She nodded to him, her face blank of emotion, and Hermes returned the gesture. Hecate bowed deeply. Aidoneus was right behind her, his hand clasped within hers.

Hecate glanced at their hands, the rings smoldering with a light of their own, and exhaled in surprise and relief. She quickly returned her features to solemn regard, but not before Persephone noticed her reaction and understood that Hecate knew. She allowed the goddess's expression to give her a faint sense of hope, and prayed that Hecate would know to say nothing.

The four stood in the dark throne room without speaking. Silvery moonlight still lit the Styx and the marshes of Acheron, and all could hear Cerberus baying at the water's edge. Only Hades and Persephone could hear the cacophony of shades, those souls in Asphodel begging her to stay, lamenting that they were being robbed of their long-prophesied queen. She tried as best she could to ignore the plaintive cries; if she listened too closely, she would be lost. Persephone knew that her husband was more practiced at letting their voices fade into the background.

Aidoneus spoke first, quiet and staid. "Shall we?"

Hermes bowed to Hades and shuffled his feet before he followed the Lord of the Dead and his queen. The four of them made their way down the flights of stairs and passageways that Aidoneus had spent a thousand mortal lifetimes crafting until they at last came to the atrium and the golden poplar tree overhanging the great palace gates. The procession to the docks was slow but brief. Hermes saw the silvery inhabitants of the Fields crowding either side of the pathway for a last glimpse of their queen, each bowed to one knee and silently weeping.

A pretty shade reached for the hem of Persephone's peplos and kissed the embroidered cloth, her eyes wet with tears. Hermes squinted. The woman reminded him of his mother's sister, Merope. Before he could get a better look, she vanished in a wisp of smoke, her apparition replaced by the tall, ghostly flowers. The mood was almost funerary. *How appropriate*, he thought.

He wanted to leave this land of sadness as soon as he could, but wilted when he remembered that by Persephone's word, there was only one way across the river Styx— and the boat was already waiting for them.

Charon stood tall on one of the creaky bracings, his oar in hand, and his hood over his head to conceal his face in shadow. His eyes shone silver, matching the light from the river. Hermes looked away from the Boatman, feeling his heavy glare. He waited, watching Hades and Persephone look one another in the eye, almost as though they were speaking to each other. Persephone leaned into his chest and he stroked her hair gently. At last, Aidoneus backed away and silently took her hand, leading her to the boat.

Hermes dropped his gaze to his feet, angrily mulling over why Demeter would do this. Hades clearly wasn't mistreating her. From what little he'd seen, they were well matched, and she had been granted a greater role in this world than a consort should ever expect of her lord husband. Hermes shook his head. How would anyone ever know the truth? Mortals and gods alike feared this place, and feared its stern master. Of course they would assume— their assumptions bolstered by Demeter's wrath— that Hades had violated

Persephone, body and spirit, and kept her here as his prisoner.

The couple ended their silent farewell and Hades picked his wife up by the hips as though she weighed nothing, lifting her clear of the water. Charon took Persephone's hand, helping her the rest of the way into the boat. Hecate appeared by the queen's side, gracefully shifting through the ether. Hermes let his winged sandals lift him and stepped in with them. He didn't dare use them to carry him all the way across the Styx and await their arrival, though it could have saved him from Charon's withering looks.

The boat lurched and Hermes sat down across from Persephone. Hades stood at the shore, his figure growing smaller as they rowed out into the river. His face was stone and he turned away suddenly, slamming the palace gates behind him.

The river was a pool of moonlight. When Hermes looked over the side of the boat all he could see was silver, and in the calmer parts of the river's surface he could make out the darker seas of the moon itself, as though the whole bright orb were filling the Styx and they were gliding across it.

"Why do you look so sullen, Messenger?" Charon's voice ground out, more strained than usual.

Hermes glanced up at him. Was it his imagination or did he see in the up cast moonlight a wet trail of tears on the Boatman's sunken cheek? He felt a swell of compassion for Charon, but Hermes had no patience for his derision. "Do you think I take joy in this?"

"I would guess you'd be very glad. You've *won* after all— haven't you, Olympian?"

Hermes gritted his teeth. "There's no victory here, Boatman."

"Oh isn't there, now? Isn't it victory when your king proves that he can break any sacred law he wants, assert his dominance over us and steal away our—"

"Charon, please," Persephone said quietly.

He was instantly silent and lowered his head. "Forgive me, Aristi."

Hermes fumed. "I was commanded to play this role and we all thought that Hades had—"

"Psychopompos," Hecate hissed. "Perhaps it's best if you hold your tongue."

Hermes shivered, visions of a white-hot torch bursting into his mind. Hecate shifted in the boat and sat upright, letting Persephone lean onto her shoulder. The young queen looked down, her emotions starting to collapse under their own weight. It took all the restraint she could summon not to jump into the bottomless waters of the Styx and swim back to him. Hecate wrapped an arm around her and held her shoulder.

"Do not despair, my queen. Look at me," Hecate said, waiting for Persephone to meet her gaze. "You have done a *marvelous* thing. No waters are deep enough to part you from this shore ever again."

She prepared herself certain now that Hecate knew exactly what she had done, and thanked the Fates that she spoke cryptically to hide her meaning from Hermes and Charon. There was more she needed to know. Things to discuss more candidly, as Hecate had said. It was her first time apart from her husband and alone with the Goddess of the Crossroads, and she knew that neither the Ferryman nor the Messenger would dare interrupt them.

Hecate could sense what she was about to ask— whether or not she carried Aidon's child with her to the world above. Her forehead tighten with concern and compassion as she gave her answer. "Blood is a dangerous thing in Asphodel," Hecate said, echoing Aidon's words from the night Persephone had first suspected she was pregnant. "It does not flow here."

Persephone wilted. If her plan today failed, she had hoped to keep a more precious memento of Aidoneus than

192

just the rings on her hand, or the jewels on her neck and girdle. Persephone grasped for possibilities. She hadn't yet arrived *in* the Underworld when she could have first conceived by him, had she? And together they had already done the impossible. "What about the grove, Hecate? Life can be created here, can it not?"

"Only in that sacred place brought forth by you and your husband. And nowhere else," she said. Persephone turned her face away to stare out into the river, frustrated. Perhaps Hecate was wrong. She ran her hand over her belly. *Please let her be wrong.*

Sensing her internal protestations, the Titaness spoke again. "The seeds of this world will bloom in the world above."

"*Which* seeds?" she asked Hecate pointedly. She was thankful for the metaphors, but Persephone craved a clear answer.

Hecate shook her head. "The waters are muddied by endless ebbs and flows and the churned-up silt from all that has transpired. The Fates alone know the answer. But after today all will know. *Nothing* shall remain the same. Only that wellspring remains clear."

The boat docked on the opposite shore and its passengers disembarked amidst a mass of shades. But instead of bowing to greet the procession of gods, the newly dead merely gawked at the mists overhanging the river. Hermes followed their wide-eyed gazes and felt ice crawl up his spine. A dark fleck was visible in the impenetrable mists, shrouded, but coming closer. He heard whinnying and saw moonlight glinting off golden wheels. Hermes stopped breathing.

It was Hades. Bearing down on them in his chariot. *Oh Gods*, Hermes thought in a panic. *He's changed his mind and chosen war.*

Hermes rose up slightly on the balls of his feet, ready to flee Chthonia, perhaps warn the others in time. Before he could move, his wrist was caught and squeezed hard by the little flower goddess, the dread Queen of the Underworld. She spoke low and calm, staring at him with her cold blue gray eyes. "Stay right where you are, Messenger."

12.

"**Y**OU *HAVE* TO SAY SOMETHING!"

"How can I?" Askalaphos brushed his fingers through his thin black curls again. "Do you have any idea what this means?"

Menoetes hushed his voice and whispered low. "It means that she stays! It means that they can do nothing to take her from us! And you intend to keep quiet and let her go, you fool?"

"*I'm* the fool, Menoetes? Can you even conceive of what will happen if anyone learns what she's done? There will be war. A war to end the cosmos! Everything will *die in fire*. And not just in the corporeal world, but here as well. You and me, our mothers, all the nymphs of the Cocytus and the Styx, the Lampades, even Nyx and Erebus!"

"It cannot be as dire as all that, Askalaphos. Now, come with me. We'll find Lady Hecate or Morpheus and get this sorted out."

"Please, we *cannot* go to *anyone* with this. I am not going to be known as the one who ended the world!"

"No, you will not, Askalaphos," a voice above them said.

The broken pomegranate fell from the gardener's hands and he stumbled back, gazing up into the darkness above.

Nyx drifted down, bathed in moonlight, to hover inches above the ground. She picked up the open fruit, examining it. A smile crossed her face and she brushed her hand through the wavering edges of the darkness that cloaked her and trailed upward into the mists and Erebus beyond.

"So she did," she said, answering the silent voice of her husband.

Askalaphos and Menoetes were bowed to one knee before Lady Nyx. The gardener stammered. "M-milady, please. I o-only wanted to—"

"Rise, Askalaphos," she said, a smile still decorating her face.

The gardener swallowed, on the verge of tears, fearing that he was about to be annihilated by the ancient goddess. "I knew I couldn't keep it a secret forever, milady, I... only... wanted to..."

She tittered. "After all these aeons, none of you seem to understand that *we see all.* My brothers and sisters and I are the earth and the waters and the air; the light, the darkness and the ether itself. Erebus and I already saw what was done. And we knew that it *would* be done."

Askalaphos permitted himself to relax, and Menoetes stopped cowering, rising slowly with the aid of his staff.

"We saw our little queen sneak out as though no one could see her. But it is night here, and I *am night.*" Nyx laughed again and clasped her hands around the pomegranate, gazing in the direction of the grove. "Those dear little ones. Their intrigues are never hidden from us. Oh, they try, though!"

The gardener swallowed. "Then... if you don't mind my asking, Lady Nyx, what are you planning to do about it?"

The goddess gave him a serene smile and held out the pomegranate for Askalaphos. He gingerly took it and cradled it close.

"Persephone ate six seeds from this pomegranate. You yourself witnessed it, son of Orphne." She drifted slowly upward. "So it is not what *I* plan to do, Askalaphos, but what you *will* do."

"Anything, milady," he said nervously.

"Meet my eldest son at the river. And go quickly. You don't have much time."

✽   ✽   ✽

"One obol... one obol... one obol..." Shades filed into Charon's empty vessel. The Boatman's incessant request for fares was the only thing Hermes could hear. The God of Thieves turned ghostly white and felt like he was about to collapse. What was to become of him? *Burn... flay... geld...* the words cycled again through his mind.

"You have nothing to fear," Persephone said softly as Charon pushed off from the shore with another boatload of shades. She released Hermes's wrist from her grasp and he let out a breath he'd forgotten he was holding.

The Messenger stood stock still on the water's edge as Hades's chariot thundered to the ground. Aidoneus pulled the reins and brought it to a sudden halt, then stepped off the back. The God of the Dead wasn't dressed for battle. He still wore his himation and crown of poplar leaves instead of his greaves and cuirass and Helm of Darkness. He had no sword. Hermes cautiously relaxed.

Aidoneus walked to the small gathering of gods by the Styx. Shades all around them fell to their knees before the King and Queen. He stopped in front of Hermes. "I've heard stories about you stealing chariots. I assume you know how to drive one of these?"

Hermes gulped in air around the fig-sized lump in his throat. "Y-yes, my lord."

"Good. You will take Persephone and Hecate to the world above in my chariot. It will be faster. Faster than even *you*, as you well know."

Hermes nodded.

197

"Heed my words and wishes, Messenger. Regardless of what you were told, Persephone returns as a queen. My queen. Bring the cart and horses to me once you are done. Is that understood?"

Hermes nodded again in affirmation, dumbstruck and relieved. Hades curtly acknowledged him, then approached Hecate.

"Stay with her and keep her safe?" he said softly. "Please?"

"Of course, Aidoneus," Hecate said, and embraced him. He stood like a plank, unmoving. She drew back and looked up at him, her eyes swimming. "My dear child, don't lose hope so quickly. We have not yet reached the widest part of the river. Much remains of today."

He wrinkled his eyebrows, perplexed.

"I expect to see you soon," she said with a nod. Aidon cleared his throat, correctly guessing what Hecate meant.

He turned slowly toward his wife, his queen, the woman he had loved and longed for through half his life, who stood proud and tall, trying to keep her lower lip from quivering. Aidoneus gathered her up in his embrace, tilting her back until her weight was supported by his arms alone, her neck cradled in one strong hand. His mouth brushed over hers, then locked against her lips. Persephone touched his face, and then smoothed back the black curls of his hair with her fingers. One of her digits wound around the lock that was never properly caught up when he tied back his hair. She mewled and shuddered, fearing that this was their last kiss. *Don't be sad, my love,* his voice said in her mind. *This is not goodbye.*

Persephone smiled against his lips. Aidoneus would follow her; she knew he would. She melted, opening to him, her tongue twining against his. He deepened their kiss with a soft and hungry growl. He drew her closer and she could feel the heat of his body and the beat of his heart through his heavy cloak. His mouth claimed hers harder and she wondered if he could taste pomegranate in their kiss.

Aidoneus pulled away from her lips reluctantly and spoke low, staring directly at her, soaking up his last vision of her in his arms. "Go, Persephone, to your dark-robed mother. Go…" he swallowed, willing himself to continue. Aidon forced a smile and brushed a stray lock of hair behind her ear. "Do not be too upset. Take heart. Be strong. No matter what they say I will always be your husband. You will always, *always* be my wife… my queen…"

Persephone framed his face with her hand again, brushing away a tear that escaped his eye.

…And I will be right behind you.

Her heart leapt into her throat and she tried to keep herself from smiling. Her eyes gave her away only to him. Aidon lifted her upright and reluctantly released her.

"Go…" Aidon whispered.

Persephone took a step back from him and walked to the chariot. Hecate offered her hand, and she stepped up into the basket. Hermes shook the reins and they were off, a thin cloud of dust twisting in their wake as they distanced themselves from the river. Soon the wheels and coursers lifted off the ground and the trailing dust was replaced by dark, ethereal smoke.

Aidoneus watched them until the crown of asphodel on her head and the glint of moonlight from the chariot wheels disappeared into the dark caverns beyond. He waited until he could hear the horse's hooves no more.

Something inside of him gave way and he let out a sharp exhale of air he'd been holding back. It burned like acid. His throat tightened and he doubled over. The sounds around him were unbearable. He could hear the souls in Asphodel crying and wailing. Cerberus whined as though he were injured, and he could even hear the Keres in Tartarus gnashing and screaming, unable to fathom that their queen was gone. He joined in their grief, his sobs coming slowly at first as he tried to hold them back, then wrenching his whole body. He dropped to his knees, lost.

He had agreed to witness his wife's last plea with Zeus. But Aidoneus knew Zeus. The King of the Gods wouldn't let her return with him— not with the lives of all the mortals at stake. If their positions were reversed, Hades wouldn't either. And Demeter's stubbornness and resentment knew no bounds. It grew hard to breathe, and he tried to calm himself again and take hold of some sense of order. He dug his fingers into the gray sands and gravel of Chthonia and he tightened his fist until he felt the rocks digging painfully into his skin. He roughly wiped his eyes with his himation and took in a deep breath, letting go of the gravel and brushing the sand off on his thigh. She would need all the strength he had to offer to support her doomed petitioning, and he would need all his resolve to let her go once all reasonable hope was lost.

Persephone wouldn't accept it, though. Despite his insistence that she not defy the rules, he was certain he would find her stepping through the ether and into their bedroom during some moonless night in the world above, and that she would be punished for it. He closed his eyes, trying to will away visions of what the gods of Olympus might do to her to keep her from disobeying and rebelling.

He listened to the pleas and cries of Asphodel. This realm needed a Queen. It needed her more that it needed him, in truth. Demeter wouldn't let her return here. A dark truth crossed his mind. Demeter wouldn't let her return *to him*. He opened his eyes again, and surveyed his realm— her realm. He'd follow her, but when he returned he would have to make sure that she wouldn't be tempted to come back to him.

He thought about Erebus. Aidoneus had never met Nyx's consort— he had become the darkness while Hades was still imprisoned, and had done so to save his children

200

from Kronos's wrath after their rebellion, aeons before the Titanomachy, had failed.

Hades would have to do the same to save his wife. He smiled ruefully. His beloved was so wonderfully obstinate and would attempt again and again to journey back to him. And back to her throne-- this realm needed Persephone as its queen. But Demeter's wrath was fixed against him, and always would be. It dawned on him: both of these things needed to be, so he would simply remove himself from the paradox.

Aidoneus shook his head. Persephone would be inconsolable, and furious at him as well.

Perhaps he could find *some* way to still be with her once he was one with his realm. Erebus wound himself about his lady wife, eternally embracing her. Aidoneus knew it needed to be done as soon as he returned. He wouldn't risk the possibility that she would be punished on his account. Chthonia would have its Queen, Demeter would have her assurance that he would never touch her again, and all would be right. His purpose had already been fulfilled, he mused. He had helped depose the Titans, and he had given the Underworld its rightful ruler. His usefulness to this cosmos was surely ended.

His resolve renewed, Aidoneus took a deep breath and stretched his hand out toward the caverns ahead.

"Aidoneus! My king!"

He heard his name called faintly behind him, almost lost amidst the weeping shades and his three-headed hound's endless yowling. The voice cracked and called out again.

"Lord Hades! Wait! Wait!"

Had someone read his thoughts? Were they determined to keep him from following in Erebus's footsteps?

"Aidon! Not yet!" A second voice above the din, this time Charon's.

Aidoneus turned toward the Styx, squinting in the darkness at a faint lamp hovering above the water. He heard the oar plunging and splashing, ripples forming all around the boat, its wake cutting deep into the water. Aboard the boat was Askalaphos, jumping up and down.

"My lord!"

"Stop hopping around, you idiot! Do you want to tip us over?" Charon hissed at him.

Aidoneus ran for the water's edge. As he drew nearer he saw the gardener hold something aloft that stopped him in his tracks. "Oh gods above, sweet one, you didn't..." he muttered to himself. He remembered the berry sweet taste of her kiss, and the heady scent, almost like wine, mingled with hers in his very clothes. "Why didn't she tell me?"

Askalaphos held a pomegranate. A well-eaten pomegranate, at that: its flesh was torn and seeds were missing. The gardener hopped out of the boat too soon and landed almost waist deep in the water, wading into the shallows and up to the shore. His teeth chattered from the cold. "L-Lord Hades! The Queen... she ate six s-seeds!"

Askalaphos prostrated himself and held the fruit up for the Lord of the Underworld's inspection. Aidon grabbed it from his hand, wide-eyed. This certainly wasn't the pomegranate he'd eaten yesterday morning. This was new. And it was hers. "Persephone..." He lifted Askalaphos up by his chlamys, almost shaking him. "Are you certain?"

"Yes, milord."

"Are you *absolutely certain* you saw her eat them?"

"Yes! Milord I'm sorry, I wasn't supposed to see. I mean, she probably didn't want *anyone* to see, but..." his excuses faded to noise in the background as Aidon turned the fruit over in his hands, his heart fluttering at the sight of it. He tried to keep from smiling or laughing or shouting joyfully.

There's only one way around this, and that is to overthrow the order of things, he had said to her. She had done it! Persephone had found a way to stay with him forever! But at what cost? It was unchangeable and unbreakable, no matter what Zeus or Demeter had to say. This was a law of nature— of the cosmos itself. Anyone who ate in the Underworld was bound to it. Even the Fates couldn't change this, though he was convinced that they had seen it coming. Persephone *must* return to him. But they weren't out of danger yet. What if Demeter didn't relent despite this evidence? Certainly even the thinnest sense of self-preservation would stop her from destroying them all. He would concern himself with that once he got there. Right now he needed to reach his wife. Though the key to ending their grief lay in the palm of his hand, Aidon's mind repeated only one thing. *Why didn't you tell me?*

Askalaphos continued to tell his tale, something about tripping over a sheep, and something else about Nyx before Hades interrupted him and thrust the pomegranate back into his hands.

"You're coming with me, Askalaphos."

"What? I—" The Lord of the Dead grasped his shoulder and started walking away from the shore, pulling Askalaphos along. "Where?"

"To the world above!" Aidoneus shouted at him and marched forward. Warmth and hope, dread and anxiety warred within him. "Hold on to that pomegranate as tightly as you can. For the love of the Fates, do *not* drop it!"

"The world above? I've never been..." Askalaphos started. Hades loomed past the shades and it was all Askalaphos could do to keep up with his long strides. "Milord! How will we get there?"

Aidoneus didn't answer the gardener, but hoisted him up under one arm. The other hand reached forward as he walked toward the caverns. Dark smoke swirled about them with every step, and they were gone.

✻　　✻　　✻

The chariot's great wheels left the ground as soon as they rolled past the entrances to the Underworld. The horses galloped silently; smoke rolling under them and marking

203

their path. Persephone looked back until her husband faded from view, and until the wan light of the moon shining through the Styx shone no more. She felt him falter, felt his despair even from here, and wished she could go back and hold him and tell him what she'd done.

Persephone lost her footing and gripped the side of the chariot again as they went around a bend. The roads to the world above twisted every which way through the earth. When she had been taken down here, Hades had opened great gaps in the earth itself— a direct route from Nysa through molten fires that destroyed her thin corporeal clothing. This journey would not be so short. These were pathways that had been carved long ago, when the cosmos itself was formed; aeons of dripping of water and welling springs had done the rest.

"I can't see a thing now!" Hermes whined.

"They know the way," the Goddess of the Crossroads replied calmly. "But if it will steady your driving and not knock us about like acorns in a bowl…"

A four-lamped torch grew in Hecate's hand and the ends lit with golden orange light. Persephone blinked, then squinted and saw stalagmites hanging overhead, and caves and crevices emptying onto roads from the world above. Through them poured the souls of the newly dead, making the days-long trudge to Chthonia, answering the call of the Styx now that they had completed their journey through the living world from womb to tomb. She thought about the poor Eleusinian bride and wished she could see all of them safely to Asphodel, but that would be her husband's work.

Hermes gripped the thick leather reins and steadied his feet on the cart. "There must be a thousand entrances! How will we know which is the right one? We could end up in Aegyptus for Fate's sake!"

"Then tell them to go to Eleusis," Persephone said, suddenly feeling queasy. Dull pain began to radiate through her from her knees through her lower back and all the way to the tips of her breasts. "You yourself have gone and come back from there, haven't you?"

"Well, yes, but there's one way down and many ways up, and I've never really cared where I've surfaced, before. Olympus is never far away…"

"Then do as the Queen bade you, and tell them to follow the path to the Corn Mother!" Hecate stated, annoyed.

Hermes shrugged and flicked the reins. *"To Demeter!"* he shouted at the shadowy beasts. One of them nickered and turned its head left and the others followed suit, hard and fast. Persephone was knocked into Hecate, who gripped her side.

She felt another flash of pain low in her belly and winced, sucking in air through her teeth. Hecate thinned her lips and looked down at Persephone. "It has begun."

"What has?" Persephone said, grasping her abdomen.

"The earth is righting itself now that one of its goddesses returns."

Persephone knitted her brow at Hecate's words and grasped the chariot with one hand, her lower belly with the other. She closed her eyes. Was Aidon behind them? Would he come? She swore she could feel him close by, but didn't turn to look. She didn't want to alert Hermes or Hecate to their plan. The feeling of her husband's presence coursed through her, gripped her with a surge of energy and made her ache sharply where they had last joined together.

She cried out and felt Hecate stroke her shoulder through the pain. Persephone felt light headed and gritted her teeth. The chariot plunged through a tunnel and the cart steadied itself. She doubled over in pain again.

Persephone smelled earth. Its warmth and richness filled all of her senses, the raw energy of the source of life flowing through her. She had been away from it for so long that it was overwhelming. The pomegranate grove had been her only source of this scent and sense below, and it was so much more potent this close to the living world.

This wasn't the cold, sterile ground of Chthonia but fresh soil and humus, aeons of plants and creatures living and dying, twisted together with the dormant roots of trees and vines and flowers waiting to awaken. Her husband's essence encircled her and she felt searing heat radiating from her womb. The cavern narrowed and the winds from the world above guttered Hecate's torches. The walls closed in so tight around them that she could almost touch the roots of the trees. When she did reach for them, Persephone felt another sharp twinge of pain and felt a small trickle of hot liquid from her core.

No...

It wasn't borne from pleasure. In the dark, she quickly reached behind the skirts of her peplos and touched her lower lips. Persephone brought her hand away and rubbed thin liquid between her fingers.

No, Fates please...

A faint light bounced through the caverns ahead of them and Persephone looked down at her fingers. They were dark. The light increased and she could see color. Red.

Blood is a dangerous thing in Asphodel.

Moon blood. Persephone saw the image blur as water filled her eyes. It was as Hecate had said on the boat. She carried no child. She never had. While they were in the world below, she never would. She squeezed her eyes shut and felt a few tears streak by her face. Her stained hand balled into a fist and she dug her nails into the palm of her hand. She willed herself to not cry.

He was following, close. She could feel Aidoneus around her and through her. She dared not look behind. They rounded another bend and a rail of light pierced the dark, almost blinding her.

The earth and all waking life rose through her in pulses and waves, just as it had when she stepped through the ether in Nysa with Aidon at her side. The light grew stronger, turned golden and her eyes adjusted. She could smell the cold tree bark, the wind and snow. And blood.

She felt the chariot slowing and looked around, the blue sky above them, the sun shining in the west, an hour or so above the horizon. Persephone blinked and saw Demeter in a dark robe, her hair veiled, with her hand cupped over her mouth, and a strongly built man with a thick blond beard and a cloaked himation standing beside her. She felt dizzy as they came to a stop and looked around at the cave from which they emerged with its sandy granite and withered husks of chaparral brush, then at the blinding layer of snow covering the dead ground.

Persephone stepped from the chariot and her foot sank into the white banks, freezing. She willed it away, and the snow vanished from around her feet. Green sprouts replaced it, growing around her in a circle, sprouting up and crowding each other. Her heart beat loudly in her ears. The pulse of the earth beat with it and she looked down at the blood staining her right hand. Roots. Soil. Life. Sprouting seeds. *Aidon...*

Doubling over with a cry, she placed her palm on the ground and felt the earth warm beneath her fingertips. She closed her eyes and felt the snow melt away, replaced with heat, with roots digging through the frost. Her womb clenched again and she cried out anew, concentrating. She heard faint trickling as water leaked under the snow; slush flowing in streams, the rivers of the world above began to thaw.

Grow.

She felt a pulse of life nearby— a crocus bulb, its green tip bursting from the hardened shell protecting it. She exhaled and pushed vitality into it, just as she had when she was Kore. Thin shoots strengthened into leaves, buds blossomed into broad purple flowers that opened to reveal bright saffron anthers. Persephone reached past that bulb until she felt another. The ground was littered with crocus bulbs, each

207

bearing precious cargo ready to spring forth and greet the sun. Other plants twisted in the dirt, their roots pushing down, their stalks and fledgling leaves pushing up. They were rooting themselves below and above.

The seeds of this world will bloom in the world above.

Blood streaked her thighs under her peplos, but she didn't care. What life she had been unable to carry in her womb, she realized, she was giving to all the earth. She felt heat and fertility spread from where her palm touched the earth, radiating out for leagues and stadia around them, across all the lands, the face of the waters and the islands. The frozen sea creaked and groaned, fissures splitting the ice. Snow melted and caved in as roots sipped its life-giving water. Warmth. Seeds. Roots. Leaves. Flowers.

Persephone gasped in a breath and withdrew her hand from the earth. She opened her eyes and stood. The gathering of gods— Demeter and Zeus, Hermes and Hecate— stood thunderstruck, all staring at her.

Persephone gazed at the altered landscape surrounding her. The snow lay in patches, and in its place grew the first hints of grass, the earth deep and rich in color, muddy and waiting to produce more. Scattered across the freed fertile ground and even bursting through the last drifts of snow were crocuses. Hundreds of them. The purple flowers were strewn all over the hillside and stretched out across the valley around the Telesterion. The trees still looked gray, their bark lifeless, but on a small olive tree close by, Persephone could see little buds with tips of green emerging from the branches. She calmly walked over, ignoring the others and touched a frail offshoot. Under the path of her fingers, buds burst open further and bright green leaves appeared. So much work still needed to be done.

"The Goddess of Spring," Hecate said quietly, interrupting the silence. A smile curled her lips. "The bringing of life above and below. It *will* come to pass, then."

208

Demeter took a cautious step forward. Persephone looked at her mother's face, the first time that she had seen her in two months. She bit her lip, conflicting emotions coursing through her. Demeter... who had endured months of anguish and pain after her only child was ripped away from her. Mother... who had always been her protector and nurturer. She had tried to save Persephone, however misguidedly, from an arranged marriage that would part them forever. Despite everything, Persephone had missed her greatly.

"Mother!" She barely heard herself shout it and ran forward, embracing Demeter. Persephone felt arms wrap around her and heard her mother's uncontrolled sobs of relief, her tears of joy at seeing her child again. They held tight to each other, weeping. She had missed her, oh how she had missed her!

Persephone knew why she had wreaked such havoc on the mortals. Men governed the world above, and a woman— even a goddess such as Demeter— was nearly powerless under their rules. It took an act of great strength and severity to make men listen, to bend them. Persephone understood. But her mother needed to return that understanding in kind, now. She needed to listen. Persephone held her, willing herself to be brave, to be strong but kind.

"Kore," Demeter cried out into the shoulder of Persephone's peplos. "Kore... My sweet, darling Kore! I thought I'd never see you again..."

Persephone held her breath and pushed gently away from Demeter's embrace. "Mother, I—"

"Look at you. Gods, look what he did to you..." she whispered, shaking her head. "You look so pale and your cheeks are so gaunt."

I've grown up, Persephone thought. *I am who I was supposed to be.* "I am well, Mother. I was never mistreated. But I need to speak to you."

"Of course, my dear Kore," Demeter said, brushing a strand of hair behind her daughter's ear. She restrained herself from tearing the asphodel out of her daughter's hair and the jewels from her throat. They were marks of Hades's ownership, his enslavement of her daughter. As soon as she could, she would give Persephone a new linen chiton, and discard that revealing black peplos Hades must have forced her to wear.

Persephone saw her mother's eyes darting to her offending crown and cleared her throat, regaining Demeter's attention. "Mother, you cannot call me that anymore."

Demeter pursed her lips and looked away, her eyes filling with fresh tears. "Kore, I know that... *things happened to you*, but you needn't bear that mark forever. We can return life to how it once was."

"We cannot. Everything is different now. I—"

"I know what happened to you, child, and it wasn't your fault that Hades raped you."

"Raped..." she said under her breath in shock.

"It's not your fault, you did nothing to provoke him, and you are *safe* now. Please know that first." Demeter gripped her arms and squeezed gently, trying to comfort her. "I love you no matter what happened to you. You're still whole; you're still my daughter. My sweet darling Kore, and you always will be. We can still—"

"*Stop calling me Kore!*" Persephone commanded, her voice assuming the tone she'd grown into the last two months.

Demeter let go and retreated several steps back. She gaped wordlessly and Persephone took advantage of her silence.

"My name is Persephone. Mother, I am here for one reason and one reason only, and you and I *must* speak plainly. You must stop what you're doing and let the mortals live. The worlds above and below have been thrown far out of balance. So much so that the King of Ephyra has escaped from the Underworld. I am here *only* to heal the world above

210

from the devastation caused in my absence, but once it is done, I need to return to my rightful place."

"Persephone…" Zeus muttered.

"No, no, it's all right, child," Demeter said shakily through tears. "You don't have to go back to that horrible place ever again. Hades has no power over you here. You are safe at last and you can heal and one day you will look back on all this without fear and it will no longer hurt. You are home, Kore. You will never have to endure him violating you ever again."

She shook her head, trying to abate her anger. "Mother, I *was not* violated. But nonetheless, I am a maiden no more. I'm not Kore; my name is Persephone and always has been. Hades Aidoneus Chthonios is my husband—"

"Persephone…" Zeus started, his voice rough with irritation.

"—And my home is with him in the Underworld where we rule *together* as King and Queen."

"Persephone, you are *not* the queen of anything!" Zeus bellowed finally. "And you are no longer Hades's wife. You are a girl child of my *oikos*, and my property. And you will obey my edicts."

"Father." She faced Zeus, throwing her shoulders back. "Before the end of the Titanomachy, you swore a Stygian oath to my husband while I was still in the womb. An oath that you kept and that we expect you to continue to honor."

He stared at her, taken aback, then stood tall again, lifting his chin. "You are not able to make that decision, girl, and I suggest you not take that tone with me. I am not only your father, but your king."

She stopped and nodded, then curtsied to him as one sovereign would to another. "My apologies, your grace," she said without fear or facetiousness and stood up again to her full height. His eyes were like hers, but far more blue. He wasn't as tall as she had remembered, but she hadn't seen him since she was a little girl. "However, I must request on our behalf that our marriage is honored and that I return to my realm to rule with Hades."

"And as you well know, *Lady Persephone*," Zeus said with a sneer of sarcastic formality, "your marriage was annulled. You have nothing to say concerning whom I chose to marry you to, nor do you have any say in the ending of it! If anything, this is a matter for Hades and I to speak upon alone."

"Then we shall," said a voice from the shadows.

13.

PERSEPHONE'S HEART FLEW INTO HER THROAT AND she turned around to see Aidoneus loom forward from the mouth of the cave. He shielded his eyes and blinked when the sunlight hit him. Askalaphos walked behind him, shaking. In their gardener's hands was her pomegranate.

Demeter threw her arm over her mouth and stumbled back, terrified. Hades made no eye contact with her, nor did he look at Persephone. He strode forward to his wife's side and faced Zeus, lowering his gaze to look at him. "My lord," Aidoneus bowed out of respect before continuing, "You well know that the lots were divided equally. You have ruler-ship over us all, but not over the rules of *my* kingdom. As such you cannot forcibly take her back once you sent her there."

Zeus turned and glared at Hermes. "Did I not *clearly* instruct you to tell—"

"He told us," Aidoneus interrupted. "Hermes stood in my halls with that pitiful scroll and told my wife and I how you broke your oath, *young one.*" The last words came out as a growl. "You hold no sway over the world below and you were bound to honor the pact we made. I expected *her* to turn against her word—" he said, pointing at Demeter.

"Now wait just a minute!" the Goddess of the Harvest said, storming toward them.

"—But not you. Surely if the *King of the Gods* cannot keep a Stygian oath, then you should not expect the fealty of those who would," he narrowed his eyes at Zeus. "What do you suppose will happen the next time your lady wife has had enough of your philandering? Or if Ares or even Athena decides to follow in your footsteps, and Kronos's before you, and depose you? Do you think I will bother to send Briareos to break your chains and subdue the gods again?"

"What would you have me do, Aidoneus? Be honest with yourself and look around. Your choice of bedmate and whatever we said at the Styx aeons ago means *nothing* when measured against the ending of all things. I had to consider the greater good. Surely you can understand that."

"And I do. But you should have brought Demeter in line before trifling with me. Instead, you unwisely engaged in a battle of wills with her that brought us all to the brink of ruin," he said, his voice dispassionate.

"We couldn't—" he stopped himself, not wanting to give away to the ruler of the Other Side how weakened by Demeter's famine they truly were. "Your obstinacy had a part to play in all this, you know. Did you truly understand the severity of all this, or were you too busy *entertaining* your bedmate? Surely your kingdom is overwhelmed right now."

"It is," he said with a nod. Zeus's accusation stung. It was true— his singular focus on her had been a way for him to ignore the devastation of the world above. But, he needed her by his side now more than ever. "All the more reason to have the God and Goddess of the Dead there to set it aright."

"The Goddess—" Zeus shook his head. "Your *consort*, you mean. What more is she than that?"

"As the Lord of the Underworld, it is my right and my wish to confer power upon her. She rules Chthonia as my equal."

"Oh, so *that's* why she wishes to stay!" Demeter interjected and folded her arms in front of her. "By poisoning her mind and promising her a throne at your side as you raped her into submission every night?!"

Aidoneus gritted his teeth, wishing with all his might that he could taunt Demeter about how *willing* her precious daughter had been to lay with him, to seduce him as many time as he had seduced her. He didn't want to embarrass his beloved by telling all the secrets of their bedchamber. Or their garden. Or their throne room. Or the pool. Or the walls and tables and a dozen other places in their palace. Instead, he scoffed and rolled his eyes at her. Demeter huffed.

Zeus spoke. "Aidon, you've let Hecate and Nyx influence you for far too long. Aren't you master of your own realm? It's *your third of the cosmos* for Fate's sake, not theirs! And yet you call *your* realm by *their* old word for it."

"The Underworld is as it ever was, and what I say is the truth. My wife and I preside over Chthonia. And what's more, while Persephone and I rule side by side in Asphodel, the true source of her power lies far, *far* deeper than that."

Demeter and Zeus both looked at Persephone in shock and leaned away, almost imperceptibly.

"Tartarus bends to her will. She has faced Titans." Hades smiled triumphantly. "And my queen is now as much a part of my world as I am. Askalaphos!"

Persephone took a step forward before her plan fell to pieces. "I ate the fruit of the Underworld, Mother!"

Demeter's legs faltered and she took a step back. "No…"

"I ate six seeds from a pomegranate—"

"Tell me you did not do this!"

"A pomegranate!" Zeus laughed. "Pomegranates don't grow in the Underworld! I've heard some tall tales in my time, but this one, Aidon—"

215

"It is the truth," Hecate said from her place beside the chariot. "For aeons the seeds lay dormant. But by your daughter's union with her husband and through their united dreams, they grew."

"Where else could you possibly find a pomegranate?" Persephone said calmly. She reached for the fruit in Askalaphos's hands and held it out to Demeter and Zeus. "Certainly not in the *living* world."

Demeter snatched it from her hand and turned it over in horror, then threw it to the ground. She gripped Persephone's arms tightly almost shaking her. "By what trick did Hades deceive you?! How did he make you eat these? Tell me!"

Persephone wriggled out of her grasp and stood next to Aidoneus again.

"You did this!" Demeter hissed at Aidoneus. "You were going to lose her and it wasn't enough for you to have ruined her for all eternity, you had to bind her to your hideous dead kingdom!"

"I did no such thing, Demeter! I didn't even *know* she had eaten them until after I sent her on her way. Persephone *kept* it from me!" He glanced at his wife, his voice gentling when it spoke in her mind. *Why didn't you tell me?*

Persephone winced at his words; spoken and unspoken, feeling a sting of guilt that she had deceived her husband, even for the sake of them all. "I ate those seeds without Hades's knowledge."

"Of course you would say that when threatened by your captor, Kore!" Demeter cried. "He forced them on you just as he forced himself on you! But we can correct this, Kore. Surely we—"

"Mother, I ate them alone, and knew exactly what I was doing when I ate them. Aidon didn't find out until after I left," she said looking at him purposefully. *My love, please... They would have blamed you unless I revealed it myself.*

They will anyway, sweet one, he answered. *It makes no difference.*

216

Demeter scowled. "You look to *him* before you speak! Why should I believe what he is obviously coercing you to say?"

Askalaphos stepped out from behind Aidoneus. He bowed to low before Zeus. "Y-your grace," he stood and nodded to Demeter, "and great Lady of the Harvest, what the Queen says is true."

"And who, pray tell, are you?" Zeus boomed.

"My name is Askalaphos, s-son of Orphne, nymph of the river Styx. I am the Queen's gardener."

"You mean Hades's slave—" Demeter snarled.

"Be silent, woman!" Zeus said. He turned to Askalaphos. "Speak."

"I..." he swallowed and breathed shallowly, looking from one powerful, angry god to the other. "I saw the Queen go out to the garden at night, alone. She didn't know I was there and must've thought she was alone in the grove. I-I panicked and hid so she wouldn't see me. Queen Persephone pulled a pomegranate off the tree and I saw her open it and eat six seeds. Just as she said. I didn't even *want* to come here, but Lady Nyx saw it too and told me I should say something. She saw her eat them, Erebus saw her—"

"Nyx witnessed it too?" Zeus asked.

Demeter's face grew red with rage. "How dare you incriminate my daughter on behalf of your master! You lie and screech and give false witness... I ought to turn you into an owl!"

Askalaphos cowered behind Persephone for protection. She grasped Aidon's hand and together they shielded their gardener. "You will do no such thing, Mother. He speaks the truth!"

Persephone glanced behind her. Askalaphos had already taken off running for the safety of the caves, not waiting around for the angry earth goddess to make good on her threat.

Demeter's face reddened and twisted in hopelessness. She burst into tears and turned to Zeus. "My lord, surely six paltry seeds isn't enough to bind my poor daughter to the Underworld! How could so few—"

"If she ate one seed or ate a thousand, it would make no difference!" Hades yelled, bearing down on Demeter. "She ate the fruit of the Underworld and is thereby bound to it for all eternity. Persephone is mine!"

Demeter faced him placing her hands on her hips, lifting her chin. "You see? *Now* your true nature comes out, Aidon. Nothing has changed about you in all these aeons. Observe, daughter, your ravisher's eternal selfishness!"

"Selfishness?!" Aidon fumed. "This from you, Deme, who kept my wife a powerless child for all the aeons of her existence, denying her everything and teaching her nothing! If you had mentioned anything about her destined role in the cosmos then it would have ignited her beautiful curiosity. You couldn't have kept your *stranglehold* on her!"

"You have no place and no right to tell me how to raise a child! What would *you* know about having children anyway?"

"You held no more knowledge than him upon your daughter's birth," Hecate scoffed quietly.

Aidoneus looked at the hand that had been holding his wife's a moment before and saw traces of blood on his palm. Persephone's blood. His gaze flew to hers, alarmed. *What is this? What have they done to you?*

Nothing, she replied. Persephone flushed with embarrassment. *It's... moon blood.*

He stared at her confused for a moment before it dawned on him. In the living world women's fertility came and went each month, following the changes of the moon. Aidoneus lowered his gaze, upset at his ignorance, and stroked her back. *Are you alright?*

Persephone thought about the stopping of her cycle, and how gladdened she was at the prospect of carrying his child, only to find out that it wasn't to be. She thought about Hecate's words in the boat, how Persephone was carrying those seeds to the world above. She realized then what the Goddess of the Crossroads meant. Any union with Aidon in the world below couldn't produce children. Instead, it had become the genesis of spring. *Yes*, she lied, fighting back tears. *I'm fine.*

"...And given the evidence of Persephone's rearing," the Goddess of the Crossroads continued, "I would say you know less still."

"You stay out of this!" Demeter hissed at Hecate. "*You* did everything you could to control my every action and desire, to run every single aspect of my life—"

"Well, at least you retained *something* that Hecate taught you," Aidon interrupted. "Gods know how little else—"

"Enough!" Demeter scowled at the Messenger, who was leaning against the chariot, scratching idly at a golden wheel. "Hermes, how could you let her out of your sight?!"

"My lady, this is hardly my fault—"

"Like blazing Tartarus it isn't! How hard was it, Messenger? Go get her and bring her back and yet you couldn't manage even that!"

"You weren't *there* Demeter! I— Have *you* seen Charon— Look, I didn't want to—"

Hecate interrupted him. "I think this has gone far enough—"

"Don't you tell me what I can and cannot say about—"

"Nothing you have to say at this point *matters*, Deme. What's done is—"

"Selfish, lying—"

"—couldn't possibly understand—"

"—meddling witch!"

"—my lady, if you would just—"

"*You* mind your own—"

Persephone listened to her husband and mother, Hermes and Hecate descend into yelling overtop of one another, their voices clashing against each other in an endless cacophony. This was going nowhere. She felt another cramp contract her womb and winced again. The mortals were still unfed and dying, and more would die unless she began healing the earth. Zeus remained silent, observing the fight. He glared coldly at Persephone as she made her way over to him.

"A fine mess you've made," he said quietly, his arms folded across his chest, "Daughter."

"The mess is not of my making." Persephone took a deep breath. "And I have a solution, if you would hear it."

"You do realize that even I am not powerful enough to undo what you did?"

Of that I have no doubt, she thought. "Yes."

"That the Underworld itself will take you even if you try to stay here?"

"But not permanently," she looked up at him, "Father."

"No," he said. "Not permanently. With the number of seeds you ate, it could only claim you for a part of the year. Which will enrage your *dear* husband, to be sure."

"I will explain this to Aidoneus in my own time. He will come to understand the value in what I'll propose to you now."

"Go on..." he said quietly, listening to the rise and fall of the others' voices and watching their manic debate: Hecate imperiously lifting her chin as she hissed at Demeter, Demeter pointing her finger at Hades, Aidoneus snarling another threat, Hermes trying to mediate, then shrugging and defending himself against their combined wrath.

"I know the plants. I've known them for aeons. Six months is long enough for the mortals to grow and harvest the fruits, olives, wheat, and barley that can feed them and their livestock for a year. I ate six seeds, Lord Zeus, and there are twelve months in the year."

"I'm listening..."

"What if I stayed in the Underworld for half the year... one month for each seed? The mortals can plant all their crops on my return, and I will remain above for the tilling and sowing, the planting and the harvest, to make sure my mother doesn't thrust the world back into famine. Then once the last harvest is over I will take my place at my husband's side. My time would be divided evenly."

He observed her and a smile played with the corner of his mouth. "You love him, do you?"

"Yes," she said. "I love Aidoneus with all my heart."

"And yet you would sacrifice half your life, your endless years with him for the sake of the mortals?"

"I would."

"Hmm," he grunted, contemplating her words and stroking his fingers through his beard.

"Your grace?" She waited until he turned to her. "This must be your idea."

"Oh?"

"Look at them. My mother will not listen to me. My husband will, but you are his king. I know he's angry, but this will mean more coming from you. He would only try to plead with me to stay with him forever, and I don't know if I could bear that right now. I know the mortals certainly cannot."

"Well, my firstborn daughter..." He snorted and shook his head. "Would that you had been born a male. You would have made a just ruler."

"I am the Queen of the Underworld." She stood tall and unflinching, despite his earlier words to the contrary.

"So you are," he conceded with a nod. "And now the Goddess of Spring, no doubt. But I meant as heir to Olympus. All I have is a cowardly, bravado-drunk boy to inherit the skies. And another girl child, and more bastards than I can count."

"I love my lot— my *husband's* lot, I mean. You will pardon my saying so, but I have no interest in ruling over the immortals," she said cautiously, indicating the throng of arguing gods.

Zeus chuckled low. "Oftentimes, neither do I."

Persephone gave him a thin smile. "Should I withdraw and let you gain their attention?"

He cocked his head at her. "We must have you at Olympus some time. There is much you could teach my other children about what it means to be one of the deathless ones."

"Thank you, your grace," Persephone said, with a reverent nod. She took a few steps back and stood off from the group, unnoticed amidst their quarrelling. The shadows were growing long. She was exhausted. Overhead, the sky quickly darkened with clouds, and branches of lightning lit them from underneath. Loud thunder rolled across the bay beyond Eleusis.

"Silence, all of you!" Zeus yelled once he had their attention. A light, warm rain started to fall, further melting the remaining drifts of snow. Hermes threw his chlamys over his shoulders and Demeter raised her veil over her hair. The rain pasted Aidon's loose curls to his forehead and drops beaded on the wilder ones. The rain didn't touch Hecate.

Demeter and Aidoneus turned to Zeus, who clapped a hand on Persephone's shoulder. "I have come to a decision."

Hecate looked at Persephone with a knowing smile on her face.

"Since she ate only six seeds, Persephone is to spend six months in the Underworld with her lord husband and six months renewing the earth with her mother, Demeter."

Aidon's eyes widened in shock and hurt, then he seethed with anger. He opened his mouth to protest, but Demeter spoke before he could.

"Unacceptable!" she yelled. "You expect me to willingly send my daughter to be defiled in the grave half of every year?!"

"This is a compromise you *must* make, Demeter! By right, Aidoneus should be allowed to take Persephone back *for all time*," he fibbed. "Count yourself fortunate that I give you even this."

"Indeed," Aidoneus said darkly. "And pray tell, why is it that she cannot return with me to our world when she is bound there by forces even more powerful than *you*, young one?"

"Because—"

"I refuse to accept this!" Demeter hissed, interrupting Zeus. "How can you continue to do this to us?"

"Persephone has no choice now. She willingly ate the fruit of the Underworld and *must* return there," Zeus said, growing annoyed at both of them. "But because *you* have devastated the earth Demeter, she will spend her first half year in the sunlit world protecting it and helping it flourish."

"This is not what you swore to me, Zeus," Demeter said. "As I said before, I will only relent if you keep your end of our bargain."

The gentle rain falling on them turned cold and slowed becoming sticky clumps of snowflakes.

"And kill us all, you silly sow?" Aidon bellowed at her.

"If that will end your ravishment and trickery of my daughter—"

"Then so be it, Mother."

All assembled looked at Persephone, shocked into silence. It was then that Aidoneus knew that Zeus hadn't arranged this deal— Persephone had. But why would she insist on spending half a year apart from him?

"If you cannot agree to this and are intent on ending the world, then you leave me with no choice but to spend the short time we all have left with my husband." She pointedly walked over to Aidoneus and stood next to him, resting her hand in the crook of his elbow.

He drew his cloak over her shoulder, covering her with his himation to hold her close and shield her from the cold. *You are playing a dangerous game, sweet one,* he said to her.

Trust me, she answered silently. "If this is your decision, Mother, then know that this will be the last you ever see of me."

Demeter's eyes grew glassy and her shoulders sunk. She lowered her face into her hands. As she started to cry, the snow melted back into a warm shower. The setting sun poked its way out from under the cloud cover and through the rain, and Iris's rainbow flooded the valley, shining in the golden fading sunlight. It was the first time Aidon had ever seen such a thing.

"Hold me a moment?" she said to her stunned husband.

"Of-of course." Aidon gathered her deeper within his himation, and she settled against him, letting herself be supported by his arms. His scent was comforting, his warmth a refuge from the chilly air, his heartbeat a soothing calm in the wake of the storm of angry voices. She nuzzled against his chest and squeezed him, smiling contentedly when he responded in kind.

Her mother's increasingly vocal sobs broke her reverie. Persephone unwrapped herself from her husband's warm embrace and kissed him on the cheek. Demeter had sunk to her knees and was sobbing uncontrollably. *She has lost her war, and she believes she has lost me,* Persephone thought.

She looked around the valley. *And we have almost lost the mortals.* The land was a patchwork of new life and lingering snow. It would take too long to grow the first crop, and if the mortals died in the meantime her sacrifice would be for naught. *The seeds of this world will bloom in the world above,* Hecate had told her.

Persephone stretched her hand out toward Eleusis and all of Peloponnesus across the bay. She closed her eyes.

Grow.

The Goddess of Spring gripped her husband's hand. He shut his eyes and felt the energy of the earth spread through him and surge into her. He thought of Nysa, when he had taught her how to travel through the ether. His knees began to buckle, and he braced himself against the ground, felt Persephone pulling at him, not with her hand but with her spirit, sapping his essence as she called up more energy from the depths. The power coursing through him made him dizzy, euphoric. When the rush subsided to a trickle, he slowly opened his eyes.

Aidon's jaw fell open. Before them on the hills and plain, bushels of asphodel sprouted up through the muddy ground, white and gray flowers opening in such numbers that they covered the land like a blanket of snow. Persephone collapsed into his side, breathing hard. Aidoneus caught her and steadied her on her feet.

"Sweet one?"

Demeter stared at her daughter and out at the endless ghostly flowers dotting the plain. "Asphodel. Of all the things in this world you could have grown, Kore..." She glared at Aidoneus. "Do you taunt me?"

"It is a simple meal for the mortals, Mother. The roots will fill their bellies. Along with Poseidon's bounty, they can survive until you and I can regrow the grain."

"We..."

"Yes," she said, standing upright again with Aidon's help. She walked to Demeter. Persephone smiled kindly, then embraced her again in a tight hug. "Mother, I love you. Even after all that has transpired. Can we please make the best of the next six months?"

Demeter brought her arms around her daughter, stunned and conflicted. She was angry, so very angry that Kore would have to return to the land of the dead, and would do so for all time. But, Kore's selflessness and resourcefulness in providing for the mortals filled Demeter with pride. She ended their embrace with a squeeze, and sighed. "We will."

She set her jaw firmly and released her daughter. Demeter trampled through the mud to stand between Zeus and Aidoneus.

"I accept the agreement. But I warn you both," she said, swinging her finger from Zeus to Hades. "She spends half the year above and half… below. Not one day longer. And to remind you of our bargain, Zeus, the crops will *wither* in her absence." She stared at Hades and slitted her eyes. "And may the Fates have mercy upon you if she is late by even a day, Aidon."

Demeter strode back toward Persephone, intent on escorting her to the Telesterion.

"I have not yet agreed to this… compromise," Aidoneus ground out. Demeter stopped in her tracks.

Hecate blanched and took a step toward him. "Aidon, please…"

"No? I expected more reason from *you*," the King of the Gods replied.

"More reason?" He loomed toward Zeus. "You expect me to accept living half a life? To condemn my wife and myself to a perpetual cycle of yearning and dread every time she comes and goes?"

Persephone stood stock-still and reached out to him. *Aidon, my love, please…*

Why didn't you tell me?

"It is no less than I'm giving Demeter," Zeus offered.

"Persephone is my *wife!*"

"She is my daughter, yet I have made peace with it," Demeter chimed in with a smirk.

"Like Tartarus you have, Deme."

"Aidoneus—"

"No!" He shot at Zeus. "You broke your oath to me! Now you try to amend that with this foul arrangement that robs me of my bride for half my life? I will not act on it— yet— but this is still a breach of our original, *peaceful* terms."

Zeus leaned in and spoke low, out of earshot of Demeter. "I have been forced to cede *enough* power thanks to *her*. I will never regain those she brought into the Eleusinian Mysteries. And I am well and truly tired of this matter and wish for things to return to what they once were, Aidoneus. So do not tempt me to reveal exactly how long those seeds truly bind your wife to your side. Think carefully before you cause further upset."

Aidoneus gritted his teeth and spun away from Zeus, knowing full well that his claim over Persephone would be reduced to a few months if he pressed. Persephone knew it too. She left her mother's side and strode over to him, taking his hand in hers. He gazed down at her, his face a mask. Even so, Persephone could feel his pain. He pointed at Zeus. "With all I've done for you and yours *since* the war, you know full well that you owe me more than this."

"So be it," Zeus folded his arms and glared at Aidoneus. "If this agreement is so distasteful to you, then I shall swear a new oath."

Hecate's face fell.

"Swear it, oathbreaker," Hades snarled.

"You are firstborn of your generation and Persephone is firstborn of hers." He paused and his lip twisted into a sneer. "I, Zeus Cronides Olympios, swear on the river Styx that if your union produces a son, he will inherit the Heavens and the throne of Olympus as my heir."

Persephone broke into a broad smile and her eyes went wide with delight. She took no notice of the pain and anger twisting her husband's features. Aidon quickly disciplined his expression, not wanting to give Zeus the satisfaction. The oath was pushed from his mind utterly when Persephone ran to him for a last embrace.

He closed his lips over hers and lifted her up on the tips of her toes to bring her closer to him. She slipped in the mud and as he tried to steady them, they crashed to their knees. Persephone giggled, and Aidon smiled against her lips, ignoring the wet earth seeping through his clothes. Propriety be damned— it would be six months before he could hold her again. In this moment, the rest of the assembled gods didn't exist, as far as he was concerned.

Demeter watched them with a mix of disgust and anger. She opened her mouth to speak, but Zeus put his hand on her shoulder. She began to wrest herself away from him, but he tightened his grip.

"Let them," he muttered quietly in her ear. "The allure of the forbidden is all they have. Speak against it, and you will only fan the flames."

"What would you have me do?" She ground out through clenched teeth. "My daughter has bound herself to a monster."

"Nothing lasts forever, Deme," he said. "She will tire of him, or he will betray her. It is only a matter of which one will happen first. Their yearly absence from each other will be too long to sustain this... infatuation. Love doesn't last among our kind. They will learn that cruel lesson eventually."

"Or you are witnessing here what shall be for all time," Hecate said, appearing behind them and startling both.

"What would you know of it?" Demeter hissed.

"Only what I can see. We are, none of us, as infinite nor omnipotent as we would like to believe." She smiled and looked on as the lovers ended their kiss. "And they shall outlast us all."

Persephone ran her fingers down his cheek, knowing that his palm had likely streaked her hair and neck with fertile earth. She didn't care. She would have him again. It wasn't goodbye. She had succeeded. And Zeus's promise held more hope for them yet.

"You should have told me," he whispered to her, "and trusted me."

"I needed to do it this way, Aidon. It was the only way to save us. To save you."

He smiled at her, though his forehead crinkled with anxiety, thinking about the long months to come. He stood and pulled her up with him. His cloak and tunic were caked with mud, as was her dress. "I love you, Persephone."

"I love you, Aidon. My dear Hades… I will see you soon."

"Not soon enough," he whispered.

"Make it sooner," she whispered into his ear, grasping at the collar of his tunic, "and perhaps we can try to fulfill *our* part in that new oath he swore."

He swallowed and his arms tensed at her words. "I will try to come to you. But we have much to do to fix all this."

With a last, soft kiss Aidoneus separated from her and walked toward his chariot. His demeanor darkened as he paused to confront Demeter. "Mark my words. After the last stalk of wheat is cut, she is mine. The Underworld will have her back, whether you will it or not. So I suggest you make that transition go smoothly. For her sake *and yours.*"

"What do you mean by that?" Demeter's voice cut like blades.

"Your chief concern should be that your new cult of worshippers doesn't forsake you when she leaves again," he said, delighting in the brief flash of worry that crossed Demeter's face. "They will need an explanation, no? As for my wife's journey, Hermes will fetch her."

"What?" the Messenger whined.

"He will be the one to take her home."

"You've got to be—"

"My daughter's *home* is—"

"The world below," Hecate finished.

Demeter held her tongue. As Zeus had said, it would only fan the flames.

Hecate matched Aidon's pace, then climbed into the chariot with him, helped up by his proffered hand. He shook the reins and the horses trotted, circling around the gathering of gods. The wheels left deep grooves in the fresh earth. When Aidon passed by Persephone, he leaned toward her. Their fingertips brushed past each other, a last touch before he made his way toward the mouth of the cave. Aidoneus looked behind him at Persephone's vanishing form, and then disappeared into the earth, leaving his love and the sunlit world behind him.

14.

THE LONG CHARIOT RIDE FROM CHTHONIA TO THE realms of mortals had left Persephone drained. Between gripping the edge of the swiftly drawn basket and bracing herself against the rigors of Hermes's driving, her muscles were sore from calves to shoulders. The confrontation with her mother, husband, and the King of the Gods had only exacerbated the strain she endured during the very creation of Spring itself. She was worn out, body, mind, heart, and soul. A soft bed and a dark room seemed the most welcome things in the warm, living world.

But rather than restful solitude, she'd found cheering throngs of starving mortals when she walked through the doors of the Telesterion. They'd thrown sheaves of barley at her feet and greeted the Goddess of Spring with happy tears, thanksgiving, and shouts of *Kore!* The Maiden. *Karpophoros!* The bringer of fruit. *She has returned!* She suspected she ought to bask in the glory. This was what she had risked so much for— the mortals would be saved, and she had earned a heroine's welcome.

Persephone just wanted to go home.

She remained tight lipped and distant throughout the evening festivities, needing sleep, something she had sorely lacked in the previous days. Her heart twisted, thinking back on her admission of love to Aidoneus, then to a joyful day in the grove followed by a sorrowful night in their room. Had it only been two days since she admitted that she loved him? Had it only been hours ago that she was convinced that she carried his child? Tears blurred her eyes when she walked up the steps of her mother's dais in the great temple, and a wreath of wheat and barley sheaves was placed on her head, covering her crown of asphodel.

They sang and rejoiced, and Persephone took her place on a newly fashioned throne, of smaller stature than her mother's. A tall, blond man Persephone didn't recognize spoke to the congregation about how fertility had returned, reassuring them that new crops would be planted, that the fields would yield twice as much as before Kore had been carried away to the Realm of the Dead.

When the moon rose high in the sky, Metaneira led her to her new bedchamber. No longer would she sleep under the stars on rushes and fertile earth, but in a room of stone and wood with a thin window. The former Queen of Eleusis, still buried in grief by the loss of all three of her daughters, had told her that the room once belonged to Kallithoe, her eldest girl, who was to be married before the winter had killed both her and her betrothed. When the woman's face contorted with sadness, Persephone threw her arms around her to comfort her. Metaneira stiffened at first, but relaxed and finally broke down sobbing, letting her sadness overflow its banks.

Persephone, despite her weariness, invited Metaneira into her room. She sat beside her, telling her about the peaceful fields where Kallithoe and her sisters resided. She described to the former queen, now Demeter's priestess, how beautiful the Fields of Asphodel were, how glorious the light of dawn was when it shone through the Styx. She described the palace and the garden wistfully. At Metaneira's insistence, she spoke a little about Hades, his strength and tenderness, and how

232

he'd spent aeons shepherding the souls and looking after them. Then Persephone shared something that Metaneira hadn't even considered— that Kallithoe's soul, that all the souls in Asphodel, would one day drink from the Lethe and be reborn to the world above.

Metaneira held Persephone's hands tightly and thanked he. This was, she said, the first true peace she had felt since the loss of her daughters. She confided in Persephone in hushed, anxious tones that throughout her service to Demeter, she had tried to be a good follower, but that some part of her felt absent until now. When Persephone yawned, Metaneira apologized for keeping her up so late, and sweetly drew back the blankets for her, tucking her in and snuffing out the oil lamp hanging next to the door before softly closing it. Persephone smiled for the first time since she and her husband had parted, satisfied far more by their exchange than any cheering throng of mortals. Still, sleep eluded her.

Before long, Persephone heard breathy gasps and the rhythmic creaking of a bed frame down the hall from her. Once she realized the source of the noises, she wrapped a pillow around her ears to drown out the lovers: the tall man from the ceremony, Triptolemus— and her mother. Her insides twisted. While she had been wrenched away from her beloved husband, Demeter writhed with delight. She wanted most of all to use the Key of Hades and escape this unfamiliar place, and crawl into bed beside Aidoneus. But she didn't dare undo the fruits of her sacrificed, all she had won.

Her restless mind drifted to her conversation with Metaneira. She was astounded that the mortals knew none of the truth about life after death and the inevitable journey back to the living world. They seemed to believe that life was a path from the womb to the grave, and death a dismal eternity spent shuffling about in darkness and loneliness. They feared that fiery torment and being torn to pieces by Keres and Erinyes awaited them if they so much as sneezed the wrong way during their mortal lives.

Hades had no priests to instruct them otherwise. The only stories about the Other Side came from self-proclaimed necromancers who could fool a crowd with ergot-induced delirium, thrown voices, and linen 'ghosts' flying on sinuous threads, more concerned with pocketing drachma than the truth of the afterlife. How would they ever learn the truth?

Persephone would tell the mortals the truth about what lay before them on the Other Side. She owed it to her husband, and to herself, to reveal the mysterious world below. She would be an emissary during her exile to the world above

She would give the mortals hope.

Her courses came again two week later, the natural way, her body aligning itself with the rhythms of the moon and smashing any hopes she had of carrying Aidon's child. After they subsided, Persephone stopped dressing in the dark colors and heavy jewels of a queen. She donned a sage green peplos, embracing her role in the world above: the Goddess of Spring. She found that it eased the minds of the villagers. She wove crocuses and lilies into her hair alongside asphodel, and later pear and apple blossoms, and at last her beloved larkspur when it finally appeared on the green hillsides.

Hermes visited almost weekly to gather lost souls. Ghosts were being drawn to Eleusis by the presence of their grieving relatives, and by the lingering hunger for food. She would ask him each time if there were any messages from her husband, but Hermes always replied the same way: he hadn't spoken with him, but he was sure Hades thought of her often. Hermes insisted that the Lord of the Dead was buried in work trying to restore order to his kingdom. Another full moon came and went. No change, no messages. Then another full moon. Nothing. Persephone began to worry that excluding Aidoneus from her decision to eat the pomegranate seeds had been unwise. Her husband knew her well. He must have guessed by now that the Pomegranate Agreement, as it had become known, was her idea. How poorly had he truly taken it? Her lingering fear was that Aidon felt in his heart that she had betrayed him.

When Hermes would ask if she had a message for Aidon, she would decline. She was bursting with things to tell her husband, but nothing she said to Hermes would be secret for long. Their marriage, and what Persephone had done to ensure that it would continue, was already the juiciest gossip among the immortals.

☆   ☆   ☆

Persephone sat under the great olive tree where the road curved, a piece of shade in the noonday sun. The days were warmer. Shoots of wheat rose green and proud in every field, their second set of leaves fluttering in the breeze.

"Persephone?"

She nearly dropped her cup of kykeon. "Athena? Athena! I wasn't expecting you!"

They embraced, and the Goddess of Wisdom leaned against the tree, running her thumb under a strap on her cuirass. Her eyes darted to Persephone's hands clutched around the clay cup. "You don't mind me calling you that? Instead of Kore?"

"What, my given name? No. I prefer it."

"Ah. I had heard… I thought that after your time there, you might not want to…"

"No." Persephone hesitated to say more. Athena looked at her cup again. "Would you like some?"

"What is it?"

"Kykeon. My mother's priests make it every day. I drink it sometimes, for their sake."

"Is it some sort of mead or wine?"

"No. Try it."

Athena took the cup from her, sipping from the other side. "Sweet, simple. It's… comforting. Are you sure there are no spirits in this?"

Persephone laughed. "It's just barley and honey, and a little bit of thyme. Mother doesn't allow spirits in her house. And the souls in Aidon's realm didn't drink wine."

Athena looked around nervously. "There were no pomegranates there either, until you arrived. At least, according to Hermes."

"Well, no. Athena, is everything alright?"

"Yes. But more importantly," she said slinking down to sit beside Persephone on the grass, "are you?"

"Of course."

"So Hades didn't force you to eat the seeds?"

"No."

Athena let out a sigh. "I had worried— Artemis had worried too— the last day we saw you, that he may have... made certain demands on you. You being his wife, and such."

"I chose to eat the seeds." She smiled. "And I'd hardly call what we had 'demands'. We..."

Athena leaned forward, waiting for the Goddess of Spring to elaborate.

Persephone pursed her lips. "Athena, whatever you might have heard..."

"No one speaks of it. At least not with me."

"So you came to me directly."

She looked down and stayed silent for a moment. Persephone emptied the cup, and Athena brightened. "I'm sorry. I was only trying to make small talk. That wasn't what I came for."

"Then what?"

"I came to ask a favor."

Persephone sat back. "I'm listening."

Athena stood and plucked an olive branch. "This."

"The olives."

"They take a full year to fruit."

"Yes."

"And they were ripening for this year when… you were taken away."

"Winter was hard on everything."

"Yes. But that's what I've come to ask you. Can you make the olives fruit before you leave?"

"Four *months*? Why come to me? Aren't they your domain?"

"Yes. But…" She sighed. "Persephone, only you can make them grow. I'm just concerned with how the oil is pressed and used. The mortals need the oil for so many—"

"Say no more."

"Then you will?"

"I won't be able to do it alone. Mother will have to help, but I can't imagine her objecting. It's important. Especially to your city."

Athena nodded. "Thank you. I knew you would understand. You know what it's like, since you're the patroness of Eleusis."

She guffawed. "I wouldn't go so far as to call me a 'patroness' of anything."

"You mean more to them than you know."

"I only make them uncomfortable."

"My city was wary of me, at first." She rolled her eyes. "They were as reliant on Poseidon as these people were on your mother. But give them time. You'll see."

※　　※　　※

Some mortals, too weak to eat, could not be saved, and their passing prompted several quick visits from Death. When Persephone and Thanatos finally crossed paths, he bowed to one knee before her, shifting from desiccated skeleton to vital youth, and when he stood he surprised him with a quick hug. She asked him for any word from her husband. Thanatos replied that he had been so occupied with hunting down Sisyphus and reaping the last victims of winter that he'd had no chance to see Aidon. Thanatos placed a

237

hand on Persephone's slumped shoulder and assured her that her husband missed her greatly. It didn't comfort her.

She was becoming increasingly frustrated by his absence. He'd intimated that he'd come to her. The days were a drudgery, the sun taking forever to set. Each night without him was an eternity of shifting this way and that. She would touch herself between her legs, trying to mimic his caress. It satisfied her, momentarily. But then she would lay alone in the dark, breathing unevenly and staring through the window at the thin crescent moon, and the craving for him, for Hades himself, grew that much stronger. No matter how fast her fingers had worked, his strong arms weren't there to hold her afterward. Her bed was not theirs. The Telesterion wasn't her home.

Each day the sun rose higher and more winter pilgrims left Eleusis to return home and rebuild. Hellas mourned its dead and the people regained their strength by boiling the asphodel roots that Persephone had sprouted in the boggy snow run-off. After the last quarter moon, Eleusis was again home to its usual pastoral residents, their numbers thinned by those who hadn't survived the harsh winter. A few Eleusinians approached her, cautiously at first, and then in greater numbers with each passing day, asking after their deceased loved ones.

Persephone told them what awaited all mortals on the Other Side, and explained the rebirth that followed. Most looked at her with glazed expressions, disbelieving her, but more and more people took comfort in her tales. A few families planted pomegranate orchards, and started leaving small amphorae of olive oil and obolos near the cave where Persephone had emerged. The amphorae were later joined by images of her and her husband: at first, grass and stick figures bound together with twine, then images carved from wood.

The offerings and devotions heartened Persephone. She was glad to bring hope to the weary mortals that floated through her days like windborne seeds. Still, she felt like an interloper in this world where she had once been adored. Celeus and Triptolemus were devoted to Demeter alone and would politely dismiss themselves from her company if she spoke of the Underworld. Triptolemus's student Diocles was afraid of Persephone, and always addressed her formally as Daughter of Demeter, with a quick nod and an equally quick excuse to leave. Not all of her mother's followers gave her the same stiff reception, and she'd found strong allies in Eumolpus and his students. Metaneira was typically reserved, but would share an evening with her every so often, and even laughed when Persephone had described fearsome Cerberus loping through the garden, chasing after a thrown stick like a playful puppy.

While she felt her progress with the Eleusinians was slow and stilted, the land told another story. Chickpeas and white beans grew amidst stocks of asphodel, and the first olives were starting to reappear, helped out of their dormancy at Athena's request. The bitter first harvest of figs was fed to the goats in a desperate attempt to keep the hungry beasts away from the growing cabbage. Sage and savory grew in small patches, plucked by the women to season and dry the fish that the men caught while the crops grew.

The mortals were growing healthier, their sallow cheeks turning blush again, their gray-tinged skin restored to a bronze sheen in the abundant sunlight. They had shown their gratitude for the land's rebirth— those who traveled between Athens and Eleusis had renamed this seaside road The Sacred Way.

✳   ✳   ✳

Persephone, chaperoned by Minthe, walked barefoot down the wide path, the packed earth warm underneath her feet. Pomegranate trees grew alongside it, their bright red flowers humming with bees. The petals were ready to drop off any day and free the fruits to swell. To the east, broad fields of golden wheat swayed in the cool ocean breeze.

With every step she took, she felt energy charge from her and through the earth, encouraging the healthy grain to grow stronger and fuller. This week would be the first harvest of wheat and barley. The mortals' despair had been supplanted by excitement to see their labors yield more grain. They sang the praises of Triptolemus and his teachings, and were preparing a festival for the longest day of the year.

Minthe bent down and ran her fingers through a clump of sweet pennyroyal that grew wild beside the path. Guilt had kept Persephone from objecting to Demeter's insistence that the nymph accompany her wherever she went. Minthe had been forced to trade herself to mortals and rustic gods for warmth and shelter during the winter. Many of her naiad cousins and dryad friends had not been even that fortunate. Her arms were thin, her wrists and ankles bony. Minthe's hair was flat and lusterless and she wrapped a light green linen fillet into her chignon to hide its thinness. She picked a sprig of pennyroyal and tucked it behind her ear.

"Minthe?"

"Hmm?" Minthe answered, absently twirling a tendril of blonde hair.

"Your mother came from the Styx, did she not?"

"From near there—Acheron. But... she left the company of the Stygian nymphs just before I was born."

"Do you know why she left?" Persephone asked, curious to learn more about her home.

"She had... performed some sort of rite with a river god from the world above. That's how I was conceived. She traveled here to tell him that he'd sired me. But my mother didn't return to the world below because she was trying to distance herself from... a regret."

Thanatos, Persephone guessed. Given his penchant for Underworld nymphs, it wouldn't surprise her. That Demeter had taken mother and unborn child under her wing didn't surprise her, either— Minthe's mother must have despised the Underworld almost as much as Demeter despised its king.

A group of mortal women, with their hair pulled back, *apodesmos* wrapped over their breasts, and linen skirts tucked about their waists, carefully marked off with twine the matured patches of wheat that would fall under their sickles later that week. One rose and waved to Persephone, and the others followed her lead, calling out "Karpophoros!"

No one ever called Persephone by her true name. They gladly used her epithets, save one— not a soul dared call her the Destroyer. She waved back at them and smiled. Most Eleusinians now treated her with the same informality as these women did, and she encouraged it. She was not a Queen in the world above, and it made talking to the mortals easier.

"Soteira! My Lady!" A voice called out. Eumolpus jogged down the road, sweating under his priestly himation and the midday sun. He stopped, breathing hard, his hands on his knees. "Last month, you asked me to look for a man. Dimitris."

"Yes? There are several who live here, but none of them the one I was looking for. I'm afraid the worst may have happened, and he perished."

"Not so, my lady. True, there are five who live in Eleusis, but did *all* of them fell a fig tree during the winter…?" He gave her a cautious half smile.

"Have you found him?" Persephone's eyes lit up.

"It was difficult. Their whole wedding party rests in Asphodel. But the few guests who survived say his bride's name was Melia. You'll be surprised. He lives close by… Just up the road, Soteira. He's never come to the Telesterion."

"Please, Eumolpus, take me to him!" She picked up her skirts to walk faster, Minthe right behind her.

They came to a stone fence alongside the road. Behind it, a row of ash trees shaded a small cottage, and they heard the arrhythmic scrape of metal against stone. They were not far from the oak glen where she had witnessed the Eleusinian wedding, Persephone realized. Eumolpus pushed through a low wooden gate and led them through the trees, where they found a young man, his features aged by grief and hunger, furrowing the rocky soil with a plow.

"Dimitris?" Persephone called out.

"Who asks, woman?" The plow stopped and the farmer wiped the sweat from his brow. He narrowed his eyes at Eumolpus and his priest's robes. "And who cares?"

Eumolpus bristled. "Show some respect! It is the Maiden who addresses you."

The man scoffed. "What has the Maiden or the Mother ever given me but misfortune?" He lifted the arms of the plow again. "Stay off my land, priest, and let me tend my field."

"How dare—"

Persephone silenced Eumolpus with a glance and he took a hasty step back to stand with Minthe by the gate. The farmer pushed muddy rocks aside, ignoring her. Persephone walked to a pile of white stones beside a fresh tree stump and knelt. "You felled and burned your family's fig tree to melt the frost and soften the earth. That was four days before winter ended."

Dimitris stopped abruptly and turned to her, his eyes wide and his face drawn. "What?"

"It was the only way to bury your wife in the frozen ground."

His forehead creased. "How do you know this?"

"Because she told me." Persephone rose to face him.

"You lie," he growled.

Persephone knit her brow, then reminded herself that this man was still deeply grieved. "You tended to Melia when she fell ill on the way back from Athens. Your wife told me how much you loved her, Dimitris."

The man faltered, then sat down on the tilled earth and buried his face in his hands. His shoulders slumped.

"Did she tell you everything else? About how your mother condemned us to wander in the bitter cold, and only offered up food when it was too late? And how I had to watch the only woman I ever loved *die*, thanks to you petty gods," he spat out at her. Persephone touched his shoulder and he flinched, expecting to be struck dead by the goddess, and not particularly caring if he were.

"All she could speak about was you, Dimitris, and how much she loved you."

He shook again, his eyes and nose running with tears. Persephone lightly placed her hand on his back. His voice cracked. "Melia…"

"I'm sorry," she said.

"Why are you here, milady?" He spoke softly. "I'm a farmer, not an initiate. Surely you'd have better luck with—"

"I'm not here to convince you to join the masses at the Telesterion, Dimitris. I'm here because Melia needs to go back."

He stared at her. "What do you mean?"

"Do you still feel her presence?"

"I try not to."

"The memories are painful, no?"

He nodded.

"You will have no peace unless you let me help you. She was drawn back to the world of the living. Melia didn't cross the Styx as you prepared her to do. She loved you, but didn't want to let go, and now she is staying here and hurting you."

"If Melia *is* here, then let her stay! At least let her— let me have that, if I cannot hold her."

"Your wife is gone, Dimitris. She needs peace. After all you did to safeguard her journey to the Other Side— burying her at home, giving her coin for passage, loving her as much as you did, please help me make sure she returns where she belongs."

"And where does she *belong* after defying Hades and escaping the Underworld? Are you tricking me into sending her to Tartarus?"

"I would never dream of doing that. Dimitris, a beautiful field filled with flowers awaits her."

She stopped when the farmer looked at her skeptically. His wife deserved more than Asphodel. Melia and Dimitris had gifted her with more than they could ever know. How frightened would she have been the first time she saw Aidoneus if she hadn't first seen the joy in *their* marriage?

Persephone gulped in a breath. What did she want for Melia? "She will have warmth; and light. Melia is going to a place where soft breezes will fan her skin and there will be grass under her feet, trees to shade her, and cool water to drink. She will laugh and smile, and know no pain or fear ever again. And one day, a day long from now, Fates willing, you will be reunited with her."

Persephone averted her eyes, her stomach twisting with the many half-truths and falsehoods that had fallen so easily from her mouth. She'd described many parts of Chthonia, some obliquely, but not any one place. She rubbed her arm and hoped that the farmer couldn't see how uncomfortable she was.

"Please help me," she asked.

Dimitris looked out over his empty field and nodded despondently. "What must I do?"

"You must let go," she said, and thought about how Aidoneus had used those same words countless times with the shades. "When she is freed of her grief, Melia will return to the Other Side, cross the Styx, and drink from the Lethe. All her sadness will be forgotten."

"What if she doesn't want to forget?" He clenched his teeth. "What if I don't want to forget?"

Persephone sat beside the farmer. "It hurts her more to keep her pain and memories. As it does for you now. One day, after she has rested in Asphodel, her soul will return to the living world."

"No one returns from there, my lady," he said, shaking his head.

"No," Persephone answered, "Death is not the end. It's just another place along the path. The beginning of another journey. You are a child, and then you are a man, and then you are an elder, and then, it is true, your flesh goes back to the earth. But your soul is eternal and will return again and again to learn more. To grow."

Dimitris shook his head. "I— how do you know this, Karpophoros?"

"Because I am not merely the Unseen One's captive bedmate when I am on the Other Side. I am the Good Counselor's wife, his counterpart in overseeing the souls and taking care of them. I am the Queen of the Dead."

He shuddered and blinked, cold racing through him, though she'd avoided referring to her husband by name.

"Can you help me, Dimitris?"

"I'll try, my lady."

A sudden clatter of shattering pottery caused the farmer to jump. "Does that happen often?" Persephone asked.

He frowned. "In truth, too many such things have happened in the last few months. Sounds, voices… I feared I was going mad."

"Do something for me," she said, remembering how Hermes had coaxed a stubborn ghost from her daughter's home a fortnight ago. "Think of her. Think of Melia as she was. Your happiest memory of her."

"Our wedding day."

Persephone smiled to herself. She too remembered the ecstatic joy they'd shared in the grove. "Hold fast to that image of her in your mind, Dimitris."

He closed his eyes and nodded.

245

Persephone stood and paced slowly to the house. The air was colder here, and her limbs felt heavier the closer she came. "Melia?"

Silence.

"It's Kore."

A charred branch clattered to the floor next to the hearth, accompanied by a low moan. Persephone balked suddenly unsure of how to proceed. Hermes had retrieved plenty of lost souls, but he had been doing so for millennia, not months. She took a deep breath. *Trust your instincts*, she thought. *Trust in your fated role.*

"Melia, it's time to go. Please." She put her hand on the windowsill and heard soft weeping. "See what Dimitris sees of you."

The cries stopped.

"You will always have your love for him. He will always be with you." The ash trees above them rustled in as if in a gust. "And before you know it you will see him again. But please Melia, it's time to go home."

The leaves murmured gently again and the air grew frigid for a moment. Dimitris wrapped his hands around his shoulders and gooseflesh prickled Persephone's arms. Wisps of exhaled breath drifted in front of them. A voice whispered through the trees... *Dimitris... my Dimitris...* and was gone.

A warm summer breeze chased the chill air, and the farmer stood, sighing heavily, letting the burden ease from his shoulders. "Soteira..."

Persephone smiled. "She went home."

Dimitris stared at the dirt, then dropped to one knee in front of her. "Forgive me, please. Forgive how I spoke to you earlier."

"I already have."

Dimitris swallowed. "Would you and your companions do me the honor of sharing a meal with me?"

"I'd love to," she said. "Will you tell me more about yourself and Melia?"

Dimitris smiled and nodded, realizing as he did that he'd grown accustomed to answering such questions with a resentful 'no.' He missed Melia, but visions of her slumped against their meager belongings had been supplanted by thoughts of her smiling as she fed him honeyed cake at their wedding. "I'd love to."

The farmer broke open a heavy loaf of barley bread. Dimitris had traded for it with his neighbor, he'd said, in exchange for a pheasant he'd shot down last week. Persephone, Minthe, and Eumolpus sat with him around his table and broke bread. Minthe ate her share quickly, despite trying to pace herself. Persephone noticed that her ribs were still prominent under her chiton.

Dimitris dug through his stores for a small cask of wine and poured it into a kylix in the center of the table. Eumolpus was unable to hide his glee, having been denied this indulgence while in service to Demeter. He soaked his bread through and savored each dripping morsel. Persephone politely declined when the wine came to her.

"There is no sun on the Other Side, yet there is light?" Dimitris asked as he took away the empty bowl.

"It's quite beautiful," Persephone said. A slightly tipsy Eumolpus smiled and gazed longingly at Minthe, who demurred and shifted in her seat. The pretty nymph nervously listened to the spring goddess continue. "I cannot describe how awe-inspiring the dawn really is. You'll see one day."

Dimitris leaned his head in his hand. "And when I eventually do, I will be reunited with my Melia?"

"Yes," Persephone answered, then thinned her lips. "And no."

Dimitris looked at her in horror. "But you said... she's not sent to Tartarus, is she?"

"Of course not, I promise. From what you've told me of her, the judges would *never* send her there." She was interrupted by loud cawing outside.

"Then what do you mean?"

"Well…" Persephone paused to consider how best to explain the effects of the Lethe when a crow landed on the fence just outside the door. It flapped its wings loudly as it steadied itself then started its cries again. The bird picked at a burlap sack slung over the piled stones.

"Damnation, not again…" Dimitris swore under his breath. He grabbed a short bow and pulled an arrow from the quiver hung next to the door.

"What's wrong?" Minthe spoke, following Dimitris.

"I didn't spend all day toiling in the field just have that creature steal my seeds!"

"Surely you don't have to kill the poor thing?" Minthe said. "He's only trying to eat."

"Trust me," he muttered, nocking an arrow. "The crows had more than enough to eat this winter."

Before Minthe could nudge his arm and force the arrow from its course, it sailed through the air, puncturing its target with a dull, wet sound. The crow fell off its perch with a shriek and lay on the ground, flapping its wings in futility. The arrow stuck straight up, impaling the creature, pinning it to the dirt.

Persephone frowned at Dimitris and picked up her skirts, grumbling as she walked to where the crow lay. "So unnecessary…"

"Soteira," he said, "You don't understand. That same crow has come here three times now—"

"Well, you finally shot him. Are you pleased?"

"No," Dimitris said, growing pale. "You misunderstand me, milady. My arrow *struck true* the last three days. He won't die."

Persephone looked at him with a mix of confusion and shock, then stood above the bird. Two holes from Dimitris's arrows gaped on its chest, each crusted with blood. The arrow pinning him to the ground stuck out from its heart. The crow stared up at her, flapping its wings intermittently. She pulled the arrow out of the ground, then freed the bird, cradling it in her hand as its breathing steadied.

Persephone could always feel the raw power of all that lay beneath the earth within her, could feel Aidon's presence at the entrance to the Underworld— the cave where she emerged and created Spring. But as she held the injured bird in her hand, she didn't feel death. The last time she had seen Thanatos was when an Eleusinian elder had belatedly succumbed to the hardships of winter and famine. She'd seen and felt death even when Thanatos was not around— after all, beings died every minute, just as flowers bloomed every minute. The gods couldn't be in all places at once. But the essence of Death was missing, as though it didn't exist at all...

"Milady?" Dimitris said. They all startled as the crow righted itself in Persephone's hand, then flew away into the highest branches of the ash tree. They heard it call out at them reproachfully.

"It's a demon!" Eumolpus said quietly, his voice shaking. "One of Echidna's brood..."

"No," Persephone finally said. "It's much worse than that." She looked at the sprig of pennyroyal tucked behind Minthe's ear. The summer heat should have wilted it by now. Instead it was as green and vibrant as when Minthe had plucked it from the roadside.

She reached her hand out to Minthe, who flinched back. Persephone curled her fingers and produced new leaves and a bright purple bud from the pennyroyal. This wasn't natural, even *with* divine intervention.

A frightful question settled heavily on her mind. Where was Death?

15.

THERA WAS AS BEAUTIFUL AS HE REMEMBERED IT. But much had changed in the intervening years. The cliffs were far sheerer than when he'd last seen them. The dropped all the way to the ocean, and part of the island looked like it had collapsed into the sea.

Less than a millennium ago, he'd heard stories of villages obliterated by great waves and molten earth. There had been a glut of new shades that day. In the following year Aidoneus and his court had heard fanciful yarns about a kingdom sinking to its new home below the waves. He'd later learned that the old, fierce empire on Crete, ruled for generations by priestess queens and consort kings, had choked on noxious fumes and been washed away. Minos had wept.

Today, the sky was sapphire blue fading into gold in the west. The setting sun was reflected perfectly in the shallow seas below. There was no special way to get to Thera— it was simply a matter of knowing which road led out where. Every island, every mountain, every valley, and every spring— every place in the sunlit world had a door to the Other Side. All roads led to Chthonia.

It was fortunate that they had chosen this island, he thought. If the journey to the world above caused too many ripples in the ether, their quarry might be alerted to their arrival. They couldn't afford the month-long chase Sisyphus had given them last time. No one could.

The hosts of Hades had been forced to take the long way in order not to disturb any of the boundaries between worlds, turning a journey of minutes into a full day of walking. Thera was far enough away from Ephyra, but close enough to Hellas that it would allow a short journey.

Aidoneus squinted, and the wind pulled a few more curls of his hair out of place. "I've never understood why the sun is always so bright on this island."

"It is the longest day of the year, my lord. Daylight is different above, especially by the sea. She was a sweet girl, but Hemera was always a bit... theatrical," Nyx mused with a smile. The shadow of Erebus curled about her, undisturbed by the light or the breeze.

He looked to the west, the last of Hemera's daylight fading on the horizon. Soon the Tribe of the Oneiroi would be able to rise from beneath the surface and help claim their missing kinsman. Their campaign to rescue him and punish his captor should have been foremost in his mind, but an entirely different matter preoccupied Aidoneus. "I doubt it seems so bright to her."

"Persephone blossomed fully in the light," Hecate said, her crimson himation wrapped around her and blowing back in the wind. Tomorrow she would change her robes to black as her final days as the Crone approached. Stringy wisps of her white hair wafted out from inside the hood.

"And then she returned to the light."

"Your bargain with the Olympians will hold," Nyx said. "They wouldn't risk losing us. My son's capture proves what dire consequences await them when our world is thrown out of balance. And Chthonia will have its Queen."

"The Pomegranate Agreement isn't what I'm concerned about," he said, thinning his lips. "It's been three months. Nothing from Hermes— not a *word* from her."

"You saw the ruin of the world when you came above," Hecate admonished him. "You know what a precarious state it was in— what she was tasked with repairing."

"Yes, I know. But she has been back in the world above for longer than she was ever with me. All the aeons of her life were lived up here, but for those two months." He looked at the sun again, watching it split in half behind a thin cloud and turn vermillion before flashing green against the water and disappearing. "I was here for only ten years. And I know how seductive the world above truly is."

"Its nectar is not so sweet to her as you think. Her heart is in Hades. The king and his realm. She would not have acted as she did if it were not." Hecate placed a wrinkled hand on his shoulder. "You underestimate how much she loves you."

"I only hope you're right," he said grimly. He would have to be cautious. Aidon had told his wife that he would come above at his first opportunity. He'd delayed because the winter had made a mess of his kingdom, and now that he was finally going to see her it was with business, not necessarily for *her*. How angered would she be at him? He'd *promised* her...

"She dreams of you, my lord," Morpheus turned to him, his sightless eyes veiled. Hypnos stood beside him, a hand on his brother's shoulder to guide him across the uneven ground. "I often wondered why you didn't ask me to send you to her, as you did the first time you saw her."

"For the same reason I didn't venture up here myself. Because, my friend," Aidon said, "if I had gone to her in dreams, I couldn't have stopped at just one night. And you have your own responsibilities to your world. As do I."

"I also imagine, my lord," Morpheus said with the rarest of smiles ticking up the corner of his mouth, "that you might not want me there to guide you together in the dream world? That your *activities* wouldn't be as... tame... as the first time I sent you?"

"No, I assure you, they would not." Five months ago, Morpheus's implication would have angered or embarrassed Aidoneus. Instead, the Lord of the Underworld gave the assembled hosts a half smile. He felt no shame now for desiring his queen.

"The Erinyes and the judges guard our home and we are in the world above now, Aidoneus," Nyx said. "If you wonder whether or not she still wants you, answer your own question. Reach out to her."

He nodded and looked about, trying to get his bearings, to speak to her thoughts directly. Aidoneus closed his eyes, and felt his wife's warm presence leagues away.

✻   ✻   ✻

"They're bringing in the wheat as we speak," Triptolemus said, pointing out the villagers to Demeter. " It is unfortunate that the barley was not ready earlier. We could have had time to ferment it before tonight, my lady."

"That might disappoint a few, to be sure."

He shrugged. "There will be plenty to brew after today. Besides— the people need bread before beer."

Persephone stooped every so often to pick up loose grains of barley. Each kernel grew full in her hand. She frowned. They were severed from the earth. Growth should have stopped the moment they were cut.

Her mother and Triptolemus discussed the decorations for that evening, how the early crocus flowers and their precious saffron had yielded beautiful golden dyes, their hue woven into bolts of wool and linen, that Eleusis would be clad in gold tonight and wreathed in olive branches.

Demeter had presented Persephone with a floral crown she'd made that morning, twined with wheat and larkspur. To Persephone's great delight and surprise, Demeter had

253

placed a single asphodel into the center of the crown. It sat next to her bed, ready for the coming evening.

Demeter asked Triptolemus about Metaneira's embroidery, whether or not she needed help, and told him how she would love to help decorate a fresh blanket for baby Demophon, to celebrate him taking his first steps the day before. Triptolemus kissed Demeter on the cheek.

She sighed, wistfully rather than with exasperation. She had grown accustomed to their affection. Perhaps in time, she thought, her mother would understand what she felt for Aidoneus. Demeter had a good example walking by her side that all men were not cruel and domineering, or flighty with their affections like her father, Zeus. Persephone's shoulders slumped. Her mother had a love like that long ago with Iasion, and had kept it from her.

"And what are your plans for the festival, Lady Kore?"

"What?" She looked up at her mother's lover and tried to remember what he'd just said. She didn't mind Triptolemus calling her 'Lady Kore'. It was how his people had always known her. And considering the fate of his sisters during the winter, calling her by her true name would be too painful. "Oh, I'm looking forward to it."

"What worries you, my dear? You've been so distracted the last few days," her mother said, petting Persephone's back. She leaned into Demeter's side.

"Something's not right, Mother. The plants shouldn't stay alive like this after they've been harvested," she said, showing her the filled-out grains. "And the things people have been saying about the fish they've caught..."

"Have you considered that the balance is just swaying the other way?"

"I don't think it works like that," she muttered to herself. She turned to Triptolemus. "Can the mortals even eat what they've caught or harvested if it cannot die?"

"The soil is more alive than it's ever been," Triptolemus said cautiously as they walked back toward the Telesterion.

He scooped up a handful of soil to examine it. "And the people are stronger than ever. No one in Eleusis has passed away for nearly a week. Why should we wish for Death to visit us again?"

The sky turned gold with the last rays of sunlight. Persephone looked at the moist clump of dirt in his hand and pulled a wriggling earthworm from it. "Because *this* little one still needs to eat. The living need the dead…"

"Honestly, Kore, must you be so morbid?" Demeter huffed. At times like this she felt that her daughter was here only in body. Demeter couldn't help but think that even though her daughter was promised to be with her for six months, she would never again see Kore as she was. The changes in her daughter were irrevocable. Persephone, somber, analytical, and forever tainted by her ravisher, walked beside her now. "This isn't anything you should be worrying about."

"But it is serious, Mother."

"Maybe your mother is right. Perhaps the balance is just restoring itself," Triptolemus timidly interjected. "An absence of life followed by an abundance of it."

"But this isn't *abundance*. Nor is it about life. We have been working to restore it, but—"

"My dear, this is a *good* thing," Demeter interrupted. "The crops are growing faster and faster."

"But that in itself is a problem! It's built on artifice. Plants must die so that others may live. Fertile soil is created that way. Triptolemus, *you* teach that at Mother's behest," she argued. The young man cleared his throat.

Demeter waved off her daughter's concerns. "There was enough suffering in the winter. This must be Gaia's doing."

"The earth doesn't just *right* itself."

"Gaia has enough sense to preserve *herself*, dear."

"But not in a way that always favors the mortals. That was why everything froze— because all fertility was leached out of the earth."

"And now it's back."

"Mother…" Persephone bit her cheek in frustration. "There's something fundamentally wrong with all this and I need to find out what it is."

"And how do you propose to do that?"

"I…"

"Thanatos is your captor's right hand— his agent in the world above. What if this is some base trick to make you go back to the Land of the Dead earlier than you ought?"

Triptolemus swallowed and stayed silent, knowing better than to get involved. Persephone scared him almost as much as she terrified poor Diocles, always speaking about the Other Side with impunity, and filling his own mother's head with fanciful ideas about reborn souls.

Persephone rolled her eyes, dreading where this conversation was turning. "My husband has better things to do than twist the balance of life and death in order to have me seek him out. And he wouldn't care for the words I'd have for him if that turned out to be true."

Demeter grumbled to herself. "It would be just like Aidoneus to do something like this. To be this selfish." Triptolemus deliberately quickened his pace and walked ahead.

"You don't know him," she said, trying to stay calm, trying not to precipitate another fight that she would ultimately lose. Her mother craved the last word. Persephone had learned early to not engage in these arguments. She focused on the sky to calm herself. The clouds were lit with flames of orange and pink. It was beautiful, but dusk here was nothing so brilliant as what she had known in the Underworld…

Demeter likewise didn't want a fight. *Don't fan the flames,* Zeus had wisely advised. She'd put up with Persephone's talk about the Underworld, had overlooked her speaking with Metaneira and even taking Eumolpus under her wing. They'd had a happy peace these last two months, and she could almost see the old innocent light of Kore returning. It shone in the way she hugged an older woman in the village or hitched up her skirts and ran barefoot down the paths between the fields. It was in the fragrant lavender and roses that she wove into her hair. The recent anxious days had marred that, her daughter consumed with the idea that something dreadful had happened to Thanatos. She'd even referred to that baneful creature as her friend.

Persephone scooped up a few more stalks of broken wheat, rolling the fat grains between her fingers. Triptolemus doubled back and joined her when Persephone motioned him over. "Here, you see these?"

Triptolemus looked at them askance. "What about them?"

"These should be dried or rotting into mulch by now… not lying here useless. If their husks cannot feed the wheat that is still alive and growing, then—"

Persephone.

It came like a breath on the wind. She stood tall, the broken sheaves of wheat falling from her open hand.

"Aidon…" Her heart raced. Her skin prickled. Every ounce of her was bent toward awareness of him— pulled in the direction of his voice.

"Who are you—"

"Shh," Persephone hushed Triptolemus and walked forward alone.

"What do you mean 'Aidon'?" Demeter clenched her jaw. "I knew it. I knew it! So calculating… he never misses an opportunity."

Persephone didn't hear her.

Persephone… Wife…

She turned in the voice's direction— southeast. *Aidoneus… Where are you?*

I am coming for you…

She sucked in a breath and she knew he could feel her worry even from so far away.

Not to take you back— not yet. But we need you.

257

His voice was clipped and serious. How betrayed did he feel? How upset was he about the Pomegranate Agreement? For the first time since they had parted, she dreaded seeing him, dreaded that her worst fears would be confirmed. She raised an eyebrow. *Who is 'we'?*

The House of Nyx. Hecate. The Oneiroi.

She straightened her shoulders. *And Thanatos? Where is he?*

He is the reason we need you.

Persephone pursed her lips. She had been right— everything was terribly amiss. She'd spent the whole day trying to explain that to her mother and Triptolemus. But her chest felt heavy and Persephone didn't know what upset her more— that he hadn't come for *her* in all this time or that his aloofness even concerned her at a time like this.

"Here, Persephone," came his voice from just ahead. The rhythmic thud of heavy footfalls followed.

His shadowy outline came into view first, quickly followed by his solid form as he removed the Helm of Darkness. Persephone's breath caught in her throat and her knees faltered before she quickly regained her composure. Hades was dressed in full armor, his golden cuirass and greaves partially concealed by a long black cloak. His expression was as unmoving as the faceplate cradled under one arm. He stood motionless and regarded her; she bit her cheek, wondering why he didn't embrace her. Or at least greet her, for Fate's sake. It had been *three months*.

Aidoneus looked past her for a moment and narrowed his eyes at the angry goddess standing behind his wife. "Calm yourself, Demeter. I'm not here to take her below."

"You have no right to be here at all, *creature*," she ground out.

Aidoneus suppressed an eye roll. Instead, he glanced at— and through— her companion. What he saw in the man's soul shocked him. He raised his eyebrows in surprise, a smile teasing the edges of his mouth. "I'm glad to see Iasion found

258

his way back to you after all these aeons, Demeter. And as your lover, no less."

Persephone turned to Triptolemus and then to her mother, who had turned white.

Triptolemus, who hadn't moved a muscle since Hades appeared, looked from one deity to the other. "Deme?"

"You knew?" Persephone asked her mother, whose teary-eyed panic affirmed her answer. "And you said nothing?" She gently addressed her mother's consort. "Do you see now, Triptolemus? It is as I told you. We all come back from the Other Side…"

Triptolemus wrenched his hand free of Demeter's and took a silent step back. "Who…"

"Iasion was Demeter's lover, destroyed by Zeus. It happened aeons ago, boy," Hades stated without emotion. "His soul crossed over. And you are he."

Triptolemus shook his head in disbelief and backed away from Demeter. "So when I told you about my dreams…"

"Triptolemus," she pleaded with him.

"…you *knew* the entire time…"

"Please, my sweet prince—"

"No!" He interrupted her roughly, then softened his voice and expression when a tear rolled down her cheek. "No. Please, my Lady. I… give me some time to think."

"Triptolemus, wait."

He spun on his heels and paced back to the Telesterion.

"Triptolemus!" Demeter helplessly watching him go. She wiped her eyes roughly with the back of her arm. "How could you…"

"How could I what?" He countered with a sneer. "Tell him the truth?"

Persephone looked up at him, her brow furrowed. *That was cruel, Aidon.*

As cruel as the agreement that separates us? Hades shot back. She blanched. Was he truly that upset with her? Was this why he hadn't spoken with her in all the time they had been parted?

259

Before Demeter could protest again, a swirl of dark mist burst into a winding gyre behind Aidoneus— a pathway over land and sea. From it emerged a woman with skin as pale as starlight, her figure wrapped in darkness that spread into every shadow. Her hair waved weightlessly. A silver-haired, silver winged youth dressed in a shining cuirass led a shrouded blind man forward. In their wake, a thousand shadows spilled forth, faceless creatures with smoky wings and glinting eyes, rising and wafting upward on the breeze like a flock of starlings. An ancient crone emerged last, carrying a four-lamp torch. With a wave of her hand, the path to the ether shut and disappeared.

Persephone walked forward silently and the thousand shadowy dream creatures, the Tribe of the Oneiroi, alighted in the fields and bowed before her. Nyx hovered next to Hecate, Hypnos and Morpheus stood at their side, the torch lighting their faces. Persephone's shoulders drew back, relief and burden warring within her as she stood before all as their ruler.

Demeter stood aghast, the color leached from her skin. The hosts of the Underworld surrounded her and her daughter. Persephone picked up her skirts and walked to Hecate, embracing her. The crone smiled as her wrinkled arms wrapped around her. "It is good to see you, child. My queen."

"Why have you come here?" Demeter blurted out. Persephone moved to stand with the hosts of Hades. Kore was slipping away from her...

"Sisyphus has captured my son, little one." Nyx's voice wavered when she spoke to the earth goddess. "Your daughter must come with us."

Persephone contemplated what this meant for the world above, then quaked when she felt her husband's presence beside her. Aidon's index finger reached ever so slightly forward and trailed along the tendons of her wrist. Persephone shivered and felt her skin prickle with gooseflesh and her insides grow molten. His touch became deliberate, his finger stroking the delicate skin. She glanced up at him. His face was still set in stone. She moved her arm out of his reach and clasped her hands in front of her. She felt sadness and alarm emanate from him for a moment before he held his emotions at bay.

"We will bring her back once this is done, Demeter," said the Lord of the Dead. "I promise."

"This was not part of the agreement, Aidoneus," Demeter seethed, barely leashing her rage.

"The agreement was that she stay above. Which she will. She is not returning below." He placed his hand on Persephone's shoulder and she turned to him. Aidoneus flinched back from her stony expression before he spoke to her. "My queen, Sisyphus holds Thanatos in Ephyra. If he escapes, it might take months to find him again. Months that no one will survive if this imbalance continues. Hypnos has a plan, but—"

"But it is the night of the feast and festival, Kore. You and I were going to celebrate together— the first time we've been able to relax for *months*. This cannot wait another day?"

"Great goddess, if you'll pardon my interruption, it is the celebration of that very festival throughout Hellas that gives us our necessary distraction," Hypnos piped up.

Demeter ignored the winged God of Sleep. Her lip quivered. "Kore, you promised me…"

Persephone felt her insides twist. Her husband stared at her, his eyes awash in sadness and longing, his face set with purpose. Nyx was calm, but Persephone could sense her distress at her son's kidnapping. Hecate looked on expectantly. Persephone took hold of Aidon's hand. "I'll go," she said quietly, trying not to look at her mother's face contorting with hurt.

"Thank you. I cannot do this without you," he said, and gently squeezed her fingers. His thumb traced over the ridge of her knuckles.

261

"Just like that?" Demeter said. "He comes to you out of nowhere, with no warning, and you disappear with him on one of the most important nights of the year?"

"Mother, I'm sorry. I truly am."

"This is preposterous," Demeter said, her voice level. "Here you stand, Hades, with all the hosts of the Under-world—"

"Not all of them," he muttered, still eying Persephone. She felt a chill crawl up her spine and knew immediately what he meant. The Keres.

"—and you expect me to believe that you absolutely must put *my daughter* in danger. And for what?"

"How little credit you give—"

"Mother," Persephone said, "the viability of the first harvest, the offerings at the festival, everything I told you about... it cannot exist without Death," Persephone answered, interrupting her husband and letting go of his hand to stand in front of Demeter. She thought about the crow with the three holes through its heart. There was no time to waste. "Sisyphus escaped from the Underworld just days before I returned to Eleusis. You must understand how important it is that the King of Ephyra be sent to Tartarus. He seeks to bring down all the deathless ones. He tried using the winter famine to his advantage to do so and now—"

"But Kore, why must *you* go?"

"Because I must."

Demeter scowled. That was the kind of answer Hades used to give her during the Titanomachy when she asked him questions. She clenched her jaw and glared at Aidoneus. The Lord of the Dead had irrevocably tainted her daughter. "Can't someone else—"

"It's *my* responsibility, mother."

Demeter held her daughter's arms lightly. "If Sisyphus captured Thanatos, then you know what he has. What he could do to you..."

"Yes."

262

Nyx spoke quietly. "Aristi, we must leave soon. The—"

"So you willingly put yourself in that kind of danger?" Demeter raised her voice, ignoring the Goddess of Night. Her grip tightened. "Sisyphus has the very sickle that Kronos used to castrate Ouranos! Daughter, please. *Please* listen to me. I cannot— I *will not* allow you to come to harm!"

The Goddess of Spring sighed and took a step back. She plucked an asphodel from the wreath in her hair and twirled it in her fingers for a moment. Demeter relaxed her shoulders. Perhaps Kore was coming to her senses.

Persephone flung the bloom to her side. She held her right hand outstretched while it settled to the earth. As soon as it touched the soil, embers radiated from the anthers, blooming into a great ring of flames. Demeter's eyes grew big and she staggered back. Persephone met her gaze serenely, her eyes rimmed with orange fire. Through her haze of fear Demeter maintained her dignity enough to cover her mouth with the back of her wrist and stop herself from screaming.

"Sisyphus *is* dangerous, mother." Persephone said as the Oneiroi lifted into the air and circled about them again. She reached out toward the circle of flames and pulled their destination closer. The walled citadel of Ephyra appeared before them in the widening pathway through the ether. The Queen of the Underworld took a step toward it and looked at her mother one last time. "But so am I."

✻　　✻　　✻

The first sounds to enter his ears were light footsteps and the scrape of a staff along the limestone floor, drawing a circle and six lines. He smelled frankincense and winced as he breathed in, feeling the chains constrict around his chest. His arms hurt the moment he moved them and he remembered that his chains laced through bone and skin, held taut to the wall on either side.

Directly below him was an ornate seat gilded with every jewel imaginable. Sisyphus's throne. He'd been hung above it as a trophy— the triumph of the sorcerer king over Death himself. Sisyphus had led a parade of nobility past him, exclaiming to all in Ephyra that he as god-king held all power in this world over life and Death.

Thanatos blinked his eyes open, his cheekbone still aching and swollen. Yesterday a woman who'd lost her son and husband to the harsh winter had hurled a heavy *kantharos* at him. He could still smell the stale wine dried on his skin. The room was windowless, and he had no idea whether it was day or night. The back of his head stung, and felt wet when he leaned back. Through the pain, he marveled that he was still injured. He'd never stayed injured— or powerless— for this long in all the numberless aeons of his life.

It had been a grand chase across continents— Europa, all the way to the eastern shores of the vast ocean, down through the deserts to mighty Aegyptus, whose people embraced the afterlife without fear and called the god of their dead Osiris. Then through the vast plains and mountains of Asia all the way to the lush valley of many rivers where the king of the dead was known as Yama. Then back to Hellas, until finally Sisyphus led him to Ephyra and snared him in a pit strung with the refashioned Chains that the sorcerer had stolen from the Underworld. Thanatos had fought hard and lost. To his vague recollection, at least three men had died at the touch of his sickle. He'd struggled until a mighty blow landed on the back of his head, sending him reeling into a dark and dreamless sleep. When Thanatos awoke a day later, he was bound in the throne room, immobile. His sickle— his *own weapon*— sat at the side of the throne, out of reach, right next to the man he desperately wanted to kill. He wondered for a moment if this was how Tantalus felt, with the illusory water and figs a finger's length away.

The scene before him had been repeated several times this week. Sisyphus was preparing for yet another mockery of the *hieros gamos*, and his intended mate in the ritual stood by, cloaked under a heavy saffron himation and veil.

"Ah, you're awake again," the god king said with a smile. "You see? It is as I told you a few days ago."

"You talk a lot," Thanatos ground out, "yet never seem to say much. But I'll humor you. What *great truth* do you have to impart upon me this time, *suagroi?*"

Sisyphus smirked at the insult. "That this is the way power changes hands. Nearly all of the Olympian children were begat on the daughters of Titans, all of whose fathers and brothers are in Tartarus, no less. Spoils of war, I suppose. The Children of Kronos handed Zeus the cosmos after the Titanomachy, and he filled it to the brim with his divine children. A wise move, to cement his claim over that of his brothers. Not a single drop of blood needed to be spilt, and all the former domains of the Titans were handed over to those loyal to him by birth."

Thanatos managed a brittle chuckle. "Is that what this farce is all about? I thought this was the only way you could get it up anymore."

The king smiled, his blue eyes sparkling. "You're awfully clever up there on your perch. If only you had been that clever when I captured you." Sisyphus motioned to the woman at his side. She let the cloak and veil fall from her shoulders, revealing long flaxen hair and perfectly curved hips. "No, Death. In truth, this is the only way one of my kind should ever copulate with lesser women."

"Your kind?"

"A father of gods."

Death laughed again until his chest ached. "Oh, where do I even begin? You honestly think that your blithering at your judgement is true, you great fool?"

"Of course. And it would have benefited your king then, in all honesty, to listen to me then. I pleaded my case in the throne room. 'Return me to the sunlit world, and I will consider you an ally and trouble you and yours no more.' If I had turned my attentions to overthrowing Olympus it would have been a boon for him. I can't imagine that Hades is terribly happy with Zeus after the King of the Gods stripped him of his bride for half the year."

"You expected us to make an exception for you? After all you've done?"

"I already explained why you should," he said. "I wouldn't have been condemned in the first place if I hadn't interceded on Asopus's behalf. But I suppose stopping the rape of a goddess isn't worth your king's consideration. Not that I should expect it *would* be, given what Hades did to Demeter's daughter."

"You know nothing." Thanatos narrowed his eyes. "By the by, do you call your bedmate a 'lesser woman' to her face? Or are you fucking yet another girl who doesn't speak Greek or Theoi?"

Sisyphus ignored him and started reciting the words of the ritual in Minoan. The woman lay supine in the center of the circle, propped up on her elbows, her legs apart. The sorcerer knelt between them.

"You know that it was women who created the *hieros gamos*, who chose *their* consorts, you mange-ridden dog, and allowed them to participate. Whatever this farce is, it is for your amusement only."

The woman spoke her words, responding in Minoan and following Sisyphus's lead. Her voice sounded familiar.

"Times change," the king replied. He removed his robes and positioned himself over the woman, reciting the last part in the ancient tongue.

"I watched that empire rise and fall as you would watch a day and night pass. You think that saying those words in a dead language makes them more powerful? Or your actions more legitimate?" He winced, the Chains tearing at his arms with every breath he took. "You can pour perfume on *kopros* all you want, but it's still shit."

Thanatos looked away when the Ephyrean king penetrated her. The woman gasped, but made no sound beyond that. Death turned back to see him rutting above her, propped up by his wrists and knees on the floor, his hips smacking against the girl's thighs as she tried to hold her position on the cold limestone. She let out a soft moan.

"Seem that's the most you can get out of her." Thanatos started laughing.

Sisyphus looked up at him with a glare.

"Am I breaking your concentration?"

The king smirked at him then dropped his gaze back to the girl, redoubling his efforts, driving harder into her.

"You're doing it wrong, you know," Thanatos called out over their rutting. "Not just the fact that you're obviously a pitiful fuck. The position's all wrong and there's words that should have been said during this part. If you or your poor partner knew anything about—"

The woman's spine arched and she let out a long sustained groan, her body thrown into extremis— faked, as Thanatos could easily tell— and as she arched, she looked at him with her wide violet eyes. Thanatos went cold. He knew that face. What was her name again? Philinnia? Lyra? Voleta…

Voleta! One of Hecate's Lampades. A nymph he hadn't seen since he'd had her almost four months ago. *Clever girl*, he thought. *I underestimated you.* If Voleta was here, that might mean she was using the ritual to distract Sisyphus… and lead her mistress, his mother, and his many brothers and sisters straight to them. They were coming to rescue him. He would only have to endure this humiliation for a matter of hours— perhaps minutes.

Sisyphus grabbed her chin and forced her gaze back to his. "Not at him," he growled. "Look at *me!*"

Voleta shook, obviously afraid of the man using her body, trying to beget on her to further his ends. Sisyphus pushed her back to the ground, knocking the air from her

267

and pinning down with his hand at her throat. Thanatos clenched his jaw when her cries turned to pain. Anger renewed his purpose, pushed the discomfort of his bindings out of his mind enough so he could think clearly.

This mating would come to nothing, he knew. If a woman lay down with Death, she arose infertile. It was one of the many reasons Hecate didn't want him copulating with her acolytes. That thought gave him some solace, knowing that she wouldn't have to carry this abomination's seed, but having witnessed Sisyphus with the *kedeshah* on Chios, Thanatos knew there wouldn't be enough time for the Hosts of Hades to find them. He would have to help Voleta, lest her sacrifice be for naught. Like the well-aimed *kantharos* from yesterday, it hit him.

He'd waited. He'd waited days to wield his greatest and most cherished weapon against Sisyphus and thanked the Fates that he hadn't revealed it too soon. He knew it would enrage him. Thanatos might suffer greatly for wounding his pride. But if it did anything to blind the Ephyrean king long enough, it would be worth it. He heard another cry of pain from Voleta as her shoulders scraped across the floor, her hips bruising. Thanatos was resolute. A sacrifice for a sacrifice.

Sweat beaded on Sisyphus's back and his face contorted, close to attaining his pleasure. Death smiled. It was worth it— worth whatever suffering he would endure. "By the way, Sisyphus…"

He grunted, at the crest of his plateau.

"I haven't had a chance to tell you…"

The king gave a penultimate thrust.

"*I fucked your wife!*"

Sisyphus doubled over with a shudder and a halted cry, his eyes wide. He fell to his elbows, his satisfaction ruined.

Thanatos grinned, laughter bubbling up from deep within, and finally spilling out. He didn't care how much the Chains shook and strained. Sisyphus seethed, his jaw clenched. He pulled away from Voleta and stood, staring at Thanatos, saying nothing, donning his robes as the God of Death hooted.

"And she *loved* it," Thanatos laughed. He felt a twinge of guilt. Merope didn't deserve to be shamed in such a way, but it was a means to an end. If he could use the night he spent with her to triumph over her murderer and send him to Tartarus, he would do just that. "My favorite part of Merope was that little mole next to her navel. And your wife tastes so, so very sweet. Like honeyed dates and wine, don't you think? Though judging by her reactions to me, I doubt you ever tasted her as thoroughly as I did. She *begged* for my cock... four, maybe five times that night. I lost count, honestly."

"Enough..."

"I fucked the very memory of you right out of her, Sisyphus!" He yelled over the shaking chains. "Merope loved it so much that she forgot all about you and had enough peace to finally drink from the Lethe!"

"Be silent," Sisyphus snarled, pacing towards the throne.

"*Keratas*!! You might have me in the Chains now, you pathetic *suagroi*, but I'll be out of these bindings eventually. But you, Sisyphus, will burn in Tartarus for eternity wearing a cuckold's horns!"

"I said be silent!" Sisyphus yelled. He grabbed a gold ceremonial *doru* from the wall beside his throne and thrust the long spear under Thanatos's ribs.

His abdomen seared and trails of light flashed behind his eyes. Pain radiated down his leg and through his lungs as he struggled to take in a breath. The wound made by the *doru* couldn't kill him, he knew. If anything could, he'd have been dead from the injuries he'd sustained already. He looked down to see Sisyphus still holding it. He laughed, painfully, his guffaw coming out with a wheeze of air.

"Is that as far in as it can go? No wonder they all feign pleasure with you!" Sisyphus responded as Thanatos predicted, jabbing the *doru* in further. He gritted his teeth, but couldn't hold back a yelp of pain. *Take it*, he thought, *take it as Voleta took it to help set you free. Keep him angry. It's the least you can do.*

The king smirked and propped the butt of the spear against a tile line on the floor. He stepped back and shook his head. "Arrogant, foolish boy..."

"We'll see," Thanatos hissed through his teeth, "won't we?"

"I have an honest question for you." Sisyphus's thin mouth broke into a wide smile. He folded his arms and cocked his head to the side. "Do you think you're buying yourself more time by insulting and distracting me, Thanatos?"

Death's face fell and his skin prickled with cold.

"I know who's coming for you," Sisyphus said. "The entire world knows I have you here. Why else do you think I would show you off like a caged beast? Hades would have to retrieve you eventually, and tonight of all nights: midsummer, the first harvest, when the boundaries between worlds are thin, would be his first, best chance."

Silence hung between them. Voleta staring up at Thanatos from where she lay on the floor. Her eyes watered, horror written across her face.

"You're mad," Death finally whispered. "What could you possibly do to the God of the Underworld?"

"That might be the best part of keeping you here," Sisyphus said. "You'll get to witness it for yourself."

16.

BOOTS PACED BACK AND FORTH THROUGH THE field, crushing grass and gouging the mud with each about face. Ares pulled off his helm for the third time, wiping his brow. It was warm and stiflingly humid this evening. The swine penned in nearby only made the stale air more putrid. The sound of the beasts rooting in the soil further stoked his impatience. "Why must we wait? And who told you we should, anyway?"

"A little bird… with three holes in its breast," Eris said with a smile.

Ares looked at her askance, then huffed and shook his head. Her tattered chiton hung off her left shoulder, the pin falling down one arm. She raised a wing and nudged it back into place. The glimpse of flesh made Ares recall their afternoon together, and he bit his cheek. Eris plucked a rose growing against the fence she sat upon and closed her fist around its thorny stem.

"You want to charge in?" she asked disinterestedly. "Charge in. See what happens. I'm anxious to see you try… Daddy."

"Damn you, I—" Ares silenced himself and fumed. He despised giving her the satisfaction of getting under his skin.

He breathed through his nose until he calmed. "You're going to tell me why I shouldn't."

"I might," she said, splaying her fingers. "But it would be far more entertaining to watch you crash headlong into the wards that sorcerer placed around the city, alert Sisyphus that we're here..." Thorn pricks bloomed red in her hand before closing. "...and see him flee all the way to the Indus, again." She smeared her palm across the white rose petals, turning their edges carmine. "I'd love to see the look on Mother's face as you try to explain your failure."

"Nyx isn't your mother."

"No, she's not," Eris giggled and shrugged. She ripped petals off the bloom and scattered them to the pigs.

"So who is?" Ares asked, immediately regretting it. The beasts shuffled around in the mud, eating the stained petals.

"Maybe my mother is your paramour. The one who says she sprung up from Ouranos's blood?"

He shook his head and snorted. "You look nothing like Aphrodite."

"How would you know? She changes her appearance to suit her needs."

Ares grumbled an acknowledgement. Eris leapt off the fence and sauntered toward the God of War.

"And Aphrodite isn't her *real* name. She is ancient and *her* divine calling is the mother of us all." Eris cocked her head to the side with a smile. "The mother of fucking... You like putting your prick in ancient women, don't you?"

"When will you stop prattling and leave me be?" Ares's face grew red, as he spat out his words.

"As soon as you tell me what it's like to fuck your mother."

He growled and lunged toward her before stopping himself and balling his fists. She threw the decimated rose over her shoulder. A squeal of pain pierced the air, and the herd converged on the fallen swine. Ares took a step backward. Eris spread her wings and clapped her hands together in de-

272

light. "You Olympians are so entertaining! A little insinuation gets you all frothy and raving, yet look at who squirted *you* out!"

"It doesn't work like that with our kind," he mumbled. "You know that…"

"Then you won't mind if I ask Queen Persephone what it's like when she fucks her—"

"You will do no such thing!" His eyes widened. "It would be *unwise* to anger him tonight. Say all you'd like about them once they've gone."

"Weren't you boasting to Thanatos a few months ago that you could rule the world below? My, how you change your tune as they approach. My poor, little Ares…" Eris stroked his clean-shaven jaw and pouted. "The brave and fearless soldier, afraid of the God of the De—"

Ares grasped her throat in one hand, pinning her to the swineherd's fence. He gritted his teeth. "If you were not immortal, I would end you right here. I'd be doing everyone a favor."

"Only one—" she gasped in air and smiled. "There's only one who can kill me."

"If only he would." Ares let go abruptly and stepped away from her. She faltered, bracing herself against the fence.

"Makes you feel a bit… impotent, doesn't it? He is the only one who can kill anything right now," Eris reminded him. She turned her back on him and rested her chin on her folded hands, watching the pigs conclude their feast and slowly spreading her wings. "I wonder… The rose couldn't die. Do you suppose that its petals live on in the bellies of the pigs? Do you think the one they turned against is wriggling in bits inside his friends? I wonder what that's like…"

Ares turned pale, acid welling up in the back of his throat.

"And how do *your* worshippers fare? The Chalcidians are at war with Thrace now, retaliating for the sacking during winter. Tell me: do they stagger about on the killing fields with great holes ripped through them? With missing limbs?" she taunted, hopping around erratically on one foot. "Do they shamble without heads, even?" She laughed, wandering aimlessly. "I'll bet they refuse to fight now, knowing that honorable death is beyond them."

"Why *else* would I be here?" Ares barked.

A breeze blew across them and the air grew colder. The sound of flapping wings engulfed them, as though a great flock of birds had descended on them. Eris smirked. "It seems our wait is over..."

"What do you m-m—"

A four-lamped torch ignited in the dark, silencing Ares. Hecate narrowed her eyes. "Two lonely jackals. Where is the rest of the pack?"

"They must have been too afraid, or are too busy celebrating." Ares folded his arms and lifted his chin. "Where is your master, witch? Afraid to show *his* face?"

"Hardly," Hades said behind him. Ares spun away from Aidoneus and stumbled. Demeter's daughter stood at his side. Ares sneered. Such a fuss had been created over this girl, and for what? She was pretty, and had a little red in her hair, which he liked, but she wasn't worth destroying the world over.

Creatures whirled about them on shadowy wings, a wisp or an outline caught in the meager torchlight, then blurred again by night. A woman wrapped in darkness with unsettling silvery eyes hovered before him. A silver-haired, silver-winged version of Thanatos, who Ares recognized as his twin brother Hypnos, walked forward with a shrouded man who stumbled when his feet touched the ground. Hypnos steadied him. "Easy, Morpheus. We're here."

"Thank the Fates," said the Lord of Dreams. "How many more pompous Olympians must we deal with tonight? I can already *smell* one of them."

Ares scowled and thought of lame Hephaestus. "You bring a blind god and three women with you, Hades? Your little flower girl, no less? You must be very confident or very foolish."

"I advise you to hold your tongue," he said. "She could be of more value here than you ever could."

Persephone smiled to herself, basking in her husband's praise. Ares puffed out his chest, but Persephone noticed the lump in his throat bob. His hands were shaking. Taken aback, she realized that Ares was afraid of her husband. Aidoneus was a hero of the Titanomachy; the God of War had never faced anything that could destroy him. Ares had only slaughtered or sided with one faction of humans or other, moving them around like stones on a *petteia* board. Her husband had vanquished Titans.

"What have you seen so far?" Aidoneus asked.

"A crow. With three holes in it," Eris said, winking at Persephone, who paled. Eris licked her teeth. "Hello, *Mother*."

"Be silent," Nyx hissed. "Abomination of Chaos."

Eris giggled. She turned to Persephone. "You might need me, you know. And you *do* know. Discord may prevail tonight if all else fails."

"How... *uncharacteristic* of the crow to share her baubles..." Hecate muttered.

"I'm not here for *you*," she jeered, scrunching her nose. "That little blood and clay king is holding my favorite fuck captive."

Hades rolled his eyes. "Ares? Anything?"

"Nothing. Mortals celebrating the harvest. Everyone is behind the walls, but none of the gates are barred... those idiots. It would be an easy thing for *two* to rush the gate and go in unseen. You have your Helm, we have our swords. As I said, you brought too many people, Hades," he said.

"I'll likely have no need of my sword."

"What? How in Tartarus do you expect to do anything once the Ephyreans know we're here? That city is a fortress!"

"Perhaps you should watch and learn," Persephone said quietly.

Ares hunched to her eye level. "And what do you know of warfare, little girl?"

"That we needn't slaughter every inhabitant of Ephyra to achieve our ends. We only need the one."

He snorted and rose to speak to Hades. "The walls are five paces thick, and the sorcerer king put up wards around the entire city! This is the time for a siege, or a surprise attack!"

Aidoneus motioned to Hypnos. "Are you and Morpheus ready?"

Hypnos nodded with a half smile. "We are. But Ares is right about one thing. The wards they hide behind need to be dealt with."

"It won't take her long." Nyx smiled, and Hecate slowly hobbled forward. Eris looked on, grinning widely while she pulled up another rose and began plucking its petals.

"Such arrogance. He hangs charms on his wall of sticks and thinks he has outwitted both the witch and the warrior," Hecate said. She raised her torch and stretched her other hand toward Ephyra. The air shifted and grew warmer, the torch blazing brighter than before. The city itself seemed to blur, then grew sharper, its lights brighter. The sound of city folk filled the air where before there had been silence. Tambourines and pipes mixed with drums and laughing voices, all celebrating the bounty of the harvest. The torch flame steadied and diminished, and with a quick puff of air, she blew it out. "Sisyphus forgets that whatever magic he wields is borrowed."

Nyx nodded to Hypnos. With a beat of his wings, he took off toward Ephyra. Sleep hovered far above the city, almost motionless. Voices went quiet and the music died down. Torches fell from men's hands at the top of the walls and spears clattered to the ground.

Morpheus smiled in his mother's direction, then raised his arms to either side. His unseeing eyes saw his own invisible world of shadows and light, each soul within the walled

276

city giving off a slumberous glow. They were empty vessels, waiting to be filled. The Tribe of the Oneiroi massed above him and wound itself into a tight gyre, then flew toward Ephyra. With the Dream Lord's guidance, the Oneiroi possessed every sleeping man, woman and child, filling them with dreams.

Ares squinted. The torches and spears along the outer wall lifted. The music began again, but the rhythm was slower and the melody broken. "What did you do?"

"I awoke them to my domain," Morpheus said.

"What good will that do?"

Hypnos alighted next to Morpheus. "Let's hope the rest of this is as easy, no?"

Morpheus smiled. "One can only hope."

Grass crunched under their feet as they made their way toward the packed earth road leading to the great city gates.

"Wait!" Ares called out. "Stop!"

The Hosts of Hades paused and looked back at him.

"Are you all mad?! Do you think to just walk in there?"

"Yes," Hades answered, annoyance edging into his voice. "Are you coming or not?"

Ares stood dumbfounded until Eris tugged at his arm. "Come on, Daddy."

Ares snarled at the Goddess of Discord and Persephone smiled to herself. His boots thudded behind them. She looked up at Aidon, whose gaze was fixed on the gates of Ephyra. He grasped her hand within his, alternately squeezing her fingers in his tight grip and gently tracing her knuckles with his thumb. He did not return her gaze and Persephone's smile faded. He set his jaw firmly when he felt her displeasure.

You didn't send any word to me, Aidon, she said. *For months. For three long months!*

Persephone, please. . . he said with a quick glance downward.

Please 'what', my lord husband?

He sighed. *There is much to discuss, wife, but we need to speak on it later.*

She bit down so hard her jaw ached. Tears filled her eyes. Then she tamped down her anger and summoned her courage. They were there for Thanatos. Everything else could wait. Aidon's fingers brushed past hers, and for the briefest moment she felt all the longing and regret seeping through the wall he'd built around him. She looked into his eyes. *You promise we will?*

I promise.

They neared the imposing gates of the city of Ephyra. Men in armor staggered listlessly about, torches and spears bobbing, their motions mimicking a sentinel march. Eris giggled.

"Be quiet, woman!" Ares growled. "You want them to know we're here?"

"They wouldn't know me from Deukalion and Pyrrha. Look!"

Ares's jaw dropped. Hoplites stood with long spears in hand and short swords at their sides, but their chins rested on their chests, snoring. Some mumbled incoherently. Ares stared at Morpheus. The Lord of Dreams grinned.

Eris sauntered past the hosts of the Underworld and opened the gates with a groan. She hummed to herself and skipped inside the courtyard. People shuffled about the square, muttering the same wordless nonsense as the guards.

One burst out in laughter, startling Ares. Two musicians played, one so out of tune on his flute it made him queasy. A number of Sisyphus's guards stood around a great barrel of barley mead, their cups sloshing fat drops of thick malt all over the ground, the barrel's spigot a wellspring trickling into the street. Their words rose and fell, but they said nothing intelligible.

If Ares were drunk, more drunk than he'd ever been in his life, this place might feel normal. But he was stone sober, and fear— that detestable emotion, his greatest and most hated frailty— clawed up his throat with every step he took. A child loped past them with a moan and only when Ares looked at the boy's face did he realize that his eyes— and everyone's eyes— were closed.

"Gods above, what dark magic is this?" he whispered.

"Something the gods above aren't capable of," Hades said. "You wanted to charge the walls of Ephyra, Ares? I give you a better strategy— walk right through their front door."

✻   ✻   ✻

Thanatos stared at Sisyphus before belting out a painful laugh. "You… are you serious? *Kill* Hades?"

"Why would I not be? I can do this to *you*, can't I?"

Death's laugh turned into a howl of pain as Sisyphus twisted the *doru* slowly, its sharp tip digging further into his flesh. Gold-tinged ichor dripped onto the floor. He gritted his teeth and looked away.

"You have no idea what you're calling down on yourself!"

"I think I do," Sisyphus said. "I know what I risk to finally end the tyranny of Olympus. Can you think of a better reason than the thousands who suffered and died during Demeter's winter?"

"A winter you made worse…"

"If so, my part pales compared to the destruction caused by the Bitch of Eleusis. Must all suffer because of a petty marriage dispute? With you here, Thanatos, all men are immortal. The equals of the gods. And once the gods are dead, we won't have to live through your famines, your plagues, war and pandemonium, old age… But a point must be made to Zeus. The gods must surrender quickly, or there will be a bloodletting that could cost the lives of all mankind. How better can I show the Olympians that I am now the arbiter of life and death than to destroy one of the three rulers of the cosmos? The *God of the Dead* no less?"

279

He twisted the spear again and Thanatos screamed through his teeth, fearing they would break with how tightly he clenched his jaw. Through pain-blurred eyes he saw Voleta stand and wrap the gold veil around her body. *Run, Voleta. Run. Get away from here.* How he wished he could speak with her where Sisyphus could not hear her— that they had the kind of bond his parents shared, or his king and queen shared. "So confident in your victory. You are the arbiter of nothing! It's only a matter of time before they—"

"They?" Sisyphus stopped and raised his eyebrows. "Just how many are coming to your aid?"

Thanatos was about to answer when Voleta filled the room with an angry cry, female, primal, and determined. She threw her legs around Sisyphus's waist, knocking the air out of him, and rained blows on his shoulders and back. The *doru* clanged loudly to the floor, and the king of Ephyra twisted fruitlessly. Voleta wrapped her arms around his neck, squeezing with all the strength she could muster. Sisyphus gripped her wrists, trying to pry the girl's arms from around his throat.

"Run! What are you doing?!" Thanatos screamed. "Run!"

Sisyphus stumbled and reached back to yank at her hair but cursed when her teeth closed on his hand. He threw an elbow into her ribs and she recoiled, loosening her grip on his throat. He reared his head back, crushing her nose. Voleta yelped as he twisted her around to capture her in his arms, then kicked her feet furiously before going limp and crying.

"Shh-sh-shh... What's this?" He cooed gently in her ear. Sisyphus gripped her jaw, forcing her to look up at Thanatos. "You cannot possibly feel sorry for this creature, can you? This baneful *thing* that killed your kin? So many died during the winter. Surely those you cared for were among them?"

A trickle of blood leaked from Voleta's nose and tears pasted strands of her blonde hair to her cheeks. She stared up at Thanatos, eyes wide and desperate, unable to free herself from the king's grasp. She sniffled and the blood dripped on Sisyphus's hand. He spun her around and let her go. Voleta stood frozen.

"But all women are compassionate creatures, are they not? Is that what this is about? Hmm?" He smiled and tenderly brushed her hair from her eyes. When he saw the rivulet of blood running from her nose and the drops on his hand, his face fell. He lifted his hand to his mouth and tasted it.

Voleta heaved a sob and started backing away.

"Lampades..." Sisyphus growled and advanced on her, his blue eyes like shards of ice.

"No, please..." Her feet failed her. "I'm not—"

"Hecate's spy. I know what the blood of a nymph looks like, girl," he said, gripping her shoulders. "And what it tastes like."

"Please..." she sobbed, and looked up at Death. "Please! Thana—"

The back of Sisyphus's hand cracked against her cheekbone, sending her to the floor. When her head hit the limestone, she stopped moving, her eyes closed, unconscious. The golden veil billowed around her motionless form and settled.

"Voleta!" Thanatos yelled.

Sisyphus turned to him, a cold smile rising on his face. "You know her."

Death only glared, frozen. *You fool, you great ignominious fool,* he thought to himself.

"But the Lampades are part of Hecate's retinue, and if legend serves, you two have aeons of enmity between you."

He remained silent, his lips pursed.

"So how is it that you know this whore?" Sisyphus picked up the *doru* and calmly thrust it back into Thanatos's ribs. "What is she to you?"

Light crackled behind his eyes and agony washed over him anew.

"How many are coming?"

"All of them!" He bellowed. *"Every last one of them!"*

"Who? The Lampades? The Stygians? The Cocytides?" Sisyphus taunted. "A whole clutch of pretty little nymphs you've fornicated with, on their way to save you?"

He screamed again, then glared at Sisyphus and spat on him. The king propped the *doru* on the floor and stepped back, wiping the spittle from his nose and cheek. Thanatos whispered to himself.

"What was that?"

"I said *bastard!*" Death snarled.

"Is that all?"

"You..." he smiled. "I welcome this. Whatever you can dream up, it only gives me more cause to kill you as slowly, as excruciatingly as I can manage, Aeolides," he said, hissing Sisyphus's birth name.

"From up there?" Sisyphus folded his arms across his chest. "That would be *quite* the thing to see."

"The torments you've designed for me will be a *festival* compared to what we will inflict on you... every day a bitter agony... until the ending of the world... And they will be here soon enough."

"And again, boy, who is this 'they'?"

"Every member of my house," Thanatos yelled. "My mother... My numberless brothers and sisters... The wrath of the Queen..."

Sisyphus chuckled and shook his head. "I have summoned enough power to hold back the House of Nyx. And do you really think I'm concerned about a little flower girl? She'll perish faster than her husband. Truly, I cannot thank you enough, son of Nyx, for all you've done for me."

He coughed, trying to ignore the pain of the *doru* digging into him. "And why is that?"

"Because you, Thanatos— and remember this when you watch each of them die— *you* delivered into my hands the means by which I can end the gods. Capturing you and keeping you here is only the honey on the cake. Why do you think I drew you out and let you pursue me when I could have more easily imprisoned your brother?" He picked up the curved sickle, adamantine, its blade flashing in the light of the column braziers. Sisyphus examined it. "You handed to me, on a silver plate, the weapon of the Terrible One. The very sickle Kronos Pantodynamos Ouranides used to destroy his own father. And because I hold you here, death exists in this room alone. If everyone outside these walls is now blessed with eternal life, then the only true power in this world is death, and the cosmos belongs to he who wields it."

Thanatos laughed softly, as much as he could without rattling the spear and causing himself more pain. "You have no idea how that works."

Voleta stirred to consciousness with a low whimper, blinking and trying to get up. A dark bruise was blossoming on her cheek and blood leaked from the corner of her mouth. Thanatos glanced back at her silently, trying to tell her to be brave. It wouldn't be long now…

"No, I don't honestly," the god king replied, twisting the sickle in his hands. He faced Voleta. "But that's easily remedied. What do you say to a demonstration?"

Thanatos opened his eyes wide. "Sisyphus, no… No!"

"After all, I can only prove its effectiveness in your presence, Death."

*   *   *

Ares walked through the agora. Flames licked up from the great raised hearth fire and people stood around it, mumbling, their eyes shut. A soldier staggered toward him,

283

spear in hand. The God of War skirted away from him and drew his sword.

"You should put that away," Morpheus said. "No sense in startling the poor hoplite. You might give him a nightmare."

"What if I did?" he said, cautiously sheathing his weapon.

"Best we not find out here and now, no?"

"They could surround us. And since they cannot die…" Hypnos answered for his elder brother. "Right now they are dreaming of exactly what they were doing before they fell asleep. At a glance it would appear that everyone is going about their business, as though we never arrived. But if you disturb them too much…"

Eris wandered over to one of the womenfolk, about to tap her on the nose. Ares lunged and grabbed her hand. "Touch nothing."

She pouted, but obeyed, following them past the agora, up the great steps and through the colonnades of the palace. The atrium beyond was wide open, its doors leading to many halls. Ares brandished his sword instinctually.

Hades nodded and reached over his shoulder to unsheathe his own. "We're not sure if Hypnos's poppies worked in here. There might be another spell cast over the palace. Hecate?"

"I cannot feel anything," she said, then smiled, pointing at a guard in the hallway who leaned against a column, flirting in his sleep with a swaying, snoring serving girl. The urn in her hand trickled rivulets of sheep's milk, making patterns across the tiled floor.

"Good," Hades said under his breath, putting his sword away.

"Wait," she said, her eyes growing wide and her lips quivering. She clutched a hand to her breast and her voice faltered. "Atropos, no…"

The witch hobbled a few steps, then ran down a hallway. Persephone picked up her skirts and followed, Nyx, Hades and Ares behind them, Hypnos helping Morpheus keep pace.

"What's wrong?" she asked Hecate.

"No, Atropos... Fates, please don't cut..."

"Persephone, get back!" her husband yelled. She slowed her pace as Ares and her husband rushed past her and they overtook Hecate, reaching the ornate double door at the end of the hall. Ares grunted and kicked its lock, the doors slamming apart on its hinges and wood splintering against the adjacent walls.

Hecate faltered, her hand clamped over her mouth, and Persephone caught her in her arms, holding her tightly. She squinted in the bright light of the braziers, peering into the room beyond the doors. Above a jewel encrusted golden throne, a pale figure was strung up in chains. She gasped. Thanatos. A spear was propped up against— no— *inside* his ribcage. Tears ran down his face and he stared, stricken and unmoving, at a crimson pile of cloth on the floor.

"Lord Aidoneus," Sisyphus addressed him calmly.

17.

A SPRAY OF RED MARRED THE KING'S GOLDEN ROBES and dripped from the inner curve of the sickle.

"Careful of the blade," Ares cautioned. "All of you, stay away!"

Hades stepped to Sisyphus's unguarded side. The god king turned to him and feinted a lunge at Hecate and Persephone, forcing Aidon to slide back between him and the women. Sisyphus bolted for the wall, wrenching a golden sword free from a jeweled display. He it in front of him, the blade shaking as Aidoneus advanced.

"You know what I hold."

"I see it, murderer," he growled, circling the Ephyrean and lowering his helm over his face. "A sword in the wrong hand..."

Sisyphus dodged to the right and Hades drew his weapon, swinging it in a hard arc toward the mortal king.

"...Made from the wrong metal..."

The blade cleaved in half in the king's hands.

"...and wielded against one of the deathless ones."

Sisyphus threw the jeweled handle to the side and blocked Aidon's next lunge with the sickle. Sparks flew when they met. Aidon's eyes widened; he hadn't anticipated the king's unnatural strength. Hades finally pushed him back. Sisyphus swung the sickle sloppily and Aidon ducked out of the way, respecting the dangerous weapon. Another lunge, and Aidon knocked the sickle off course, giving ground as Sisyphus hacked at the air between them. Aidoneus vanished from sight and Sisyphus stopped his advance, turning about. "Coward!"

Sisyphus turned his attention toward Ares. The God of War stood frozen, his eyes trained on the sickle, his sword shaking in his hand. Sisyphus advanced on him, the sickle held low at his side. The God of War backed up and felt his heel hit the wall.

"Ares. I'm sure your father will take me just as seriously when his only—" His breath and speech were cut off. Blood soaked his robes and a glint of metal pierced through his chest from behind. Sisyphus looked down in shock.

Aidoneus appeared behind the king, his hand gripping the mortal's shoulder. He shoved the blade further between his ribs to the hilt with another wet slice, then pushed Sisyphus off his sword and onto the floor. He stood for a moment over the still and crumpled body and stepped over it, shaking off the blood, making his way to Ares's side.

"You all right, boy?" Aidon placed a hand on his shoulder.

"Voleta, sweet child!" Hecate cried, letting go of Persephone and running for the pile of crimson fabric in front of the throne. Persephone followed her. As she drew closer, the air left her lungs. The cloth was dyed by blood, parts of the veil still gold, and a fair-haired girl lay inside it. Hecate picked her up, cradling the girl to her chest and repeating the nymph's name over and over through her tears.

"Hecate," Thanatos slurred. "Hecate, I'm sorry. Please forgive me! Voleta... Voleta..." he mumbled, echoing Hecate, his head lolling to the side.

Hecate held the girl and Persephone pulled the spear from Thanatos's side. Her eyes blurred with tears. Sisyphus had slashed the girl's throat open from ear to ear. Hecate supported Voleta's lifeless head, tipping it forward before rocking her body in her arms.

"I'm sorry…" Thanatos kept repeating. "Please…"

Nyx and Hypnos flew from the doorway to Thanatos's side.

The Goddess of the Night turned and gasped. "Hades! Behind you!!"

Aidon whirled, his sword held at guard. Sparks flew as curved blade met heavy bronze, and the light illuminated Aidon's horrified face. Sisyphus grinned and Ares crowded toward the wall, open-mouthed and wide-eyed. The king spoke, calm and measured. "Merope was a Pleiade, a daughter of Atlas, was she not?"

Hades landed a kick to his gut, hoping it would break the king's grip on Thanatos's sickle. Sisyphus rolled and stood, weapon still in hand, and Aidoneus circled him so he stood between his wife and the Ephyrean sorcerer. "Abomination…"

Persephone stared at Sisyphus, seething. He had killed Merope. He'd killed the poor girl lying in Hecate's arms. He was trying to kill Aidoneus… her husband… separate them forever… Everything she'd fought for, everything she'd done, would be meaningless. The Queen took a step toward her husband, balling her fists, feeling fire rise within her.

"Merope was only a nymph," Sisyphus said. "Their kind is only immortal within sight of their domain. I chose well when I married her. She and her sisters were creatures of the stars. And now I draw my immortality from the heavens above."

He stepped toward Aidon, the sickle held out in front of him. Ares mustered his courage and slunk away from the wall, stalking like a lion.

"Where I'm sending you, there is only darkness." Aidoneus shifted from foot to foot, flourishing his sword and feinting to hold Sisyphus's attention, not affording Ares a glance lest Sisyphus notice his approach. Zeus would never forgive him if his only son was maimed. Or killed.

"So long as the stars shine in the sky, I will be deathless," he declared with a smile.

"Then you can be deathless without an arm!" Ares charged, slicing upward with his sword. Sisyphus startled and turned as the blade caught on the curve of the sickle and wrenched it from his grip. The sickle skittered across the floor to the wall.

Sisyphus turned pale, and sprinted after it. Hades reached toward the sickle with his open hand and it wavered and vanished in smoke, pushed into the ether. The Ephyrean stopped short.

Hades and Ares advanced on him, swords drawn. Sisyphus closed his eyes, muttering an incantation in Minoan. A golden crack stretched along the wall, and he stepped through and disappeared with it.

Aidoneus stopped in his tracks.

Ares threw his helm loudly the floor, stomping his feet and cursing with every word he could find in Greek and Theoi.

Persephone stalked forward, her fingernails digging half moons into her palms, her jaw set tight, and her eyes burning with unshed tears. "No…"

Hecate raised her head. "My queen…"

Nyx called out to her. "Persephone, please!"

"No…" Persephone snarled. Suffering surrounded her. Disorder, death, the danger the condemned man posed to her husband. Aidon had protected *her* first and foremost. He'd endangered himself because of *her*. Persephone's throat tightened and her shoulders stiffened. A flood of unwanted images of what might have been raced through her mind. She tore her asphodel crown from her head and threw it to the floor. "No more!"

The crown burst into flames. Fire whirled across the floor, twisting like the great river Phlegethon, growing under her control. Hades stepped back to his wife's side and Ares crowded against the arm of the throne. Persephone closed her eyes and concentrated, seeing silver strands of light and a warm glow of crimson stretching in every direction. She found the shadow of a man. It was just like her practice with Aidon, passing objects back and forth through the ether, except this one was in motion. Sisyphus was trying with all his might to fly over land and sea, fleeing them. She could hear the same chanted incantation growing closer, closer as she bridged the space between them.

She reached out with her consciousness and grasped at his ankle. Sisyphus yelped and struggled as she gripped him harder, reeling him out of the ether, up through the maw underneath. She heard his frightened cry come closer, then cease once it was above her. When Persephone opened her eyes Sisyphus, the sorcerer king of Ephyra, was pinned against the ceiling of his throne room, gasping for air.

"Enough!" she yelled. Her irises were circled with flame.

His breathing steadied and he looked down at her. She could see astonishment flit across his eyes. He'd expected that Aidoneus had dragged him from the ether. Sisyphus smiled at Persephone. "Demeter's daughter," he crooned, then snarled at her husband. "Hades! You still send your whore bride to deal with me? A sniveling concubine? How did you and yours fare the last time you did such a thing?" He was trying to break her concentration, Persephone knew— to escape back into the void.

Persephone felt her husband's rage building beside her and placed her other hand on Aidon's arm to calm him. She saw Voleta, lying cold and limp in Hecate's arms, then thought about Merope. Her friend's voice echoed in memory from the depths of Tartarus, telling how this man had nearly destroyed her to cheat his way out of his fate. *He drugged me with black henbane so I couldn't cry out and broke my legs so I couldn't escape.*

She felt her essence wrapped around Sisyphus, holding him to the ceiling. Persephone focused her power on his legs, and with a snap, she shattered one bone, then the next. His cries filled the chamber and he writhed in pain, his body wriggling against the forces that constrained him. "I have never seen anyone more afraid of their end than *you*, Sisyphus."

He whimpered between labored gasps.

"What's the matter? Have you no more to say to me than 'Demeter's daughter'?"

"Mercy... Mercy, please, I don't deserve—"

"As you showed mercy? The pain you suffer now is a reminder, the first of many, of what you did to Merope. To others."

She looked down at her ring of fire, twisting with silver threads, and willed its path to Tartarus. Black flames twisted at its center, then a shrill chant, growing louder from the Pit. *Praxidike... Wanakt-ja... Wanakt-ja...*

Ares yelped and clapped his hand to his mouth before he could scream again. Black diaphanous creatures emerged from the Pit, crawling through the flames and across the limestone, filling the throne room. They crept up the walls, latching onto the stones and the ceiling, surrounding Sisyphus until the hall was black.

"Mercy!" He stared into their pupilless eyes. "Please, gentle queen, I beg you!"

"Gentle?" Persephone asked. "It is true what you said. I am my mother's daughter, she who visited great wrath upon men when I was parted from her. I am also the Queen of Curses— the one who silences the voices of men. What sort of mercy do you think I have for you?"

"Please..." he sniveled as a Ker pulled the golden circlet off his head and started playing with it. The toothy creature hissed at him and tossed the crown to one of its sisters. "I don't want to—"

"Silence!" She stared up at him. "You murdered Voleta and Merope, and many more; you raped your own niece, you stole from Gaia herself, and for what?"

"For mercy… Asopus's daughter… I don't deserve…" he said. "Voleta attacked me. Merope… I wouldn't have touched her if she hadn't—"

"You blame your miseries on women?" She recalled how Sisyphus had dismissed her at his own judgement, and a smile curled her lips. "The same was done to Pandora, you know. The wife of Epimetheus. It is a delightful tale you mortal men dreamed up. They say that she was the first woman. She was given a jar she must not open, and was cursed by my father with curiosity to see what lay within. They say she let loose all the evils of the world and that her sex would forever be a plague upon mankind. But one thing within that fabled jar was not allowed to escape."

"Please." A Ker tested the air with its tongue near his eye and bared its teeth.

"What was it, Sisyphus? What did Pandora hold back?"

Another Ker hissed into his ear, drawing a claw lightly across his cheek. "Hope," he said weakly.

"You ask for mercy. I shall give you hope, instead. You've spent your whole life trying to avoid the flames of Tartarus. So if you can complete one task for me, I will set you free."

"Persephone—" Aidon warned, then stilled when she glanced back at him.

Trust me. She continued. "In the Fields of Punishment, there sits a great stone. If you can roll it uphill and out of Tartarus, then we will release you."

"August Persephone, my queen, thank you, I—"

"I'm not finished," she said. "There is a reason the condemned are told in my husband's court to abandon all hope when they are sentenced to Tartarus. Hope is the greatest curse there. All you will have is desire, the *illusion* that you can possibly escape. Your obsession with escaping your fate will follow you to the Pit. The stone will roll down upon you every day and you will keep pushing, mindlessly, endlessly, for all time."

His eyes widened, finally understanding her. "Curse me with anything else. Anything else... Please!"

"Aeolides, who calls himself Sisyphus, King of Ephyra."

The flames below him started to glow with the pale pulsing light of Ixion's wheel, and the Keres gripped his wrists. When they grasped his shattered right leg he let out another contorted scream. The Keres pulled him from the ceiling and dangled him over the Pit.

"I, Persephone Praxidike Chthonios, sentence you to Tartarus, where your mind will burn with hope, your body will be broken by your task, and your tale will be a dire warning for anyone who tries to escape my husband," she said, and looked over the yawning edge of the Pit. "Kottos!"

Yes, Praxidike... His voice boomed.

"Take him!"

The flames reached forth, darker and hotter. Sisyphus's open mouth was fixed in a scream but she couldn't hear him. The Keres chants drowned out his voice as they flapped madly about. *"Wanakt-ja! Praxidike!"* they called out in high-pitched unison, *"Wanakt-ja! Wanakt-ja! Wanakt-ja!"*

A great stony hand emerged from the widening flames, the palm splayed open. The Keres dropped him and Kottos's fist closed around Sisyphus. As his fingers slowly shut, Sisyphus struggled and cried and beat at the tightening cage of the Hundred Handed One. His face, his garments, his body were stripped of light, leaving only a faceless shadow behind. Kottos's fist lowered itself back beyond the ring of fire and each Ker made a last sweep around their Queen and dove in after it.

By her will, the path swirled shut, the flames quenched, and silence filled the room. Persephone stood stock still, her hands quivering at her side, her breath uneven. She heard a rattle of bronze armor plates from the throne and turned to see Ares staring at the spot on the floor where Sisyphus had been dragged to Tartarus. His knees shook as though he were about to collapse, and his face was pale as the moon. Only his arm leaning on the golden throne held him upright.

A warm, familiar hand reached for Persephone's shaking one, then traveled up her arm to rest on her shoulder with a comforting squeeze. She spun around and wrapped her arms around Aidoneus, his eyes wide with surprise.

"Persephone..." He brought his arms around her with caution, remembering her ire in the fields beyond Ephyra. He felt each breath she took in, felt her relax with each one. She needed him. His heart leapt; she was in his arms again. He was tempted to kiss her on her head, but dared nothing more than simple comfort. He brimmed with confusion and longing, and knew she could feel it too.

She pulled away from Aidon and stared up at his face. *Soon?*

As promised, wife.

"We need to see to Thanatos."

"Of course," he nodded.

Hypnos broke the silence and spoke first, his mouth dry. "M-my queen? There's quite a bit more chain here than what Sisyphus stole from us."

"He enchanted an alloy," Aidoneus said under his breath. He pulled out his sword, tossing it hilt first to Hypnos. "That should cut through it."

While Nyx held Thanatos aloft, the God of Sleep swung the blade down on the Chains and sliced neatly through them. Nyx wrapped her arms around her son.

"My sweet boy," Nyx said into his ear. Thanatos just stared at Voleta's limp body, cradled in Hecate's arms.

A tear fell down his cheek. Nyx stroked his forehead and willed his flesh to pull back from his bones, revealing his true manifestation in the world above.

"There's too much…" he slurred as the chains fell through his arms and wings. "Mother, there's too much to do…"

"Just rest, my child," she said, descending with him. The darkness that wavered about her wrapped around Thanatos, holding him gently.

"Voleta…" He shuddered, reaching out to her.

Nyx looked to Hecate, pleading with her. The Goddess of the Crossroads thinned her wrinkled lips and sighed. Her face softened and she somberly inclined her head toward Death. Hecate rested her fingertips on his bony shoulder. "This wasn't your fault, Thanatos. She knew the risks."

"Hecate… I'm so very sorry…" he whispered, then sobbed dryly. Hypnos unclasped his chlamys and Nyx laid him within it. "She wasn't near… when she died, her spirit… it's my fault. She never would have… I don't deserve your forgiveness."

"Just rest, Thanatos." Hecate gathered her arms around the nymph's body. "I'll take her home." With that, she vanished into the ether and Voleta with her, bound for Chthonia.

Morpheus leaned through the doorway. "My Queen? I fear there's something amiss outside."

Persephone looked around the room. All were there, save Hecate and…

They heard a distant scream. Ares finally had enough voice to speak. "Eris."

"We have to leave. Now," Persephone commanded. Hypnos cradled Thanatos in his arms and flew through the halls ahead of everyone.

Morpheus, guided by Aidoneus and Nyx, gasped as they ran. "Nightmares. I can see them."

"Can't you call back the Oneiroi?" Persephone asked, grasping her long skirts to run. Ares deliberately trailed far behind them.

"Not unless the mortals awaken."

They reached the colonnade and stopped. The entire marketplace was aflame, tradesmen staggering about, shouting and babbling, with torches in hand. Musicians still played and soldiers cut at the air with their swords, fighting against enemies that weren't there. Children wailed and screamed, huddling together. Ares finally caught up, then stomped ahead of them when he saw her.

"Eris! Damn it, woman!"

She leaned against the raised hearth of the agora, her arms wrapped around a hoplite soldier who passionately kissed her in the midst of his dream.

"I told you not to touch them."

She rolled her eyes. "But they taste so good when they're asleep!" She turned back to her mortal companion and locked lips with him again, her hand wandering up the inside of his thigh.

"Eris, now!"

She unceremoniously dropped the unconscious soldier to the ground and folded her arms across her chest, walking toward them. Her wings spread, silhouetted against the burning marketplace. Eris cracked a wide grin when she saw Thanatos held in his brother's arms.

Leaning over, she placed a kiss on his exposed teeth. "Get well soon, lover. We'll see each other again when you're rested."

"No, we will not."

"You say that every time," she cooed, tracing his rib cage. He squirmed away from her touch. Hypnos bristled at her.

Flesh, painful to manifest thanks to his injuries, spread across Thanatos's body. He wanted to look her in the eye. When he opened his, he looked squarely into hers. "I said no, Eris. I will never visit your bed again. Not now, not at aeon's end, not ever."

She pouted and stood upright, backing away as he slipped the bonds of his flesh again and curled up against Hypnos in peaceful sleep. Eris opened a pathway through the ether behind her, its edges forever collapsing in on themselves in a chaotic geometry. A pert smirk twisted her features. "Until we meet again…"

Ares surveyed the gods of the Underworld, his face solemn and pale. He gave them a respectful nod, then quietly followed after Eris. The gateway shut behind them.

Ephyra burned.

"Don't look now, but if we don't leave we'll be over run," Morpheus muttered. His blind eyes perceived what they could not. Soon after he spoke, sleepwalking mortals, locked in nightmares, pointed in their direction. They screamed and railed, unintelligible, shambling toward the palace steps with their eyes shut.

"We can't just let them burn," Persephone worried. "Hypnos, can you wake them?"

"It will be utter chaos."

"At least they'll have a chance."

"Will *we?*" he asked, nodding his head at his unconscious brother.

"Persephone, find us a way out of here," Aidon said quickly. "Hypnos, *wake them.*"

An asphodel grew through a crack in the steps and a great ring of fire bloomed as soon as the first flower opened. The mortals drew closer, tripping on the palace steps, some falling to be trampled by others. She ignored them and pulled Eleusis closer, bridging the divide. "Now!"

Hypnos closed his eyes and pulled back the veil of sleep he'd cast over the city. The caterwauling stopped and all voices and motion ceased. Mortals dropped where they stood, and the thousand shadows of the Oneiroi leapt from their bodies and flew away, disappearing into the blackness of night. Slowly the people of Ephyra awoke, softly at first, then to great alarm as their marketplace blazed. Burning olive oil filled the air with thick black smoke, and embers landed on thatched roofs. A young man shouted directions at three soldiers, fetched large pitchers of water. As the Ephyreans organized themselves to douse the flames, the chthonic gods walked, unnoticed, through the ether to the fields of Eleusis.

Persephone knelt where Hypnos had laid Thanatos on the ground and smoothed her hand over his brow. "Is he going to be all right?"

"Yes," Nyx said, hovering over him. She looked up at Aidoneus. "Physically, it shouldn't take long. But…"

"Thanatos will recover, my lady," Aidon said stonily. "He'll protest, but I don't want him active for at least a few days."

"Are you coming with us?" Hypnos asked.

Aidon glanced at Persephone. Her eyes were wide and expectant. "No. But I'll be back home soon enough."

"Not too soon, I hope," Morpheus said with a smile. "I imagine that you and the Queen have a bit of catching up to—"

Hades's glare was palpable and Morpheus cut himself short.

"Little one." Nyx smiled at Persephone. "If you ever doubt your true place in this cosmos, remember tonight. Until we see each other again, my queen. My lord," she nodded and a great dark path opened behind her. Nyx's sons followed her, and the starless gyre wound shut on itself.

Then they were alone.

18.

CHIRPING CRICKETS AND FROGS WERE A DEAFENING chorus, and the smell of night blooming lilies filled the air. The silence between Hades and Persephone stretched on. He slowly inhaled.

"Persephone…"

"Why did you not come to me?"

"Wife, if I came to you I would have never—" Aidoneus tightened his jaw and narrowed his eyes at her. "Why did *you* not send any word to *me*? You saw Hermes often enough."

She creased her brow. "What could I have said? Should I have told him everything I wanted to say to you for him to repeat to all of Olympus?"

He started shifting from foot to foot, then paced a few steps. "I don't care what the Olympians think."

"But I do!"

"Why? Are you ashamed of what they know about us? About what you feel for me?"

She softened. "Of course not, Aidon."

"Then what is it?" He came to a stop.

"You have no idea how much easier it is for you," she muttered, shaking her head.

He looked at her incredulously. "Easier?"

299

"Yes!" She straightened. "You have the refuge of Chthonia, but I have to live *here*. The Olympians gossip, and it's not idle. They know that I am— that *we are* a weakness for each other. Our marriage is their greatest source of curiosity right now, and I endure all sorts of questions, even from someone as staid as Athena. And the things my mother—"

"Oh, *damn* your mother and her precious opinions to Tartarus!" She flinched, and he paused to calm his voice. "Surely she recognizes that you are a woman now. A married woman."

"Barely."

He shook his head. "You could have at least written to me."

"I don't know how to *write*, Aidon," she reminded him. "I barely know how to read!"

Aidoneus exhaled and looked away. He could have kicked himself for forgetting.

"Even if I could write, what would stop Hermes from reading every message I send to you?"

"He's not allowed to do that."

"Do you think that would stop him? I've been so tight-lipped about our... life together... that any information about us is more precious to them than gold!"

Aidoneus saw tears form in her eyes. "Persephone—"

"Do you have any idea how desperate I was to hear from you? You said you'd come to me."

"There was too much to be done."

"Do you think my tasks were any less? I thought you resented me, Aidoneus. Maybe even *hated* me."

"What? Why?!"

"Because I hid my plan from you. Because I ate the pomegranate seeds without telling you."

"Do you think so little of me, do you think me so fickle as to hate you for *that*?"

"When I hear nothing from you for three months, what *should* I think?"

"What would you have me do? Let all the things that I wanted to say to you privately come rolling off Hermes's tongue?"

He'd asked her that same question moments ago, and she'd responded in kind. She took a step back, the same understanding softening his features, too. Persephone did not want to fight. She just wanted this to be over so he could hold her, but she needed answers. "You missed me, Aidon, but not enough to come see me?"

"I missed you plenty," he answered, his brow furrowing.

"Then why not just once?"

"Because I would never have gone back! For Fate's sake, Persephone. It was hard enough for me to leave you up here in the first place."

"Dreams would have enabled you to——"

"I've hardly slept. Between the glut of shades and... your absence..." He took a cautious step toward her. "It's been nearly impossible."

She looked down, forgetting how restless he had been before she came into his life, and worried that it was worse for him now that she was gone. His sandaled feet and greaves came to a stop in front of hers. She could hear him breathing and felt the tension in their bodies humming between them. Persephone felt his walls crack and come tumbling down, leaving him raw and exposed. She slowly lifted her gaze to meet his. Her husband's eyes were awash with emotion. "Aidon..."

"Enough." His voice was rough. "Enough words for one night..."

He pulled her against him, almost knocking the wind from her, and their mouths crashed together haphazardly. They moulded together, hands lacing through hair, teeth gently pulling at lips, tongues intertwining. She surrendered. A whimper of relief was answered by a halted groan from her husband. They could barely breathe, and Aidoneus pulled away with another nip of her lower lip.

"I've missed you…" he whispered against her cheek, his voice shaking. "That's all there is to it. I've missed you terribly, sweet one."

She relaxed. "I don't want to argue with you, Aidon. Not when we have such a short time together. But I cannot just leave this matter unfinished and expect everything between us to be all right when I come home." She brushed her fingers over his jaw line. He held her, his eyes betraying his vulnerability. "Do you understand?"

Aidoneus nodded. "I do. My love, I'm so sorry I did not contact you. After we parted, I worked day and night for over a month to restore our kingdom. When that time had passed, I simply didn't know what to say. And I couldn't have Hermes just unfurl a scroll and read off everything I've held back." He cupped her face in his hands. For the first time since he'd appeared in the world above, he smiled for her. "Persephone…"

"My love, I—" Aidon swept a thumb across her lips.

"Sweet one, it's all right. Let's not dwell on what has passed. We'll find a way to do better in the future."

"I barely had enough time to plan what I did," she said, tears welling up in her eyes. "I thought I did the right thing by not telling you."

"Perhaps you did." He kissed her forehead. "The state I was in… I would never have let you go if you'd told me you'd eaten the seeds."

"And I gave no thought to how we would keep in contact with each other once it was done."

"How could either of us have? We had no chance to prepare for this."

"I knew I couldn't use the Key…"

He raised his eyebrows. "Safe to say, the Olympians will know that you have the Key soon enough."

"I don't think you'll have to worry about my safety anymore," she said before a grin quirked her mouth. "Something tells me I won't ever have to worry about poor Ares."

"If he were mortal, he would have soiled himself."

Aidoneus held her as she laughed. Her smile widened and her eyes squeezed shut. When her mirth subsided and she wiped a tear away from her face, he moved in to kiss her, feel her, taste her. She was warm against him, even through the armor. When he pulled back, her eyes were unfocused and dark. He cleared his throat, pulling himself back from his own growing need for her.

"Back to the matter at hand… the last three months weren't your fault, Persephone. Or mine, in truth. One moment we thought we'd be inseparable, sweet one, and the next we were apart. As for the pomegranate, you did what you had to." His eyes glimmered and he looked away, deep in thought. Turning back to her, a half smile played on his lips. "Do you remember the day we first judged that miserable charlatan? Before he escaped?"

"Of course," she said licking her lips. "And what part of that *conversation* would you be referring to, husband?"

"Not the part you think," he said, but grinned hungrily anyway. "I speak of learning together."

Her lips parted in realization and delight. "Learning to write from Minos, you mean?"

"His people's language is long forgotten. Perhaps even by the gods. If we could write to each other in that tongue, we wouldn't have to worry about Hermes or anyone reading words meant only for us."

She looked away from him. "But I have so far to go… I can barely read as it is."

"We have eternity," he said. "And I can take some time in the next three months to learn. I shouldn't be nearly as busy as I have been."

"This coming week may be... interesting," she said "I'm sure there are many who are belatedly beginning their trips to Chthonia."

"Undoubtedly."

"What have you been doing all this time? I wish I had been there to help."

"I spent much of my time on the far shore of the Styx... bending the rules."

She tittered and shook her head. "What?"

"There were many we received during the winter without coin for passage. It wasn't their kin's fault they hadn't been buried properly. Too often there was no one left to bury them. I couldn't, in good conscience, strand so many souls and deny them peace."

Persephone leaned her head against his chest as he kneaded his fingers along her shoulders. She listened to the counterpoint of his heartbeat behind the armor and the hum of life in the air. The crickets sounded so much like the constant twittering of the shades in Asphodel. If she shut her eyes it was almost as if she were back home. "You gave them coin for passage?"

"Yes. And since I was busy with that, I did as you wished with the judges."

"What do you mean?"

"I will no longer judge the wealthy and the powerful. The world is changing and there are too many of them. You were right. The best way to prove to the mortals that death makes equals of them all is to have the judges see to them equally. The ones from Europa now go to Aeacus, and the ones from Asia to Rhadamanthys. Minos has the final vote if there is a dispute. I intend to keep it that way unless you have a better suggestion," he said, feeling her shake and sniffle once. "What's wrong, sweet one?"

"Nothing," she said, wiping a tear away. "Only that you actually listened to what I had to say."

"Why would I not listen to my queen?" He grinned broadly at her, and Persephone traced the smile lines framing his eyes and shook her head.

"You haven't been sleeping, Aidoneus."

"Not often, no."

"Have *their* voices returned in my absence?" She paled at the idea of Kronos whispering rebellion to her husband after all that had happened.

"No, sweet one," he said. Relief washed over her. "The reasons are far more mundane."

"Mundane?" She twirled a loose curl.

"There's a great deal of work to be done. Chthonia is *still* crowded with souls, and I've let many be reborn to the world above. But more frequently I…"

He sighed and dropped his head. When he met her gaze again, his eyes were lidded and dark and Persephone felt tension return to his arms. Aidon leaned forward, his breath ragged against her ear.

"I've longed for you, Persephone. That, above all else, is what keeps me awake at night. The absence of you beside me… beneath me."

Her knees went soft and her heart raced. "I'd… hardly call that *mundane*, my lord."

"No," he scoffed. "I suppose not."

"It certainly hasn't been a mundane concern for me…" She tilted her face toward his and kissed him again, lightly, pulling back ever so slightly when he tried to deepen it. If she gave in now, she would lose herself in him. And there was still so much more she wanted to tell him, so much she wanted him to see. Persephone smiled broadly and grasped his hands in hers, walking backward. "Come. I have something to show you."

"That way leads to the Telesterion," he said, digging his heels into the earth. Above all else, he wanted to avoid another encounter with Demeter.

305

"Not *just* the Telesterion." She reached into the ether with a small flash of flame and quickly fading sparks to produce her Helm— the one Aidon had given her the day before they journeyed to Tartarus. "Come with me."

She disappeared before his eyes as she lowered the silver helmet onto her head. The grass rustled beside him and he turned in the direction of the sound. He felt her hand stroke his jaw line and neck, and heard her giggling when his eyes grew wide. A warm and unseen hand tugged at his.

"Come!"

"Patience, wife! Let me find mine," he said as he looked for his in the grass. He turned quickly, fearing that someone had stolen it, cursing his carelessness, before he heard her laughter again.

"You mean this?" she said, drawing it out from under her mantle. It hung in midair, held by her invisible hands.

"Thank you," he said with a smirk, snatching it. *Don't think for a moment I'm letting you get away with that.*

Then come after me, she replied through thought. His eyes lit up at the challenge. She stood still, then took off with a giggle, stalks of grass shaking in her wake.

Aidoneus donned his helm and disappeared. He didn't need to see her to know where she was headed. He could hear her, he could feel her, and he could follow her scent of narcissus and pomegranates drifting on the still air. As they ran toward Eleusis, he could hear flutes and lyres, a drum and the shake of a koudounia as the villagers celebrated their first harvest. In front of the Telesterion and through the streets of Eleusis, men and women danced separately, but his sharp hearing could discern laughter and flirtation between villagers not as willing to maintain the bounds of social separation.

A pair of giddy lovers dressed in saffron chitons dashed past him in the opposite direction, escaping the fires and torches for the privacy afforded by the open fields, the night sky, and the stars above. Aidon jogged after his wife, nearly

306

losing her trail in the incense wafting from the temple. He looked about the crowd for signs of her, then felt a hand grasp at his.

"Come on," she whispered. "It's not much farther."

The music faded into the background, a steady muffled drumbeat and a melody from the flute amidst the singing. Aidoneus and Persephone carefully scaled the rocky hillside north of the temple. She lifted the faceplate of her helm and perched it atop her head, becoming visible to him again. He followed her lead so he could be sure of his footing, but his helm still covered his face, his cloak hiding all but a single arm and a glint of his cuirass. Persephone held his hand and gathered up her skirts with the other, one pale foot carefully following the other, trying to find the scattered steps in the darkness.

"You climb these rocks barefoot?" he asked.

"Of course," she said, smiling. "I always did so when I was Kore."

The incline gentled and they soon came to a short wall of stacked stones and blocks of marble. Mason's tools lay propped against one of the walls. This was an unfinished temple. "I know this place…"

"I'd hope so," she said. "It's where we emerged and struck the new Agreement."

He frowned. "It's where I lost you for half the year, every year. Why bring me here of all places, Persephone?"

"Look." She paused and he turned in the direction she faced. All was silent except for the distant music in Eleusis. Her husband's eyes widened and his mouth hung open. Persephone spoke. "You said you weren't worshipped in the world above. You told me how you would be blamed for all that happened, how the mortals would never know you…"

Aidon shook his head and removed his helm, laying it on the ground beside him. Before them on a raised altar stood two life-size statues— his likeness and hers, carved from ash trees. They faced outward together, he standing slightly behind her, one hand gently holding her shoulder, the other cupped beneath her upturned hand. Cradled in her hand was a single, perfect pomegranate flower. Persephone's free hand held a long stalk of asphodel. Her face was serene, his looked stern.

Fresh wreaths of poplar leaves and asphodel flowers crowned their heads and boughs of cypress lay at their feet, perfuming the air with their spicy scent. It mingled with the sweet smell of narcissus and pomegranate flowers that were strewn about the altar. Footprints littered the ground. This place was well visited and, judging from the crispness of the wreaths adorning their heads, recently and carefully tended.

Persephone's hand intertwined with his, and the statues blurred. He quickly wiped away the tears that moistened his eyes and gazed down at her. "How... Persephone, have you..."

"Yes," she answered softly. "I wasn't expecting them to create all this, though. It was built by students of one of my mother's priests. My priest, in truth— Eumolpus. He said it would take too long to work with marble; so this is temporary."

"A shame. I quite like the ash wood." Aidon took a step closer to look at the embracing statues and saw amphorae of olive oil stacked near the base of the altar, offerings to his realm. "So that's where all the oil has been coming from."

"Mortals have made offerings to the Underworld before, though. Haven't they?" She remembered how he'd used the oil to slick back his hair, and shave his thick stubble.

"Only small libations," he answered. "Nothing like this. Olive oil has been appearing in the great hall of the palace of late. What have you told them of our world?"

"The truth." Persephone leaned against his arm. "That they are reborn above. About how peaceful Asphodel is, how you are firm but kind, a shepherd of souls."

"*Sto Theo, kai Thea,*" he said, reading the inscription carved into the platform below.

"Is that what that says?" she said, a smile broadening across her face.

"To the God and the Goddess; yes. Unsurprising. We're rulers of the dead. They will not call on us by name, or write our names, for that matter."

"What about that one?" she said pointing to a heavy marble cornerstone at the entrance. She only recognized the first letter, *pi*, the same letter that started her name.

Aidon squinted to read it. The word *Plutonion* was scratched roughly into its surface to mark where the chisel would eventually do the rest. "The Rich One…" he said with a smirk. "Or rather, the sanctuary of the Rich One."

"They're not talking about gold, Aidon. That had little value here during winter. They call you the Rich One in Eleusis because you helped bring fertility back to the earth. You're more than just the God of the Dead."

"Hmm," he grunted in acknowledgement and thinned his lips.

Persephone pointed to a much smaller cave littered with copper coins. "That one they dedicated to Charon."

"Oh?" A wide smile broke on Hades face and he laughed. "Oh no, I can't…"

"What's wrong?"

"If I tell him they built this, I'll never hear the end of it!"

"Oh, poor Charon; he should know, Aidon," she said and laughed with him. "Fine. Hold off until I come back. It will amuse me to no end to see his reaction."

He turned toward her and cupped her face in his hand. "You've done the impossible, my love."

"What do you mean?"

"You've found a way to bridge the divide between our worlds. This is the first temple they've ever built where I am even mentioned. You've created a way for the mortals to know us as we are."

"I couldn't just stand by and let everyone speak for me, or for you. My mother had more than enough to say about our relationship during the winter. But I wanted the Eleusinians and all of Hellas to know that—"

He lifted her against him and silenced her with a kiss. Persephone gave in, holding him to her, grasping at his cloak, pulling him closer. He drew his shaking hands along her waist to her hips. "Persephone…"

"That I love you," she whispered.

He gathered her close and kissed her again, and Persephone relaxed in his arms, her legs going limp and heat pooling in her belly.

"I love you, sweet one," he said when they separated to catch their breath. "I often thought about how it was barely two months you were with me… the blink of an eye compared to the long aeons I've lived. But it feels as though a piece of me has been missing without you there."

"I know…" She shook her head, her eyes watering. "Aidon, I'm so sorry, half the year was the best I could do…"

"No, my love. Don't ever apologize for what you did," he said, then looked away. "Do you regret it? Forever tethering yourself to the Land of the Dead? To me— after knowing me for such a short time?"

"Of course not," she smiled at him. "You forget, it's my world too. Your palace is my home… your bed is my bed."

He kissed her again, harder this time, and she felt his fingers bunch in the fabric of her peplos. His lips played with hers, her tongue stroking his, boldly deepening the kiss. He pulled away from her and breathed shallowly, his pulse drumming in his ears. When he finally spoke again, his voice was low and vulnerable. "Can we…?"

"Here?"

"Anywhere." His hands retraced their path up her waist. "I need you."

"I can think of no better place," she said with a smile. "This is your sanctuary— your home in this world, after all."

"Our home," he replied huskily, brushing his thumb over the outline of a taut nipple peaking against her dress.

She gasped and pressed herself to him, her body flush against the cold, muscular outlines of his cuirass. "How do I remove this?"

"If you want, I could change the armor back to my robes," he said, his mouth twisting into a lusty half-grin. "Or I could just will it off my body."

She looked at him in surprise. "I don't recall you doing that before, Aidon. And I can think of several times where we would have benefitted from that expediency."

"I like the ritual of removing clothes," Aidon said against her neck, planting a soft kiss behind her ear. "Of revealing each inch of your skin… of discovering and knowing you one part at a time. And I love the expression on your face when you reveal mine."

"As do I," she whispered, impatiently running her fingertips over the edges of his armor. "Show me how to take this off…"

Aidon unlaced one of his gauntlets, and Persephone copied him with the other, albeit more slowly. She bent down and examined his greaves. He helped her by effortlessly pulling one forward, the metal springing back into the shape of his leg. Persephone removed the other. She quickly untied one of his sandal straps, then the other, the leather thongs loosening and falling around his ankles. She tossed the greaves aside next to the other pieces as he stepped out of his sandals and kicked them away.

Aidoneus unpinned his cloak, letting it drop to the ground behind him. She traced her fingers over the tensed muscles of his exposed arms and the veins winding their way to his wrists. He covered her hands with his, moving them to his sides, her fingers brushing over the straps that held his cuirass securely to his body. She kissed him and started working the leather through the bronze fasteners, three on each side.

The first strap took the longest; the others followed quickly once she figured out how to unlace them. Aidon lifted the strapped shoulders over his head as she pulled it up from the bottom. The golden carapace crashed loudly to the rocky ground.

Persephone jumped back and glanced about. Aidon chuckled at her reaction. "Afraid of being discovered, my love?"

"Only a little. I know that no one is coming here or looking for us. They're all celebrating in the village. But, still..." she said, gazing off toward the glowing lamps and torchlight surrounding the Telesterion. She could vaguely make out what they were playing. It was the same song from her childhood— the one Charon hummed the first time she traveled the Styx in his boat, nestled into her husband's side.

"Come, wife."

She turned abruptly as he spread his cloak over the ground, the embroidered edges snapping against the thick wool before it billowed out and settled. He rose, and Persephone looked longingly at him, his tunic clinging to his form thanks to the warm summer night and his closely fit cuirass. His desire for her was evident. Persephone sauntered over to him, then slowly brushed her hands down the wrinkled fabric covering his chest. "I was thinking that we could do away with any barriers between us and the ground."

He raised his eyebrows at her, his voice rough. "This is hardly a clover field. Your back will be raw before I'm done with you." His last words came out strangled, and she reached for the edge of his tunic and lifted it. He took over once she raised it past his waist, and flung it away, pins and all, then untied his loincloth and let it drop to the ground in front of him.

Persephone stepped back, her eyes glassy, her breathing heavy as she beheld him naked in the dim light. Her mouth went dry. "Y-you forget my love, we are in *my* world..."

She stretched out her hand and the cloak flew away, settling in a heap with his tunic. In its wake were tufts of soft grasses and downy moss, clovers and small white flowers. They spread out under their feet, rising up from the dusty earth to cover the whole floor of the Plutonion.

"…And if I want to make love to my husband pressed against the earth, *our* domain, then I'll do just that."

"We must go to Nysa, sometime," he ground out. "When the sun is up."

"And have Helios see us?" She circled him.

"I'm sure he's seen stranger things than a man and his wife joined in marital bliss," Aidon turned toward her with every step she took, their movements like a dance.

"Even if said man and wife are creatures of the Underworld?" She giggled when he shrugged. "You've fantasized about us together there often, haven't you?"

"Of course," he said, looking her up and down. "How else do you think I've managed to get any shred of sleep these past three months?"

Persephone stopped and looked at him askance. Her lips formed a silent 'oh', understanding his meaning. She thought about her nights spent alone when her hands would wander beneath the sheet to mimic his caress. He must have done the same, perhaps even to completion. A riot of provocative images filled her head. "Show me."

"First things first," he crooned and snapped his fingers.

Her tightly wound hair relaxed and fell, and cool air nipped at the small of her back. The gentle breeze wafted against every inch of her skin and Persephone shivered. Her flesh broke out in small bumps and the tips of her breasts hardened almost painfully.

Persephone looked down at her body, now as naked as his, then to the pile of his clothes. Hers were folded neatly atop them, willed there by him in an instant. She laughed, but her mirth immediately subsided when she saw the tight set of his jaw, and his fingers clenching and unclenching at his sides.

"Forgive my impatience, my love," he said raggedly. Aidon stepped toward her with every intent of laying her out on the soft earth. "Three months is long enough…"

"Ah-ah," she said, taking a step back and holding a finger out, teasingly.

"Persephone," he growled.

"Show me," she whispered. "Tell me how you found solace in my absence."

"Tell you?" he whispered back. "About you how thoughts of you, your skin, your warmth drove me mad every night?" He reached for his groin, wrapping his fingers around his shaft and caressing upward, then slowly squeezed the swollen head and pulled back. Aidon hissed and gritted his teeth.

Mesmerized, she watched him touch himself with his palm upturned as though he were offering it to her. The tip seeped and glistened, his essence slicking over the head with every pass of his thumb. Persephone licked her lips and inched toward him. He placed his other hand on her lower back to pull her even closer, the tip trailing wetly against her belly on every down stroke. Her eyes traversed his body from his intense gaze to the motions of his hand and the tension knotting his forearm.

"About how the… *culmination* of this cold pleasure was the only way I could find any rest at all," he continued, "about how it left me euphoric but empty, with my seed in my hand instead of filling your womb or your perfect mouth?"

Undone, she dropped to her knees in front of him and batted his hand away, replacing it with her hand and lips. Aidon threw his head back with a shuddering moan, then gently laced his fingers into her hair when the tip of his cock touched the back of her throat. His legs nearly gave out when she took him deeper still.

314

She hummed in enjoyment, intoxicated by his taste and scent, the feel of his coarse hair against her nose and lips, the awareness that he shuddered helplessly above her. Persephone traced her fingers across the lines from his waist to his hips, the slight protrusion of his hipbones, his thighs, his flanks, holding him to her as she copied the fervent motions of their lovemaking.

"Oh gods… sweet one, you're killing me…" he groaned, his head thrown back, his eyes squeezed shut. Watching her would end him.

You cannot die, husband… you're immortal, she teased him.

But we can go mad, Persephone, and right now you're driving me out of my mind…

She looked up and stroked his shaft with her fingers, smiling at him. "With waiting or wanting?"

He pushed at her shoulders to send her onto her back, then dropped to his knees and lay astride her, the tip of his cock prodding against her entrance. A buck of his hips slid his hardness along her aching bud. Persephone wiggled her thighs and clawed at his chest. He ground against her again and she swore she felt every vein and contour of his length brush over her lips. She tightened her legs around him, her body quivering, canting her hips upward and urging him to enter.

"Hmm," he mused with a mischievous smile. Aidon drew back with a kiss on the tip of her nose. "What of you, my love?"

Her teeth chattered from the absence of his heat. "Please…"

"What did you do on nights when you missed me?" She mewled when his fingers teased a puckered nipple, then traced an uneven path down her stomach to her thatch of hair. "Did you touch yourself as I did?"

"Yes…"

"Here?" He petted her mound and dipped his fingers into her warmth.

She could only close her eyes and nod, shaking at his touch.

"And here?" Aidon swirled the pad of his thumb over her bud, causing her back to arch and her thighs to squirm. "And imagined me taking you here?"

He pushed two digits into her and she curled forward toward him. "Yes!"

He pulled out and tasted her, licking his fingers with a low hum of appreciation, before pushing her knees further apart and diving in for more.

"Aidon, please! Please!" She gripped his scalp as he rolled his tongue over her sex from entrance to apex and back again to spear inside. Her taste was sweet like honey, intoxicating like pomegranate. He held her hips steady and lapped at her fervently as her hands became fists in his hair. A steady chant... *Take me, take me, take me,* rolled through his thoughts, a plea from hers.

He didn't stop, not until he felt her thighs shake and her voice call out his name. Her head tilted back and her channel thrummed and ached with need, waiting to be filled. Only when her climax started to subside did he rise up the length of her body, burying himself to the hilt in the same movement. She clasped her legs and arms around him and cried out her approval as he groaned against her ear.

She pulsed and fluttered around him, a great wave surging over them both. The fullness of the living earth rose up through her and wrapped itself around him completely, heightening his every sensation. The current she commanded was electric and delirious, grasping at his very soul, as though the pull of life itself would swallow them both if he didn't act on their desire. He responded in kind and set a devastating rhythm, fast and deep, giving no mercy to either of them. Persephone gripped at his skin, her body wracked with aftershocks of pleasure, heightened by every quick thrust.

Her nails raked his back and he grasped her thigh. Every plunge into her produced a throaty cry. He planted one hand in the soft grass, pushing harder. Aidon felt that same swell of waking life flood into him and back through her. He was lost to pleasure, oblivious to anything that existed outside their sanctuary.

His lips met hers and their sounds were muffled and breathless as he felt ecstasy build torturous, almost painful. His back arched and fire burned up the length of his spine, color and light and the vague outlines of a thousand narcissus blooms filling his last coherent thoughts. He shouted her name to the stars above, then collapsed on top of her, his eyes shut and his breath hot against her tangled hair.

Persephone lay still, letting the pull of the earth subside, breathing onto his neck and running her fingers through Aidon's locks until his weight grew too great and she pushed at his shoulders. He released her reluctantly and rolled onto his back, taking in great gasps of air and holding her against his side. When Aidoneus opened his eyes, he stilled. Larkspur, crocuses and small clumps of narcissus grew all around them, spread across the whole of the Plutonion, and even creeping up on the hillside above. "Sweet one? Did you—did we just…"

Persephone wearily opened her eyes, looked in the direction of his outstretched finger and laughed, sitting up and planting a hand on his chest. "Not what I intended, honestly…"

"Explaining these flowers to your mother will be a walk through Tartarus, no doubt."

She stopped and buried her face in her hands with a groan. "I don't want to think about that right now."

"Apologies." He sat cross-legged beside her. "But it does beget an important question: what time are you expected back?"

"Dawn, at the latest," she answered, looking off toward the east, hoping that she wouldn't see light on the horizon for a while yet. Her face fell. "What time must you leave?"

"Probably around then. Chthonia needs me," he sighed. "The natural order will resume now that Thanatos is free. And after he returns to his duties, we will be *very* busy. I will also pay Tartarus a visit to ensure that the punishment you designed for Sisyphus is being carried out to the letter."

She felt his seed shift inside her and hope sprang up in her heart. It was a few days past her peak of fertility, but there might still be a chance, and perhaps tonight they could make a child together— conceived in the world above. "Then we have a few more hours…"

"And I intend to make the most of them." He lay on his back in the grass with a broad smile. "But what you called forth from the earth was… exhausting. Give me a few minutes to recover, wife."

She lay on him and listened to his heartbeat, then traced her finger over his chest. Her hand wound its way down to his thigh and traveled inward, stroking the seam of his scrotum and his softened penis. She smiled and played with the skin at the tip, then combed through his coarse thatch of hair and traced its path up to his navel and back again, caressing him with no intention of arousing, just a desire to explore him.

Nonetheless, he didn't stay soft for long, and she heard his heart pick up tempo and felt him thicken in her hand. With a firm kiss, he let her know that he was ready, and she straddled him and lay on his chest, slowly sinking down onto him. Aidon held her hands so she could balance, her softly lit face framed by the waves of her hair and the starlight above, an image he wouldn't soon forget. He sat up to hold her, both barely moving, immersing themselves in slow, languorous pleasure, indulging in a feast of intimacy after their months of famine. When they grew anxious for release, he turned her over and filled her from behind. His chest grazed against her back and one arm wrapped securely around her waist, their knees and hands pressed to the earth.

Afterward they lay hand in hand, staring up at the stars, and the music at the Telesterion finally died down. The lights there dimmed and they were left with crickets and starlight. Persephone told Aidoneus about sending Melia's ghost back to Chthonia, and Aidoneus told Persephone that their pomegranate grove was in full bloom, that he would often retreat to its beauty at day's end to think about her. He spoke about studying the ritual of the *hieros gamos*; she expressed her desire to write and pondered how they would communicate for the next few months.

Aidon muttered about wanting her scent caught up in his clothes to take back with him. Persephone gladly obliged, laying out his cloak and wrapping it around them. They huddled within, limbs entangled. He peppered kisses all over her heated body. Aidoneus made love to her sublimely and slowly, withdrawing every so often and prostrating himself to worship the apex of her mound with his lips until she begged for him again. They peaked close together, and Aidon lay back, fitting her against his side, gathering his cloak around her as though it were the sheets of their massive bed. He started to nod off, blissfully drowsy and content, trying to keep himself conscious so they wouldn't awaken at noonday to curious Eleusinians or an angry Demeter.

He stroked Persephone's hair, hoping she would sleep in his arms, under the stars. He'd carry her unseen through the Telesterion to her bed if she did. "I love you, sweet one," he murmured. "I'm counting the days until you return."

"I am as well. I love you, my dear husband." She closed her eyes and nuzzled up to him, petting his chest, her limbs heavy, her words slurring from sated exhaustion. "I want to give you a child, Aidoneus. A son. I want to fill our home with your sons and daughters."

He said nothing.

"Aidon?"

Hades stared at the sky, wide eyed and silent until Persephone finally fell asleep.

19.

"LYING WITH THAT CREATURE WAS MORE important than keeping a promise?"

Persephone gaped at Demeter. Three days had passed since her return from Ephyra, each one filled with silence between mother and daughter. She knew this was long overdue. Still, Persephone had expected more subtlety. Her face grew hot, and she felt her stomach sink.

"That... Plutonion your little band of fanatics built was *covered* with—"

"Larkspur and narcissus, yes! I don't deny any of it!" Persephone's voice echoed through the empty hall of the Telesterion. She calmed herself. "And I don't regret it."

"How could you?"

"How could I what?" Her eyes narrowed to slits. "Spend a night making love with my husband, who I hadn't seen for three months?"

"You weren't—" Demeter took a breath. "He is *not* your husband. He abducted you and your marriage was—"

"Enough, Mother! Zeus reversed his edict. At least my *father* knows how to keep an oath."

"Yes, that makes one among us."

320

"I didn't *swear on the Styx* to sit next to you in that pretty little chair for the festival! That was your idea. I had more important things to take care of."

"Like that selfish monster's carnal needs? And next to *my* temple no less! Thankfully, when Diocles told me about the burst of new flowers, he didn't know what you did there, but *I did*." Their existence was even more of a blow than anything else. Only an act of love between an earth goddess and her chosen mate could have grown those flowers. Demeter herself had done so with Zeus, a great field of poppies springing up beneath them on Crete so very long ago. "It isn't enough that you admit to lying with him. Now I'm forced to see the evidence of your fornication so close to—"

"The same way I'm forced to hear you fucking Triptolemus?"

"Language!"

"What else would you call it? For three months I've had to listen to your bed creaking down the hall from me!"

Demeter's face grew red. "You are the bedmate of a violator and call him your husband, you call your defilement 'lovemaking'! What has he done to force you to tell me these lies, and tell them to yourself?"

"I had a choice to leave Hades, to leave the Underworld and never return, yet I ate the seeds to remain with him. You lie to yourself because you can't stand when I tell you the truth." She turned to walk away. "You have no idea what you're talking about, Mother."

"Don't I? Helios told me how loudly you screamed, that you cried out for *me* to save you when you were abducted. And don't think I was deaf to rumors about what that monster did to you before you even arrived in the Pit!"

Persephone stared at Demeter, her voice like ice. "And why was he compelled to abduct me? Why was he forced to consummate our marriage so hastily, Mother? Answer me that."

Demeter stopped breathing.

321

"You're not the only one who hears things."

Her mouth was dry, her eyes glassy. "I didn't—"

"Because he got there first."

"I would never have—"

"Wouldn't you? What was I to become?" She paced a slow circle around Demeter, fighting to keep her anger at bay. "An oak?"

"Kore..." She gentled, her eyes filling with tears.

"A laurel like Daphne? No, it would have to have borne flowers. Pear, then?" She sneered. "Pomegranate, perhaps?"

"Stop..."

"I think I would have rather liked that."

"Please..."

"To be a pomegranate tree..."

"Stop it!"

"No! This is yours! *Own it!* I was to be bound to Aidoneus whether you liked it or not and your last desperate scheme nearly ruined my chances for a happy marriage. Fates be praised I found it in my heart to trust Aidon after he did what had to be done!"

Demeter stayed silent.

"And it wasn't even a fit of madness! Merely the last flourish in a lifetime spent sheltering me from men and sex."

"I only wanted to protect you," she whispered.

"By forcing Daphne's fate on me? By taking away my free will?!"

"You don't understand what was at stake!"

"You tried to subvert the will of the Fates, to hide me from the man I was betrothed to in the womb, and you never even told me! You never bothered to tell me about Iasion, you forced Kyrene to leave, you banished the Oriades, sent away my friends, forbade me from speaking with the mortals... You... you yanked me away from my home in Nysa when I started to bleed, and barely told me anything about *that*! I thought I'd done something wrong!"

Demeter had nearly forgotten Kyrene, the warrior nymph that bore an ill-gotten child by Apollo. It was as though Persephone were emptying a storehouse filled with all the anger she'd harvested over the aeons. "I sacrificed *everything* to raise you well. I kept you safe, Daughter. Do you think that recluse would have rushed to protect you if you attracted the attentions of Ares, or Apollo, or Poseidon? You have *no idea* what sort of pain I prevented."

"You're right. I knew nothing about the dangers around me. And I was helpless because you never taught me how to protect myself!"

"There were things I taught you—"

"To become invisible *to mortals*. To grow brambles."

"What else was I supposed to do?!"

"You could have taught me to escape, to travel the ether to safety. But you couldn't have me running away or relying on myself, could you?"

"Worse could have happened to you there!"

"What, exactly? Discovering the goddess I was born to be?" She folded her arms across her chest and raised her chin. "That I'm more powerful than you are?"

The Harvest Goddess clenched her teeth and the room chilled and darkened. Persephone leaned back as her mother took a slow step toward her. "Do not forget, little one, that I am aeons older than you. I challenged Iapetos the Piercer *before* the Titans were bound in chains. You will not disrespect me so."

Persephone flinched, her fists still tight. "Respect is earned, not given, and you've never had the decency to show *me* any. Stay away from me."

Demeter's shoulders slumped. "Kore, you don't mean that."

"I'm forced to *stay* here with you," she hissed as her vision blurred. "Not *speak* with you or see you. No agreement can force me to do that!" Persephone wiped the back of her hand across her reddened face, brushing tears away. She gulped around the acidic lump in her throat and muttered her thoughts aloud. "Gods above, I cannot wait to go home again..."

"But... your home is with..." Her face fell.

"Home!!" she shouted. "Where I'm called *Persephone*. Where my husband loves and respects me!"

"Kore, please..."

"Stop calling me Kore, *you selfish sow!*"

Her mother stood frozen, her jaw slackened and tears brimming in her wide eyes.

Persephone stared forward, frozen, her throat tightening. She picked up her skirts and bounded up the stairs, fleeing the hall and her mother's quiet weeping. She slammed her door shut and crashed down on her bed, curling up into a ball, waiting for Demeter to angrily fling the door open and demand an apology.

Nothing.

Persephone— Kore, by any measure of how powerless she felt— shuddered and wrapped her arms around her chest. She buried her face in the pillow and bawled.

*   *   *

Demeter collapsed in the greenhouse behind the throne room, sobbing. She was furious with herself. Zeus had told her to not fan the flames. But with that argument, she might as well have thrown Kore bodily into Hades's arms. She huddled, her knees to her chest, the front of her peplos damp with tears. She didn't see the growing light as the door slowly opened, nor did she hear it shut. Demeter only felt strong arms wrap around her shoulders, and heard Triptolemus whisper comfort and reassurance into her ear.

That night, Persephone heard the groaning of the bed frame in Demeter's room, and guessed that her mother and Triptolemus had made amends. She didn't want to ask how or why— it was none of her business, just as her marriage shouldn't be any concern of Demeter's. Persephone wrapped her pillow around her ears to muffle their reconciliation.

She and her mother didn't speak to one another for days after, parting ways each morning to attend their duties. Persephone nurtured the second planting and Demeter made sure the first harvest grew strong and full in its bounty. Mortals and nymphs surrounded Persephone throughout her waking hours. She grew used to the company of Eumolpus and Minthe, and was often joined by a pretty Oceanid named Daeira who was three months along with Hermes's child. Even so, her separation from Demeter made her feel isolated. Worse still, the constant companionship made her miss her husband all the more.

The week after his departure, Persephone was filled with hope and trepidation, wondering if she would quicken with Aidon's seed. All the flowers had fallen from the pomegranate trees in Eleusis the night after their coupling, and little bulbs of fruit started to appear on the branches. She took it as a sign. Many of the women in town were as fertile as the fields they tended, and the countryside was full of wives— and a few soon-to-be wives— with radiant smiles and growing bellies. She'd spoken with many about their glad news. But when she shared with them that her husband had been sending souls back from Asphodel to be reborn, many had recoiled in fear.

A few did understand and would give her a wistful smile, saying they wondered if the life they carried was a lost loved one returning to them. Persephone answered honestly, that she did not know— that no one could. One woman, a student of Eumolpus, had said that she planned to name her child Plutus if it were a boy, the closest anyone could come to honoring her husband. There were already a great many Artemisias and Hephaestions, Dimitris and Apollonas living in Eleusis. Why not a Plutus?

Persephone fantasized about what she would name their child if he'd given her one that night under the stars. Of course she would consult with Aidoneus, but her mind happily wandered from name to name as she walked through the fields, filling the plants with renewed life.

Persephone finally settled upon a potent one: Zagreus. 'King of the Reborn'. It would fit perfectly, given his parentage and the destiny accorded to their eventual son by Zeus's oath. She giddily wished that she already knew how to write so she could tell Aidon of her idea. More sober reflection reminded Persephone that despite being the Goddess of Spring, fertility personified, she searched for signs of whether or not his seed had taken root in her fertile soil.

The next morning, she awoke to both bed sheet and sleeping chiton stained with blood. Minthe came to wake her and heard her weeping. Persephone lay with her head in the nymph's lap, and Minthe petted her hair while the goddess cried inconsolably. Persephone said as little as possible when Minthe asked what was wrong. It was better to not divulge too much to Demeter's faithful servant. The naiad patiently listened to her broken sobs, reassuring her that all would be well. At noonday, Persephone finally arose and washed, sponging her thighs. She wadded a rag inside an itchy loincloth and donned her clean peplos, then resolved that she wouldn't let any more flights of fancy get the better of her. She would speak plainly with Aidoneus, and together they would decide on how best to conceive.

When she'd made her desire for his child known in the midst of hazy afterglow, he'd remained silent. Was he reluctant to have children? Things had certainly changed since she'd first contemplated the idea of a family with him. Perhaps he desired to talk with her further about it, but had wanted to let her rest. His silence was likely borne of consideration.

Practical questions replaced fancy and loomed over her as she tended the growing crops. How would they raise a child? More importantly, *where* would they raise it? Would the babe travel with her, or stay at home with Aidon? What would her mother think? Would Demeter welcome Persephone's child knowing that Hades had sired it?

Demeter came to her the next morning and sat at the edge of her bed. Her weight shifted the mattress, and Persephone stirred from sleep, bleary eyed. A hesitant, almost penitent smile crossed her mother's features. Demeter held a warm cup of honeyed kykeon, and Persephone could smell a strong dose of ambrosia, pennyroyal and willow bark wafting from the ceramic cup.

"Minthe told me your courses came," she said quietly. "Here. This will help you feel better."

Persephone sat up slowly, her hips and lower back still sore, and reached for the offered drink. "How?"

"When taken with ambrosia, the same herbs and tinctures that make humans well can also affect us." Demeter smiled, trying to reassure her. Persephone regarded at her skeptically. The Goddess of the Harvest folded her hands in her lap and looked down. "It… it is your private life. I should not have said anything. I have my concerns…"

"I *know* you have concerns."

"Rightfully so, considering—" Demeter's voice climbed in pitch before she held her tongue and took in a deep breath. "Daughter, you were right."

"About what?"

"I often speak of— and suffered from— your father's hypocrisy. But if I have my own private affairs and chastise you for having yours, then I am no better than he."

Persephone lifted the cup to her lips and sipped a long draught, the ambrosia mingling with the honey, thickened by the barley. It filled her belly with sweetness and warmth, hiding the bitterness of the herbs. "What assurance do I have that you won't interfere again? That you won't heap scorn on my husband or our marriage?"

"None, truthfully."

Persephone snorted into the cup and took another sip.

"Only that I… promise to try."

She looked up and set the cup down. The cramps eased and the pain lessened as the pennyroyal and willow bark took effect.

"Kore, I'm sorry."

"But not enough to call me by my real name."

"I called you that for aeons. You've..." she swallowed, the words heavy in her mouth. "You've been... *Persephone* for only a few months. Please give me time. I cannot change my ways overnight."

"Mother," she said with a strained smile, "can I ask you to change one thing right now?"

"You can ask."

"Please stop disparaging my husband." She watched Demeter's lips thin. "I know how you see him. The *whole world* knows how you see Aidoneus. But I know him, I know the full, unfettered truth of him. And I love him."

Demeter nodded slowly without meeting her eyes, her forehead creasing.

"He is my other half." Her mother sighed plaintively, and Persephone felt waves of frustration rolling off of her. She took her mother's hand in hers. "Just as Iasion was... just as Triptolemus is... *your* other half."

Demeter grimaced. "Triptolemus... he is a good man. Iasion was a good man— a great comfort to me. But as for my other half..." Tears formed in Demeter's eyes. "I chose poorly. My choice gave me you, and you've given me more joy than I thought possible, but I chose poorly."

"But you have someone who clearly loves you now."

"Yes," she said. "But he and I will exist for eternity. And love doesn't last that long. I learned that in the most bitter of ways. It will only be a matter of time. Centuries, if I am fortunate..."

Persephone was about to declare her bond with her husband eternal, to argue that love could last forever, but she stayed silent. What did she know of loss and betrayal? Demeter had loved and been abandoned in her most vulnerable

328

hour, then had loved again and lost. If Persephone boasted about her idyllic marriage, she would only hurt her mother. "I am sorry for what I called you."

Demeter blinked back tears and stared out the window. Lines of worry melted from her face. She smiled, then laughed.

Persephone leaned back, confused. "Mother?"

"No, it's all right. I forgive you. I just remembered something from long ago." Persephone inclined her head to listen as the Harvest Goddess continued. "Your husband called me a selfish sow once."

"Mother…"

"I promise I am not speaking ill of him." She brought the back of her hand up to her mouth and laughed again. "It was a long time ago, when I was young and foolish. I deserved it… somewhat. I was with Hecate when they slew Kampe. He'd stumbled back to camp, his hair singed, gashes all over him, his cloak still smoking. And I bounded over to Aidoneus and practically shook him by the armor, begging him to tell me that Zeus was unharmed."

Persephone's mouth quirked into a half smile. Demeter never spoke about the war except to exalt her father. And even at that, she hadn't heard those tales since she was a little girl.

"Oh, the rage I put him into!" Demeter guffawed. "Hecate held him back and I was crying and crying… You should have heard the tongue lashing she gave him afterward, and seen his face when he had to apologize to me."

Persephone giggled, imagining diminutive Hecate scolding her towering husband.

"But I *was* selfish back then. Rebellious and childish." Demeter snorted. "If I had known then what I know now about your father, I wouldn't have given a fig about his fate."

Persephone snickered and drew Demeter into a tight embrace. She swallowed the lump in her throat. "I love you, Mother."

"I love you too, Daughter." She relaxed. "Even if it comes out all wrong."

"I know."

"I'll try. I promise." She patted Persephone's back. "Do you feel any better?"

"I do." She leaned away, a grin spreading across her face. "Can I... blame my harsh words on the phase of the moon?"

"You can." Demeter's eyes lit up. "Are you feeling well enough to travel? I hear Thassos is lovely right now."

20.

FOR THE NEXT TWO MONTHS MOTHER AND daughter did not argue. Demeter didn't fuss over her, or pepper her with questions or insinuations. Persephone didn't object to Minthe remaining her companion.

Hermes came on each full moon to visit Daeira and deliver gifts for Persephone from Aidoneus: first, an assortment of six jeweled hairpins, then a beautifully embroidered wool shawl woven from the fibers of the world below, and lastly a blank papyrus scroll and stylus pen. Demeter held her tongue. She said nothing when Persephone braided and snipped a lock of her hair for Hermes to take back to the Lord of the Dead. When Eumolpus or Metaneira or one of the Eleusinians mentioned anything about Hades, his realm or the afterlife, Demeter remained tight-lipped and let Persephone speak her mind and heart.

Three days before Persephone was to make her journey to the Underworld, Demeter stood in her daughter's room, watching Persephone twist her hair into an elegant chignon and secure it into place with a gold and garnet hairpin.

"Why, of all places, would you go to Olympus?" she asked her daughter.

"I was invited," Persephone said with a smile, tucking a loose strand behind her ear and adjusting her floral crown. She'd chosen an arrangement of asphodel and crocus, and put on the necklace and the jeweled girdle that Aidoneus had given her. She changed the color of her peplos to a rich gold, letting the garnets, rubies and fire opals stand out on their own. It was a dress for harvest— for the time between her dual role as Goddess of Spring and Queen of the Underworld. Her coiffured hair and jeweled raiment made her vaguely uncomfortable. This was as finely as she'd ever dressed, save for the ceremonial robes and jewels worn in Hades's court at judgement.

Persephone giggled to herself. She half suspected that Aidon had transferred the responsibility of judging the wealthy and powerful to Minos, Rhadamanthys and Aeacus just so he would never have to wear uncomfortable ceremonial attire in his throne room again.

"What's so amusing?"

"Nothing... a memory."

"Who summoned you to the mountain, anyway?" Demeter asked softly, folding her arms. "I received no such invitation."

"My father," she answered cautiously. "He told me I should visit, and I think now is as good a time as any."

"But you leave in only three days."

"Exactly," she said with a smile. "Tomorrow the wheat reaping begins, and I likely won't get to visit Olympus while I'm below. This is my only chance."

Demeter shook her head. "That place is a viper pit. Fornication and gossip are the Olympians' only currency. There is a reason I go as rarely as possible."

"Then I should find that out on my own, no?"

Demeter exhaled sharply through her nose. "No, you shouldn't *have to* find out on your own— that's why I'm warning you. It's not safe— especially if you value your marriage and your privacy. Besides— it's unwise to journey there alone as a woman."

Persephone barely suppressed an eye roll. She wrapped her pomegranate-colored shawl around her shoulders. The mornings were crisp and dewy now, and she guessed it would be even cooler on the top of Olympus.

"Who is accompanying you?" Demeter said, following her downstairs through the Telesterion and into the great hall. She was tempted to ask if Hades was meeting her there for another tryst, and almost drew blood biting her tongue.

"Athena. She's coming here first. And Hermes said he'd meet us there."

Demeter's lips thinned at the mention of Metis's daughter. She still blamed the Goddess of Wisdom for passively aiding Hades when Kore was abducted from Nysa. "Be careful, Daughter."

"I promise I'll be alert and cautious, Mother, and I won't stay too long. I'll return before nightfall." With that, she gave Demeter a hug and a kiss on the cheek, then started for the door. Persephone stepped outside, listening to a lonely sparrow chirp. A great flock of noisy terns flew overhead, bound for the south.

"Persephone?"

Spinning around, she saw the source of the voice, none other than the Patroness of Athens. Athena leaned against the walls of the Telesterion, wearing a sky blue peplos held to her body with a silver cuirass. Her hair was coiffed to hold up a hoplite's helm that she wore tilted on her head like a crown. It was a lighter, more ornate design than Persephone's, made in Hephaestus's forge, not those of the Cyclopes.

"Athena!" Persephone stopped awkwardly in front of her, remembering that the gray-eyed goddess wasn't as affectionate as she.

Athena surprised Persephone by giving her a tight embrace. "My dear cousin, I've missed you… How are you?"

"I'm well, and you?"

"Likewise. What a beautifully woven shawl... a gift from your husband, I presume?"

*   *   *

They walked down the Sacred Way, hand in hand, stopping every so often to observe menfolk getting a head start on the barley. The women had resumed their traditional roles inside the home, preparing for harvest, grinding grain into meal, no longer out in the fields. Many had grown heavy with child. Persephone missed seeing them.

"I've been watching how everything has progressed since you returned," Athena said, "and it is simply beautiful. Even I can feel the life in the crops. The greatest part of the harvest is soon, yes?"

"It is, and thank you," Persephone said, then sighed. "It hasn't been easy."

"I can imagine. But is the difficulty in managing the crops or managing Demeter?"

Persephone's eyes went wide and she guffawed, clapping a hand to her mouth. She glanced sheepishly at Athena, whose nose scrunched when she smiled broadly. Persephone shook her head and spoke. "I... Mother and I get along well enough, and it's been better these past few months, but I don't think we'll ever see eye to eye on... several things."

"Ah..." Athena said. She grew solemn and looked at the ground. "There's something I've been meaning to ask since I saw you last, Persephone. Can you forgive my inquisition when I was here five months ago? I had heard things. We'd all heard things."

"I know."

"And it was wise of you not to divulge anything. I apologize for my motives in desiring your confidence. I prodded you for too much information."

"You're forgiven. Aidoneus doesn't care what anyone on Olympus says about him. And seeing how hungry everyone was for the smallest morsel of news once I returned, I can understand why. Speaking of, I still haven't heard from Artemis," she said. The road bent around a centuries-old olive tree, its boughs filled with spear-shaped leaves and heavy with purple and green fruits.

"Give her time. She's… uncomfortable around *married* women." Athena reached up and plucked an olive. "I'm indebted to you for bringing these trees to fruit so quickly."

Persephone shrugged. "They're very important. I'm happy you asked after them when we last spoke. You care very much for the people of Athens, and this is their greatest crop."

"Yes," Athena smiled. "But more importantly, it helps me keep my claim over Attica. Without it, Poseidon would have tried to steal its worshippers from me."

Persephone quirked an eyebrow. "Truly?"

"He is… not to be trusted," she said, furrowing her brow.

"To be honest, I'm surprised. Aidoneus always has good things to say about him."

Athena snorted. "Perhaps so, but your husband is a *man*. It's different when you're a woman, especially a *free* woman dealing with him."

"Hmm," Persephone acknowledged, remembering her mother's bitter feud with Zeus, the lengths she had gone to in order to be taken seriously, and all that their struggle had damaged. Such suffering it caused, she thought, this conflict between male and female…

"I would likewise have cautioned you to stay away from Ares, but I doubt he'll give you any trouble after how you dealt with Sisyphus," Athena laughed. "He was quick to boast that he disarmed that wicked man but oh, the riot we had with him on Olympus when we found out from Eris! Well, partly from Eris. Hermes let slip what Hypnos told him…"

Persephone half-listened to her go on about it, laughing at Ares's expense. She trained her features into what was becoming a practiced smile. Persephone would have to tread lightly on Olympus and be careful with whom she spoke. Her mother was right. Gossip was their currency.

As for their other tender, she was sure that fear of her husband would keep her safe from any sexual advances. Hades's frightful reputation would keep her from harm. But if she revealed the depth of his affection for her, it might endanger her. Her shoulders sank. She would even have to be careful about how much she shared with Athena. They stopped on the road once they were clear of any mortals. Athena raised her right hand, ready to open a path to the home of the gods.

"Allow me." Persephone smiled and summoned an asphodel bloom from the ground, which burst into a swirl of flame, creating a gateway through the ether. She drew their destination closer, the gardens of Olympus coming into sharp relief.

"Well then..." Athena gave her a wide-eyed grin, impressed. "After you, Queen of the Underworld," she said with a playful bow.

"No, I insist, Patroness of Athens," Persephone smiled. They giggled and Athena walked forward, holding Persephone's hand.

They were met with blinding light and lush gardens when the gateway closed behind them. The trees and shrubs were carefully manicured and more symmetrical than anything that Persephone could have imagined, as though each tree had been clipped to expose their eternal fruits perfectly. She saw apples— a rarity in Attica— figs, dates and pomegranates, each fruit exactly like the other, growing above perfectly flat grass lawns where every blade seemed to be cut to the same length. An olive tree grew with only enough twists in its limbs to allow someone to easily scale it and pluck its dark purple fruits, which were all the same shape and shade. Persephone had only known these trees to grow untamed, at the whim of rain and sun. She discovered that she didn't really need her shawl. The temperature was... ideal.

"Glorious, isn't it?" Athena said, breaking her contemplation. She picked up the skirts of her peplos and walked up the perfectly hewn marble steps.

Persephone followed, and they entered a vast atrium, fronted on all sides with colonnades and murals of plants and animals. Water bubbled up from a spring in the center into the rectangular basin of a fountain. Its soothing trickle was accompanied by a lyre and flute played by two women in diaphanous linen chitons, golden beaded nets gilding their coiffured blonde hair. The delicately plucked strings and the clear tones of the flute filled the air with a soft, almost slumberous music.

Athena traversed the atrium with the Goddess of Spring in tow, and the musicians stopped mid-verse, genuflecting before the goddesses. "Persephone, these are Erato and Euterpe, the muses of poetry."

"My lady," they said in unison and bowed.

"It's a pleasure to meet you."

"May we continue?" one said.

"...Of course," Persephone answered, surprised that they had asked her permission.

They curtsied again and started their melody anew. Persephone wondered if everyone would be so formal here. They walked on, passing into a great symposium hall. She balked. This was the throne room of Olympus... the same one she had seen in the vision Kronos had given her in Tartarus. There was a grand dais with twelve steps, upon which sat the throne of Zeus, and Hera's seat three steps below his. A banquet table spread out on one end of the hall, strewn with amphorae of all sizes, each filled with wine, nectar or olive oil. Ambrosia was piled beside round loaves of bread, a great wheel of goat cheese, grapes, and figs. Great cuts of cooked, seasoned meat sat on the table: lamb, goat, and the fruits of the sea— the smells of which were overwhelming. Persephone felt nauseous. Though she would never begrudge the mortals their meat, neither she nor her mother ever touched it. None of the immortals *needed* to eat; they feasted for pleasure. Feasts arrived by way of libations and sacrifices, so food seldom, if ever, appeared in the Underworld. Aidon never partook unless it was a special occasion, like the first ripe pomegranate from their grove.

Mingling alongside the table and throughout the room were a host of immortals so finely clad that it made her feel plain. On her first day in the Underworld, she had thought the jewels Aidoneus had given her to be extravagant. But the gods and goddess, as well as their retinues and attendants, looked... over done. A few glanced at her, some out of curiosity, some in recognition. Over strains of music from every corner of the room she could hear faint whispers of 'Persephone', 'Hades' and 'Demeter'.

Persephone suddenly felt herself missing the Underworld more acutely than ever. Though her husband was the Rich One, his domain the origin of every jewel and pin and fine gold chain adorning these Olympian gods, Aidoneus never made a show of it. She thought of the diamond and sapphire ceiling of the grotto pool under the palace. To him, jewels were not evidence of power or prestige. Instead, he carefully chose what he thought most suited something, or best complemented someone. Persephone touched her necklace and smiled.

"I have to warn you, Persephone, not everyone here is worthy of your time," Athena said as they walked through the atrium arm in arm. "You should stay away from Apollo. He'll only flatter you, and he doesn't take rejection well. Hermes is a *notorious* gossip, as I'm sure you already know. And don't trifle with either Hera or Aphrodite."

"Ah."

"No one has seen Hephaestus the last few days. He's been working on some commission he refuses to talk about, but he once tried to—"

"So I should only stay with you, then?" she asked, tilting her head.

Athena looked at her and thinned her lips sheepishly. Persephone gave her a half-smile and the Goddess of Wisdom laughed. "Oh, listen to me go on! I must sound like your mother. Forgive me, Persephone. Speak with whomever you'd like. You hardly need my protection anyway."

"Athena! A word with you!" Ares barked at her, a cup of wine in his hand. His face immediately paled and fell when he glimpsed Persephone.

"Thank you," she said and gave her cousin a quick kiss on the cheek.

"I ought to see what that great fool wants from me this time. Another silly wager, I'd guess," Athena said, hugging her. "Be careful, all right?"

Persephone nodded and they parted ways. Scanning the room, she didn't see Hermes anywhere. It wasn't like him to be late, and he had said he would gladly help her navigate the sea of new faces.

After a moment of standing alone, a beautiful young man approached her. His figure was lithe, his skin oiled and perfumed, and his chest smooth, as though every errant hair had been plucked. His only garment was a short chlamys, one side thrown back over his shoulder and the other scarcely concealing his nether regions. An inadvertent downward glance confirmed Persephone's suspicions and she blushed. Indeed *every* hair on his body had been plucked. "Can I interest the lady in a cup of nectar?"

She'd never felt the effects of nectar— ambrosia wine— having only eaten the food of immortality in its unadulterated form. It was best to keep her wits about her here. "No, thank you. What is your name, if I may ask?"

"Ganymede, milady. The cupbearer of Zeus," he said with a slight nod. "If you'll pardon my saying so, I've never seen you here before. Might I ask the resplendent lady's name?"

"Persephone!" A voice boomed from a nearby divan. Zeus. She barely noticed Ganymede back away from her fearfully at the utterance of her name.

"Your grace," she said softly and bowed low to the King of the Gods.

"Oh, we'll have none of that formal nonsense here... we're family!" He clapped a broad arm over her shoulder and smiled, showing his teeth. His beard was not streaked through with nearly as much white as the last time she had seen him, but he was still a far cry from the ancient yet youthful refinement of her husband. Zeus was wrapped in a gold-embroidered royal purple himation and his breath reeked of wine. The blonde nymph he'd left behind on the divan set down both their cups, folded her arms and pouted.

"Indeed we are, your grace."

"Whom can I introduce you to?"

She was shocked by his informality. Wasn't this the very same man who had called up rank and title and tried to cow her into submission to his rule not six months ago? "Well, I've already met quite a few. Hermes, ahh... Ares, Athena, and Artemis, of course..." She trailed off.

"Since you're bound for the sunless world in less than three days, I should introduce you to Apollo. Come," he said, shepherding her with a hand at her back, moving her across the room.

She heard hushed voices as she passed by groups of immortals. "Demeter's daughter..." "No wonder she hid her away! If only I had gotten to her before..." "Poor thing's beauty will shrivel away down there..." "Did she really? I heard he *forced* her to eat..."

Persephone passed an exotic, golden skinned woman of impossible beauty fanning herself. Her eyes were rimmed with kohl and a diadem balanced on her head with golden strands weaving an intricate pattern across her dark hair. Deep in conversation with her attendants, she laughed lightly and spoke with a hint of an accent. "They can't be *that* interesting! It's probably him on top with the lamps out and their chitons on every time!"

One of her girls leaned in. "No, my lady! Hermes swore up and down that he saw—" The woman shook her fan at the girl who promptly fell silent, and watched as Persephone walked past. The Queen of the Underworld glared at the woman. She stared straight back, serene, her gaze piercing all the way through Persephone, seeming to draw her in. Persephone flinched and averted her eyes, her cheeks burning.

"Who was that?"

"Aphrodite," Zeus answered, his voice flat. "Someone can introduce you to *her* later."

Persephone fumed. The Goddess of Love herself had been brazenly gossiping about her husband and their love life, of all things. Why in the name of the Fates did *any* of these fools find her intimacy with Aidon so interesting in the first place? She shook her head. The next three days couldn't pass fast enough.

Zeus and Persephone finally stopped in front of a sunlit divan with a golden-haired man and several women draped across it. He was in the middle of a song, telling a story about love unrequited with a flawless tenor voice and a silver lyre. Two of the women, who Persephone recognized from the courtyard as Erato and Euterpe gazed longingly up at him. Apollo glanced at Persephone and winked, his melody uninterrupted. She raised an eyebrow. Was anyone in Zeus's court *not* completely shameless? He ended his final verse with a slowly plucked chord. When he finished, Zeus, the women and Persephone clapped for him. Apollo stood and bowed low, his eyes traveling up her body as he rose.

"Persephone Karpophoros Chthonios, daughter of Demeter, may I present Apollon Lykeios Delphinios, son of Leto."

She curtsied to him and he bowed exaggeratedly low once again, then gave her a wide smile filled with perfect teeth. "Apollo, please. And I believe we've met before."

"We have?"

"We were only children, then. I think I gave you flowers— larkspur of all things— and recited an ode to you." He chuckled. "Your mother was furious!"

"Forgive me. You're now the god of...?"

"Prophecy, music, light, the healing arts..."

"That's... quite the list of accomplishments."

"This from a fair goddess who is both life and death at once."

"I'll leave you two be. I have a feeling you'll get on famously!" Zeus said. He paced back to his divan, then bellowed a laugh and buried his face in his companion's cleavage as she smiled and squealed.

Persephone's mouth twisted contemptuously. Where was Hera, his queen? A hand on her shoulder interrupted her thoughts.

"There goes Father Zeus again..."

"You disapprove of him?"

"Naturally," he said and shrugged. "But, if he begets on that silly nymph, that could be one more ally on our side. Not of noble blood, but we shouldn't split hairs..."

"*Our* side?" Persephone swallowed and looked at him with alarm. Was he openly talking about rebellion? Another war among the gods? "What do you mean?"

He cracked another disarmingly beautiful and calculated smile. "Oh, don't be so serious, Sephia!" His face fell slightly when her features twisted. "Should I not call you that?"

"Persephone, please."

"Persephone then. And what a contradictory name for one so very radiant. Don't be so grave, darling. I'm not sug-

342

gesting anything like open war. Everyone here is subtler than that, as you'll come to learn. Here— give us a smile."

She imagined for a moment what Aidoneus would do with this silly boy if he knew that he was attempting to use his charms on her. Picturing Apollo begging for mercy finally turned up the corners of her mouth.

"There's a good girl," he continued. "What I mean is that Zeus's... fruit plucked from less *legitimate* branches of the Olympian tree should stick together. You're already friends with Athena and my sister, Artemis, and Hermes, if I'm not mistaken."

"Yes." She looked around for Hermes. "Speaking of, have you seen—"

"Good!" He interrupted. "We shall be friends too."

"Friends?" So it was *friendship* he wanted... Maybe, Persephone thought, she was taking his behavior the wrong way. The Olympians seemed to be from a world set far apart from her and her mother, not to mention her husband. His forwardness could have been learned from Zeus and the others. What else had she heard about Apollo besides Athena's brief warning? Artemis rarely spoke about her brother. She knew of his pursuit of Daphne. The nymphs she'd known had had a checkered acquaintance with him. Except for one... "We may yet have another friend in common."

"Do we, now..." he beamed. "And whose acquaintance might we share, radiant one?"

"Do you know Kyrene?"

He looked at her blankly. "Who?"

"She was a friend of mine long ago. She mentioned you once. That you and she were... lovers."

"You blush so charmingly, but sadly, I cannot recall her. Are you sure she and I..."

Persephone swallowed. "Ah... yes. She said that you found her in Libya—"

343

"Oh, now I remember! The lion tamer girl! Yes, she was..." he ran his hand back through his curls. "She was something. Kyrene had a son, I believe?"

"Aristaios."

"That's right... the beekeeper, cheese maker... busy little god, isn't he?"

"I've never met him," she admitted. "Sadly, I haven't spoken with Kyrene since she conceived him."

He laughed. "Then that's another thing we have in common."

Persephone's face fell. "Never mind. I thought you might know where she was."

"Heavens no," he said dismissively. When she frowned he tilted his head toward her. "I didn't mean it that way, Persephone. She's probably wrestling lions in Libya right now. And I find my present company far more... engaging."

"I see."

"But speaking of him, Aristaios prepares the most *wondrous* delicacies. Have you ever tasted cheese and honey together?"

"I cannot say I have," she said. Most families in Eleusis owned a goat, perhaps two, and maybe had some extra milk during kidding, but rarely turned that into cheese. Apollo flicked his wrist toward a serving girl, then motioned Ganymede to their side. The girl held up a golden tray piled with dates stuffed with soft goat cheese and drizzled with honey. Apollo grabbed a full cup from Ganymede.

"You simply must try these. They go so well with the nectar," he said, picking up a date. She reached for one, only to be blocked by Apollo. "Ah-ah... allow me."

He drew closer to her, his lip curling into a half-smile. Apollo lightly caressed the back of her arm and lifted the date to her lips. Persephone took a full step back from his reach. "Apollo..."

"What's the matter? You don't want a taste?"

"I… yes. But this is… You know that I'm married, don't you?"

"Of course I know. *Everyone* knows." He rolled his eyes. "I'm only asking you to take a bite… to sample… to try something new."

"That's not all you're asking of me."

"You are a bright flower indeed."

"So state your intentions."

"You'd prefer I speak plainly?" He pulled his shoulders back. "You make such a beautiful addition to Olympus and I want to introduce you to all its potential. You are a queen, Persephone. You can do what you want, when you want, *with whom* you want. No one expects you to abstain while you're away from him. And it would be a sin to be so selfish with your charms. Is that plain enough?"

She wanted to run from the room, but she refused to let Apollo think he could intimidate her. If word got around, her troubles with the rest of the gods would be endless. "I find myself… steadily occupied when I'm in the world above. I have *many* responsibilities."

"But you work so hard! You miss out on all the delights the world has to offer. There are so many different fruits to bite into, and so many who would be willing to show you how. I humbly beg the opportunity," he said, taking a step closer, the date inching toward her lips.

She turned her head aside. "Opportunity abounds, my lord, but I'm not interested. I have my husband."

"For six months of the year…"

"For always."

"Persephone, open your eyes and look around you… Zeus is married. Aphrodite is married, and Hermes has Penelopeia, but they also know that there is greater pleasure to be had in… sampling. The monotony will wear on you over time, as it does to all. And time is all we have, radiant one. Why chain yourself to that… *corpse*—"

345

"I beg your pardon?" The words exited her lips with a hiss.

He laughed lightly at her reaction and shook his head. "What else does one call a god who doesn't eat, sleep, or lust after women?"

"A faithful husband!"

"Whom you are with only half the year..."

"I don't consider my fidelity to be 'chains', Apollo. We teach the mortals—"

"The mortals? Oh, the peasants are faithful, but their kings are not. We are deathless, radiant one, and such constraints are mere curiosities to our kind. I know that as an... earth goddess... you rarely spend time among *us*. Especially since your mother tends to shun Olympus for lesser beings. You have a golden chance to experience pleasure... *real* pleasure..."

She raised her brows. Now she was certain Aidoneus would tear him to pieces, if he weren't too busy laughing. Perhaps he would do both. "Real pleasure?"

"You are a rare fruit ripe for plucking, radiant one, and this room is *filled* with eager harvesters. I thought to offer honesty before someone else beguiled you. There is so much you could have while you're here... if only you'd allow yourself to be free."

"And you intend to liberate me?"

"It would be my honor, fair goddess. If discretion concerns you, I will honor that as well. Surely for one who has *already* tasted forbidden fruit..."

She folded her arms and cocked her head to the side. "And yet there isn't a single fruit here that tempts me, Apollo."

His comely smile resolved into a sneer. "A hearty meal will leave your belly full, but you'll know hunger again soon enough. Such a shame to pass up this feast. I can't fathom how that crusty rind of stale bread pleases you so."

"I guess you never will," she said plainly. His countenance grew smug and dangerous, regarding her callously.

"Sweet, innocent Persephone..." He drew out her name. "You lie with one man, him of all men— and think you know what it will be like after ten years... a thousand... of *nothing*."

"I wonder if you would dare say any of this to him directly."

"He'll never come here. You are so naïve... a goddess of fertility latching on to a king as infertile as his kingdom. I can see it in your eyes— smell it on you— how badly you need to be taken by someone who can give you what your heart *truly* desires."

She felt fire rise within her as she stared at him, wondering if the Phlegethon lit her irises. She calmed. He wasn't worth any more of her words. Persephone relaxed her arms to her sides and rolled her hips, pushing her bosom forward. She drew out an exaggerate sigh and gave him the most contrite of smiles. "Perhaps."

"Oh?" he said with surprise. His eyes glinted as his gaze traversed her curves.

With a slow bat of her eyelashes, she spoke again. "Ganymede?"

"Y-yes milady?"

"I've changed my mind," she said, not taking her eyes off Apollo. She bit her lower lip. "I think I'll... *sample* some of that delectable nectar after all."

The god's fingers twitched and the corner of his mouth rose as Persephone extended her hand to accept the cup. She held his rapt and hungry attention as she brought it to her lips...

...and flung its contents all over him. Those nearby gasped and tried to suppress nervous laughter. Apollo stared down at his drenched clothes. So did every other pair of eyes in their corner of the room. The flute and tambourine stopped.

For a long moment, no one spoke.

"You... you contemptuous little *bitch*!" He snarled, drawing more of the hall's attention. His eyes narrowed. "*I am one of the Dodekatheon!* When Zeus hears about this you won't be received on Olympus ever again!"

"You say that to every girl who scorns you," said a female voice behind Persephone. "No wonder the women you pursue have a habit of turning themselves into trees!"

The tension in the room snapped like a lyre string and the immortals roared with loud laughter, snickers and whispers spreading throughout the rest of the room. Apollo stood open-mouthed. His face turned red and he stomped off toward the garden, shoving both Ganymede and the serving girl aside. Sticky dates rolled across the floor.

Persephone turned to see who her savior was. Her jaw dropped— it was none other than Aphrodite. She beckoned to Persephone. "Come. Let's away from this racket before another one of these Olympians underestimates you."

✻   ✻   ✻

The Queen of the Underworld followed the Goddess of Love outside to an airy pavilion overlooking the garden. Aphrodite uncoiled on a cushioned divan.

She motioned a girl over. "Khrysothemis! Wine for both of us." She gestured at the seat and stared up at Persephone. "Please. Sit."

The girl came forward with two golden cups and filled them with dark wine. "It is pomegranate," Aphrodite said. "I think you will like it."

The Queen of the Underworld frowned. "I heard what you said about me and my husband."

"I know. And I want to apologize, Queen Persephone. Please sit. Drink."

Persephone sighed and sat tensely on the opposite divan, folding her hands in her lap.

"I was mistaken," Aphrodite started. "When I looked into you, you felt it, yes?"

"I… I did."

"Have no fear. It's my business to know these things. The two of you share a stronger bond than I have seen in many, *many* aeons. It was wrong of me to doubt your passion for each other."

She blinked at the Goddess of Love. "If I hear you correctly, then, you're apologizing for accusing us of *prudery* instead of apologizing for gossiping about us in the first place?"

"Is that the apology you would prefer?"

"Yes!"

"Then I apologize for that too. I shall speak no more of you or your honored husband."

"Well, thank you very much," Persephone said, getting up to leave.

"Persephone…" Aphrodite pleaded softly. She stopped. "I promise to you I shall not. Though I cannot lessen your pain when you hear petty gossip from the mouths of others."

Persephone sat down again and stared at her lap. "Thank you for what you said… to Apollo. I don't know what else he would have done in his anger."

The Goddess laughed and lifted her cup to her lips. "I did him a favor. If he so much as touched you, your husband would have his testicles. And only because those would be the only parts left of poor Apollo once *you* were through with him." She swirled the wine in her cup. "I know who you are, *Praxidike*."

Persephone pursed her lips. "I take it you spoke with Ares."

"He… may have curled up in my bed some months ago and whined about Sisyphus and flames and the Keres. It reminded me of stories told about you elsewhere. Where they call you Ereshkigal."

Persephone sat upright. That was one of the names Merope had used.

In the easternmost islands of Hellas and the lands of Phrygia your name isn't Persephone— it's Perephatta. Beyond Phrygia, in the crescent land of the two rivers, you are called Ereshkigal.

Aphrodite nodded. "Yes. The Queen beyond the Seven Gates, ruler of the Land of No Return. Irkalla. Taken there from a flowery field above to rule with her consort Nergal," Aphrodite said over the rim of her cup. She tittered at Persephone's wide-eyed reaction and smiled. "Sound familiar?"

"The land of the fertile crescent… that's where you come from?"

"No," she said. "It was where I went when the Tyrant seized power."

"But if you're from here, then why do you look…"

"Eastern? Because something within you wishes to see me that way. But to my Ares, I appear thusly."

Persephone reeled back and nearly knocked over her cup as Aphrodite transformed within the blink of an eye, her hair now silken straight and the fiery color of the setting sun. Her eyes were still heavily rimmed with dark kohl, but had changed to a steel gray. A smattering of freckles dotted her lightly tanned cheeks. Aphrodite giggled.

"And to Hermes…" Her hair curled tightly again and became flaxen gold and lustrous, her irises green with golden centers; her were lips fuller. With a shake of her head, Aphrodite's hair and complexion darkened once more. She grinned and held Persephone's empty hands within hers.

"Y-you—" Persephone could hardly form words.

"I am as they desire to see me. I suppose it comes from being born of the many seeds of Ouranos."

"So the story about the sea foam…"

"Is true… depending on who you ask. But my story in the eastern lands as the Red Goddess, Astarte, is also true. And as for how *you* see me, Queen Persephone, I was first known in those eastern lands as Inanna. And Ereshkigal was my sister." She gave Persephone a wide, starry-eyed smile and warmly squeezed her hands. "We shall be sisters here too, yes?"

"I... Aphrodite, I'm flattered, really, but I honestly don't know you," she said, raising an eyebrow.

"Ah, but you do," Aphrodite said, sitting back and swishing her wine in the goblet. "You used my methods to deceive and humiliate Apollo. And you used my ways to seduce your husband that moonlit night on your balcony, when he was too shy to ask you to do what he truly wanted."

Persephone felt her cheeks grow hot and looked away.

"Take no offense. It is my place to know these things. We are connected, Persephone, through fertility in the world above most acutely. And you are stronger here than you imagine."

"I only," she said quietly, "grow flowers when I'm here."

"You bring the *seeds* to flower. In that way, you and I are more similar than you think. My domain lies within the flower as well. It is in the bee, humming inside the blossom. It is in the sweet nectar and pollen he stirs within it to start the fruit. My son and I, in that way, sow the seeds. He certainly sowed the seeds for you and your beloved."

Persephone thought about the golden arrow and gave her a cautious half smile. Aphrodite was earnest, at least. She sensed that most women reviled the Goddess of Love, and that although she had a great many attendants, she had few friends.

"There is a sweet tale the mortals have. About how they were first created together as one, *hermaphroditos*, that they had two equal hearts, two minds, both a phallus and a vulva, or two of whichever. But fearing their power, fearing that the mortals were connected *too* perfectly, Zeus came with his thunderbolts and split them apart. They say that one part spends its lifetime searching for the other. They say I made one such being, sired by Hermes, of all men."

"Is Hermes Eros's father?"

"No," she said, her face falling. "And neither is Ares. My son's father was from far away." Persephone read the sadness in her eyes as Aphrodite put down her cup. "And he lived a long time ago."

"What was his name?"

"Dumuzi," she whispered, looking down. She closed her kohl-rimmed eyes and took a deep breath. Aphrodite let it out, then returned her gaze to Persephone and forced a smile. "You and your husband are also split souls, yes?"

"I believe that," she said. "My mother, not as much."

Aphrodite laughed, hiding her teeth with her fan. "Have you yet performed the *hieros gamos*?"

Persephone blushed again, staring down at her dark reflection in the untouched cup of wine.

"No, then? You should. Of any of these Olympians, *you two* should. My *hieros gamos* created my son."

"Do you think ours would?"

"Do what?"

"Give us a son."

Aphrodite's lips tightened. "I know not. And I am not the one to ask such questions."

She thought back to Apollo's snide words... *naïve little girl*, he had said... *a goddess of fertility latching on to a king as infertile as his kingdom...* "Who else could answer that for me but you?" Persephone said incredulously, her brow creasing.

The Goddess of Love put her hand up. "Please do not be angry with me. We're sisters."

"We're *not* sisters! I don't even know you!"

Aphrodite turned up her nose. "Yet you ask me questions only those closest by blood or bond should answer?"

"I don't understand you." Persephone stood up. "You insult me, you apologize, you call me your sister, you say that love, desire, the *hieros gamos* itself are your domain, yet you

352

can't answer a simple question about it? Do you do anything but contradict yourself?"

Aphrodite narrowed her dark-rimmed eyes and set down her cup of wine. "I cannot answer it because your question is far from simple, little queen."

She tightened her fists, then took in a deep breath. "I see. Thank you for your hospitality."

"I apologize, that was rude. Persephone—"

"It was my own fault," she snapped. "Asking you, of all people, whose affairs behind your husband's back are legendary!"

"So you repay rudeness with unkindness? Now I *know* we are sisters," she said. Persephone wilted, mapping the hurt on Aphrodite's face.

"I'm sorry," she said, embarrassed.

"I began with an assumption about your marriage, you ended with an assumption about mine. Fitting."

Persephone felt her throat closing up. "I'm sorry, but I've had quite enough of this place today," she said, her eyes welling with tears. "Again, thank you for helping me earlier. I need to speak with my mother, obviously."

"Wait, Persephone! Not yet!"

Persephone didn't listen. She turned on her heels and left the pavilion. Behind her, she heard Aphrodite calling for an attendant to take away the untouched cup of wine.

From a distance, Persephone peered between the columns of the throne room, trying to see if Hermes had arrived late. He was supposed to meet her here! Shaking her head, she wandered into the garden, unwilling to wait any longer. She nearly knocked a bunch of grapes from its vine when she passed under a trellis, making her way toward the orchard where she and Athena had first entered the great citadel of the Olympians. The Messenger had forgotten her, and left her to stumble through this snake pit.

She brushed her eyes with her shawl, then wrapped it tightly around her shoulders, quickening her pace. From the

353

other side of a hedgerow, she heard a clucking, choking noise, followed by a gasping whimper.

Persephone slowed and peeked around the corner. She immediately regretted her curiosity. Erato knelt in front of Apollo, Euterpe stood to the side, their clothes scattered on the grass. Euterpe messily kissed him as he groped at her breast, with his other hand fisted in Erato's hair as she bobbed in front of him. A vein pulsed in his neck as Apollo broke off the kiss, and his eyes met Persephone's. She stood frozen. His lip curled before he thrust violently into the muse's open mouth. Erato made that horrible choking sound again, then gasped when he pulled away from her.

Persephone shook her head and stormed away from their exposition, her face burning as hot as the Phlegethon. *Real pleasure, indeed*, she thought as she hastily opened a pathway back to the Telesterion.

✲   ✲   ✲

"How was Olympus, dear?" her mother asked that night.

"Terrible," Persephone said, her voice muffled, her forehead resting on her folded arms at the small vanity. Demeter sighed and walked into Persephone's room.

"I'm sorry."

Persephone had been expecting 'I told you so' or 'I warned you, didn't I?' or any number of other admonishments. She tilted her head up, staring at her warped reflection in the bronze mirror. Demeter pulled the jeweled hairpin out of her chignon, wavy locks falling around Persephone's face.

"They aren't like us," Demeter said, picking up a comb. She unraveled Persephone's tresses and slowly combed out her daughter's hair, starting at the ends and working up until the teeth went through smoothly. Persephone relaxed her shoulders. "They are… nothing like your husband, either."

She sat up. Was Demeter contrasting Aidoneus *favorably* with the Olympians?

"You know what I speak of." She looked away from Persephone's questing eyes in the mirror, her own filling with tears as bile crept up her throat. "Whatever... whatever else he *is*, he is not like *them*."

Persephone turned, clutching her mother's hands in hers. She was not expecting to hear this mere days before the Pomegranate Agreement would send her back to the Underworld. She'd wagered that a thousand years would pass before she heard anything like this— even an inkling that her mother accepted her marriage. Persephone lifted her mother's hands and kissed Demeter's knuckles, happy tears clouding her eyes.

Demeter tried to stop herself from crying. "At least by... by marrying him, you don't have to be at Olympus as often as I. At least you are saved from their lies and gossip and endless affairs when your father calls up the members of the *Dodekatheon*. You're not forced to witness his..."

Demeter shook her head, unable to finish her sentence. Persephone wrapped her arms around her mother's shaking shoulders. Tears ran down her face and she buried a quiet sob in the warm folds of Demeter's mantle. "I'm going to miss you too, Mother."

"I only have three days left with you."

"We don't have three days." She squeezed her mother's shoulders. "We have forever. I love you. Married or not, I'll always be your daughter."

21.

"SING! YOU MAIDENS AND YOU MOTHERS, SING with them: Demeter greatly hail! Lady of much bounty, of many measures of corn!" Diocles said aloud, walking along the Sacred Way with a pitcher of milk. He poured it on the ground as they walked, offerings to the earth itself. Demeter and Persephone followed, crowned with diadems of wheat and barley. The village women laid down the husks and stalks for them to walk across, and priestesses held a painstakingly embroidered linen canopy over their heads on wood poles. Persephone resented the honor— it blocked her view of the sky, and she had very little time left to see it.

Triptolemus and Eumolpus walked closely behind them, followed by Celeus and Metaneira holding Demophon, who delightedly chewed on his finger and wriggled about, twisting his head this way and that, watching everyone gathered at the sides of the road. A procession of Diocles's and Eumolpus's students trailed after, holding fresh and full stalks of wheat and barley, swinging censers filled with frankincense.

As the procession passed each field, the menfolk of Eleusis picked up their sickles and started reaping and threshing, piling the mature grain onto oxen-driven carts bound for the mills. A single cart stayed in the fields with them, filled with barrels of barley mead, and men lined up to quench their thirst each time they hauled away a heavy bundle of grain.

Elsewhere, young girls and boys scaled the trees, picking figs and pomegranates. The sweet scent of over-ripened juices filled the air whenever a fruit fell from their small hands. Goats and chickens made short work of what tumbled to the ground. A portion of everything gathered was set aside, and several of Eumolpus's students carried sacrificial baskets of pomegranate and figs, barley, dates, and olives to the Plutonion. Diocles's followers carried bushels of wheat and barley, as well as a few piglets and lambs to the Telesterion.

Diocles continued as they walked, pouring out more milk. "Save this people in harmony and prosperity, and in the fields bring us all pleasant things! Feed our kin, bring us flocks, bring us the corn-ear, bring us the harvest! And nurse peace, that he who sows must also reap."

Persephone glanced up at her mother, who smiled at her and squeezed her hand. They walked on, the rustle of wheat sheaves, the slice of sickles keeping time with the songs sung by the Eleusinians. The fresh cut stalks were bundled, the Eleusinians' stores stacked high in the agora. Women shook the wheat and blew the chaff from the corn, the empty husks scattering across the roads and floating through the air. By nightfall, the exhausted workers had retreated to the center of town to celebrate the brewing of barley. Flutes and lyres played as drums pounded out a rhythm, the laughter became raucous the more they drank, and fires blazed against the chilly air.

"If you don't mind, my lady, I think I'll turn in early." Triptolemus gave Demeter a kiss on the cheek.

"Of course. I'm tired as well. I shouldn't be long." Demeter and Persephone sat on their thrones, crowned with wheat and surrounded by offerings of grain and fruit. Pomegranates were the only things missing— piled in great numbers at the Plutonion, but not allowed inside these halls by Demeter. Persephone understood.

"I'm glad we'll be together tonight and tomorrow."

"I wouldn't trade it for anything." She smiled, but her eyes were cast down, and Persephone could see the line of her lips tightening.

"I know we only have a short time left," Persephone said, grasping her mother's hand. "But when I return, we'll spend more of spring and summer together. It won't be so hard for the mortals while I'm away this time, right?"

"This bounty will carry them through the winter while you're gone," Demeter said. Persephone sighed. "Kore, you understand why I must do this, don't you? Why Zeus cannot be trusted unless I hold him to his word?"

She nodded, her forehead tightened. "I do."

"Things are going to change for them."

"What do you mean?"

"We are beings that grow when change occurs; not by passage of time. The Titanomachy changed us, having children changes us, but little has done so since. I worry about what this cycle of seasons will mean for all of us, now. We... Me, you, *him*... We are responsible for that."

Persephone contemplated her mother's words. It had taken her aeons to grow into a young woman, and such little time to mature into her role as the Queen of the Underworld once she arrived there.

"Are we in danger?" Persephone said, alarmed. Had Zeus introduced her to Apollo to try to keep her in the sunlight and away from Aidon for more time each year? To circumvent his oath and keep the deathless ones from being affected by a cycle of seasons?

"I hope not. Your father is opposed to all this," she said waving her hand at the Eleusinians celebrating around them. "That much I know."

"They will have to adapt."

"They won't like it. Their children will grow up faster, they will receive fewer offerings each winter. Everything... everything is different now."

"I don't see change as a bad thing." Persephone smiled. "And I wonder what else the cosmos has in store for me."

"In what way?"

"Once... I have children."

"You mean by..." Demeter slowly turned to face Persephone and blinked.

She had taken a calculated risk by bringing it up, and expected a measure of disapproval or anger. Not the confusion and concern twisting Demeter's features. "What's the matter?"

"He didn't say... Hades didn't tell you..." She tightened her jaw and snapped her head forward.

"Tell me what?"

"That selfish... that self-centered..." She spoke through clenched teeth.

"Stop, please. You promised."

Demeter set her jaw in stony silence.

"Just tell me."

"Aidoneus cannot sire children. I thought he would have at least told you *that*."

She grew cold. *A king as infertile as his kingdom,* the God of Prophecy had said. The room started to spin.

"Come," Persephone said, standing.

"Where? Why?"

"Anywhere else. I don't want to discuss this here," Persephone said, nodding her head at the mortals. Her eyes brimmed with tears. Demeter must be lying. Her mother was angry that she was going to leave the day after tomorrow. Persephone knew that these three months of peace were too good to be true. She steeled herself for an inevitable fight. "For both our sakes. And theirs."

Demeter nodded and stood. They bowed to their attendants and the celebrants, then walked to the small room behind the great dais.

Persephone shut the door, muffling the music outside, the beat of drums making the wood door vibrate on its hinges. She wiped away her tears with her shawl and took a deep breath. "I know you hate him. I *accept* that you hate him. But to say something like this—"

"I swear on the Styx it is true."

Her eyes narrowed. "That is… quite the oath, Mother."

"Daughter, I have no reason, no desire to lie to you about this. Not when I could be so easily disproven." Demeter gave a heavy sigh and lowered her head. "I don't want to fight. Please. There is no need."

Persephone turned from her mother, her eyes and throat burning, arms folded tightly around her chest.

"I don't want to stop you from having children— I can't. I don't even want to discourage you. I would care for any children you bore as though they were my own."

"You need to tell me everything, then," Persephone said, her stomach dropping as she faced Demeter. "Surely you understand why I find it hard to believe you."

Demeter averted her gaze from her daughter's palpable hurt. She could feel Persephone's eyes boring into her. "Please, Daughter. You and I have had a very long day. Can we discuss this tomorrow?"

Persephone relaxed her shoulders and tried to breathe evenly. "Tomorrow, then."

Demeter's mouth was set in a grim line, her eyes filled with compassion. "Get some rest, dear."

Demeter left the greenhouse and quietly shut the door behind her. Persephone stared at the beds of fallow soil, her ragged breathing the only sound in the room.

✧   ✧   ✧

Aidoneus cannot sire children.

Persephone walked through the fields. It was her last day above ground. In the distance, she could hear Eumolpus joking with Minthe, who managed a titter at his words. She turned in their direction and saw Minthe clasp her hands behind her back and rock on her heels, and Eumolpus nervously tousle the curls of his dark hair. Soon enough, she mused, they might become lovers and have piles of fat curly-haired children.

I thought he would have at least told you that.

Perhaps Minthe would be with child when she returned. Minthe finally saw Persephone staring at them and nodded to her. She forced a smile and nodded back, then looked up at the sun.

A king as infertile as his kingdom.

What did that arrogant Olympian know anyway? What did any of them know? No one knew anything about her husband, but her. The sun was starting to drop in the sky, just past noonday, and Persephone knew that in a matter of hours she would see Aidoneus again.

I want to give you a child, Aidoneus. A son. I want to fill our home with your sons and daughters.

He'd said nothing that night. Persephone took long strides to catch up with her mother. The menfolk were clearing the last patches of wheat from the field, the women shaking the heavy grains in wide woven baskets. Translucent husks drifted away on currents of air, as surely as snowflakes would in a month or two, as surely as petals and pollen would when she returned. Soon silos would be filled. Mills would grind all winter long. The people would eat. Their winters would be spent planning, weaving, making babies.

"It's tomorrow," she said, words catching in her throat. Persephone paced next to Demeter, along with Diocles, who carried a censer in her wake, and a student who poured kykeon onto the fallow ground as an offering.

"So it is."

"Are you going to explain what you said last night?"

361

She motioned to the Eleusinians. "Leave us."

Diocles bowed to her and skirted away, avoiding eye contact with Persephone.

"Daughter—"

"Before you begin," she said, "I need honest answers. If I had a child by Aidoneus, would you accept it as your grandchild?"

"Yes," Demeter said, without hesitation.

"And if I wished to raise it in Chthonia, would you still love it?"

"Yes."

"Can I trust what you will tell me?"

"Yes, Daughter," Demeter said, starting to grow exasperated.

"Then you need to swear it. To me. If you love me, swear to tell the truth."

Demeter took in deep breath. "I, Demeter Anesidora, daughter and inheritor of the bounty of great Mother Rhea, swear on the River Styx to tell you the truth about your ability to bear children. All of the truth."

She expected Demeter to flinch, but her mother stood resolute. Persephone faltered, her heart beating out of her chest. "Why can I not have a child with Aidoneus?"

Demeter sighed. She was sworn to answer, but knew the truth would hurt her daughter. "He rules the Realm of the Dead. He is Hades and Hades is him, and there is no life among the dead."

"But that's not true," Persephone said, the corner of her mouth peaking into a hopeful smile. "There is a grove of pomegranates there now. And they are very much alive."

"It is not a part of that world. If they grow there, they arrived with you," Demeter said, shaking her head, trying to gentle the news. She could still see a spark of hope in Kore's expectant eyes and it pained her to know that Persephone herself had asked her to extinguish it with her answers. "The grove you say grows there is not possible in that world.

362

These are laws that have existed since Chaos formed that realm from the Void."

"But… Thanatos… Hypnos… Charon, the Erinyes, Morpheus, all the children of Nyx… they were conceived and born, all the thousands of them, while Nyx ruled the Underworld—"

"And the night sky. Her domain was more than just the world below. And there was no Death until Thanatos came to be."

Persephone sunk, and anger buoyed her up. Her throat started to sting again and words became painful. "But there *is* life there *now*. It could happen, and everything you *think* you know—"

"My dear, if it were to be, it would have happened as soon as you…" Demeter could barely say the words. "…*had congress* with him."

Persephone ground her teeth together.

"You were conceived on your father's and my first time," Demeter continued. "Most divine children are. And yet… all the time he had you down there… no doubt you engaged in many opportunities to…"

Go ahead, Persephone thought, balling her fists. *Ask. I'll tell you everything*, she fantasized, her jaw clenched so hard it hurt. *In detail. Congress indeed! We made love. We made love twice a day. Three times. Once we stayed in bed all day until I was raw and he couldn't bid himself to rise again— and we could only lie in each other's arms, exhausted. I loved it. He loved it. And we loved each other with hands and lips and tongues, and still have a thousand other things we want to try. We would flirt and make one another blush when we spoke of how much we wanted each other. And when we didn't make love, Mother, we fucked. He fucked me sweetly. Gloriously. Hard. Until I screamed his name! He wasn't satisfied until he brought me to ecstasy and I wasn't satisfied until he cried out and filled me with his seed!*

But that was the crux of it. His seed. It was the truth of what Demeter had left unspoken in her passionless dismissal of their conjugal delights. Her father's pursuit of nymphs, goddesses, and mortal women seldom lasted beyond a single coupling, yet his children were strewn about the earth like wild oat grass.

Eight months had passed since Aidoneus had first taken her in his chariot— outside the boundaries of the realm of the dead. Even if Hecate was correct and conception wasn't possible in the Underworld, she'd been at her peak of fertility on the way there. They had met at midsummer in the Plutonion. But they had coupled when the moon was waning and she was past her cycle's fertility. And surely something as momentous as conceiving a god didn't always happen at the first opportunity...

"We've never actively tried to conceive a child," Persephone said demurely.

Demeter pursed her lips and shook her head. "It happens if it's supposed to happen. If it *can* happen. There's no *trying* about it, Kore."

She clenched her teeth. Her anger rekindled and flared into a roaring fire. "I've asked you so many times, Mother, to please stop calling me that. Kore means maiden. And if we're talking about my— my marital life with my husband— then obviously—"

"You asked *me* about children. About your duties as his wife."

"My *duties* as..." she looked away and shook her head.

"Yes, your imagined duty to bear him a child. Because honestly, I have no idea why you would willingly do so, since you must divide your time between worlds. Besides— the last time a god from below begat on a goddess of the earth, they brought forth Typhoeus, who nearly destroyed—"

"Enough!!" She stilled when a few villagers looked up at them and then hastily returned to their work.

"Kore, you asked me to swear to tell you—"

"I'm not speaking about this anymore! You've proven over and over that you know nothing about my husband."

Demeter softened. The last thing she wanted was for her daughter to leave upset with her and have Aidoneus whispering hatred and lies in her ear until the snows retreated. "Daughter, forgive me. This must be very difficult for you, knowing that tomorrow you must leave the sunlight and all life behind."

"I—"

"You're overwrought, and here I am making it worse." Demeter grabbed Persephone in a tight hug, her daughter's arms pinned to her sides, before drawing back and resting her hands on Persephone's shoulders. "I'm sorry."

Overwrought? I'm the Queen of the Underworld and I'm not a little girl anymore! She looked down at her bare, mud stained feet, her toes curling in the drying grasses. "I'm… The past few days have been long."

Triptolemus was trudging toward them, a broad smile on his face. He carried a dark clump of dirt with cutting from the strongest wheat crop sticking out of it. Demeter gave him a wide grin and Persephone forced a smile.

"Come," Demeter said. "We'll go back to the Telesterion and rest. I'll make you a warm cup of *kykeon*… you'll feel better, I promise."

Persephone sighed.

* * *

"Tomorrow is not here yet. You're here. You're safe with me," he whispered, sinking into her. "I love you, my lady."

His lips tasted of her, and her body still convulsed with the pleasure he'd given her. Demeter raised her hips and wrapped her legs around Triptolemus's back. His arms gripped her shoulders and she clung to him, but didn't meet his gaze. She tried to clear her mind, push away everything that she'd talked about with Persephone. She squeezed her eyes tightly and whimpered with pleasure into the hollow of his neck. She loathed herself for thinking about the god who had captured and captivated her daughter at a time like this. Every time she tried to banish her worries, they came back tenfold.

Hades had *lied* to Kore, and once her daughter knew the truth she would be broken, would hate him, but would still be forced to shuffle between worlds instead of leaving that deceitful monster forever. Would he drag her heart and hopes across the ages as she tried in vain to get with child by him? Would he blame her so he wouldn't be forced to answer her about his own infertility? Demeter shuddered, futilely trying to stop herself from weeping. Here she was in the warm arms of her own lover, yet tears streamed down her face.

"Demeter?" Triptolemus breathed raggedly. She turned her face away from him, ashamed. "No, no no, my light," he soothed, and traced the line of one of her tears with his rough thumb.

"I can't stop thinking about… I'm sorry…" Her voice came out far weaker than she intended.

He kissed her again, chastely. "Do you want to stop?"

"No…"

"I won't be offended." He tentatively pulled away from her. "You've been through too much today."

"My prince, please…" She dug her heels into his lower back, pushing him deeper. He let out a long gasp.

"Are you sure?"

"I need this. I want you," she said. *I want you to sleep soundly beside me*, she thought. "Please…" *I don't want to speak about this.*

He gripped her hip and pushed forward. "I love you, Demeter."

She moaned, tensing around him, concentrating on the sensation of him moving within her. When her thoughts drifted to the future, she would clench around him again, drowning her worries in waves of pleasure. Her head rested on his shoulder and his breath quickened. He swelled and grew harder, his thrusts more erratic. Demeter squeezed and

366

rippled around him, and Triptolemus's body stiffened and bucked. His skin was smooth under her touch and she laid kisses on his shoulder and collarbone when he collapsed upon her, a last shuddering moan lost in her hair.

With a contented sigh, Triptolemus pulled free from Demeter, lying beside her. He pulled her back against him and drew her into his embrace, an arm supporting her head, the other cupping her breast. Demeter lay still, listening to his breathing, the heat of his body behind her and the cool trail of his seed on her thigh.

"I'll be here for you," he said. "And she'll return sooner than you think."

"I know."

"We have all winter together, my love. In a week, we'll finish building the second granary, and all will be well for the mortals." He kissed her neck. "And I'll be here with you until spring comes again. I promise... I won't leave you. Teaching our methods to the people in Scythia and Illyria can wait..."

Triptolemus drifted off. Demeter lay in his arms, her eyes wide open.

✻   ✻   ✻

Persephone lay in bed, thankful that the noises had stopped, and anxious to be alone with her thoughts. She would see Aidon tomorrow, and all her questions would be answered. Hermes would take her there— Hermes, who had let her twist in the wind during her visit at Olympus. She'd have words for the Messenger when he arrived to escort her tomorrow morning.

Demeter would likely not conceive by Triptolemus. Unlike the licentious gods, it was rare for a goddess to do so with a lesser being. Hypnos had kept poor shepherd boy-turned-immortal Endymion in eternal slumber so that he might sire children by his lover Selene, the great Titaness of the moon. Triptolemus might be immortal, but no divine

367

blood ran through his veins and no half-sisters or brothers would be forthcoming for Persephone. Her forehead crinkled. Was that why Demeter kept insisting that Persephone's union with Aidoneus would produce no offspring? Was she jealous?

Hades and Persephone were equals, divinity flowing through them since birth. And the deathless ones seemed to effortlessly produce children. Poseidon and Zeus had countless demigod and immortal offspring. She had been between the tides when Hades had first taken her, and should have conceived then, if her mother's words were truthful.

Of course he will tell you the truth... if you know which questions to ask.

Kronos's words splintered through her. Persephone hadn't even considered children until after Tartarus.

I can give you what he cannot.

She froze, curling her arms around herself. Hades had nearly lunged at Kronos when he'd said it. She'd thought nothing of it at the time. Persephone contemplated the vision she'd received there, when Kronos had tempted them: Aidoneus enthroned at Olympus with her by his side, heavy with child.

Persephone, don't listen to him!

Aidoneus had broken her trance and in the vision Kronos sat by her side. A wave of nausea passed over her. The Tyrant hadn't been showing her heavy with her husband's child, but with his own child. The desire to have a child with Aidon had been planted like a splinter in her mind, and the Tyrant must have thought that she already knew that her husband could not...

Tears streaked her face. Persephone thought about her father's peculiar new oath to them, that their son would inherit Olympus. If he knew the truth, why would he say such a thing? And wasn't his son Ares his heir? He was at least legitimate. Why not Athena? She was easily Zeus's favorite. She remembered the look that had crossed Aidoneus's face when Zeus had spoken, the hurt that had twisted his features. The same expression of anger and hurt crept across her face as she lay in bed.

Zeus hadn't made the oath to make amends. He'd said it to bring his vassal, her husband, back into line after Aidon had caused so much trouble. Persephone sobbed quietly. There would *be* no children. Not above ground, not below.

Ten years... a thousand... of nothing, the God of Prophecy had spat at her.

Every mention of children she'd ever made flashed through her mind. Aidon in the pool after their last practice, wincing when she'd said that she wasn't innocent to how babies were made... Hecate's vague dismissal of a possible pregnancy in the Underworld... the stopping of her cycle and its violent return when she came above. His utter silence when they last lay together... Aidon's admission that he had eaten the food of the Underworld as penance for nearly unleashing the Titans.

As atonement for what I'd nearly done, I ate the asphodel roots in the fields to eternally bind myself here and took the name Chthonios.

She stopped breathing. Did the fruits of the Underworld render one unable to bear children? Did he know and willingly do so to punish himself? Acid welled up in her throat and tasted sickeningly like pomegranate. In binding herself to her realm and the man she loved, had she unwittingly destroyed any chance of having children for all the long aeons of her life to come?

It made no sense. The nymphs of the Underworld bore children. Askalaphos and Menoetes were both children of the Stygian nymphs. Minthe herself was born from a nymph of the Underworld.

He is Hades and Hades is him, and there is no life among the dead.

He ruled the Dead. He was Lord of the Dead, she thought to herself. Persephone burst into tears, unable to control her confusion and sadness any longer. Her chest hurt, her nose ran, she huddled into a ball and cried. What a little fool she had been, to think it could be otherwise. How silly her denial must have sounded to her mother. She would have to face Aidoneus tomorrow. What could she possibly say to him? Should she say anything at all when she herself was uncertain of what sort of future any child of hers might have? She rolled over, taking the sheets with her and pulled a pillow to her face to bury her sobs.

✻   ✻   ✻

Demeter listened in the dark. Triptolemus breathed slowly and heavily against her neck, but she could hear her daughter. A tear rolled down her face and she scowled.

How dare Hades do this to her Kore? If he had been honest with her, would she have bound herself to his kingdom? Or would Kore have walked away from him and returned to the light, never looking back? Aidoneus had robbed a mother of her child, and had robbed her child of being a mother. He would steal all Kore's happiness, his selfishness leaching her dry as the centuries passed. And once she had become as empty as the chaff blowing on the cool breezes outside, he would grow tired of her and take another.

Demeter got out of bed, hastily pinning a chiton across her shoulders and wrapping a himation around her to keep out the chilly air. She padded across the floor, then slowly closed the door so as not to wake Triptolemus. Demeter lifted the hood of her himation over the mess of her loose hair and picked up an oil lamp in the hallway, lighting it as she walked.

She paused outside her daughter's doorway. The sound of Kore's barely muffled choking and sobbing filled the hallway. Demeter's eyes brimmed with tears. There was nothing to be done. Kore would not listen to her, just as she had not listened this afternoon, just as long ago Demeter had not listened to Hecate's warnings about Zeus's nature. Her daughter would go below tomorrow, likely confront her husband and his heartbreaking lies, and have to stay below with him, either watching her imagined happiness crash down around her or timidly believing his falsehoods.

Demeter and Kore would be condemned to this, coming and going, waiting, dreading, for eternity. And every time she returned, Demeter would see just a little more of her daughter left behind, consumed by the dead and their inexorable master.

She knew what had happened to Sisyphus, and how it had been Persephone's doing. Her daughter was strong, but Aidoneus would weaken her over time. Without him, she could rule the Underworld by herself as its Queen if there was any truth to what Hecate or Nyx believed. But stubborn Kore would persist, fed by lies and false hope until all the light within her burned out and her joy turned to ashes in her mouth.

It couldn't be allowed to happen. Surely a clean break in their attachment was more merciful than that miserable fate. But her daughter seemed to love her new husband and would never rule the Underworld without him. Not unless something devastating and irreversible were to—

Her eyes widened. Her feet carried her from the hallway, down the steps to the center of the Telesterion and out the great double doors. She glanced around the narrow walkway and the row of small cottages south of the great temple. Turning on her heels, Demeter quickly paced the cold streets, her feet bare, her face and hair cloaked. When she came to a simple dwelling next to a trickling brook, she stopped, taking a deep breath.

Demeter pushed open the door, and stood over the sleeping girl within.

"Minthe."

"Hmm?" The naiad rubbed her bleary eyes. "My lady! You're still awake at this hour?"

"I have something to ask of you." Demeter set the lamp on Minthe's table and leaned on the side of her bed. "Your beloved mother died of a broken heart. I helped her in her hour of need, and when she passed, I bound her spirit forever to the poplar trees in Thesprotia so she wouldn't have to return below— a *living* monument to the injustice done to her. If you ever wanted retribution for what she suffered, and for what you suffered by losing her…"

Minthe sat up, her eyes wide, her skin prickling. Demeter slowly shook her head, her eyes brimming with tears.

"If you *ever* loved me or my daughter, if you ever cared at all for Kore, you will do *this* for me…"

22.

C ELEUS AND TRIPTOLEMUS, DIOCLES AND EUMOLPUS, stood waiting, a long oak box before them. When the first light of dawn touched the Telesterion, each stepped forward and placed a object in the box: a full blade of wheat, an eggshell, a crocus bulb, and finally a clay phallus. To the initiates of the Eleusinian Mysteries, this signaled the beginning of winter, and the promise that spring and fertility would return again.

Persephone got a final look at the crowd before Eumolpus draped a long saffron veil over her face and down to her waist, then placed a crown of asphodel and crocus on her head. She was glad that the gathered masses could no longer see her. Her drawn and tired expression had been mistaken by the townsfolk for reticence— they suspected she did not want to return to the Underworld and her lord husband. Persephone feared that her puffy red-rimmed eyes had tainted everything she'd accomplished since returning to the world above. Even loyal Eumolpus looked at her ruefully. She needed to speak with Aidoneus to confirm with the man who had sworn on the Styx to always tell her the truth whether or not they would be able to have children… and whether or not he'd known all along that the answer to that question was 'no'.

Most of the Eleusinian priesthood dressed in funerary indigo, but Eumolpus's followers discreetly wore nuptial saffron chitons underneath their dark robes. The irony didn't escape Persephone. She held a heavy bouquet of poppies, crocus, asphodel, echinacea, and narcissus so broad that she could barely see her feet. Celeus and Metaneira guided her from the Telesterion to the Plutonion. They looked ghostly through the thick veil, like the shades they would one day become. A *koudounia* rang behind her, carried by a little girl cloaked in indigo. A funeral. A wedding.

Diocles spoke between the shakings of the bells. "I sing of lovely-haired Demeter, great goddess, of her and of her slender-ankled Kore whom Zeus, all-seeing and loud-thundering, gave to the Receiver of Many to wed…"

Persephone half-listened to the hymn that Diocles had busied himself writing over the last few weeks. Though she feared she would trip over her own feet, she was thankful for the covering. All eyes were focused on her at a time she would much rather spend alone, reflecting on her impending journey. The procession arrived at the door of the Plutonion, now standing fully enclosed by marble blocks. Offerings were piled against the outside walls nearly three paces deep. There was barely enough room for her to walk to the entrance. The procession and music stopped.

Eumolpus stepped forward and raised his hood over his head, the assembled acolytes doing the same. He waited, listening to the wind and seabirds before he spoke. "No man, once the earth has covered him and he has descended into darkness, the home of Persephone, has the pleasure of listening to the lure of the piper or of raising wine to his lips. So too we have forgone wine as our sacrifice and have filled the home of Plouton, the Rich One, the Receiver of Many, with the fresh bounty and fruits of our labors to mark the return of his cherished bride." He cleared his throat and unrolled a scroll. "The Archon of Athens sends two score amphorae of oil to thank Karpophoros, the bringer of fruit, for the bounteous crops of olive. To Plouton and Kore, the beekeepers of Kekropis give honeyed kykeon. The great house of Ceryces, long the servants of the Mother and the Maiden, offer pomegranates, the fruit that bound the Maiden forever to the world below and to her husband's side. The house of Antiochis offers figs, the first of all fruits to appear. The house of Pandionis offer dates and pomegranates…"

Persephone stifled a yawn as Eumolpus listed every offering from every illustrious family and tribe in Attica.

"I wish you would reconsider," Demeter said quietly as the list of offerings droned on.

"Taking Minthe with me?"

"Daughter, you are a queen. All queens have servants."

"We don't have or need servants."

"What about Merope?"

"She was a friend and my guest."

"…Who attended to you. As all the nymphs living along the rivers of the Underworld should."

"They are their own creatures. I would feel silly ordering them about."

"Nonsense," she said under her breath. "You are in every way equal to Hera, and should act the part. Even her humblest servants are goddesses in their own right. Would it be so terrible to to take a mere nymph under your wing?"

"It wouldn't be *terrible*, but—"

"It would be like sending Minthe home."

"I don't know if Minthe would call it that. She was conceived above. She was born above."

"Her entire family is below. And she often told me she would like to see her aunts and cousins one day."

"What has prevented her from doing so?"

Demeter looked at her feet, her voice low. "It was my fault. I forbade her."

Persephone nodded. Demeter was trying. She was trying so very hard, and Persephone was surprised that her mother hadn't broken down crying. Three months ago, Persephone had dreaded this day, fearing that Demeter would scream hysterically and try to drag her bodily away from the door of the Plutonion.

How things had changed.

She turned her gaze to Minthe, who seemed to be the only congregant who wasn't fidgeting or yawning while waiting for Eumolpus to stop talking. On the contrary, he held the pretty naiad's rapt attention.

"For six months, then," Persephone muttered.

"You'll try having a servant?"

"I suppose it could work. Then she could be back among the mortals for half the year."

"I doubt it she'd miss them."

"I would beg to differ," she said, nodding her head at Eumolpus.

"The priesthood in Dion has let it be known that the Loud-Thunderer, father of the Maiden, has promised the island of Sikelia to her as a wedding gift..." he said to the crowd.

The corner of Demeter's mouth turned up. "We shall see."

Persephone smiled. She wouldn't reduce Minthe to waiting on her. The girl would wander freely. Though not *too* freely, she worried, imagining what could happen to Minthe if she ventured too close to the Lethe. But surely her family would welcome and care for her.

When the priest had finished listing offerings, Demeter gave Eumolpus a curt nod.

His shoulders slumped and he drew in a long breath. "And finally, the great Lady of the Harvest, Demeter Anesidora, commits Minthe, daughter of the river god Kokytos, into the service of her daughter, to attend to the great Queen Beneath the Earth, Soteira, savior of mankind. Know this, all who hear these words! Those who journey below, return to the world above, just as that which is planted will be reaped and the seeds sown."

Eumolpus produced a crocus bulb from his robes and rested on his haunches, digging up a handful of earth and burying the bulb in front of the Plutonion. He stood and one of his students poured goat's milk from a wide kylix over the newly planted bulb.

"For the Maiden's return!"

"For the Maiden's return," answered the Eleusinians.

Persephone looked at her mother, her eyes watering. She dropped the bouquet and wrapped her arms tightly around Demeter, who held her and shuddered, trying not to cry. The Goddess of the Harvest bit her lips together and stepped back, then lowered an indigo veil over her face so the Eleusinians wouldn't see her weep.

A hand stretched forth from the doorway of the Plutonion. Persephone flinched before realizing that it was Hermes. She gazed one last time at the crowd of mortals, then nodded to Minthe, who picked up her skirts and trudged after her, her eyes cast to the ground. The congregants stood silent, waiting. Persephone took the God of Travel's proffered hand and stepped over a large pile of pomegranates just inside the threshold.

Once inside, she let her eyes adjust to the darkness. Sunlight filtered into the Plutonion from a high clerestory at the roof of the cave, and small lamps lit the walls, illuminating the statues of her and her husband. Their images were crowned with laurels and poplar, pomegranate leaves and asphodel and draped in finely loomed saffron robes. Minthe shut the door behind them.

"Gods above; is he going to drone on like that every year?" Hermes whispered, a half smile on his face. "And this temple to you and Hades! Best one I've seen so far. Not surprising, of course. You wouldn't believe—"

"Where were you three days ago?" Persephone asked angrily, tearing off the cumbersome veil and the flower crown with it.

"What?"

"When I was on Olympus. You said you'd meet me there and keep me safe. You *promised me!*"

"Listen, I'm sorry."

"Do have any idea what Apollo said to me?" She balled up the veil and threw it to the floor. Persephone looked around the room. Every corner was piled with amphorae and pithos of all sizes, leaning against one another, fruits, wheat, oil, coins, clay and straw figurines, flowers…It was almost impossible to move.

"By now, *everyone* knows what Apollo said to you… and how you rebuffed him. I hear Aphrodite took a liking to you!"

"What was so important that you let me be fed to the wolves? What do you think my husband would say if—"

"It was an errand for your husband that delayed me." Hermes said, his brow knitting.

Persephone calmed, her shoulders sinking. "I'm sorry."

Hermes gave her a half-smile. "Don't be. I can't imagine the last few days were easy for you." He cautiously patted her shoulder then peered at the nymph standing behind her. "Who is this?"

The naiad pushed a blonde lock of hair behind her ear. "Minthe."

"Really…" He smiled. "Are you a Leimenid or a Potameid, perhaps?"

"Cocytid."

"Ah, so you're going home, then?"

"One could say that," Minthe glanced away, rubbing her arm. She narrowed her eyes at Hermes. "Daeira is doing well."

"S-she… that's good. Good."

"If your child is a boy, she said she'll name it Eleusis, af-ter the town."

"Wonderful. I'm glad."

"Stop trying to seduce my handmaiden, Hermes." Perse-phone smirked at him, then sighed in frustration. "I don't understand why you even need to take me to the Under-world. I could simply open a path to the throne room and there I would be."

"So why didn't you?"

"I…"

"You've had ample opportunity. And for months every-one on Olympus has known that you are able to do so. Why hesitate?"

Persephone swallowed. "I had promises to keep. I didn't… I needed to be here for the mortals. I-if my mother knew that I was sneaking away to the world below…"

Hermes smiled. "Whatever you say."

"Should I just take all of us to the palace?" Persephone said, shifting from foot to foot. "My way is faster."

"I would feel more comfortable following your hus-band's orders," Hermes said, raising his eyebrows. "He commanded me to bring you to the shores of the Styx."

"Why?"

"It's a surprise." He smiled and held out both his hands. "Ladies?"

Minthe cautiously gripped his fingers, and Persephone followed her lead.

"Hold on tight."

Hermes lifted off the ground, and Persephone felt as light as a feather, her feet rising effortlessly. The room blurred around them, and the little lamplights streaked past her vision. Minthe shrieked.

Persephone felt pulled and pushed all at once, the wind itself too slow to touch them. The room was gone. Shapes appeared and disappeared almost as quickly as Persephone could recognize them. She saw the roads through the earth, stalactites hanging overhead, endless caverns through which they dodged this way and that, and a few souls drifting toward the world below. Blackness consumed the blur of caves and pathways rushing by. The waking, breathing life of the sunlit world lay far behind her, and she inhaled the familiar cool mists and wet earth of her home.

✻   ✻   ✻

Hermes alighted on the far side of the Styx. Persephone was so accustomed to seeing it crowded with souls that she didn't recognize the banks. Asphodel grew there again, tall and thick, rebounding quickly now that the droves of hungry shades were gone. Persephone knelt and plucked a single ghostly flower, tucking it into her chignon.

"There. That wasn't so bad, was it?" Hermes said to Minthe, who was shaking, either from the journey or their new surroundings.

Persephone clasped her hand. "Minthe, it's all right. This is home."

"H-home..." The nymph took a deep breath. "Is it always so brightly lit?"

"During the daytime in Chthonia, the Styx is..." Persephone trailed off. It was nighttime in the Underworld. The great River was supposed to be dark. She looked out across the brightly lit water.

Thousands— no, *thousands of thousands* of floating flames lit its broad expanse, drifting on the calm currents from as far as she could see upstream out to the endless dark sea of Oceanus. They looked like stars flickering in the night sky. Great bursts of white light flickered and sparkled in the river's reflection. She looked up through the mist to the palace beyond. Every causeway, every tower and passage of the palace burned brightly, lit with torches of white *magnes*... the unquenchable flame that guided her descent into Tartarus. Persephone's mouth hung open.

380

"Again, I apologize for not meeting you on Olympus three days ago. I was helping Hades procure... this. And bringing Hephaest— nevermind."

She barely heard Hermes. Persephone stood shocked silent when a familiar chorus began in her mind. *Soteira... She had returned!... Metra... Annessa... She came back! She came back!... The Queen has returned! Thea! Aristi! Aristi Chthonia!*

Through the Key of Hades, the noise of the rejoicing shades was almost deafening, but only the Queen and her King could hear them. Where was Aidoneus?

Husband? She reached out to him, her voice hesitant. There was no reply, just an impatient, delighted energy emanating from the opposite shore. Persephone closed her eyes and felt him, could feel his heart pick up rhythm at the sound of her voice in his mind. She could feel him shifting from foot to foot, tampering down the urge to swim across the Styx to meet her. She smiled, and could feel him smiling back.

A long boat parted the flickering lights, drifting toward them silently before the prow scraped loudly against the shore. Persephone's shoulders relaxed and she smiled. "Charon."

He bowed low to her. "Aristi Chthonia. Do you have any idea how glad I am to see you, my queen?"

She reached for his hand and stepped into the boat. He curtly nodded at Hermes, who dipped his head in respectful acknowledgement. Charon then reached for Minthe and froze, cocking his head to the side and peering at her when their fingers touched.

"Aren't you the daughter of the one who never came back?"

"I... M-my mother was from here, yes."

"Ah. Minthe." He gave her hand a tense squeeze. "It is good... though unexpected... to have you returned to us."

The Boatman pushed off the shore, the craft drifting toward the palace. Persephone leaned over the side and saw small ebony floats holding clay oil lamps, softly bumping into one another in the wake of Charon's oar. They were drifting through a sea of dancing lights, glowing in the thin haze cast out over the bottomless reaches of the river. She sat in awe. She melted. How had Aidon managed all this? He must have planned her homecoming for months. Persephone relaxed back into her seat and changed her saffron peplos to a dark burgundy. She felt the tension of the past week leave her body, as though a millstone slung about her neck had dropped into the river. Persephone was home. She could speak with him about her concerns later. Her mother had surely misled her. Aidoneus would confirm that.

"My queen," Charon said, "Did you ever hear the tale about the nymph that used to tend the great poplar tree?" Minthe snapped her head in his direction and was met by Charon's burning gaze.

"I have not."

"Remind me to tell you that tale one day," he said, eyeing the naiad. "Soon."

The tree he spoke of overhung the palace gate, glittering gold in the multitude of lights. The opposite shore came into focus through the misty air. An assembly was gathered to greet her. Thanatos and Hypnos stood side by side, crowned with white poplar leaves. The God of Death looked somber— a great weight about him. Their mother hovered above the ground behind them, the darkness of Erebus twined around her. A young Hecate smiled at her, her waves of deep red hair laced with beads of selenite, her dress white. Behind them, Lampades nymphs dressed in red and crowned with asphodel wreaths and anklets carried torches sparking with white magnes, dancing and laughing. Translucent shades appeared and disappeared like trails of smoke, smiling and crowding each other. They peered around the river reeds and tall stalks of asphodel, eager for a glimpse of their queen, the youngest shades giggling and toddling about.

In the midst of all of them, Aidoneus stood motionless, a gentle smile playing on his face, his hair pulled back loosely and a crown of golden poplar set on his head. His himation was a deep burgundy, perfectly matching her dress, and as the boat drew closer she saw an open pomegranate cradled against his chest. His demeanor was calm and staid, but she could see the lights reflecting in his eyes. Her heart pounded. Persephone was distantly aware of the boat scraping against the rocks below, barely felt Charon's long fingers lifting her trembling hand, helping her stand up and disembark. She felt weightless, her gaze never leaving his, her feet light on the ground when she stepped clear of the boat. Everyone standing at the Styx dropped to one knee, the Lampades's many torches lowering, their heads bowed for the Queen's return. Everyone him, whose eyes were locked with hers. He slowly extended his hand, beckoning her forward.

The voices of Asphodel quieted and for a moment it was just the two of them. She floated, her body pulled toward Aidoneus, his eyes drawing her closer. She took his hand.

"Welcome home, my queen."

Aidon broke into a broad smile, his visage blurred as tears filled her eyes. His arms wrapped around her, lifting her onto her toes, and their lips met. Persephone closed her eyes and she heard cheers and applause, the shouts and clapping barely registering as she fitted against his chest.

He kissed away a happy tear that had trailed from her eye and spoke low in her ear. "I missed you so much, sweet one."

"Aidoneus…" She held him and sniffled, her voice cracking when she spoke his name.

He quirked an eyebrow. "Is something the matter?"

She swallowed. "Just a bit… overwhelmed. I wasn't expecting—" She looked around and laughed, wiping the tear away from her other eye. "How did you do all this?"

"I had some help from Hermes." He smiled, his eyes sparkling. "Come… there is much I wish to show you."

As they turned toward the palace, Charon beckoned his brothers to his boat. "I need you to keep a close eye on someone."

"Who?" Hypnos asked. "The Queen's new handmaid?"

"If she is anything like her mother, yes."

Thanatos smirked. "Even if she were, nothing will come of it."

"That's my hope, little winged one," Charon said, grasping Death's shoulder. "But when has my intuition ever led us astray?"

✻   ✻   ✻

Hades and Persephone led the procession through the gates of the palace, toward the lilting notes of tambourines, pipes and lyre strings. Hermes followed at their heels, chattering about developments in the world above. "They piled up pomegranates around a cave entrance in Illyria, too. And you heard about the new temple in Ephyra, I take it?"

"The Nekromanteion," Aidon muttered. "I heard."

"You wouldn't believe the number of offerings they laid in the Plutonion," Persephone said, holding his arm as they crossed the courtyard.

"I might," he said, stopping at the doors to the great hall. Askalaphos and Menoetes stood on either side, their heads crowned with poplar leaves. Menoetes held his head high, intent on looking as dignified as possible. Askalaphos leaned against the wall and grinned widely at the Queen. With great effort, they pushed open the heavy doors, and Persephone gaped, taken aback. The hall was warmly lit, filled from wall to wall with offerings from the world above, amphorae and pithos of kykeon and oil. Their path was a soft carpet of white asphodel flowers, purple myrtle blossoms, deep green poplar and laurel leaves.

At Hecate's behest, the torch bearing Lampades danced inside and scattered among the waiting Stygian nymphs, the Erinyes, Morpheus, and other children of the world below.

Each guest wore a crown of asphodel or poplar. As the queen entered, the music stopped and Aidon's guests bowed. When she passed, they joined the procession and filed into the throne room, where great tables were piled high with olives and dates, innumerable pomegranates, and great baskets of figs. Persephone was shocked to see an enormous plate of ambrosia— one that could have only come from Olympus— in the center of the table.

"That was a wedding gift for both of you from Hera, of all goddesses. I delivered it here three days ago," Hermes said, inclining his head toward Persephone. "There's a temple to both of you in almost every village, it seems, all of them overflowing with offerings. And in the countryside, wherever there was a cave or a spring, I would see handmade idols of a god and goddess with pomegranates and asphodel piled high next to them. You two keep on like this and you'll make the Olympians jealous!"

Hermes tittered, but his words made Persephone cringe, remembering her dealings with the Olympians.

"This is your doing, sweet one." Aidoneus turned to his stunned wife and smiled. "Without your words and deeds, this would never have happened."

She laughed joyously and wiped a tear from her eye. Her efforts in Eleusis hadn't been in vain. For months she'd struggled to replace the mortals' fears of the world below with hope for peace and rebirth. Many had recoiled from her message, but those who did not had carried her tales with them when they left Eleusis.

Persephone and Aidoneus made their way up the dais. Stygian nymphs embraced Minthe, smiling and wiping away tears as they greeted their long-lost cousin. For the first time since they had arrived, Persephone saw the naiad smile. The Queen sat back on the light filigree of iron asphodel her husband had wrought into a throne. Aidoneus sat beside her on his throne of ebony and held her hand.

A fiery-haired man with a lamed leg, whom Persephone recognized only from description, shuffled toward the dais with a large wooden box. Hephaestus quickly dipped his head in a bow, then smiled up at the rulers of the Underworld. "Queen Persephone," the God of Fire and the Forge started. "I have known your husband and his generosity for aeons. All the materials I have ever used for my labors originated within the earth, his domain. It is with great joy that I created and now present his gift to you."

He opened the lid of the box to reveal a golden diadem, crafted into a thousand tiny poplar and laurel leaves wound about each other and etched with veins. The assembled crowd gasped collectively, and whispers rippled through the chamber. On the strong yet delicate crown sat six large rubies, each haloed with garnets, glimmering like moonlit pomegranate seeds. Around them sat an array of diamonds set in the shape of small asphodel flowers, the petals' veins defined by rows of tiny fire opals. The diadem gleamed on its bed of black linen and Persephone covered her open mouth with her hand. Aidoneus walked to Hephaestus and quietly thanked him, then ascended the stairs of the dais and stood behind his wife's throne. He waited until all were silent, then drew a long breath before speaking softly.

"When I was given this realm, it came with the promise of someday having a queen, a daughter of the Olympians, to rule beside me. It took me some time to adjust—" He was interrupted by muffled snickering and sarcastic mutters from the sons of Nyx. Aidoneus smiled at them, then continued. "But after long years of war, I came to appreciate the peacefulness of this world. I grew to love its beauty, its many riches. I learned to care for its inhabitants and for the souls of the mortals. I thank you, Hephaestus, for making this gift for my wife… a crown befitting the Queen of Asphodel and Tartarus, and the Goddess of Life and Death."

Aidoneus set the jeweled crown softly on his wife's head.

"But there isn't a jewel in this crown, or in this kingdom, that compares to her beauty. The peace this realm brings me pales in comparison to the calm and happiness she brings me, and I will never love anything in this cosmos more than I love her."

He resumed his seat beside her. A tear fell down her cheek and he brushed it away with his thumb. "Welcome home, wife."

Persephone threaded her hands into the hair at his temples and pulled his face toward hers, kissing him firmly. The room broke into applause, accompanied by a whistle from Hermes.

Aidoneus turned to the gathered crowd. "And I expect all to attend our wedding ceremony!" The crowd cheered, and Persephone froze. Wedding ceremony? They'd discussed one briefly before she'd left, but hadn't planned anything so… momentous. And there was so much she needed to ask him first. "But for now, feast! All of you! E-except those from the world above." A few laughed, and Hermes and Hephaestus exchanged looks of warning. Music and conversation filled the room. The Lampades resumed their dance, crimson handkerchiefs linking their hands in a wide circle.

Persephone swallowed. "Aidon…"

"Yes, my love?"

"I need to speak to you, privately."

"Of course." He smiled at her, then leaned in close to her ear. "I've been waiting for three months to speak to you in private."

He nipped at her earlobe and she shivered, then pulled back.

"What's wrong?" His face fell.

"Before we…" Persephone stared at him for a long moment, listening to the revelry surrounding them. Her mouth lifted into a forced smile. "Nothing. It's not important."

"Are you sure?"

"It can wait." She kissed him again. "I love you."

"I love you, too," he said. He looked away and she felt him stir with emotion. When his eyes met hers again, they had those same flecks of gold she had seen when she first confessed her true feelings for him. "It feels as though it were longer and... I can hardly believe I have you here again beside me."

"Aidon," she smiled and her eyes were refreshed with more tears. Discussing children could wait. He had worked so hard, so long to plan this grand welcome for her. He had missed her, profoundly, as surely as she had missed him, and it showed in every glimmer of light that greeted her, every careful preparation he'd made, the weight of the diadem on her head. Though the splinter of doubt stuck within her, in this moment she would celebrate their reunion. She smiled broadly. "Can you believe it? The pomegranate worked! I'm actually here... we're still married..."

"They are weaving us a new tapestry. To celebrate our marriage."

This is where we started, Persephone. And one day Clotho, Lachesis and Atropos will weave a tapestry that tells our story.

"The Fates? Truly?"

"A continuing gift from them, they say, for my allowing them to reside in this realm. They wove the last tapestry aeons ago. This one shows you and I in the pomegranate grove, Nyx told me. But she said it almost looks like we're in the world above, there are so many green things growing. The whole scene is framed in narcissus and golden arrows."

"I don't think greenery is out of place... the grove is still covered in grasses and moss. A flower *did* grow there." She blushed hotly, recalling the last time both of them were there, and exactly *how* that flower had appeared. "They...er, it's fit to hang in the main hall isn't it? I mean, they didn't portray us in the midst of..."

Aidon threw back his head and laughed. "Nyx said we are standing side by side, not unlike how we are depicted in the Plutonion." He brushed his nose past her cheek and kissed her again before whispering into her ear. "But if you desire, we could commission something like that for our bedroom. Though I cannot imagine that any artist could truly capture how beautiful you look when you—"

"Oh, Aidoneus, honestly!" she said smacking his chest.

He captured Persephone's lips again, then opened his eyes and peered around her, a scowl briefly crossing his features when he pulled away from her. "And this is?"

Persephone turned to see who had interrupted them. "Oh! Forgive me! Minthe, I want to introduce you to my husband, Aidoneus."

Minthe swallowed and curtsied low. "My lord."

"You brought a servant with you?"

"After a fashion," she said. If she mentioned Demeter's insistence on bringing her along, it would ruin the evening. "I consider Minthe a friend. A companion."

Aidon gave the woman a brief nod. "Any friend of my wife is welcome here. You are a naiad, no?"

"I am. Cocytid."

"Ah," he said, squinting at her. She looked familiar…

"I'm not really from… I know I don't look it, milord. I'm too fair. But m-my mother was fair, so…" Minthe's eyes grew as wide as saucers. She stumbled back as Alekto, one of the Erinyes, meandered over to the dais, *kantharos* cups in each hand, wings spread behind her.

"Are you going to sit here and make eyes at him all night," she asked Persephone, "or are you going to go out and greet your guests? Some of us came a *long* way…"

"Don't tease my wife, Alekto," Hades said with a smirk. "We'll greet everyone soon enough."

"The Iron Queen cannot take a jest?" Alekto smirked at Persephone. "Here I was, certain that Praxidike's patience with us was as bountiful as her will. That's what Kottos said, at least. Anyway, you *must* taste this!"

389

Persephone raised her eyebrow at the cup Alekto thrust in front of her. "Wine?"

The daemon snickered. "Not exactly. Nothing ferments down here. What's sacrificed to the dead cannot rot!" She smiled at them, her tightly wound hair glistening like coiled asps. "But this is as close as it gets. It's the juice of crushed pomegranate arils mixed with nectar. That sky queen's idea, according to Hermes."

Hera's gift, made with the ambrosia she'd sent. *Drink no wine, eat no bread...* Persephone pulled her husband's gaze to hers quizzically, saying nothing.

"Not a regular thing, mind you, but I thought we could drink to your return." His accompanying smile calmed her concerns.

"Thank you," she said, accepting the cup. A sip of the nectar swamped her senses and she felt grateful she hadn't tried any on Olympus. Her husband took a long draught, finishing the cup quickly.

"I told Tisiphone and Megaera to keep that little dog Hermes occupied so he wouldn't nip at your heels all night long. Besides— I have an inkling that Tisiphone secretly likes him. Or likes torturing him. We'll see." Alekto placed her splayed fingers over her heart. "And why haven't you paid us a visit in Tartarus? Surely if you can look on the Hekatonkheires' ugly faces you can stand to spend some time with *us* when you come below the Ouroboros. Oh! I thought you'd be happy to know that we're keeping that wicked little king busy with his boulder." She laughed and clapped her hands. "I *loved* it! Even better than what your husband devised for Tantalus. But truly, come visit us. We'll give you a better tour of the place than this dusty old bag of bones, that's for sure!"

The King of the Underworld snorted and shook his head. "Thank you, Alekto."

"Any time." She bowed to him and skipped away toward her sisters, calling out over her shoulder. "At least dance already, will you? So the rest of us can?"

Aidoneus chuckled and offered his wife his hand. She stood with him, and they descended the steps to the floor together. The Lampades wove a wide circle in the center of the room, their feet tapping out the simple dance, ten steps forward, two back, to drum beats and clapping, and the shrill melody of the pipes. Hermes stood between Megaera and Tisiphone, stiff as a board, muttering something to them. Tisiphone smacked him on the back and bellowed a laugh, exposing her sharp teeth. Hephaestus shuffled quietly to a corner of the room, favoring his right leg; Hecate sauntered up to him and said something that made him smile.

All eyes turned to the center of the hall as Hades and Persephone made their way into the midst of the circling Lampades. The music changed to a slower *syrtos*, and Aidon clasped his wife's right hand within his and turned in a circle with her. They wound around each other, and he led her into a twirl before grasping her close and spinning with her in his arms. They laughed and others joined them in dancing and revelry.

No one noticed the pale nymph slip from the room.

✠   ✠   ✠

He is a creature of nothingness. Master of all things dead. Taciturn. Cold. Demeter's words solidified her resolve. *He will sap the life from her. All that is warm and good. And she will let him because she loves him with a love that cannot be returned. My Kore will become nothing more than a husk.*

When Charon had taken her hand, Minthe feared that he would see into her soul and toss her off the side of his boat. The Styx had no bottom. She would have sunk into the unknown waters for eternity. She shuddered and drew in a long breath, summoning her courage. It had to be done. It had to be done to save Kore from centuries of torment...

the same agony her beloved mother had endured... a love that could not be returned, offered to one who was incapable of such a thing.

Only you can accomplish this, Minthe, the goddess had said. *You are ageless, faithful one, and when you return, once you've saved my daughter, I will make you deathless as well. You will be the new Goddess of Sweet Herbs.*

It was frigid here, compared to above, and goose flesh prickled her skin. She crept along the wall and felt solid stone behind the tapestries and searched for a gap that could lead to a staircase. Persephone had mentioned such hidden entries when she had described the palace. Minthe pushed her hand against a tapestry portraying tall cypress trees and celery grass. She met no resistance and stumbled forward. Behind the heavy curtain, a flight of torchlit stairs wound upward.

...framed in narcissus and golden arrows...

It would simplify so many things. She had to find it. Everyone knew that Hades had been struck by Eros, the golden arrow's indomitable power compelling him to abduct Kore from the fields of Nysa. Persephone once told Minthe that Hades had kept the golden arrow on his person until she discovered it. She'd said they quarreled over it, and he'd kept it safely hidden in their room thereafter.

But where?

The stairs ended at a set of double doors, a golden poplar tree carved into the wood. Minthe clenched her teeth at the symbol and pushed through the door. Cool air wafted into the darkened room from the terrace. The sound of revelers came from far below, nearly drowned out by the rush of the waterfall. Two divans were placed opposite each other and two goblets filled with pomegranate and nectar sat between them on a small table covered in olives and fruits and goat cheese.

Minthe took a deformed red stalk of barley out of the pocketed fold of her peplos and ground it between her fingers before emptying the fine granules into both cups. The powder curled and drifted down into the liquid. She held her dusty hands away from her body and walked outside to wash them in the freezing water. Then, Minthe scampered back inside afraid that someone below might see her.

A subtle glow came from the corner and she followed the line of light cast across the mosaic of stones on the antechamber floor. The naiad pulled open another door, warmth flooding out from within. A raised, curtained bed dominated the far wall, asphodel and myrtle petals strewn about its black sheets. A great fire blazed in the center of the bedroom, ringed by an obsidian hearth, its bright orange flames flickering off the walls. Something moved. She shrieked and clapped her hand over her mouth. Thousands of chunks of polished amber held within the walls, entombing insects and small creatures of which she'd never seen the like. Their shadows danced in the firelight.

Other than the bed, the room was spare. An ebony chair, a marble table and washing basin, no amphorae, no jars, no boxes to store anything. She twisted her hands and glanced about the room. Surely if Hades were to hide anything that significant and powerful, it would be here in their inner sanctum— the most secure place in the Underworld, possibly in all of the cosmos.

She sighed and peered into the hearth. What she saw made her heart leap into her throat. The golden arrow lay in the midst of the fire, untouched by the endless purifying flame of the Phlegethon. A god like Hades would be able to reach through the fire unscathed but she would be badly burnt if she attempted it. Minthe searched the room, looking for anything to pull the arrow from the flames, at least enough so she could reach it. She snatched a long razor from the wash basin and turned in over in her hand. Minthe unbound the cloth that held her tresses in place, wrapped it around her hand, and dipped it into the basin, soaking it with cold water.

The naiad returned to the fire and drew in a breath, willing herself to endure this. She darted her hand into the flame and moved the arrow closer, using the razor as a poker. The cloth came away steaming. She winced and darted in again, hooking the arrowhead with the blade and drawing it out. Her fingertips burned. She made another thrust and the arrow flew from the hearth, clanging to the ground.

The cloth caught fire and Minthe shook it loose from her singed hand with a yelp, dropping it into the fire. Smoke twisted through the room, smelling faintly of pennyroyal and spearmint. Minthe threw the doors to the room open, letting the smoke disperse, then carefully hid the arrow beside the bed and ran from the room.

23.

PERSEPHONE SCOWLED. "DEMETER SAID NOT VISITING was *my* idea?"

"Believe me, dear queen, I was not so easily fooled," Hephaestus said with a smile. "No one was. But in her own way, your mother was wise to keep you away from the mountain of the gods. Oftentimes, I find myself wishing I could make my home elsewhere."

"Why don't you?"

He thinned his lips and looked down.

"Aphrodite." She sighed. "Hephaestus, I'm sorry."

"Don't be." He snorted a laugh. "To be honest, I find the reason we are married to be more insulting than any ill-gotten child or dalliance on her part." Persephone blinked in surprise, and Hephaestus chuckled. "You and I both were married away for duty's sake. Would that my arranged marriage had turned out as well as yours."

Persephone glanced at her husband, who was smiling, visiting with Thanatos and Hypnos, a freshly emptied cup in his hand. His eyes met hers and he stopped listening to the sons of Nyx until Thanatos waved his hand in front of Aidon's longing gaze. Hypnos belted out a laugh when their king turned back to them, his cheeks crimson. Persephone giggled before turning her attentions back to Hephaestus. "Why not insist she remain faithful?"

He shook his head. "It isn't in her nature. I would as soon ask that of Aphrodite as I would try to pin the seafoam that birthed her to the shoreline. When she returned to Olympus from the East, Zeus chose me because I was the *safest* mate for her. Ares, Apollo, and Hermes all vied for her, but with the power she holds, a union with any one of *them* would have driven us all to war. Your father at least knows that I cannot rise against him. Fates… I can barely rise at all."

Persephone tittered uncomfortably at his self-deprecation. "Do you… You already know I spoke with her…"

"Yes, she told me all about it. And rest assured, I don't begrudge you befriending her. On the contrary, if you were her confidant, it would be a great relief. She doesn't share a bed with me, but desires to share everything else, it seems, and I often find myself counselling her on matters I have no wish to hear about."

"Is there anyone to give you comfort since she refuses?"

He shrugged. "I made my vows and my nature is to adhere to them. There was one I had my heart set on before, who felt kindly toward me in turn, but that time has passed."

"Who?"

"Her name is Aglaea, youngest of the Kharites. An attendant of my wife, no less." He shifted on his feet. "And I won't dishonor either of them."

Persephone was about to respond when Minthe sauntered up to them, her long golden hair hanging loosely about her shoulders. She gave Persephone a wide smile, rare for her. Persephone was relieved that the naiad seemed to be enjoying herself. Perhaps her mother was right to encourage her to bring Minthe here. She eyed the cup of pomegranate nectar in the naiad's hand. "Are you sure you should drink that?"

"Why ever not?"

"For the same reason I'm not," Hephaestus chimed in.

"I am Cocytid," Minthe said. She took a long swig of the nectar and smacked her lips. "Even if I ate every morsel of food here, I could still venture above. And as far as I'm concerned, I'm home."

Persephone smiled, relieved, then hugged Minthe. The naiad stiffened as the Queen of the Underworld embraced her. "You have no idea how glad I am to hear that. I was so worried that I had agreed to something you didn't really want, that I was pulling you away from... from..."

"Eumolpus?" Minthe pulled back and smiled. "He... I wouldn't worry about *that*. If I am here, and he will one day come here as all men do, what's the difference?"

"It isn't the same, though. I don't know if Mother told you, but the mortals drink from the Lethe when they arrive. He will still be Eumolpus, just not as you know him to be..."

"Couldn't *you* make that different?"

If I could, she wanted to reply, but her mouth had grown dry. "Asphodel is what it is for a reason," she said, echoing her husband.

"Yes," Minthe agreed, looking away toward Hypnos, Thanatos, and Aidoneus chatting in the corner. "Some things will always be as they are..."

Her words puzzled Persephone.

"Do I have your permission to... to roam a bit? To visit my kin?"

"Of course you do! I don't expect you to be constantly by my side the entire time you're here. Truthfully, I don't need a servant, despite what Mother thinks."

"Thank you." Minthe nodded to her with a smile and walked away into the crowd. Persephone lost sight of her among the dancing Lampades. Her eyes met her husband's and she smiled at him longingly.

✻   ✻   ✻

"Your majesty." She curtsied low.

Aidoneus turned to acknowledge her. "Minthe, is it? You needn't be so formal. Have you met Thanatos and Hypnos?"

The naiad gulped, glancing from Death to Sleep. "Milords."

Aidon would have hesitated to introduce any woman to Thanatos, but since he'd been freed from Sisyphus, he'd heard no complaints from Hecate, no tales of conquest from the world above. When Aidoneus discreetly mentioned it to him, Thanatos simply stated that he wouldn't let anyone else endure Voleta's fate… that his days of chasing women were over. He'd scarcely touched the food and drink. It was an aftereffect of all that he'd suffered, Aidon reasoned, a season he would pass through eventually. In the meantime, The Lord of the Underworld was enjoying the peace that it brought to his court.

"I-If you will pardon me, my king," she started nervously, "may I have a moment alone to speak with you?"

Thanatos folded his arms. "What about?"

"A…" She gulped in air and fidgeted. "A private request from the Queen."

Aidon waved off the twins and smiled at Minthe. "If it is a 'request' from my wife, then I don't see why not."

Minthe looked up into his eyes, made warm by mirth and nectar. His features weren't displeasing. He towered over her and his shoulders were broad. His fingers were long and manicured but looked rough from aeons of swordplay. His hair was swept back from his face by his crown, but fell loosely in tight waves about his shoulders, curling at the ends. He smelled of warm earth and cool cypress.

She contemplated what it would mean to be the mistress of a powerful king, sharing his chariot, his palace, his bed…

Warmth and desire trickled through her. She felt a sharp ache between her thighs at the thought of him pinning her down, prying them apart. Minthe looked at the glint of golden poplar on his crown and shook the idea from her thoughts. She should be revolted by this. This was duty, not desire. If she dwelled on it, on *him*, it would destroy her, just as it had destroyed—

"What was it you wanted to tell me?"

"I..." Minthe blushed and collected her thoughts, then motioned Aidoneus so she could whisper in his ear. He obliged and dipped down, amused that the girl would be so nervous delivering a simple message. "She asks that you leave the hall quietly."

"Why?" He said softly.

"Sh-she wants to speak with you in private, she said. In your chambers." Minthe cleared her throat and whispered, her breath hot against his ear. "Without any clothes."

Aidon's eyes briefly widened before he schooled his reaction. He stood up and swallowed the lump in his throat. A smile teased the corner of his mouth and his voice purred when he responded. "Tell your mistress I will do as she bids."

Minthe shuddered and gave him a nod. She backed away slowly, then skipped away to leave him standing alone. Aidoneus glanced toward his wife, who was laughing in conversation with Hermes and Hephaestus. She caught his gaze and smiled at him mischievously, knowingly. Nectar swam through Aidon's head, mingling with desire. Three months ago they'd only had a matter of hours to enjoy each other; it had scarcely been enough to sustain him. He'd spent so much time carefully planning her return. Though enjoyable, the welcoming celebration had quickly dissolved into tedium, beginning the moment he caught a glimpse of her on the waters of the Styx, Charon dutifully rowing her closer, and closer, and closer... At last their long, celibate drought would be ended and she would be in his arms again. He knew she could feel his eyes on her from across the room. Persephone nibbled on her lower lip in a way that made his fingers twitch at his sides, and another part of him twitch beneath his robes.

"Aidon?" Thanatos interrupted his lustful reverie.

"Beg pardon…" He muttered awkwardly, his voice rough before he cleared his throat. "Friends, if you will excuse me…"

"Of course," Hypnos said with a smirk. Aidon nodded stiffly to them and slinked off toward the break in the tapestries that lead to the royal chambers.

"I don't like it," Thanatos said quietly, his arms still folded.

"Don't like what? I'm surprised those two made it *this* long without sneaking off somewhere for a quick—"

"Not that, you dolt. The nectar's affecting you even more than it's affecting *him*," Thanatos scowled. "They share a bond. Why in Tartarus would Persephone send some servant girl to say something that could be said where no one else can hear?"

Hypnos mulled over his brother's words, then snorted and shook his head. "You're paranoid and melancholy. And it's getting tiring, brother. Why don't you go find yourself a willing nymph and—"

"He didn't even stop to consider that. He's as cock-led as you are…"

"Oh, please. I never in a thousand aeons thought that I would hear *you* judging *anyone* for *that*," Hypnos said, punctuating each word with a poke at his brother's chest.

"You're intoxicated. And if I'm wrong, why is she still talking to *him*?"

Hypnos glanced at Persephone, who laughed when Hermes pointed up at the ceiling and gesticulated wildly. "I don't know. Politeness? …Or maybe she's frustrating Aidon a little so that he won't be able to help himself once she gets there? After all, absence makes the heart grow—"

Thanatos pushed him aside and stalked off in search of Hecate.

✢   ✢   ✢

The antechamber smelled faintly of fresh herbs and living things. Aidoneus closed the door behind him. With a quick brush of his fingers he lit the torches, their flames smoldering orange, barely illuminating the room. He thought about Alekto teasing them earlier. Gods forbid if she or her sisters were flying around outside. He didn't want to turn his private reunion with his wife into a spectacle.

"Persephone?"

His voice echoed off the domed ceiling and his stomach pitched with anticipation. Was she already here and hidden? Was she on her way? He grinned. *Without clothes*, the little nymph had whispered. She could be here now, watching him.

His heart leapt and danced as he imagined laying her atop the myrtle and asphodel blooms he'd scattered across their sheets this morning, her hair fanned out on the pillows behind her. Aidon unwound his himation from his shoulder and draped it over the divan. He pulled his crown off his head and set it on the table next to the two cups of pomegranate nectar he'd poured earlier. Beside them sat morsels of food from the feast. He'd prepared it for her himself, eager for her to sample everything Chthonia had received in sacrifice because of her. Aidon wanted to make sure that once they entered this room, there would be little reason to leave it. For days, perhaps.

He unclasped the fibulae holding up his tunic and fumbled with the belt, dropping the rest of his clothing on the divan before unlacing his sandals and pushing them underneath the seat. Aidon ached. His breathing was shallow and his pulse drowned out the rushing water outside. He shivered and faced the doorway she would open any minute. He glanced down; his organ throbbed and pointed straight at it.

401

Aidon swallowed the lump in his throat and shifted from one foot to the other, waiting for her to make her appearance. When he'd gone above, he had mentioned studying the *hieros gamos*. What if Persephone expected a soul-melding, ecstatic performance from him tonight, akin to the night they'd shared the Key? What if, in his zeal, he took her too fast? What if he was careless and hurt her?

Aidon snorted a laugh. Of all the preposterous things in this cosmos, he thought: him— nervous about being with her! He began pacing the room again, shaking his head. Only once had he ever been anxious with her— the first time they made love in her bed. Aidoneus had wanted it to be perfect, just as he had strived to make her homecoming perfect. Persephone had denied that anything was troubling her, but Aidon could sense her anxiety as though it were his own. He had felt it surge through her when he'd announced their impending wedding ceremony.

His stomach dropped and he froze. He recalled their night in the Plutonion— those last words she'd spoken to him, and his silence that followed. Was that why she had told Minthe to summon him here instead of reaching out herself? Aidon combed his fingers over his scalp. He had to relax.

He stared at the prepared food and drink, the dim torchlight smoldering red in the cup's reflection. His mind was already swimming with too much nectar, but a bit more might calm his nerves. Aidon snatched up a cup and gulped down half its contents.

The orange lights in the room left trails across his vision. He rubbed his eyelids and shook his head. The trails remained, then thickened and grew brighter. His fingers felt numb. Aidoneus tried to draw in a breath, but his chest constricted. Sweat broke out on his forehead. He stumbled backward. Distantly, he heard the clay cup shatter as it hit marble, the remaining nectar and pomegranate splashing across the floor. The trails of light blazed. His stomach clenched, and the spilled dark nectar on the floor started creeping toward him— following him. The slain demons of Echidna, his faithful guard dog's monstrous brothers and sisters, flashed through his memory. Their blood lurched across the floor. *Murderer... murderer...* The wet snap when Kampe's neck broke. The screams of the Golden Men... Iapetos's son, Menoetius, falling into the nothingness below Tartarus, falling forever. The Titan's cry became his own. He clapped his hands over his ears, but still the screams echoed. The blood chased after him, spreading across the map of his kingdom, rivers of blood he'd shed during the war. He heard weeping.

No... no...

Next to the golden poplar tree engraved on the chamber doors, he saw a pale nymph crouched, heavy with child, her face contorted and streaked with tears. Her fingers reached in his direction, his name a plea for mercy on her lips...

No, Fates, please...

He retreated toward the bedroom, the light streaking toward him. *Destroyer... murderer...* His weight slammed against the door as he stumbled into his bedroom. His knees started to give out and the muscles in his legs seized. His fingers twitched. The roaring fire was all consuming, raging like a great furnace, filling the room. He lost his balance and his back met the wall. The creatures inside the amber twisted and screamed all around him, their pincers and teeth cracking against their translucent cages, shattering their prisons. They leapt to the floor and skittered toward him. Aidon cried out and shambled to the bed, threw himself on it, and closed his eyes.

This isn't real... this isn't real... Persephone! Persephone, please... where are you?

He burned and froze. His limbs wouldn't respond to his will. They twitched, splayed out, his heart racing, his stomach roiling as though the scorpions and centipedes from the walls were tearing him apart from the inside.

"Hades…" The voice was velvety and female.

This wasn't real. The nectar had been poisoned. He had to fight it.

"Why so afraid, Hades?"

With all his strength he tilted his head up. "S-sweet one? Persephone, d-don't drink…"

"The nectar?" A pale woman with flaxen hair came into view, slim-figured and naked but for a crown of golden poplar. His crown. Her form wavered in the firelight. "Ergot is a curious thing. Mortals see the most monstrous visions before they die of it."

Her voice… he knew that voice. He knew that pale figure and those poplar leaves… Please, Fates, don't let it be her. Of all the memories sent to torment him…

Help me…

"Your minister, Thanatos, is rumored to take kykeon laced with ergot on occasion… just enough to give him visions, but *never* with nectar. That affects a god the same as it affects a mortal, no? And though you feel like you're dying, though perhaps you'd welcome that release, Hades, you simply won't get it, will you?"

He sputtered trying to form words. "You're n-not real."

"Oh, I am. Or perhaps it's a memory you see?" She giggled, sauntering closer. "Mortals react to ergot by doing the most peculiar things— accusing the old women in their villages of witchcraft and stoning them." She lowered her voice. "They are often struck mad— haunted by old memories."

"You're not her…"

The naiad's face was blurred, her features twisted by his memories of another. "Tell me. When you see me, what haunts *you*, Hades?"

*　　*　　*

Persephone…

She felt cold. Aidoneus was panicked and confused— she felt as though his alarm were her own. She looked around the room for her husband, trying to find the source of his voice.

Persephone, please… where are you?

"Aidon?"

Her eyes widened and Hermes stopped his story. "Didn't Hades leave a while ago?"

"I thought he was talking with Thanatos and Hypnos…" She turned and saw Thanatos looming toward her, Hecate by his side, trying to keep up with his long gait.

Help me…

"You know," Hermes said, "I've never seen him so happy. It's almost stra—"

Thanatos shoved Hermes aside, his eyes wild. "Go to him. Now."

"Where is he?! Where is my husband?" Persephone's skin felt clammy, prickling with fear.

Hecate closed her eyes. "Upstairs. Hurry, my queen."

The ether flashed and her helm appeared in her hand. She put it on and disappeared from the view of the immortals before bounding up the stairs.

I'm sorry… please… I'm trying to stop… but she…

She? Persephone's heart raced. What was he talking about? *My love, what is wrong?*

No answer. Persephone pounded up the stairs, faster and faster, too distraught and distracted, desperately willing herself to bridge the space between them as she ran. She failed.

Please tell me! What has happened to you?

His lone word made her whole body flare with rage.

Minthe.

*   *   *

The naiad's hips swayed from side to side, her blonde hair cascading over her shoulders and breasts. Aidon convulsed, illusion and delirium transported his tortured mind to the days after his arrival in the world below. He recalled the beautiful nymph who tended the poplar tree in front of

405

the palace, the poplar crowns she fashioned for him from its leaves, the friendly words exchanged, the loneliness she'd admitted to him. His visions darkened, showing how their acquaintance had soured, how she had wanted him as a lover instead of a friend.

"You are *not* Leuce," he managed, speaking around his thick tongue. "She died long ago in the world above."

"But before she was banished, *by you*, Leuce told you she loved you." Minthe climbed on the bed, astride one of his twitching legs. "She told me how she offered herself to you. Leuce was no idiot. She knew it wouldn't last, that you were destined for another. But instead of letting her go gently…"

Aidon remembered that distant morning. He remembered how temptation had almost won over him, how he had nearly broken his vow and given in to her. How Leuce had crawled into his bed, naked and warm, had caressed him to wakefulness, how he had angrily shoved her away. The words she had spoken were etched in his memory. *Aidon I know what I am*, she said, *I know who you are. But for just this brief time, please… My king, my sweet lord, let me care for you… ease your troubled mind… take me please… I offer you my innocence…* He had bellowed for Leuce to leave his room at once. Hades had told Hecate to send Leuce away, even before her training as an acolyte was complete, to lie with a river god in the world above. He refused to speak with her or any of the other Underworld nymphs after she left. Hades saw Leuce only once after that, months later. She was pregnant, bawling, waiting at the shore for Charon to row her away from her home, never to return. Of all the sins he'd ever committed…

"…you had her raped by another." Minthe's face came into focus above him. Her scent, sweet and sharp, made him gag. "Your coldness created *me*, Hades, and I watched my mother die slowly of a broken heart, cast off and exiled by the man to whom she'd confessed her love."

"Minthe." Aidoneus swallowed. "Y-you— Leuce was…"

"My mother."

"I never… Minthe, I didn't— I'm not…"

"I know you didn't sire me. My mother was abandoned, rejected, then taken in a ritual she did not want by a man she did not want. When I was born, Kokytos refused to acknowledge that he'd sired me. And when I sought his help in winter, he threw me out to his court to be used day after day like whore. Thank the gods that the Corn Mother saved my mother, and when she died, Demeter was able to bind Leuce's spirit to the poplars of Thesprotia to keep her soul from returning to this wasteland."

"I didn't know…"

"Coward. It was so easy to send her off, wasn't it? An inconvenience to be discarded. And now you have your spoils of war, your plaything… the daughter of the goddess who was our salvation, the innocent girl you ruined to keep beside you."

"I didn't…"

"Liar. Everyone knows! Everyone knows what you did to her. And her mother knows and I know that you aren't capable of love. You destroy, despoil, break, and ruin. You are incapable of compassion or regret. It is simply your nature," she said, inching up his body to straddle his hips.

"Not with her… not w-with Persephone…" Through the cacophony of pain and illusion, the Harvest Goddess's plans, executed by this simple pawn, came into sharp relief.

"Defiler. Do you, does *anybody* honestly believe that you can change like the flip of an obol, as though aeons of being the cold unforgiving ruler of Tartarus could be erased in an instant? I will save her from you. I will *break her heart* to save her from you."

"Why would-d you do this to her?"

"Because finally, my mother's spirit will be able to rest. In Leuce's name you will reap what you've sown."

Aidoneus saw the fire blazing around them, rippling with scalding heat. Minthe pulled her prize from behind her back.

407

Its shaft glinted gold, and she aimed it straight at his heart. He tried to sink into the mattress, tried to put distance between the golden point and its target. If it pierced him...

He mustered all his will, trying in vain to keep the golden arrow's proximity from affecting him. Fire flooded his loins. She felt him stir underneath her. She grasped his flesh stroking him with delicate fingers. He quaked, her touch the only relief from the poison coursing through his veins. He let out a soft moan, his senses overwhelmed by the mix of ergot, the arrow, her touch... Aidoneus narrowed his eyes, shutting out the visions, the pain and pleasure. He wouldn't give in so easily. "Persephone... s-she will know. If you do this, she'll know how it w-was done."

"That will be quite a thing to explain to your wife, when she comes in the room and sees you fucking me. Don't fret, Hades. She'll be here any minute."

Minthe pushed back his foreskin, ready to impale herself on his length. Her heat, her flesh quivered above him. He tried to writhe out of her grasp. "What you wish to do— this is suicide. Minthe, for your sake and mine, don't do this. I b-beg of you. Everyone will know..."

"You are cut from the same cloth as all the other licentious gods," she hissed, gripping his phallus and centering herself above him. "Who would ever believe you?"

"I would," a female voice growled behind her.

Minthe flew backward, her hair yanked by an invisible force. She flailed, kicking Aidon hard in the side. He curled up, shaking, his body succumbing to pain and poison. Through the haze of hallucinations, he saw the lights in the room and beyond extinguish. All light was gone but for one: the writhing body of a screaming woman bursting into white-hot flames.

＊　　　＊　　　＊

In the hall and gardens below, the torches and brazier lights, the lamps carefully set on the Styx and the *magnes*

408

burning atop the towers went dark all at once. Sound ceased, and Hermes was left mute mid-sentence, along with all the other guests of the Underworld. Long, silent moments passed.

A pained wail, female and filled with anger, echoed from the chambers above. When the scream subsided, sound returned to the hall below. A single torch appeared in Hecate's hand, the only light in the chamber. She cajoled the shrieking Lampades, fruitlessly trying to calm them. The Erinyes spread their wings and alighted, hissing curses. Thanatos gestured to his brother. Hermes's knees shook, and he glanced from one daemon to the next. Hephaestus grabbed his arm, startling him.

"We need to leave," the God of the Forge muttered. "Now."

"Y-yes," he said, his mouth dry. Hermes looked upward in the direction of the royal chambers. "What *was* that?"

"My mother once screamed like that." Hephaestus tugged at Hermes arm. "But when Zeus was caught with another woman, Hera didn't silence and darken the world. We are strangers here, Hermes. We don't know what she's capable of if Hades did what I fear he did."

Hermes looked at the creatures surrounding them, their eyes glowing in the light of Hecate's solitary torch. "Best we find out later."

He grabbed Hephaestus and flew from the terrace across the river, past milling shades and onward to the caverns leading back into the sunlight.

24.

PERSEPHONE'S HELM CLANGED AGAINST THE floor.
Her throat was raw. Before her lay a pile of ashes. Her
hands shook. She could smell the burning hair, charred
bones, and entrails of Minthe, whom she trusted, whom her
mother had insisted attend her. Persephone gasped in air, her
skin prickling.

She had brought this upon them. She'd confided in Demeter. Demeter had insisted on sending Minthe. And
Minthe...

Aidoneus lay on his side, his body seizing, a thin foam
bubbling from his lips. His eyes stared into nothingness.
"Aidon!" She ran to him, her eyes blurred by tears. "Fates,
no... please... Aidon, what's wrong? Aidon!!"

He looked up at her, his eyes unfocused and his arm
flailing toward her, glancing off her shoulder. "The n-n-
nec— the nec— Don't... don't..."

The nectar. Persephone ran to the antechamber. A piece
of clay from his shattered cup cracked under her sandal. All
the lights in the room flared to life with a pass of her hand.
Persephone dipped a finger in the full cup on the table, her
digit wet and coated in red powder when she pulled it away.
She rubbed the grit between her fingers and sniffed it. Perse-

410

phone had known every plant for as long as she could remember. Not just the lovely flowers like larkspur, or the
herbs and roots for eating and healing, but also those for
numbing, like willowbark, or even poisoning, like hemlock
and foxglove. She knew the countless wispy molds and fungi
that grew on the plants, and every good and poisonous
mushroom. But beyond all of them, she knew the dark red,
deformed barley that grew after late rains and spoiled her
mother's crops, the stalks tainted and deadly, burned before
children could find them.

"Ergot."

She ran back to Aidoneus and laid him back, placing a
hand on his chest. She could feel the poison moving through
his veins, through his mind. "Lie back… lie back, my love."

She covered his body with hers, lying atop him and feeling the rush of the bad herb moving through his blood. She
laid her head on his chest, listening to his shallow, uneven
heartbeat. Persephone closed her eyes and concentrated.
"Hold still… hold still… I'm right here with you…"

The life she brought with her from the world above radiated from her until it filled the room, pulsing with green and
growing things. She poured the concentrated energy into
him, felt it spread through him like fire, the ergot burning
away like a leaf landing on hot coals. Under her splayed
fingers, she felt his heartbeat slow, steady, and soften. His
breathing deepened and his limbs stopped shaking. She
opened her eyes and looked into his. His pupils shrank and
she could see the dark brown of his irises. "Aidon."

"Are you real?" He cupped her face in his hands.

Persephone started crying. "Yes. I'm real."

"Show me you're real… That you're not another illusion."

She kissed him hard on the mouth, sobbing. *I'm real, my
love.*

He rolled with her, holding her underneath him, gathering her in his arms and trailed his lips over her collarbone,

burying his face in her hair. Hades stopped and sat up, his jaw clenched, relief quickly replaced by anger. His voice growled low. "Where is that wretched girl? I will *ruin* her for this."

At that, Persephone burst into tears, her mouth open, moisture spilling down her temples. Aidoneus quirked an eyebrow, not sure what he'd said to make her react so. He stroked her forehead.

"No, no, my love, nothing happened between us. You saved me. But she…" Where was she? Aidoneus glanced around the dark bedroom. Had the vision of Minthe burning been real? He stood and walked to the hearth, passing his hands over it, rekindling the Phlegethon flame. When the room filled with light, everything was as it once was… the room didn't blaze like an overheated furnace, and all the little insects and creatures of long ago were still frozen in the stones covering the walls and ceiling. His eyes widened when he saw little purple, hooded flowers and uneven waxy leaves bursting from the walls, growing from the spaces between the amber. Aconite. The poison that was in him had transmuted, living and growing harmlessly on the walls of their bedroom. Persephone cried on, curling into a ball on their bed.

On the floor was a black pile of ash— now become rich soil, and sprouting from it was a bright green sprig, its scent pungent and disturbingly familiar…

His eyes widened and he stared at his wife. She had killed the naiad. Healing him, purging his body of ergot and filling the room with her life-giving energy had brought the little plant to life within Minthe's remains. Aidoneus shook his head, his teeth grinding together. With the flick of his wrist he summoned his clothing, his himation winding around him and darkening to a midnight black.

One hand scooped up the little mint plant and the other tugged his wife to stand. "Come with me."

"I didn't mean to…" Persephone choked through her sobs. "Aidon, she was going to…"

"I know."

"I should have said something. My mother sent her with me to s-serve… I'm so sorry! This is all my fault… my fault…"

"It's not your fault."

"Are you angry with me?"

"Not with you."

He pulled her with him down the stairs and through the palace, past the last of their guests, before stopping in the empty stableyard. Only once they were there did he let go of her hand.

Aidoneus grabbed the staff from the side of the gate and hammered it against the ground as hard as he could. The stones in the center of the yard broke apart and fell away, and Persephone could hear the whinnying of horses, the rumble of chariot wheels.

*   *   *

The sun was high in the sky. Demeter sat alone outside the Plutonion, twirling a crocus in her hand. Her veil fluttered in the chilly breeze.

Frost had already started climbing the barren stalks of wheat. She touched the crocus flower and it wilted; she let it tumble to the grey, fallow ground. Would her daughter hate her for this? She worried at her lip. If Kore was angry with her, then so be it. It was better than watching her shrivel like that purple flower.

She walked into the empty fields, reaching under her veil to brush away her tears. Her eyes felt raw. How would she endure the next six months, not knowing how Kore fared? She had no doubt of her servant's commitment, or her desire to avenge her mother, Leuce. Even so, perhaps it had been a mistake to send Minthe.

Demeter stopped at the oak tree where her daughter's shrine had once been. The shoots had been uprooted last winter by mortals desperate to fill their empty bellies. Husks of larkspur, killed by the cooling evenings, stuck up out of the earth. She shuddered, remembering the day Kore had been taken from her, how she had torn out the plants that had grown around her sleeping daughter. A single asphodel still grew at the base of the tree and Demeter plucked the last ghostly bloom clinging to its stalk.

The earth trembled.

A crack split the ground. The sound of crumbling stone was deafening. Smoke jetted from the yawning chasm. Her stomach dropped and Demeter staggered, bracing herself against the oak. Four great black chargers thundered from the depths of the cold earth. Her hand covered her mouth and her knees failed her.

She wanted to run. She couldn't run.

A golden chariot followed the four horses, its rider shrouded in smoke. Demeter heard her heart thud in her ears, but steadied herself and stood her ground, tight lipped, ready to face the Lord of the Dead.

As the smoke cleared, she saw a form clinging to Hades. Her daughter. Tears streaked Kore's face. She stood on the quadriga's platform, holding her husband's arm and shaking, her gaze unfocused. Aidoneus stepped off the chariot and marched toward Demeter, cradling something against his chest. Demeter took a cautious step back, then stopped and balled her fists. She would not run.

Hades flung his parcel at Demeter's feet: dark soil and a fragrant little plant. It smelled sweet and familiar. Demeter's eyes widened and she stared at the mint in horror. Her mouth went dry.

"You... you murdered her..."

"I did nothing," he said. "If you want to know where this came from, look to your daughter."

414

The Goddess of the Harvest glanced up at Kore, whose eyes were tear stained and bloodshot. She stared at her mother, unmoving. In that moment Demeter knew.

"Shame on you," he hissed. "Shame on you, Demeter! Do what you will to me. Hurt me, send your minions against me, take all from me, but for Fate's sake *leave Persephone out of it!*"

Demeter flinched, her lip quivering.

"She turned her friend into a pile of ash. You've made your daughter a murderer." Aidoneus paced in front of her.

"Hades——"

"She *killed* that nymph! A girl she trusted. You sent your servant to do your dirty work because you cannot leave well enough alone! You sowed betrayal and infidelity... *violence* because you were too jealous to let your daughter become her own woman. And for what? To destroy every remaining shred of trust she placed in you? How dare you do this to her!"

"She..." Demeter choked on the lump in her throat. Her eyes burned. "Kore would never——"

"She walked in on *your* servant, *Leuce's daughter* for Fate's sake, poisoning and violating her husband!"

"Poison? B-but I never told Minthe——"

"What did you *think* would happen?! I would never stray from my wife, and Minthe would never *dare* tangle with me when my wits were about me."

"My daughter would have never killed *anyone* if not for your influence! The power you have over her... She wouldn't have killed Minthe if you hadn't already tainted her."

"Tainted?"

She stabbed her finger at him. "*You* know all about killing, don't you Aidoneus?"

"I have slain tyrants and monsters, Demeter. But you outdid me in ways I never imagined. Not with your two hands, no. But you starved the earth, and man and beast alike died by the scores of thousands."

"To keep you from ruining her!"

"Ruining..." He shook his head. "This from the woman who would have obliterated her precious Kore to keep her at her side..."

"I could never hurt her in the ways you could! At least with me her heart would be safe from what the gods—"

"I am not like them!" Aidoneus bellowed, pointing toward distant Olympus. A vein stood prominent on his forehead and his face grew red. Demeter cowered, shielding herself from him with upraised hands. "I waited *aeons* for Persephone! There is nothing in this cosmos that could turn me from her! I love your daughter. I always have and always will love her, and her alone." He drew in a breath, trying to calm himself. "You know that. I am sorry Zeus treated you so poorly. Truly I am. But I am *not* him, I am not *them*, nor will I ever be. Deme..." He spoke gently, his voice low. "Deme, deep down you *know* that."

Demeter stared up at him, her face drawn and pinched. She broke like rain. The goddess hid her face in her hands. "Aidon, I... I didn't—"

"Shame on you Deme, for what you did," he said again through clenched teeth. "And mark me... my wrath will fall upon you tenfold if you *ever* hurt her again."

"I didn't mean to—"

"But you did." Persephone stepped from the chariot, her voice as unsure as her footing. Minthe, burning in a flare of white and green until there was nothing left, flashed through her thoughts again and she shuddered. She could still smell charred bones, acrid, pungent and sweet. She wondered if Minthe's final scream would follow her forever. Persephone calmed herself. The wind whipped around them. "I've always known you to be wise. But you're blinded by your hatred for my husband. Did you think your plan wouldn't hurt me? Hurt me *and* you? The Agreement says that I am above for half the year. It says nothing about me staying by your side."

Demeter paled. "Please… Daughter, you must forgive me."

"You said I needed servants." A tear rolled down Persephone's face. She lifted her hand toward the fragrant little mint plant and it dug itself into the rough soil, rooting and sprouting, spreading across the ground. "Now Minthe will serve me forever. She will be your constant companion in summer *and* winter to remind you of what you did. And if you choose this path again, Demeter, know that you will lose me forever, and it will be your own doing."

"Kore…"

"If you are in Attica, I'll be in Thrace. If you are in Peloponnesus, I'll be in Macedonia. If you are in Hellas, I will be in Illyria. If you cover the earth, I will raise flowers and shoots from beneath the soil."

Demeter averted her eyes from her daughter. The Goddess of the Harvest knelt before the Queen. She curled forward and wept, reaching out to touch her daughter's right foot in supplication. "Persephone…"

She tried to hide her surprise. Demeter had never called her that.

"Persephone… please forgive me," she sobbed. "I'm sorry. I'm so sorry."

"Swear it. Swear that you will never interfere with my marriage ever again," she said.

Her husband sneered. "An oath from her isn't worth—"

With a glance, Persephone silenced Aidoneus. She turned back to her mother, placing a hand on her shoulder, and spoke low. "Swear it."

"I swear on the Styx… for as long as we live, I will never harm you." She choked on her words, acid welling in her throat. Tears streamed down her cheeks. "I will never harm your husband, or your marriage, ever again."

"Neither will you speak against it…"

Demeter shuddered. "And I will... I swear on the Styx I will not speak against your marriage. Ever. Oh gods, Persephone, I'm... I'm..."

"Rise, Mother."

She stood before her daughter, her eyes cast to the ground. "Daughter, will you ever find it in your heart to forgive me?"

"Forgive, yes. But trust... I need time." Persephone smiled faintly. "Fortunately, the deathless ones have nothing but time."

Demeter stood frozen. Persephone wrapped her arms around her mother, drawing her into an embrace. Demeter sobbed anew. "My dear sweet child..."

"I understand why you did what you did. That doesn't make it right."

"When he came to Olympus I thought I would never see you again," she cried. Her eyes opened wide as she thought about all the mortals who had passed, the starving faces looking up at her when she was grieving. "Gods, what I did... what I had to do just to be able to see you... You were gone... gone..."

"Deme..." Aidoneus spoke quietly. "Do you remember when we forged our pact? It wasn't meant to take away Persephone then, and it isn't now. I am as I was, and I'm not cruel enough to deny you the company of your daughter anymore than I can deny her yours."

"She was married to *you*, Aidon. And your home is beyond this world. Beyond me for all time." Demeter shook. "She would join your house and leave me forever. It... it is that way for all women."

"That is *their* world." he said. He bit at his cheek and sighed, glancing at Persephone. His wife would want him to make some concession. Aidoneus looked at the ground. "Demeter, I should never have involved Zeus. I thought I was doing the proper thing; I should have gone to you directly."

"Zeus is her father."

Hades scoffed. "He did nothing to raise her. *You* were her mother, her teacher, her protector. I should have respected that. And I should have gone to you alone."

"I don't know if I would have…" The Goddess of the Harvest sniffled around half-formed thoughts and wiped her eyes with the edge of her veil. "But now… the Agreement…"

"We cannot undo it, nor should we. It would make Zeus think he can break oaths whenever he pleases," Aidoneus said with a half-suppressed smirk. "Moreover, I could never deprive my wife of the sunlit world. Persephone needs it as much as the world above needs her."

Demeter's mouth went dry and she paled. Persephone turned to face her, her brow knitted, her anger rising. Had Demeter hidden her role in this world from her throughout her life, claiming it instead as her own?

"Wife," Aidoneus said gently, petting her shoulder. "Your mother didn't know. Everything has changed. Because of the seeds, because of the Agreement, this world now relies on you to grow new life."

Persephone's shoulders slumped and she looked to Aidoneus. "So we can never be free of this, then. I will never be able to come and go at will."

"No, much though I wish it was so. After you left, I inquired everywhere for a means to keep you for longer each year. I learned from Nyx, who consulted the Fates themselves, that this is *your* divine role, now. You are the Queen, but you are also Spring. Death and Life."

Demeter wrapped her arms around her body, shaking. "This is my fault."

"No," Aidon said. "This is *ananke.* This is the way it was fated to be. These cycles, the seasons, everything."

Demeter stared north, toward Olympus. "Gods age and change when the world itself changes. Now it will change constantly and nothing can stop that."

"After we made the Agreement, I'm certain Zeus knew this would happen."

Demeter and Persephone turned to Hades, each of their faces mirroring the other's worry.

"As King of the Gods, Zeus is more privy to the will of the Fates than any of us," he continued. "There was a reason he didn't give Persephone to me outright once she reached womanhood. He hoped I would forget; that I would be too busy with my kingdom, or that some woman below would tempt and distract me. He couldn't have known that Persephone's existence would be intertwined with new life springing up from the earth, the seasons and the gods changing, otherwise he would have never agreed to the marriage. But he surely knows now."

"With the Agreement, with the Eleusinian Mysteries, we have taken from them," Persephone said. "They didn't forgive Prometheus when he stole their fire. Will they retaliate against us?"

"Possibly," Aidoneus said. "But subtly, knowing them."

It would be foolish to underestimate them. Persephone drew in a heavy breath. "We can't survive like this, pitted against one another. I am not asking you to forgive each other after all these aeons. But please, in the name of your love for me, at least agree to a truce."

She looked to Aidoneus first, who nodded curtly to her. Her mother's jaw tightened and she cast her eyes to the ground. "I will."

Persephone grasped Demeter's hands, a faint smile on her face. She threw her arms around her again and felt her mother's stiffness melt away, overcome with quiet sadness. Persephone could feel guilt and resignation emanate from Demeter, but also a weight lifting from her chest. Persephone squeezed her tighter. "I love you, Mother. I'll see you in six months."

A tear rolled down Demeter's cheek. "I love you too."

Aidoneus headed toward the chariot. The horses idly nibbled on the mint sprigs dotting the ground but came to attention as their master approached. He climbed onto the chariot and offered Persephone his hand. She stepped in front of him, secure between his arms. With a shake of the reins they were off.

*　　*　　*

"I still don't trust her."

"I don't expect you to," she said as they descended through Erebus. "As I told her, I don't fully trust her either."

"But you trust me?"

She remained quiet.

"I know something has been eating away at you, Persephone."

She gave no answer.

"I can feel it. You know I can."

She swallowed, the pungent smell of mint still permeating his clothes. "Not now."

"Please, just tell me."

"I've gone through too much today, Aidon. Can it wait?"

He stiffened. "Of course."

They rode through the darkness, and Persephone turned to face him. She tugged at his himation until it fell from his shoulders and pooled around his feet.

"Sweet one?"

"I'm sorry," she said angrily, her voice shaking. "I just can't stand her scent on you any longer."

"Is that what's bothering you?"

"Yes," she lied.

"It's not, though."

"Who was Leuce?"

"She was a nymph that once tended the golden poplar tree at the palace entrance."

"What was she to you?"

421

"Nothing. To her dismay." He paused, and she could feel shame wash over him. "Leuce wove crowns for me. I had acquainted myself with everyone who served the grounds when I arrived. I befriended her, but she was not content with that. One morning, she offered herself to me and I spurned her. I sent her away. Or rather, I had Hecate send her away."

"Were you tempted by her?"

"Only for as long as it took me to wake up and recognize that *she* was touching me and not—" He cleared his throat. "She was trying to arouse me while I was dreaming."

Persephone leaned into him. "What did you dream?"

"You know whom I was dreaming about," he said roughly. Aidon recalled the dream, recurring and persistent, one that had haunted him before the golden arrow, before Kore, Persephone, came into his life. "It was always brief visions and flashes, never anything complete. But I... I often dreamed that we... that I was with..."

Persephone felt for his face in the dark, remembering when she had first made this descent with him, her linen dress burnt to ashes, her limbs wrapped around him. It had been so long, and all she could think about was her relief when she had healed him, the ardent, protective love he had expressed when he defended her, and how he'd humbled himself in front of Demeter. Her fingers brushed over his cheekbone and he turned quickly to the side to kiss her palm. Persephone grabbed his head with both hands, winding her fingers through his hair, and brought his lips down over hers.

Aidon tightened the reins in one hand and brought her closer with the other, feeling her legs inch up and wrap around him. His tongue pushed into her mouth, stroking hers rhythmically.

"I don't want any trace of *that woman* on you," she hissed against his lips. "I only want *my* scent on you."

His blood burned when he kissed her, but blazed hotter at her words. She was jealous. That potent knowledge filled him with renewed desire, and he felt guilt boiling up underneath his growing need. He'd never tasted her jealousy before, and he thought how Zeus had used that foul emotion to control Hera all these aeons. His musings were banished when her nimble fingers reached under his tunic. He closed his eyes, his voice thick. "Persephone…" She wrapped her fingers around him and slowly stroked up from the root, circling her thumb over the tip. He had to make sure, before his ability to think rationally was overthrown. "Sweet one, after all that has happened—"

Aidon, please… Her tongue silenced him and twined with his as she gripped him. His free arm pulled her closer. *I need you.*

He dragged her up his body, her heels digging into his sides before her legs wrapped around him. She hoisted her skirts above her waist and felt his palm land on her rump to lift her higher, then reach under to massage and lightly squeeze her vulva. She ground against the tips of his fingers, her hips gyrating against him.

He listened to her impatient mewling against his neck as he trailed his fingers through her labia. Aidon caught her scent, sweeter than any honey or nectar. A fresh surge of need instinctively bucked his hips toward hers at the thought of tasting that sweetness again when they were safely home. Persephone locked her lips against his and yanked the last of his clothing from between them. She felt the tip of his cock prod against her, seeking entry. She wiggled atop Aidoneus, drawing a frustrated groan from him. "I think," he said gruffly between kisses, "that from now on I'll retrieve you myself from the world above."

"I would like that," Persephone whispered into his ear. She sank down, listening to the air rush from his lungs as she joined with him at last. She felt his fingers dig into her thigh, lifting her up before thrusting deeply. She cried out, filled and fulfilled, quivering around him, milking him with every rise and fall.

"Perhaps we could make this our yearly tradition," he said, breathless and hot against her neck. His tongue trailed along her jaw line. Persephone closed her eyes in silent agreement and arched her back, sighing against his searching lips.

Her questions could wait…

25.

"SHE HAS QUESTIONS." THE VOICE WAS A REEDY whisper.

"They all have questions," a richer voice said.

"Their questions will never stop," a third female voice chimed in. "The trees hang with fruit. And who will pluck the seeds but her?"

Persephone sat up, clutching the bed sheet to her palpitating heart. Aidoneus breathed slowly, his eyes closed, undisturbed. She had woken frequently, throughout the night, vaguely aware of tossing and turning next to Aidon. Her body was attuned to the world above, where it was still daylight. Her reunion with Aidon had pleasantly exhausted her, but it was a shallow substitute for deep sleep. The voices haunted her.

Three voices.

They had never spoken to her directly, but she knew deep in her soul to whom those voices belonged. Persephone slowly scooted to the edge of the bed so as not to wake her husband, and her skin prickled when her feet touched the cold stone floor. She'd grown too used to the warm wood, thick fleece, and summer breezes of her mother's home. Persephone shut the curtain and padded across their bedroom, hastily pinning her peplos at the shoulders, and fumbling in the dark to tighten the thongs of her sandals around her ankles. She donned her shawl and wound her hair up as she walked through the antechamber, then down the steps to the throne room.

Pomegranates, olives, figs, and amphorae of oil and kykeon still lay about the hall, as though time had stopped in the wake of their hasty departure. The lights were dim. She gazed up at the dais.

"You won't like what they have to say."

Persephone whipped around to see Hecate, dressed in white.

"Their answers will be as clear as a silt bog and will drown you just as surely."

She thinned her lips. "Even so, they will be more clear than the answer you gave me six months ago."

"My queen, consider what you're about to do."

"If *ananke* is unchangeable, what harm could come of speaking with the Fates?"

Hecate smiled. She'd heard those same words aeons ago. "More than you know. Your husband could answer better."

"If you truly don't want me to go," Persephone said, standing tall, "then you will answer me plainly."

"My queen..."

"Are Aidoneus and I able to bear children?"

Hecate's shoulders fell. "I cannot answer that question."

"Why not?"

"Because I do not know the answer."

Her brow knit. "Then I'm left with little choice but to speak with them."

The Goddess of the Crossroads shook her head. "That choice will turn you into a cistern that can never be filled."

"They're just words, Hecate." The Queen paused, staring at the ground. "You know the way, don't you?"

"Persephone..."

"You know how to reach the Cave of the Moirai. You, Nyx, my husband, abide by *ananke*, no? The very will of the Fates?"

"We do. Which is why you should ask your husband."

Persephone's eyes clouded with tears and her throat tightened. "I can't."

"You fear asking him, yet would go to those whose words you should fear above all else?"

"What if Aidon doesn't know the real answers?"

"Aidoneus knows what they told him," Hecate said, grimly. "The words of the Fates drove him like a ship against a rocky cliff when he first arrived here." Persephone frowned. "We feared his mind might never be clear again. In some ways it is still clouded. He loves me like a mother, but your husband's wrath would be great if I set you on that same course."

"Then that tells me all I need to know. I won't betray you if you take me to them."

Hecate cocked her head to the side and peered at her. "They visited you in dreams."

"Which means that they invited me to come and will tell me the truth."

"They will not lie, but neither will their words be etched in stone. Their world is as fluid as ours. Many threads lead to them, many threads lead away. To them, even the gods are dust. Fibers and felt. Threads, twined and twisted about, then guided into the loom. And those paths change direction, just as yours did when you ate the pomegranate seeds." She stared at the Queen. Persephone stood resolute. Hecate sighed and willed a torch into her hand, the end lighting as her fingers brushed over its tip. "But I already know this river, much as I foolishly try to resist its currents. Nothing will change your mind, will it?"

"Not before the Styx flows backwards."

427

"Follow me, then." The Goddess of the Crossroads vanished from sight, and Persephone startled, the room growing dim as Hecate's torch faded with her.

Hecate never really leaves the ether. She is its goddess—as much a ruler of all the spaces and pathways between the worlds as I am ruler of the Underworld.

Remembering Aidon's words, Persephone stretched her hand forth and fire swirled before her, dilating and burning wildly at the edges. The great crimson and silver twisting expanse of Hecate's home appeared before her. She stepped through and faltered, barely keeping her footing, distracted by vertigo.

"You bridge this divide often." Hecate's voice came from all directions. "Have you never visited my home without knowing your destination?"

"No."

"You have much to learn, then." The red-haired goddess coalesced before her. On either side of the Goddess of the Crossroads were faint outlines of her younger and older self, each holding torches. Vertigo struck Persephone and Hecate caught her hand as she lurched backward. "Steady."

"Where are we going? Why can't I just step through?"

Hecate chuckled to herself. "You are more like him than you know."

"You took him there?"

"Aidoneus demanded I do so. I could not dissuade him, either," Hecate said, the smile erased from her face. "We are going to the Cave of the Moirai, at the headwaters of the Styx."

Persephone raised a quizzical eyebrow. The Styx flowed so deep and endlessly, She didn't think it had headwaters.

"Everything in this cosmos has a beginning. And everything begins and ends with the Weavers."

Persephone stumbled forward, falling onto solid ground. She lay there for a moment before she could replace the air that had been knocked out of her. She brushed gravel from

428

her stinging hands, then stood and shook the dust off her peplos.

Where was she?

The hazy sky was a deep red, half way between day and night. Was it twilight, or dawn already?

"Hecate?"

She was alone. Her voice sounded empty. Fog obscured everything, making the space around her feel small and confined. There were no mountains, no rivers, no asphodel. There was no glow from the Phlegethon and no light from the Styx. A stream of water bubbled and sloshed against the pebbles underfoot.

It's been here since Chaos gave the cosmos form from the void. It is the mother of all waters above and below the earth. Persephone understood, her skin turning to gooseflesh when she realized where she was. This inconsequential trickle of water was the mighty River Styx.

Time— the past and the future— was unknown here. She stood in a space beyond all concept of time, perhaps before Chaos, perhaps after the death of the Deathless Ones. As soon as that clarity dawned, the mists lifted to reveal a sharp cliff, impossibly smooth, extending higher than she could see. Faint reflections whirled on its surface and Persephone squinted at them. Grass waving on green meadows, a calm sea dotted with islands under a blue sky, then the passing sun and moon, and other heavenly bodies in a riot of colors. She saw more stars than she'd ever thought possible turning about one another, then a hand grasping at skin, lovers pulling each other closer. The images flashed so quickly that she could barely discern them. She saw herself, staring at her own reflection on the cliff face, her brow knitted. Beside her was an opening in the rock, wide and deep. Had she not seen it before? Or had it appeared suddenly and soundlessly?

This was undoubtedly the Cave of the Moirai. When the gods prayed, they would do so to the ones who dwelled here.

Persephone peered around its edge and inside. Within, the voices of three women hummed, the song drifting toward her, echoing through the chamber. It was the same lullaby sung by Iasion, by her mother, by Charon, across the ages to where she stood. She swayed, mesmerized, their voices blending with the voices of everyone she had ever known. They stopped.

"It won't do to stand there," a reedy voice echoed, calling out to her.

"No, no it won't," a richer voice chimed in.

"She'll stay without as long as she needs." The last voice was lower.

Persephone took one step forward.

"There, you see?" the last voice said.

She took a deep breath and another step, walking toward the warm glow of a single oil lamp. The floor was damp and the cold seeped in through her soles. The old song resumed. Mud started to weigh down the edges of her peplos and her sandals stuck to the floor.

She reached out for the side of the cave, but the closer her fingers moved to its surface, the further it receded. She felt dizzy, her eyes deceiving her, and pulled her hand back, trudging forward toward the flickering flame. Shrouded women came into view, their faces obscured by darkness, their hands working quickly. One held a drop spindle and sent it spinning as her fingers nimbly twisted the black felt into thread.

"Greetings, Kindly Ones," she said, dipping into a low curtsy.

"So formal, little one…" said Clotho, the woman with the spindle. The wool felt she twisted in her hands was so dark and fine it was nearly invisible.

"She is only showing respect," Lachesis said, pulling the thread from Clotho's fingers as it was formed. Aquamarine, bolder than any dye, flooded through the newly formed thread as she determined its length.

"The Theoi have no respect for *ananke*. Including this one." Atropos snipped the measured piece and twisted the end to keep it from unraveling. "If she did, she would not be here."

Persephone swallowed. "I… I respect *ananke*."

"Do you now…" Clotho said. "Even if it meant the end of the cosmos itself? Even if all you loved ceased to be and everyone you knew turned to ash?"

Her lip trembled. She had no answer.

Lachesis smiled and measured a new thread, this one emerald green. "Don't worry, little one. None of your kind can answer those questions honestly."

Persephone recalled Aidoneus's revelation that coming and going at will from the Underworld was not possible, thanks to her new role in the world above. She expelled a tense sigh. "What am I?"

The three paused and glanced at each other. "It is not often we hear that question."

"Because most think they know."

"She knows too, but there are many answers for her." The spindle spun again and more thread passed between their hands.

"The Destroyer."

"The Maiden."

"The Queen."

"A mother…" Lachesis's voice said. "You are mother to many, little one."

"And mother to none."

Persephone shifted uncomfortably. Of course they already knew what her most pressing question would be. "Mother to many?"

"Half the year, when you nourish, half the year when you comfort."

"But the little threads are in your care, always."

"And what about my husband?"

431

Atropos looked to Clotho. "The seeds cannot return to the earth without them."

"Either of us?" Persephone asked.

"Your husband. And you. You do not play your role alone."

"He is your equal and counterpart. In this you saw the true nature of the cosmos."

"Together you are mother and father. Rulers of the eternal realm, male and female."

"The seeds of the earth are passed from him into your care."

"It was ever to be that way."

"Maiden no more, yet you are the Maiden when you walk the Earth. The little threads still call you Kore—"

"They are too frightened by my real name," Persephone said. "They dare not call on She Who Destroys the Light." Mother to many. Mother to none. Together you are mother and father. She swallowed hard, afraid of what they would say to so direct a question, but she needed an answer. "Will I ever give Aidoneus a son?"

"The earth is your womb, Aristi Chthonia."

"But as for your own hystera…"

"…the gift and sacrifice of fertility is yours to share with Hades…"

"The King and the kingdom."

"For just as the earth cannot harvest without your mother…"

"…it cannot replenish without the sacred union of Aidoneus and Persephone, or your journey between this world and the world above…"

"…and for so long as the seed rises to the earth to spring forth as new life…"

"…that new life cannot take root within you."

Persephone could say nothing. Her head tilted forward and she felt tears fall onto the damp ground. She wept immovably, silently. She felt the black sorrow— the finality—

wrapping itself around her heart, but she refused to give in. There was no room for sympathetic appeal of any kind here, least of all that achieved by sobbing. For all their implacability as governors over the dead, Hades and Persephone were as reeds bending in the wind compared to the Fates. She knew this. Still, the tears fell.

"She doesn't ask to change her fate," Clotho observed as she twisted the fibers together.

"This one is wise," Atropos said with a sharp snip of a dark red thread. "She understands *ananke*."

"She knows and accepts that we are only its stewards," said Lachesis as she drew out another long piece behind the one cut by her sister. It became a golden yellow in her fingers.

Clotho looked up, the small flame faintly lighting her compassionate, ancient face. Her fingers still nimbly worked the spindle, turning the wool into thread. "Child, take heart. We have not finished speaking."

"We never finish speaking."

"So much weight given to words already spoken. Too much weight."

"What do you mean?" Persephone said, quietly wiping her face with her shawl.

"There are infinite threads."

"Woven in infinite patterns."

"In our basket lie the threads for Hades and Persephone's children."

Persephone snapped to attention. "What?"

"Not immutable."

"Not yet, at least."

"So much still to undertake before they can be woven."

Her tears started again, only this time they welled up with hope. "We will have children then…"

"Woman, take heed," said Atropos. "We have not finished speaking."

"We never finish speaking."

433

"The words, they do not weigh enough. The threads are already heavy."

"Words are words. Threads are threads. And those threads can spoil to felt once more to spin again."

"Please just tell me!" She cried, wavering between hope and oblivion. Hecate was right. She shouldn't have come here.

"Patience," they said in unison, their voices dark. Persephone shuddered and dropped slowly to one knee, then the other, the cold mud seeping through her clothes.

"My apologies, Sparing Ones," Persephone said, planting one hand in front of her and bowing her head. "Forgive me. I only seek to make sense of what you say. If there are threads for our children—"

"One, who is twice woven, cannot remain your own."

"Two, the ether bound, who shines the torch in darkness."

"Three, the blessed harbinger, who reaps the reaper's heart."

"All at last aeon's end," they said together, "And all to end the aeon."

Persephone stood slowly, watching the Fates' handiwork, one thread twisted, another snipped, hands moving, measuring, casting a wealth of colorful strands one by one into the straw basket at Lachesis's side.

Three children...

"I... you said..." Persephone stammered incredulously, "I-I don't understand..."

"We know," they answered in lilting, sing-song unison.

Lachesis spoke the moment Persephone began to step back. "She is going to leave, now."

"She thinks she's heard enough."

"Should we tell her more?"

"No, let her go."

"There remains much to be done..."

"...by two in the dark."

Persephone didn't know if the Fates were dismissing her, or if she was actually preparing to leave. It didn't matter, she realized. She curtsied once more, and lifted the hem of her peplos out of the mud. The low light outside beckoned her. As she stepped closer, the horizon brightened, becoming daylight, then grew brighter still. The clouds grew distant and wind whipped across the barren ground.

She breathed in the icy air, shaking like a newborn, and squinting as she emerged. Hecate stood beside the cave, her cloak wrapped tightly around her, the ends flapping in the gale. Persephone licked her lips, ready to apologize, ready to tell Hecate she was right, she shouldn't be here—no one should be here.

"I know," the Goddess of the Crossroads said quietly before Persephone could speak. She extended her hand as the wind grew stronger. "Come," she said, "that is our sign to leave, and we should do so before it comes to pass."

"What, exactly?"

"The creation or destruction of the cosmos. I don't know which. Perhaps both. All these aeons and it is still unclear to me when we are."

Hecate closed her eyes and the ether swallowed them whole, the whirl of the Void a comfort. When the Goddess of the Crossroads finally released her, she was standing alone in the throne room. There was no mud staining her dress or caking her sandals. Her hair wasn't damp or blown out of place and the room was still flooded with darkness, just as it had been when she left it. Persephone turned on her heels, and ascended the narrow staircase, eager to return to the safety of her bed.

26.

"HE WAS A RUNT. HECATE THOUGHT THAT
Echidna would kill him when he was born, so she
gave him to me to keep and to improve my mood, I think."

"A runt? I can't even imagine him being called *average*,
much less a runt!"

"His paws were enormous— I knew how big he would
get one day, but for a time he could fit in my lap. Would
curl up on me and fall asleep when I was judging shades.
Three little heads snoring in unison, with three tongues pok-
ing out. He wasn't a very intimidating guard dog, at first—"

"Obviously," she guffawed.

"It's too bad he outgrew his spots..."

"Is *that* why you named him Cerberus? I'd wondered..."

"Yes," Aidoneus said. "Not very creative, I know."

"At least you didn't name him 'Three Heads'!"

He laughed and moved closer to her. Their conversation
had meandered wildly since he'd settled beside her. They had
spent the morning and afternoon making love, talking about
everything and nothing, and sampling the bounty sent to the
Underworld by the mortals.

Aidon felt as though the intervening time hadn't passed
at all, that they were as they had been before the pomegran-

ate seeds, when she was supposed to be his for always, instead of this strange half-life they would play out until the end of time. He knitted his brow momentarily. The thought that in six short months she must leave again drove needles into him. He pushed it from his mind and focused on her instead, committing to memory every hair that had been pulled out of place, every eyelash framing her slate blue eyes, the gentle slope of her nose, the soft bow of her lips. The pain faded the more he studied her.

Persephone lay on her stomach, propped up on pillows and a soft black fleece, her arms folded under her chin, relaxed and sated, and gazing at him. Aidon leaned on his left arm, lazily tracing shapes on her back with his index finger. She smiled at him.

"You're wondering what in the world I'm doing right now," Aidon said.

"You read my mind."

"Not a hard thing to do these days." He bit his cheek. Something worried her, something increasingly palpable. He gave her a concerned look.

She giggled.

"While you were away I got a head start on learning how to write to you in the old tongue."

She relaxed again. "So is that what you're doing to my shoulders right now? Writing to me?"

"Mm-hmm."

"What does it say?"

Aidon slowly traced the outlines of two glyphs, sounding them out as he wrote them. "I love… you…" he whispered. She buried her face in her hands and smiled, feeling her cheeks flushing hot, then turned back to him. He drew three more symbols, quicker and with a practiced hand. "Persepho-neia."

"Persephoneia?"

"It was the closest I could get in their language. And it's graceful. It suits you."

Persephone blushed again. She rose up on one elbow, but he gently pressed her shoulder back to the pillow, stilling her so he could continue writing.

"Will you..." He drew the next two symbols and whispered as he traced their patterns into her skin. "...marry me?"

She froze. "What?"

"Will you marry me, Persephone?"

"I... we... Aidon, do you mean a *wedding*? We've been husband and wife for eight months, now. Far longer, if you consider that we were betrothed aeons ago."

"By the laws of the world above. We are both *quite* aware those can be broken at will."

"But we're still married. We just spent the whole day doing... *married things*."

Aidon laughed, then drew in a slow breath. "Persephone, I never asked if you wanted to be my spoils of war, or if you wanted to be the bargain I made with Zeus and Demeter. I ask you now, as my equal, as rightful Queen of the Underworld, if you want to be my wife."

Her face fell. He was serious.

"I never asked your permission."

"Aidon—"

"I didn't. I *stole* that decision from you when I abducted you. I wish to return that choice to you."

She was quiet, then shifted again to sit up, facing him. "My love, when you announced at the welcoming celebration that we would have a wedding ceremony..."

"I know. I knew as soon as I said it that I should have discussed it with you first."

"You know that I love you, Aidon. Perhaps after all this, after Minthe, my mother... Should we wait?" In her heart, she didn't want to wait; she wanted him to say 'no'. But she needed to confront him about the truth first... and delaying that was far more comfortable.

He sensed the doubt in her voice and raised an eyebrow. "If that will make you more comfortable, we can postpone. Do you still *want* a ceremony?"

"I do." She hesitated. The time to speak was now, but she swallowed the questions raging inside her and gave him a nervous smile. "Maybe a smaller ceremony? Instead of inviting everyone who lives in our kingdom?"

Aidon chuckled. "Anything you wish. We can even have just the *hieros gamos* itself, if that is what you want. Alone. Without anyone bearing witness."

She felt her breath catch and tears clouded her eyes.

"Is that what you still want, sweet one?"

She nodded. "I do. I do, my love. But I've seen the Rite and its lasting bond... go terribly wrong. My parents..."

"I am not him. You are not her."

"I know. But why is the ritual so important to you?"

"Because I want to seal myself to you. Permanently." He rubbed her back. "I have wanted to since the night we shared the Key."

"To bring us closer?"

"Yes."

"I am already bound to you, Aidon. What more?"

"I trust you and I love you. I want us to relinquish everything that separates us, every possible thing that could stand between us."

"Truly?"

"I swear it."

It was inescapable now. Persephone took a deep breath. "Aidon, if we are to go through such a ritual, if we are going to bind ourselves to each other completely, then we need to know and consider everything about each other. You told me once that you would tell me the truth, you swore upon the Styx to do so, and I likewise should do the same for you."

"You don't have to, my love."

"Yes, I do. I certainly don't want to be less than you, but I don't want to be some statue set upon a pedestal, either. I am as imperfect as anyone else."

He felt his stomach drop, worrying where this could lead. "I will accept it then."

"Good." She stared at him and took his hand within hers. "I, Persephone Praxidike Chthonios, Queen of the Underworld, Goddess of Spring, swear on the Styx to tell you the truth, no matter what the consequences, and withhold nothing."

He nodded and brought her hand to his lips, kissing it.

"I need the same from you, Aidoneus. That you will withhold nothing and tell me everything."

"Everything," he said. "I swear it in turn."

She took a deep breath. "I visited the Fates."

He froze.

"I asked them about children..."

Aidoneus stood up from the bed and paced the room, his hands raking his scalp. "Hecate took you, didn't she? I swear by the Styx, when I see her next—"

"You'll do no such thing. I demanded she take me, Aidon. Just as you once demanded *she* take *you*."

"Then you know."

"That it is more than likely that we cannot have—"

"That I *lied* to you."

"You didn't *lie* to me, Aidon. I never asked."

"But *I knew*. I lied by omission, Persephone." He exhaled with a shudder, then stood still, his jaw clenched.

"Aidon..."

"I know what they said!" His voice broke. "Gods above, of all the truths my father ever tried to use against me, it was that staying here, becoming ruler of the Underworld would make offspring, heirs, *a family*, impossible." He stared at her.

"What if it's not true, my love?"

"It *is true* and I made it so. I ate the asphodel to bind myself here for penance! But I didn't realize until after I'd done

440

it that consuming the food of the dead, making this place a part of me… Then you… Persephone, I stopped you from tasting the pomegranate *for a reason* that morning in the grove. If you had eaten that seed you would have shared my fate," he said, rubbing his eyes. "But I didn't tell you *why* I stopped you because I thought I would lose you. And when you ate the seeds on your own…"

"Aidon…"

"You're a goddess of the earth. Of fertility, for Fate's sake, and the consequences of eating the food of the dead are *eternal.* My silence, my cowardice robbed you of…" He turned away from her and went silent. His back shook and his head dipped as he crumpled forward. He tried to take in a full breath and calm himself. "I'll go."

"What do you mean?"

"The palace is yours. This is a vast kingdom. You were meant to rule here, and during the winter I can find another corner of this realm to—"

"Aidon, stop," she said, her voice firm. His fists were at his sides, his muscles taut, his knuckles white. Persephone rose and walked across the bedroom to him. As she approached tension knotted his body further. "Face me. Please face me, Aidoneus."

He turned slowly and brushed his hands over his face and back through his hair, trying to quiet the despair raging within him, to salvage some shred of dignity in front of her. This might be the last he would ever see of her. Persephone brought her hand to his cheek and he closed his eyes.

"You know that I love you."

He shook, his words coming from behind gritted teeth. "You bound yourself here, to me, without knowing the whole truth. I destroyed any chance you ever had to bear children."

"I forgive you."

He opened his eyes, his voice a harsh whisper. "Why?"

She smiled at him. "You're behaving like you forced me to eat the seeds."

"Isn't that what I did? Slowly and methodically? By seducing and tempting you and letting you fall for me without telling you all of what I knew? What would you have done if I had told you?"

"Aidon, had you told me all you knew, I would have eaten the seeds anyway."

He stared blankly at her, not sure he'd heard her correctly.

"My lord, I love you. More than any… *possibility*, more than any future plan. The Fates laugh at our plans, anyway. I love every flaw, every virtue that outweighs those flaws a thousandfold. You were afraid I would reject you; you were only trying to keep your heart safe."

"I don't deserve your forgiveness. You've never withheld anything from *me*."

"Did you wade into the Lethe while I was gone?" she guffawed. "Don' t you remember? Until the last few days I was here, I hid my heart from you because I was afraid. I feared many things— that you would tire of me once you'd won me. You know that. I slept beside you, I made love to you, I spent every free moment with you, but I couldn't admit aloud that I loved you." She bit her lip and stared at the floor. "But what you didn't know was that after we returned from Tartarus, I discovered that I hadn't bled while I was here and because of that I thought I was with child by you."

"Oh, sweet one…"

"I didn't tell you what I suspected. And it made telling you I loved you so much more *complicated*." Her voice cracked. "I didn't know what to feel, or what to say, and I didn't want to say anything to you because I was afraid you would abandon me, that you didn't want that responsibility. I was afraid that our child would grow up as I did."

"You must know that I would never do that to you. I would cherish any children we had."

442

"And I would never leave you or stop loving you for not giving me a child."

The fire crackled in the hearth and they stood before each other for a long moment, saying nothing. Aidon took a step forward and reached for a loose tendril of hair falling down her breast. He brushed it behind her back and pulled her tight against him, feeling her sigh in relief as she wrapped her arms around his back.

"Don't you understand?" she said. "You asked me if I wanted to marry you. I accept. I freely choose you, Aidoneus."

He kissed the top of her head. "Even if it means we cannot have a family?"

"You shouldn't believe everything the Fates told you."

"I'm afraid I have no choice."

"Even if they told me something different?"

He scowled. "Their words are never meant literally. If they gave you any hope, you need to let it go. It will only ruin you."

Persephone shook her head and took his hands in hers, guiding him back to the bed to sit beside her. "When you spoke to the Fates, what did they say to you?"

Aidoneus thinned his lips. "They told me that those who rule Chthonia do not have heirs. That is the fate of 'those who share in the bounty of the souls'."

"What if our child is meant to rule the sky instead?"

"Zeus said that to—" He calmed his angry voice. "It was an empty oath meant to silence and shame me."

"Or he unknowingly speaks the will of the Fates. Tempting them..."

"*Please* don't let their words go to your head. Curiosity about my destiny nearly destroyed me. The Fates told me that I would bring you here against your will, that I would have you but *not* have you, all of which has come to pass. They said that I would bring sorrow and destruction to the mortals..." He shook his head. "Gods above... I *ate* the

443

fruits of the Underworld, the 'bounty of the souls', just as they predicted I would. *Ananke* is inescapable."

"They also told me that you and I would have not one but *three* children, Aidoneus."

He narrowed his eyes. "Is your continuing love for me bound up in this idea that we *might* have children?"

Persephone stroked his arm. "My feelings for you are unchanged whether we have no children or a thousand. I loved you before the idea was ever planted in my head."

"Then why are you trying to convince me of this, Persephone?"

"Because they mentioned more than just children. They first told me about our role in this cosmos. You are not bound to this realm, to its 'bounty' and rule alone. You are not just the Lord of the Dead."

He snorted and looked away from her. "Of course I am. It's what I was fated to be... Well, after a fashion. I am the consort to the *actual* ruler of the Underworld."

She leaned against him. "But that's the very thing they said, Aidon. You are neither greater nor lesser than I. The Fates said we hold dominion over the earth and everything beneath it as equals."

"As I said, their words are not meant literally."

She reached for the plate Aidon had set at the edge of the bed after he had fed her dates and figs for breakfast. She held an olive up to his mouth. "Then consider this."

He nibbled it from her fingers and bit into the briny fruit. "What about it?"

"It wouldn't be here if you didn't share in my role in the world above. You aren't just the King of the Dead. Poseidon has the sea, Zeus has the sky..."

"We all *thought* the third lot would be the earth," he said, chewing the olive. "It wasn't."

"Perhaps that's because the earth is too big. Maybe it needed to be governed by something greater than just *one* of the Deathless Ones. Perhaps it needed to be ruled by a union of opposites."

He spat the pit into his hand and set it on the plate, then raised his eyebrows at her. "Intriguing, but if you'll please forgive me for doubting that…"

"There is a new order to the cosmos. Nothing will ever be the same again and we'd be fools to think anything would be after a union as significant as ours."

"Which would be?"

"Well…" she braced herself, ready to feel her husband's antipathy. "Demeter is responsible for the harvest. The season of harvest, no?"

He thinned his lips and grunted in acknowledgement.

"And you discovered that since the order of all things has changed, the earth cannot renew itself without me returning to the world above in the Spring."

"True," he said.

"The Fates told me that we are the ones who bring fertility up to the earth. Because of us, *together*, I… carry the seed of the earth when I return to the world above each spring."

"Carry the seed of the…" His ears grew hot and his throat closed.

She licked her dry lips. "Symbolically, of course…"

"S-so by virtue of us…" he tried to clear the growing lump in his throat. "When— because you and I… the earth is fertile?"

She fell to the side, giggling. His face burned and she could feel the heat from where she lay. "After this afternoon, and all we've done to 'ensure the fertility of the earth', you still blush, Aidon?"

A smile curved one side of his mouth, revealing a few white teeth. She sat up, relieved that his embarrassment wasn't worsened by her teasing. His eyes widened and he rubbed the back of his neck. "Well, I had never considered that the… *consummation* of our love had meaning to anyone beyond you and I."

"It wouldn't have, before. But the cosmos has shifted. Forever. For us, for the mortals, for the Olympians… What do you suppose it will mean for us down here?"

"Well, for the immediate future, it means I will gladly… *perform* my part in our new divine role eagerly. And vigorously," he said, his eyes lit with passion.

Persephone bit her lip as her mind conjured images of Hades eagerly and vigorously fulfilling their divine purpose.

"After all, the mortals depend on us!" he said, raising his voice and eyebrows in mock urgency. Persephone doubled over again, holding her sides as her laughter pealed through the room.

He gathered her up in his arms and scooted them back toward the pillows, lying down side by side. Aidon brushed Persephone's hair away from her face while she spoke. "As for marriage, there is something I would like to ask of you."

"Name it and it's yours," he said, smiling.

"I want to see you more often. In a more permanent place. A home for us in the world above."

The corners of his mouth tensed. "It's bad enough that you're away for half the year. My prolonged absence would be dangerous."

"I'm not suggesting that. And I don't intend to make you shoulder the burden alone." She held up her left hand, the Key sparkling in the sanguine light of the hearthfire. "I have an instantaneous way back here and could come for a night or two or if I am… urgently needed. But not while the mortals are sowing crops or during the last days of harvest."

"That leaves us a fairly narrow span of time. And I doubt that a few nights every six months will suffice for either of us."

"Not nearly."

He bit at his cheek. "I'll come above. But for Fates sake, I don't like risking Demeter or her priesthood walking in on us in the Plutonion. I can't imagine that would endear me to your mother. Nor would it strengthen her truce with me."

"So not there, then?" Her face fell. "That's our home among the living."

"We could meet there sometimes. And the Telesterion is... not what I had in mind either. What about Nysa?"

"Mortals can't go there. We might as well be at Olympus."

"I'd as soon drink the blood of a hydra than go there."

She smirked and pinched his side. "I wasn't suggesting that. But one of the reasons we should make time above is for the humans. We— I need to be among them in Spring and Summer."

"Thera?"

"It's so remote..."

"The mainland, then."

"What about Locri or Sikelia?"

Aidoneus snorted and tucked his hand under his head. "And you think Thera is remote..."

"There's farmable land there."

"This might not be to your liking, but Thesprotia is distant enough from Eleusis. Its rivers are named for mine, and before the Mysteries, most of the sheep and oil sacrificed to my kingdom came from there."

She ground her teeth. "Leuce's resting place."

"Persephone..."

"I know." She sighed. "Besides— it's still within Hellas and not *too* far from Mother. But in terms of permanently settling, we might as well take advantage of the fact that Sikelia is *mine* now."

"How did that come to pass?"

"A wedding present, from Zeus."

He rolled his eyes. "An island for a goddess queen's bride gift? You merit nothing less than a continent."

She giggled, rolling onto her stomach.

"It's a silly thing to say, I know. You know my feelings on that subject."

"I hope that our world and our ways will have at least some influence on the mortals. They already have, but not how you would prefer, I think."

"How so?"

"Athena told me that men in her city have been taking their brides away in chariots. Some will toss their new wife's flower crown— and one time a *girdle*— to the crowd before whisking them away into their house."

Aidoneus flopped onto his back and covered his eyes with one hand, massaging his temples.

She poked his side. "Not what you had in mind, I take it?"

"The furthest from," he said. "They re-enact when I rapt you away from Nysa?"

"Apparently."

"I fear that despite all your efforts the mortals will never really understand anything about me, or this place, and that things will only grow worse."

"They may," she said. "But that might depend upon you. Come above. Be who you truly are to them— Plouton— the God of Riches and Fertility. The God of the Earth."

He gave her a strained smile. "I can try."

"Be my husband in this," she said, grasping his hand. "If you detest the way things are above, then help me change those things. Look at what I did in six short months. Mere words to a handful of people. I thought they didn't believe me, but they know the truth now: death is not the end."

He examined her, watching her eyes flare with possibility. "I will. I'll be your husband, your king and your consort. In this and in all things."

She laid her cheek on the pillow and relaxed when he stroked her back. "Tell me your thoughts on the ceremony."

He nestled closer to her. "Which part?"

"The *full* ceremony."

✻   ✻   ✻

448

"Cerberus! Cerberus, down!"

The great guard dog skidded to a halt in front of his mistress and sat on his haunches. Persephone gathered up the little black lamb that huddled at her feet for protection. It shook, wobbly legged, and curled up against her bosom. She patted its head and it gave an indignant bleat to its pursuer. Cerberus barked again, snarling, his fangs bared. The lamb squirmed in her arms.

"No! Stop scaring him," she commanded her husband's dog. Cerberus flopped to the ground, resting his center head atop the other two. He let out a rumbling whine. "You can chase after the others, but this one is Menoetes's pet! You know that, you adorable beast."

Persephone reached for one black head and scratched behind his ear. Cerberus's tail thumped on the ground, shaking the Fields of Asphodel and scattering the shades away from them. He stretched his back legs and yawned, then shook himself and trotted away to watch over the Acheron.

"Aristi! Aristi," the bondsman called out. His shepherd's staff smacked against the tall stalks as he ran. Menoetes was out of breath by the time he stopped, and hunched over. "Thank the gods you found him, my queen."

"You should really build a better fence for little Rodi," she said, smiling.

He chuckled and took the tiny lamb from the Queen's arms. "He continues to be nothing but trouble. You know that *he* was the reason I ran into Askalaphos and discovered your half-eaten fruit, milady?"

"So the King told me," she said with a smile. "How is your mother, Menoetes?"

"Still feasting, along with the rest of the nymphs," he said as they strolled back to the gardens. "You were most generous, sharing everything the world above gave to *you* with all the nymphs and daimones in the kingdom."

She laughed. "Did you expect me to eat a palace full of fruit by myself?"

"Well, no," he said sheepishly. "But Askalaphos and I weren't expecting that you would give us so many olives. He's quite fond of them, milady."

"I heard he's been sharing them with Nychtopula."

"Ahh, yes..." Menoetes said with a smile. "If he can stop lamenting that he cannot get olive trees to grow in Chthonia, and if he can get it through his thick head that she wants more from him than olives..."

"Perhaps I should tell him there will be more next year." Persephone opened the garden gate and walked ahead of Menoetes. Rodi drifted to sleep in the crook of his elbow, content to be home. She looked at the pomegranate grove, the fruits ripe and red, and took a deep breath. Aidoneus stood within, speaking with Hecate. He glanced in Persephone's direction and she could feel him smiling at her. They had spent the last few days opening their thoughts to each other, even further than they naturally could. They were able to feel each other from across the palace, across the Fields, even on opposite sides of the Styx, just as easily as they could when they were intimate. She smiled back at him.

"Pardon my asking, but shouldn't you be preparing for tonight's ceremony, my queen?"

"We have been preparing all week." Persephone had spent the first few days sleeping, trying to readjust herself to the cycles of day and night in Chthonia. The rest of her time she'd spent consulting with Hecate and Nyx, and practicing the vows and words of the ritual with Aidon. After discussing the details of the ceremony and the *hieros gamos*, Aidoneus and Persephone had agreed to abstain until the night of the wedding.

It hadn't been easy, especially with their thoughts consumed with the details of the ritual. Three nights before, they'd awoken flush against each other, and without thinking Persephone nipped at his lower lip. Aidon firmly kissed her back, their mouths greedy for each other, their tongues rehearsing the motions of lovemaking. His hands had swept

450

across her body, touching and electrifying every inch of her skin, liquid fire spilling from her womb. His phallus was as hard as stone between them. He delighted in her moans, teasing her mercilessly with quick fingers, no matter how much she tried to gyrate out of their path. Her body wanted something besides fingertips.

When her nails dug into his flank and pulled him closer, he'd separated from her with a growl and leapt out of bed. Aidon stormed over to the wash basin and quickly doused himself with its contents. Persephone barely suppressed a laugh when he yelled and cursed at the shock of cold water. He stood drenched and breathing hard, his passion dying down, then mumbled something unintelligible and grabbed his himation, slamming the door behind him. Persephone lay on the bed, letting her heartbeat slow, and drifted off. When she awoke, she found him curled uncomfortably on the divan outside their bedroom, his cloak muffling his snoring.

The following night, Persephone decided it was best to retreat to her old room to avoid temptation. She hadn't been there in months— not since they began sleeping beside each other. The memories of that first month together made Persephone toss back and forth for half the night. In the wee hours of the morning, Aidon threw open the bedroom door, stark nude in the dim light. Despite her protests, he hoisted her squirming body over his shoulder and carried her all the way back to their bedroom, a hand planted firmly on her bottom. Aidoneus tossed Persephone on the mattress and pulled the covers over them both, then promptly fell asleep, his arm heavy across her waist.

She smiled and opened the door to the palace. The new tapestry hung from the high ceiling, depicting husband and wife in an emerald field with an azure sky, framed by the pomegranate grove, the center portrait encompassed by a meandros of narcissus and golden arrows. In each corner was a scene from the past year: Kore standing in a newly-sown barley field, a butterfly in her hand; Hades pulling her into

451

his chariot; Persephone holding a pomegranate in one hand and six seeds in the other; and lastly a portrait of her mother and father, her husband and herself reaching the Agreement and completing the circle of the year. The tapestry of Hades and Persephone's marriage was complete, buffeted on all sides by the seasons— summer and autumn, winter and spring.

"My queen?"

She turned to see Hecate behind her.

"It's time."

27.

IN THE END, THEY CREATED THEIR OWN CEREMONY.
Aidon didn't want the marriage ceremony of the city folk
of Attica— 'the slave rite', as he called it— that ended with
him dragging her by the wrist into his bedchamber. And
Persephone joked that there wasn't enough time before the
full moon for him to fight all the Olympians and thus prove
himself capable of protecting his new bride like the Lace-
daemonians did. Their ceremony was to be a coronation of
the King and Queen of the Underworld as much as it was a
wedding ceremony.

Nyx and her sons would witness, and Hecate would prepare Persephone and preside over the ceremony. The Witch
Goddess led Persephone to her old chambers, where they'd
first met. She undressed the Queen and helped her stand in a
large basin, then doused her with warm salt water before
drying her with fresh linens and plaiting her hair into a
coronet of braids. The white witch rubbed a perfumed oil
infused with frankincense and sweet bay laurel into every
inch of her skin, then scraped the excess off with a metal
strigil. Persephone knew that Aidoneus was undergoing similar ritual bathing and preparation with the help of Thanatos
and Hypnos.

We're gods. To whom would we swear ourselves?

"You decided on a ceremony with few vows," Hecate noted.

"Our vows will be the *hieros gamos* itself." Persephone shivered, rubbing her arms. The oil was warming, but not enough to stave off the pervasive chill of the palace.

Hecate unfolded a short chiton so heavily dyed with saffron it was as dark as the little orange anthers from which it drew its color. The finely woven garment shimmered and slithered over Persephone's curves almost weightlessly. Hecate held two fibulae in her mouth and gathered up the cloth, pinning one shoulder, then the other, before standing back to admire her handiwork. "A wise choice. You and your counterpart see the *hieros gamos* in a very different light than your mother did."

"She was only doing what she thought best," Persephone said. "When Demeter chose Zeus, she was acting out of love." Hecate wound a simple sash of saffron cloth around her waist as a girdle.

"Indeed," she answered flatly, unfurling an even greater measure of cloth to drape over Persephone's shoulders as a mantle. The edges met the floor. "Is your *hieros gamos* to be only an act of love? Or is it to be something greater?"

Persephone knitted her brow. "From what everyone has told me, the Rite by its very nature produces 'something greater'. I was the product of my parents' union, after all."

"Are you suggesting that this could mean children for you and your husband?"

Persephone looked away.

"Do not be afraid of hope, Persephone. Hope is a hard-forged blade, keen and shining. Used recklessly, it will maim and scar; but wielded with finesse, it will give you the power to carve a destiny of unsurpassed glory."

"The Fates said that we might have three children."

"That may well be," a lilting voice said from the corner of the room. Nyx appeared from a haze of darkness and

454

floated across the room. "But beware their favor and prophecies. It is not meant for creatures like us to fully grasp what *ananke* has in store for us."

"What should I expect?" Persephone asked nervously.

"Nothing you *could* expect, dear," Nyx said. "Even I know not what. Erebus and I, on our first Rite, believed we would merely unite our souls, but we also received a child. *The* first child born from our generation. And each subsequent union produced more still. Your mother sought out love. She birthed the Queen that had been foretold since Ouranos's downfall. You, Persephone, already have love. This rite will create more than the sum of what either of you alone possess. Remember that tonight."

Nyx and Hecate took either side of a bright saffron veil and tucked it gently into Persephone's braids, instead of over her face, leaving her vision clear. Nyx then produced two crowns of olive and laurel, narcissus and pomegranate leaves. One wreath was woven with asphodel.

Your bridal crown is beautiful...

Persephone froze. She had tucked asphodel from the grove into the wreath Artemis had woven before Hades had taken her. And the night she ate the seeds, before Persephone ascended back to the living world, her dream featured the very crowns Nyx held.

They were lying in the pomegranate grove, entangled in each other's arms, markings gouged into the ground around them...

This night, like every twist and turn of her life, had been both freely chosen *and* preordained. She nodded, finally understanding.

Hecate stepped back and clasped her hands together, her eyes sparkling. "Wisdom and beauty. Your husband is a fortunate man, indeed. Come."

Persephone took Hecate's hand and walked down the winding steps. With a flick of her wrist, Nyx opened the great doors leading to the garden and the pomegranate grove beyond. Hecate led their way. Persephone felt like Nyx, euphorically floating toward the grove as her feet glided down the pathway, her heart beating harder the closer she came to Aidoneus. She took a deep breath, trying to calm herself. The Styx lit the mists of the Underworld in a dazzling array of golds and purples.

Gravel crunched under her toes and poked at her heels. This time, Persephone barely noticed. She watched as dark red seeped into Hecate's trailing robes, bleeding over the white and signaling the apex of the full moon.

Nyx brought up the rear of their small procession, carrying the wreaths and soundlessly floating inches off the ground. The darkness that twined about her grew and spread above them, becoming night in the Underworld. Torches smoldered along the palace walls and on the tops of the garden enclosure, illuminating their path in gold. Moonlight turned the grove silver. Leaves rustled as Hecate parted them.

In the midst of the grove stood her lover, her husband, her king, barefoot, clad in the same saffron as her, but with a deep purple, gold-embroidered himation wound about him. His hair hung loosely down his back and he gripped his staff tighter when their eyes met.

Morpheus and Charon stood to either side of him. The Lord of Dreams was unmoving, his face hooded. He held an obsidian knife in one hand. Charon's head was also hooded, but he swayed gently, the Styx a part of him even when on land, and his hand wrapped tightly around a kantharos of its water. He shifted his stance and smiled at her.

Hypnos and Thanatos parted, allowing Hecate to lead Persephone to Hades, then took their places, each wedding guest standing in front of a tree in the grove. In their right hands, each of Nyx's sons held half a pomegranate plucked from the sacred grove.

Aidoneus straightened as she approached, and Persephone could feel his nervousness, his heart beating out of his chest and overflowing. *I love you*, she said, and felt him calm.

And I love you. His face remained serious.

456

She gazed up at him. I'm going to become one with this man, she thought, her stomach fluttering.

Indeed, sweet one.

You heard me… She smiled at him. *That means that all of your innermost thoughts…*

…are an open scroll, he finished for her. *Naked. All you need do is read me, as I can read you.*

Hecate took her place before them, waited for Aidon to hand her his staff, then motioned for them to turn. Persephone and Aidon slowly walked toward Nyx hand in hand, their bare feet padding through the moss and soft grasses of the grove. When they reached the Goddess of Night, they knelt together, their heads bowed.

"Before the Tyrant, I ruled this realm with Erebus as my consort and husband. Freed by Aidoneus the Liberator, I passed on the Key, abdicating my power over the Underworld to the first born son of Kronos, hero of the Titanomachy, and fated consort of the Queen. The world below was ever meant to be ruled by a Queen, one who had been promised to us since the downfall of Ouranos. That time has come, by the will of the Fates."

A smile teased the corner of Persephone's mouth and she grasped Aidon's hand.

"But the Fates do not always reveal themselves in the manner we think they ought. Clotho, Lachesis, and Atropos revealed *ananke* to our prophesied Queen, and told her that she and her husband share equally in the rulership of this realm, in their fate, in their responsibility to the souls above and below. And it is with this knowledge that I ordain not just a Queen and her consort, but a King and Queen to rule side by side."

Nyx lifted the crowns over her head and placed her slender fingers on Persephone's scalp.

"Persephone Praxidike Karpophoros Chthonios, Queen of Asphodel and Tartarus, Goddess of Life and Death, do you accept responsibility over all the souls above and below as the Queen of the Earth?"

"I do," she said.

"Do you pledge yourself to them and promise to rule by your husband's side as his consort and equal for all eternity?"

"I do."

"Hades Aidoneus Plouton Chthonios, Receiver of Many, Lord of Souls, God King of the Underworld, do you accept responsibility over all the souls above and below as the King of the Earth?"

"I do," he said.

"Do you pledge yourself to them and promise to rule by your wife's side as her consort and equal for all eternity?"

"I do."

Nyx placed the wreaths on their heads and drifted back from them. "Rise as one— as the Rulers of the Earth," she said. "Make your vows, and consecrate your union as King and Queen."

Hades and Persephone faced each other, then walked to their respective attendants. Persephone took three seeds from the pomegranate held by Hypnos while Hades took three from Thanatos; then the queen took three more from the fruit held by Charon and the king received his from Morpheus. They returned to stand again before Hecate.

They each cradled six seeds with their fingertips, held aloft and offered to one another.

Their priestess spoke. "As these seeds bound you to this world, let them also bind you to each other as husband and wife."

Persephone lifted her seeds to Aidon's mouth as he did the same to hers. She felt a shiver course from her wrist to the pit of her stomach when his lips touched her fingertips and felt a similar frisson echo within him. Hecate took the stone blade from Morpheus and held it with its point down before the King and Queen. They interlaced the fingers of their left hands around its blade. Hecate took the kantharos from Charon and held it aloft.

"As the water of the Styx bound you together at your betrothal, it binds you now, a second time," Hecate said. The Priestess pulled the knife out of their grasp quickly, scoring their palms, blood against blood, and shook it into the water, washing it clean.

Persephone kept her eyes locked with Aidoneus and bit back a whimper. The only sign that he'd felt the cut was a momentary tightening of his jaw. He grasped her hand tighter, silently lending her his strength as they bound themselves together—flowed into one another. The wounds healed. Their rings smoldered with a faint red glow and Persephone felt her heart beating in time with his.

The water in the cup darkened and tinged red, imbued with their combined essence. When it purified itself and reflected the moonlit clarity of the great River, Hecate continued. "When you take these vows you will bind yourselves a third time, everlasting and eternal through the sacred rite of *hieros gamos*. But before that consummation you must consecrate yourselves to each other, and drink from the Styx as you swear upon it." She handed the kantharos to Aidoneus first. He held it between them and spoke his vow.

"I swear upon the Styx to love and to cherish you. To honor and protect you as your consort, your king, and your beloved. With this oath I bind myself to you eternally, and by drinking the water of the Styx, I become your lord and your husband."

He brought the cup to his lips and drank. His brow furrowed. The Styx was pure yet bitter, a reminder of the gravity of any oath made upon it. Aidoneus passed the cup to his wife and she drew in a ragged breath.

"I swear upon the Styx to love and to cherish you. To honor and protect you as your consort, your queen, and your beloved. With this oath I bind myself to you eternally, and by drinking the water of the Styx, I become your lady and your wife."

She took a heavy sip and felt it settle in her stomach, watering the seeds she'd eaten from her husband's hand. It wound through her heart, crashed through her veins, and made the grove waver in her vision before it drew back into sharp focus as the Styx became a part of her. Persephone passed the cup to Hecate.

The Priestess returned the staff to Aidoneus, who clutched it in his right hand, then placed Persephone's left hand on it below his. Hecate turned husband and wife away from her, to face their witnesses.

"Before these hosts you have sworn yourselves to each other as King and Queen, husband and wife. But as male and female, god and goddess, your union consummates without witness," Hecate said. "There remains much to be done, by two in the dark."

Nyx cloaked herself within Erebus, and each of their sons stepped back and out of sight. The torches along the garden and castle walls snuffed out and Hecate pressed their hands within hers, her grip firm and comforting. She faded into the ether, a proud smile brightening her face.

They were alone. Aidoneus stood quiet and staid, letting his eyes adjust to the faint moonlight. Shivers raced through Persephone and her mind churned, tumultuous, her heart beating quickly.

Be at peace, my love, Aidoneus said. Persephone felt her pulse slow. He stroked her cheek. "Remember… as I said, I will guide you."

She nodded. He pulled at his himation and Persephone gently moved his hand away to unwind the heavy cloth herself, pushing it off his shoulder until it fell in a heap on the ground. He wore a saffron *chitoniskos* underneath, girded at the waist with a strip of cloth. She pulled the veil from her braids and it floated down to lay atop his cloak. Her mantle followed, and Persephone was glad to be free of its weight until she shivered in the cool night air.

So beautiful, he thought, knowing she could hear him. Aidon smiled at her, then took the staff in hand and dragged the end in a wide circle, ensconcing them within the grove. Persephone watched his eyes, his gaze unflinching as they stared at each other. When he returned to her and closed the circle, she felt a sharp vibration root her to the ground beneath them. The life within the grove was enclosed, sealed between them.

She took a hesitant step toward her husband and unhooked the pins at his shoulders, letting the tunic fall past his waist before she unfastened his sash and it dropped at his feet. Her chiton came next, and he twitched when she revealed her flesh, forcing himself to breathe steadily to calm himself. He focused, feeling her, opening himself for her to experience every sensation coursing through him.

Persephone felt the strength in his hands as they gripped the staff, the tension in his legs, the soft earth under his well-worn feet just as she felt it beneath her own. She pulled the simple ribbon from her waist and cast her garment next to his; both now wore only the laurels crowning their heads. She stepped deeper into the circle, and Aidoneus traced a smaller one within it, walking in the opposite direction, the staff etching a deep mark into the grasses and moss, trenching the soil like a plow. The Key shone brightly on his hand.

Aidoneus felt the ground below him pulsing, breathing with life once the second circle was closed. He could hear his wife's heart beating. He could feel her delicate fingertips resting on her hips, the breath she'd just exhaled, the tingling in her stomach. His eyes met hers and he gave her a brief smile, then began carving the last markings into the earth. He started at the tree where they had been crowned King and Queen and crossed the grove, drawing straight lines between three trees and returning. He then started again at the tree where they had taken their vows as husband and wife

461

and dragged lines through the soil in the opposite direction, joining the remaining trees.

When he set the staff down, they stood within a star that represented the union and conjunction of male and female. The pattern mirrored the little stars on each pomegranate hanging heavy above them. She felt his knuckles brush the earth, his feet sinking into it as he rose. She retreated to her side of the circle and felt his shoulders relax as he took his place opposite her.

"I am the sky and you are the earth," Hades began. "When and where I am the sky, then and there you are the earth."

"I am the earth," Persephone repeated, "and you are the sky. When and where I am the earth, then and there you are the sky."

They stepped toward each other, pulled inexorably to the center of the star. She let go of all fear, all trepidation, any worry that she might get it wrong. The moment Aidon felt her relax, he started speaking the ancient words.

"What I tell you, let the singer weave into song. What I tell you let it flow from ear to mouth. I tell you softly: come, my beloved. My beautiful one, come with me," he recited, his voice just above a whisper. He felt her, felt her envelop him in everything that was her, her scent, her sound.

"The trees create their early fruit," she said, her mind filled with a vision of the dark soil coaxing the new seeds to spring forth, their leaves to unfurl above the fertile ground. "The blossoming trees spread their sweetness. The fallow season is passed," she said, drawing him closer until their hands interlocked at their sides. "The rains are over and gone. My beloved is mine, and I am his."

She was reminded of when he'd shared the Key with her, how close they had needed to be— within each other, skin to skin and thought to thought— for it to pass to her. With just the touch of his fingers, she felt that same current flowing between them, the unrelenting pulse of life beneath them, drawn to and from the earth. The Styx wound through their veins, the seeds unfurled, their hearts beat, their bodies warmed, their essence was imbued with all the energy that coursed through the worlds above and below.

She felt him thicken and rise between them and molten heat charged from her womb. He trembled as he lifted her chin, then canted his head until his lips met hers. She shook as she shared his kiss, overpowered by the sensations coursing through both of them.

He feathered his lips along her neck and felt her pulse echoing in his veins. He could feel the trees surrounding them, the fruits growing heavier on their branches, the seeds ripe, the fruits pregnant with their multitudes.

"Come, my beloved," he said, his voice rasping, "my beautiful one come with me."

He knelt down and kissed her womb just below her navel, and their minds were simultaneously filled with visions of creation, and the visions from outside the Cave of the Moirai. He sat in the center of the grove before her, his phallus rising from his lap, his hand reaching up to hers, beckoning her to join him in the center of their circle. She grasped his fingers and straddled him, his arm holding her aloft as she slowly made her descent. Aidon held her against his chest and she hovered just above him and wrapped her legs around his torso, trusting his supporting arm. The tip of his phallus prodded her vulva, waiting and ready for the final words of the rite to be spoken in unison.

"Put your hand in my hand," they said together, grasping their left palms between them. His voice shook. "Put your hand on my heart. Sweet is the sleep of hand to hand. Sweeter still the sleep of heart to heart."

He released her and she opened to him, their last connection made, their bodies shuddering together. Persephone threw her arms around his neck and whimpered in his ear, her voice no longer under her control. "Oh, my God…"

"My Goddess," he whispered roughly against her cheek. Aidon lifted her up with aching languor before dragging her down upon him again. They cried out together, sensations expanding. The grove filled with their presence, concentrating their pleasure and charging it back through their bodies. Their hearts slowed as one, echoing the timing of each thrust. Their breathing synchronized. Their eyes closed and they felt everything. Their eyes closed and they saw.

The seeds burst above them, the drops of juice ignited, fire trailed from them like falling stars as they dripped to the ground. A breath, a thrust, a heartbeat. Hades and Persephone were surrounded with light and flames, the branches spreading with white fire. She held him, he held her closer. Sensations became an inseparable whole, a graze of skin, a brush of lips, fingernails digging into flesh, hardness, softness, every chill that raced up the spine and every flash of heat, all fused together.

The fruits above them opened one by one, bathing them, anointing them. Fire rushed across their skin. It poured through their souls, merging, coalescing. It burned their laurel crowns and the sparks flew off like innumerable stars, surrounding them. They moved in perfect unison, building and destroying, ceasing and starting, crashing through each other. Flames licked and consumed them, lost to one another in holy fire.

They saw themselves distantly in visions— the past. They were an infant being ripped from Rhea's arms, her screams wild, her eyes red as she tried to wrest the babe from her husband. They were born a second time, expelled by Kronos into the midst of war. They were at the great meeting and the *hieros gamos* on Olympus, and Persephone's conception. They ran carefree through the fields. They sat on the ebony throne of the Underworld. They were within their first dream, shared in Eleusis. They were falling, falling through the earth, holding each other in the darkness of Erebus.

They were ferried across the Styx.

The good mortals— the ones who were especially brave or kind. There's no place for them? Persephone had said.

They shared the Key.

And sacrifice their usefulness to the world above? Won't the living world only deteriorate if we cloister them here? Aidon answered.

If they decided to leave, they would have that right. And new souls are made here every day. They can take the place of those who wish to stay. People can change, Persephone reminded him.

If we could, what would we do differently? What would you want? Aidon asked her.

She will have warmth; and light, Persephone had said to Dimitris. *A place where soft breezes will fan her skin and there will be grass under her feet, trees to shade her, and cool water to drink. She will laugh and smile, and know no pain or fear ever again. And one day, a day long from now, Fates willing, you will be reunited with her.*

They were the seeds. Spring rose from the earth, melting the snow, a thousand crocuses, a field above filled with asphodel. She gripped her husband's hand to create them, his soul reaching through hers, replenishing the earth with her. Somehow she'd known then— she'd known all along. They carried the seeds of the world below to the world above, then carried the fruits of the living world to the land of the dead. They were the single narcissus opening in the grove and the flowers bursting forth in the Plutonion. It was their doing— always, together.

The future. Hades and Persephone sleeping amid narcissus dappled with sunlight. Both are in their antechamber where he is kneeling before her, his fingers reverently tracing the curve of Persephone's swollen womb. And another vision, where she is holding a swaddled infant close to her breast. A girl with white curls is gripping her finger and toddling beside her through the palace garden, where they meet with Aidoneus who is holding a smiling little girl with messy dark locks perched atop his shoulders. She pulls his hair. He looks up at her with the eyes of a proud father and laughs.

The future. Persephone and Hades on the Styx, her doubled over in pain and clutching her womb, her shaking hand stained with blood, Hades holding her, panicked and trying to reassure her all at once, Charon crying out for Hecate. Persephone weeping inconsolably, crumpled on the floor, a wooden box shrouding a beating heart clutched to her chest, begging them not to take it from her. Hades staring up into Erebus, watching a thousand, thousand flaming scrolls rain down from the mortal world and into his kingdom, his face contorted into helpless anguish. Persephone running to his side to comfort him.

The future. The mortals. War and the fall of Ilium. Conquest. Famine. Slavery. Death. But amidst the darkness, the light of understanding. Tolerance. Wisdom carried by well-rested souls. A distant city, a great library, a great many peoples coming together. Ignorance, destruction, a stupor of thought, then a great rebirth. Time lumbers on, and the world changes with it. Loud, enclosed chariots without horses and immense, towering buildings crowding against one another. Some are squat with columns taller than those of the grandest temples, billowing dark smoke into the air. The temples of the gods above lay in ruins, stripped by wind and sun. They are forgotten. But in Eleusis, a bustling inn with strange glass ovens and metal mechanisms and oddly-clothed people staring at tiny, brightly lit tablets. Aidoneus and Persephone meet there dressed like the mortals, greeting each other with a kiss before sitting down at a table by a window.

Silence.

The present. They opened their eyes. They opened their eyes as one. They were themselves; they were each other. Aidoneus and Persephone saw darkness, absolute and endless, then rills and sinews of light twisting like faint branches all around them. One point, brighter than all others, rushed toward them, expanding in their vision— carried closer without effort.

Stars wheeled and danced below them, winding in a slow gyre. The wonderment of it all stunned them silent, and in that moment they knew. They were witnessing All. Life, Love, all things that bound existence. They were darkness and light. Rebirth and death. Male and female, in perfect conjunction with the power to make and unmake the cosmos itself.

Male and Female. Hades and Persephone. Names, an unending chain of what that duality of creation represented to all mortals coursed through them. Chaos and Void. Gaia and Ouranos. Anu and Ki. Shiva and Shakti. Ku and Hina. He and She. They were a thousand other names, to a thousand other peoples, with the power and responsibility of all creation at their fingertips. Their own private wishes seemed small and petty compared to this great expanse of Everything. Totality. Conjunction.

The twisting arms of the great spire of light streaked past them in their brilliance, filled with stars and worlds beyond account or reckoning. They saw the outlines of seas, the snow-capped peaks of great mountain chains with shining rivulets trickling down their sides. The thin layer of night sky clung to the earth, its edges cast in sunrise and sunset, and the shallow seas and deep oceans wrapped around an endless, curved expanse of earth. They were so very small, but their burden and purpose were great. They knew so much and so little.

"They need Us," She said to Him. "And We need them. We must take them into Our care."

"They are tired and need rest," He said. "Their lives are short."

"You asked me once," She whispered, "what I would change."

"Yes," He said. He felt Her thoughts within His and wanted to stay forever, perfectly connected and enlightened, but knew that They couldn't. Their responsibilities to all the souls, living and dead, were too great. "And so it shall be.

Let Us give them that comfort. Against all the cruelties of the world."

"How will we do that, Aidoneus?"

"Together." She felt his arms around her again and his breath against her ear. "Let go, Persephone."

They surrendered. Her body crashed against his and their consciousness fell through sky and water and land, down through cracks of molten earth, through darkness and light until they stopped, silent. Aidoneus and Persephone stilled and shuddered, utterly spent, and collapsed into sleep and dreams in each other's arms.

*   *   *

The trees, their fruits, the seeds of the earth watered the ground. A great mist hung above their sleeping forms and as they dreamed, earth and sky birthed themselves and turned to gold.

The sun rose high, the moon followed, walls crumbled and turned to dust and the grasses beneath them covered the ground, spreading out from the roots of each tree. They grew, against and over each other, teeming with life.

The sun rose, the moon followed. A new shoreline lapped with tides cycling in and out and endless islands rose from the waters. The moon set, the sun rose. They lay underneath the expanse of light and dark, the growing trees and shrubs, the flowers, the creatures they nurtured.

Under the wheeling heavens, trees and grasses, forests and meadows grew up. The sun, the moon, the sky, the earth, cycling, reeling, turning over the length of a thousand millennia set against mere moments. An endless flash of dark and light, setting sun, rising moon, aeons of time dissolving into hours.

It was done. All went dark. The dream of creation was ended.

A meadowlark twittered on the branch above her, and a breeze, warm and fragrant, drifted across her face. She felt the rise and fall of his chest under her cheek, his arm wrapped around her. She cracked her eyes open and her vision was filled with wavering yellow and white. When she blinked they came into focus. A thousand narcissus flowers bobbed in the breeze. Persephone stirred, and was immediately pulled back into the arms that had encircled her all night.

"Too early, wife," Aidoneus mumbled. The lark called out for its mate again and he opened his eyes, confused, then squinted. The sky above them was as blue as sapphires. He froze and tilted his head up. Their dreams… He leaned forward on one elbow, his heart racing. "We…"

"Are we in the world above?" Persephone sat up. Had the *hieros gamos* transported them? She rubbed her eyes. Above them, pomegranate leaves shook in the breeze, and dappled the grove with sunlight. Beside them, under the thick growth of narcissus flowers, a gouge scored the earth. "Aidon! We're still in the grove! How…"

"Stay here," he said, his brows knit with concern. Aidon squeezed her hand, and walked to the edge of the grove, peering out through the branches toward the palace. There sat their home and gardens, the stone wall, all just as they should be. He stepped outside and circumnavigated the trees. The grove itself glowed brightly, brimming with sunlight. "Persephone?"

"I'm here!"

Aidoneus pushed the pomegranate branches aside and entered the grove again, squinting in the sunlight. His eyes were wide, and he surveyed their surroundings, astonished. "Wife… we're still in the garden, in our grove, but…"

They stood, holding each other close. The markings he had made in the earth were still there, as were their clothes. Persephone grasped Aidon's hand, his jaw hanging open as he contemplated the ritual. Their connection, the expanse of the cosmos. Their desire to take their place as caretakers for the mortals, to offer a reward for a life well lived. Aidon walked beside his wife, hand in hand to the green edges of the grove. The stone wall at its side had been replaced by thick shrubs. She pulled back a branch to reveal what lay beyond. Hades and Persephone stood awestruck.

Before them was a great meadow teeming with grasses and wildflowers, butterflies and bees humming from one bloom to the next. The sky was blue, interrupted by small puffs of white clouds. A deer bounded across the field, followed by a few more, and doves flew from branch to branch between oak and ash trees. Trees bearing pomegranates and olives, figs and apples, and exotic trees with peaches, walnuts, and oranges dotted the landscape. Persephone took a cautious step outside the grove, Aidon following close behind, her hand intertwined with his. They soaked in the sunlight.

Beyond the great field, waves crashed against tall cliffs, much as they had on Thera so long ago. Lush islands dotted an aquamarine sea, stretching out to the horizon. He closed his eyes and felt the sea air on his face, heard the waves pounding the rocks, and the distant cries of pelicans and cormorants.

Persephone poked her finger into the warm earth. Roots took hold and dark green leaves spread out from her fingertips. She lifted her fingers and wound her wrist upward, the stalk creeping toward her hand. A bright purple bloom sprang from the top.

She remembered her first day in the Underworld and all her ill-fated attempts to make asphodel bloom in the great fields. But this was not the Fields of Asphodel. It was somewhere else. A fiery copper butterfly drifted in from the grasses and settled atop the flower. Persephone grinned.

This place was within the Underworld, and yet a world apart from it. It was rebirth: an everlasting realm of life encompassed by death: a new, third portion of Chthonia. Through the *hieros gamos*, Hades and Persephone hadn't created a child.

They'd created Paradise.

Persephone observed their surroundings, understanding the weight of what they'd ushered into being. "This is meant to be the mortals' place of rest and reward, Aidon. What should we call it?"

"Elysion," he replied without hesitation. Her eyes widened in surprise and he kissed her on the forehead. "After Eleusis. Where I fell in love with you."

Her eyes filled with fresh tears and she wrapped her arms around him. Aidoneus stroked her hair, then cupped her cheek and kissed her, holding her close as another breeze rippled across the grass and their sun-warmed skin. She laid her head against his shoulder, watching the little butterfly fan its wings and suckle at the thistle. "The Elysian Fields…"

He rested his arm across her shoulder. "Not what I'd imagined we'd awaken to, either. The Fates laugh at our plans, sweet one. Or so you told me once."

Persephone sighed. "It will take time to gather all the worthy souls who belong here. Surely those already sent to Asphodel deserve a second chance?"

"You and I will find them together, my love. Though… I don't *quite* mind having Paradise to ourselves. At least for today."

She giggled, and he herded her toward their grove.

"And perhaps *my* plans, my certainty that we can't have a family, are also laughable," he said.

"What do you mean?"

"If you and I can create an entire realm of life in the Underworld, sweet one," he said, turning again to survey the Elysian Fields, "then making a baby should be easy, no?"

She guided his face down to hers, his lips upon her lips, tasting their shared joy. Aidoneus wrapped his arms around Persephone, lifting her up onto her toes. She took his hands within hers, tugging him back to the shelter of the grove. "There's no harm in trying."

This tale continues in THE GOOD COUNSELOR.

Acknowledgements

This novel, and the one before it, *Receiver of Many*, is the culmination of one of my lifelong goals: to publish a book that people liked. I started posting the first draft of *Receiver of Many* online for free, every Wednesday at midnight in serial format and the reaction I got from my readers blew me away. They, dare I say, *loved it*... And supported me through the entire process from its initial debut in Fall of 2012 to the last posted chapter in Fall of 2014. For those who read this for free and bought it anyway, this book is for you.

I want to thank the folks who patiently took the time to review and provide feedback on each chapter of the first draft, namely, C. Thorne and L. Wilder. Next, I want to thank Sophia Kolyva, who was my greatest resource for most of the Greek translations, and helped fix my atrocious Greek grammar. Efharistó polí! And much thanks to fellow authors M. M. Kin, Eris Adderly, Titania Oliver, and several others who provided encouragement and insight.

In January 2015, I launched a successful Kickstarter to publish *Receiver of Many* and *Destroyer of Light*, and it is by the backing and contribution of many, many wonderful people that you are reading this today. A very special thanks to Kathryn B., Astrid Broady, Kenzie Capri, Shannon Cooper, Claire Starrs Daly, Stephanie Gilman, Lizbeth Hevia, Elaine Ho, Rostine J.M., Ivy K., Melanie Beth Keffer, Katherine A. Morgan, Bea Payumo, Sarah Rice, Ben Rico, Victoria Rybnick, Kate S., Alyss Scollard, Jessica Smith, Tran T., Kit Ilanya Turner, Tylar Voss, and Abby Woodworth for their generous support.

I also owe a huge thank you to my dear Kim F. (who you especially have to thank if you're a fan of Thanatos as he appears in my book). A special thanks to the wonderful Asphodelon, who provided artwork for the Kickstarter and for collaborating with me on *Bringer of Spring* and just being an all around amazing artist and friend. And to my darling Elizabeth Crowley, who graciously went through the book, line by line, twice, hunting down type-os before both *Receiver of Many* and *Destroyer of Light* went to press. My eternal gratitude goes to the fantastic Morgan Bondelid who designed the beautiful covers for my books. And last but certainly not least, my dear husband Robert, who started content-editing the book while we were dating, and faithfully carried the editing through the busy times of our engagement and into our marriage. His dedication is written into every chapter, and he has been my greatest source of support and inspiration.

So thank you, everyone, for making *Receiver of Many* and *Destroyer of Light* possible. This book and its predecessor, *Receiver of Many,* would not exist without you.

About the Author

Rachel Alexander has been a resident of California all her life and finished her first novel at age 16. She co-wrote a play that won awards from Bill Moyers of PBS and the University of Southern California. She received her Bachelor of Arts degree in English Literature and Literary Criticism from Principia College with an emphasis on creative writing.

When not writing, Rachel can often be found sewing corsets, overstocking her spice cabinet, and petting chickens. She is married and lives in San Carlos, CA with her wonderful husband/editor.

Prologue from THE GOOD COUNSELOR

The following is the prologue for the forthcoming novel The Good Counselor, *sequel to* Destroyer of Light.

"He won't be long," she said, pausing at the door.

Persephone grasped the handle and the aged hinges creaked when she opened it. Warmth and incense, the scent of mint and parsley, flooded out from the other side. She stood in the doorframe, and many pairs of tear-streaked eyes met hers.

"My lady," a frail voice said from the bed that dominated the center of the room.

"Hello, old friend," she smiled.

"Gods, it's good to see you again."

"And you as well."

"To think... I am only a child compared to you... a mote of dust, Soteira, yet I grow old while you stay evergreen, no?" He chuckled around the rattle in his throat and managed a smile for her.

"You're mean more to me than you give yourself credit."

The venerable priest squinted at her, then his forehead wrinkled with worry. "My lady, it is two days past. Shouldn't you be with your honored husband by now?"

"He understands, Eumolpus," she said, shutting the door and walking over to the bed. His students and family cleared a path for her and Persephone sat down next to him, stroking thin wisps of white hair away from his liver spotted forehead. "This time you're coming home with us."

"I will only be another shade in Asphodel..."

"No," she soothed. "You're going to Elysion."

"I do not deserve it, my lady."

"Of course you do. With how good you are, with all you've done…"

"I served you for almost seventy three years. But my youth was not so piously spent." He frowned, every breath harder to take in. "When I was seventeen I plied an unwilling girl with drink until she lay with me. I whipped my servants with little provocation, I forgot sacrifices to the gods and—"

"We are, all of us, the sum of our parts, good and bad," a baritone voice said from the back corner of the room. He removed his helm, becoming visible to all within. Hades watched twenty pairs of eyes widen, then avert. The dark robed mortals knelt and bowed to him, some trembling in fear. Eumolpus's eyes widened and he stretched a knobby hand out to his lord.

"Eubouleus," he whispered, using one of Hades's many epithets.

"It's alright everyone," Persephone called out to the frightened Eleusinians. "Plouton is here as a friend."

They knew Persephone well, many since birth, but even members of her priesthood were wary of the Unseen One. They crowded to the other side of the bed when he advanced the room to join his wife. Aidoneus managed a thin smile. "My queen speaks the truth. Do you think anyone who goes to the Elysian Fields is pure as snow?"

He smiled and coughed again. "Of course not, my lord."

"Then how do you suppose I would welcome a mortal who has done more for my wife, more for all of Chthonia, in his short life than anyone who has lived before or since?"

A smile spread across the old priest's face and his breathing gentled.

"We had a question for you, Eumolpus," Persephone said, blotting sweat from his forehead with the corner of her shawl.

"I might have an answer," he smiled. Though his eyes were dulled by cataracts, Persephone saw the same sparkle in them from long ago.

She looked up at Aidon who carefully removed a gold foil scroll from his robes. Persephone took it from him, unrolled it and held it out for Eumolpus. "Charon has been finding these in the mouths of the dead. We wondered if you knew who would give these out. I've never seen their like in Eleusis."

He nodded and squinted at the text. Eumolpus turned to his youngest son. "Keryx, will you read this for me?"

The gray haired man took the scroll and unrolled it. "It's in Thracian."

Eumolpus closed his eyes and shook his head, already guessing at its author.

"…But on the other side, from the lake of Mnemosyne, you will find water flowing fresh. Say: 'I am the son of Earth and starry Heaven, but my parentage is heavenly: know this you too. I am dry with thirst and dying. Give me quickly then water from that which flows fresh from the lake of Mnemosyne'." When Keryx finished, he looked at his father, confused.

The old priest merely nodded. "I know who writes these. He was my student several years back, practically a boy. The son of a Muse no less, and it's rumored that Apollon is his father. Came to Eleusis intrigued by the idea of rebirth before he left for the island of Samothrace and the temple there. He had his own ideas about what greets those who journey across the Styx."

"Should we be concerned?" Aidon asked. "Is he doing this for material gain?"

Eumolpus shook his head and coughed violently. "No… no. His heart is in the right place. But I believe you should seek him out, regardless."

"Why?" Persephone asked.

Eumolpus breathed in again with the rattle in his throat growing louder. He waved toward the door. "All of you out," he commanded, then raised his palm before anyone could protest. "Every soul in this room knows as well as I that death is not the end. I will see each of you again in Elysion. Keryx, you stay."

They left, filing out quickly, his eldest granddaughter weeping as others ushered her from the chamber. The door shut behind them.

"My lady," he said with a smile. "I know you have long desired a child."

Persephone leaned in. "Yes…"

"The one who wrote that… he is gifted. Given his lineage, his intelligence, it doesn't surprise me. There are rites that his order oversees—"

"Eumolpus," Aidoneus stopped him quietly. "My wife and I have tried… many methods already. Spells, rituals, traveling throughout the known world…"

"Aidon…"

"Persephone, no. Sweet one, we go through this once a decade, to no avail. I'm not going to stand by and watch you be crushed by false hopes yet again."

"This is different, my lord," Eumolpus strained. "It is a fertility rite like many others, but in it the Samothracians invokes one who is not yet born. An heir to the earth and heavens— a god of life, death and rebirth."

Hades and Persephone exchanged a long glance and leaned in to listen to Eumolpus.

"It requires sacrifice. There have been successes. A king and his barren queen have already—"

He was cut off by another round of coughing, so violent it bowed his back. His breathing became labored. Persephone looked up at her husband, her eyes pleading with him.

Aidoneus sighed. "What sort of sacrifice?"

"I know not. But it must encompass…" He took one gasping breath, feeling lighter, euphoric. "…what you are… your most heartfelt desire…"

"What is the man's name?"

Eumolpus saw the lamps around him glow more brightly, the incense thicker, like fog, obscuring his last vision. He could feel warmth, like sunlight, and heard the laughter of childhood friends, long gone. He closed his eyes, exhaling a last word. "…Orpheus."

Printed in Great Britain
by Amazon